THE GOOD LISTENER

BY THE SAME AUTHOR

To the Lions
The Dead Line
The Hunt and the Kill
The End of the Game
The Last Truths We Told

THE GOOD LISTENER

HOLLY WATT

RAVEN BOOKS
LONDON • OXFORD • NEW YORK • NEW DELHI • SYDNEY

RAVEN BOOKS
Bloomsbury Publishing Plc
50 Bedford Square, London, WC1B 3DP, UK
Bloomsbury Publishing Ireland Limited,
29 Earlsfort Terrace, Dublin 2, D02 AY28, Ireland

First published in Great Britain 2026

A catalogue record for this book is available from the British Library

ISBN: HB: 978-1-5266-9457-7; EBOOK: 978-1-5266-9720-2

2 4 6 8 10 9 7 5 3 1

Typeset by Six Red Marbles India
Printed and bound in Great Britain by Clays Ltd, Elcograf S.p.A

FSC
www.fsc.org
MIX
Paper | Supporting
responsible forestry
FSC® C018072

To find out more about our authors and books visit www.bloomsbury.com
and sign up for our newsletters
For product-safety-related questions contact productsafety@bloomsbury.com

Alex Marrache, Alice Wood, Becky Knox, Collette Lyons,
Cressida Pollock, Ellie Collins, Imogen Lister, Jessica Sheehan,
Katrina Lintott, Laura Millar, Laura Smith-Roberts,
Tess Hardick and Rachel Vanns – bluebell woods and
copper beeches and 'It's EMOTION, Katrina, go with it!'

PROLOGUE

At first, it is only the most casual of questions.

Later, these minutes will be dissected second by second. They will be torn apart and stitched together in a thousand different ways. But at first, it is only a question.

'Is Lyra having her face painted, Tabitha?'

Lyra's brand-new little friend had certainly suggested face painting earlier. Several of the children running around the festival field are sparkly fairies, rebel pirates, noble tigers.

But Tabitha – now a glittery butterfly – shakes her head.

'Was Lyra with you when you went over to the face paint stand, Tabitha? Did you see where she went instead?'

Tabitha considers. 'Can I have an ice cream?'

'Or was she with you, Daisy?'

The woman's tone has changed almost imperceptibly. But Daisy, an emerald dragon, is only two, and she couldn't say where Lyra was, even if she knew.

The mother looks round the folk music festival with that first hint of worry. Surely, there is nothing to worry about. Surely.

There are flags and smiling faces and tents framed with bunting. In the far distance, there is the rolling moorland, bright in the cool spring sunshine.

There can't be anything to worry about.

Surely.

But Lyra isn't in the craft tent. Lyra isn't over by the pizza van either. The mother is moving faster now. Not quite a run, but she is breaking into a few jogging strides here and there.

'Have you seen a little girl?' she asks for the first time. 'She's wearing a green jumper and blue jeans.'

Heads shake.

Has she found her way onto the bouncy castle? No.

The woman is running. She is pushing people aside, politeness gone.

'Have you seen a little girl?' Already the phrase has taken on a terrible familiarity. 'She's wearing a green jumper and blue jeans.'

A man shakes his head and flips a burger.

The terror is boiling up now, impossible to contain.

'Lyra!' she starts to scream. 'Lyra, where are you?'

There are so many people on the village green. There are little girls everywhere the woman looks. But not *her* little girl.

The woman's panic is spreading through the crowd now. Other mothers look around for their children, and clutch them close with a superstitious dread.

The police arrive as the mother sprints around the village green one last time, ricocheting off small clusters of people. Everyone knows by now, everyone is looking. Everyone knows there is no easy solution anymore.

No *Oh, she was with Tabitha's mum all along!*

No *Oh, she was watching the dog agility with Daisy and her dad!*

No. Lyra is missing and the police do not know where she is.

The sun has gone in now, and Dartmoor is covered in mist.

'Her name is Lyra,' the mother whispers. 'Her name is Lyra and she is six years old.'

1

I know I have to stop. I *know*. If my wife knew, she'd… I don't know what she'd do. She'd go absolutely mental for starters. And then she'd leave me.

I've lost so much. I haven't even tried to work out how much. I mean, it's thousands. Tens of thousands. It might even be hundreds of thousands now.

Alright. I know it's hundreds of thousands.

But *still* I can't stop. Even now.

Because in the middle of all this, in the middle of this complete and utter disaster, there is still this little tiny voice right in the back of my mind. *You could get it back, you know? Maybe your luck's turned, just a little, and* now *is the time to strike?*

I hate myself.

I hate myself so much.

****

Losing a child… It goes against nature, doesn't it? I was meant to go first. *Me*. I can't… I don't… I'm sorry. I can't—

****

I find myself hovering in the aisles of the village shop. I wait because if there's someone behind me in the queue, she'll have to hurry. She'll have to whizz everything through the scanner, bleep the card, shove everything into the bags, and off I'll go.

But if she's not in a rush, and if there's no one else queuing up, she takes her time and we can have a chat. Tamsyn, her name is. Although I only know that from the label on her uniform.

Isn't that ridiculous? The person I talk to the most in the whole world, and I only know her name from a stupid piece of plastic. *My name's Tamsyn. How can I help?*

I'm sure that to her I'm some sweet old duck. *How are you, love? Do you need a hand with those bags? Bit heavy, aren't they?*

It's humiliating. I feel, well, shame is the word. Eighty-seven years on this planet, and what do I have to show for it? Everyone else has friends, family. But my daughter moved to Australia. And most of my friends… Well. Last one standing, aren't I? Just bad luck. Ha.

Yes, isn't it cold out today? Yes, I'm looking forward to a nice cup of tea and a sit down. Thank you so much, Tamsyn.

It's meaningless. Completely meaningless. But all the same, I find myself waiting in the aisles. Waiting until the shop is empty and Tamsyn has got nothing better to do.

I wait because Tamsyn's the only person I'll speak to all day.

****

I don't say much. You don't need to most of the time. People just want to talk.

I murmur a few words now and again. *I'm so sorry. That must be really difficult. You're being so brave to get through this. No, of course it doesn't matter if you cry! That's what I'm here for.*

When a call finishes, I listen to the dial tone for a few seconds just to make sure they're really gone, and then I straighten up in my seat and uncrick my neck. If it's been a tough call, I might put my phone on hold for a short while. I might pull off the headset and step into the little kitchenette off the main room. As I walk out of the main room, I might gesture to Sally: *cup of tea?*

I know Sally well enough by now to know how she likes it. Milk, two sugars, nice and strong. We've done a lot of shifts together, seem to get paired up a lot.

If it's been a really hard call, I can speak to Simeon. Simeon and Alys run the Exeter branch of the Good Listeners. I can tell Simeon what I've heard and how I feel. I rarely need to do that though. I've been doing this for a year now. Not much shocks me anymore, and we'll have a debrief at the end of the shift anyway.

Instead, I'll hand Sally her cup of tea and she'll smile her thanks.

Then I'll sit down and I'll pull on the headset. I'll take the phone back off hold and I'll wait for it to ring.

It will ring. It always does. I'll press the green button and I'll smile, because you can hear a smile in someone's voice. And then I'll say those words that I've said a thousand times before.

'Good Listeners. Can I help?'

2

It's nearly 1 p.m. and the end of my shift. I can hear Rosie and Boris out in the lobby. There is laughter in their voices and Rosie sounds very slightly out of breath. She's coming to the end of a story about her new puppy, an untrainable Vizsla.

Handover time. Sally already has her phone on hold and I'm just coming to the end of a call.

I'm speaking with Jackie. She's one of our regulars, although she doesn't know I know that. Every call is a brand-new contact as far as we're concerned.

Jackie is a kleptomaniac. She can't stop stealing from the nice shops in Exeter. Princesshay is her favourite hunting ground at the moment, although she'll go over to Guildhall too. She lives in one of the big houses in St Leonard's and rings us up wracked with guilt at least twice a week.

I walked around St Leonard's once, looking up at the double-fronted stucco houses and thinking about Jackie. As she weeps about swiping a bracelet from Pandora, or snatching a handbag from Oliver Bonas – 'Why do I do it? Why can't I stop?' – I feel a surge of pity, despite the double-fronted stucco.

'How would you feel about asking someone for help?' I ask her gently. 'Telling a therapist, or someone you trust, about what you're doing and how you're feeling about it?'

'I can't,' Jackie chokes. 'I just can't.'

* * *

They look like doll-houses, some of those houses in St Leonard's, with their perfect Georgian proportions and elegant little porches. I imagine Jackie's house crammed with stolen shoes and filched lipsticks. As her expensive voice rattles on, I can almost see her crouched on top of her magpie hoard, with her blonde highlights and her glossy red nails.

Not that I know what Jackie looks like. But you can't help guessing.

Because, actually, I do know quite a lot about what Jackie looks like. Two months ago, she told me she ran – 'practically sprinted' – home to St Leonard's after snatching a Chanel nail varnish. *Rouge Noir*. In a call a few weeks ago, she told me about stealing some Olaplex hair conditioner for her highlights. 'Blonde Enhancer,' she added, as if this was important.

Because it is important to her.

So, I know that Jackie has blonde highlights and glossy dark red nails and lives in St Leonard's.

People tell you more than they realise.

I wonder if Jackie's husband has even the smallest clue what she gets up to while he's at work.

He must know.

Or perhaps he just doesn't want to know.

Perhaps that is why Jackie is calling me.

'You take care of yourself,' I tell Jackie. *One minute*, I gesture to Simeon. *Less, probably*. 'I can hear that you're going through a really difficult time and I am very sorry about that. You can always call us, whenever you need to, day or night.'

A sniff. 'I wish I could stop.' I can hear the elocution lessons in Jackie's consonants. 'I hate myself. *Hate* myself.'

The phone goes dead. I put the line on hold.

'All okay?' Simeon is standing next to me.

'All fine.' I make a quick note on the piece of paper in front of me. 'Jackie again. Poor woman.'

'Poor woman,' Simeon agrees. Although Jackie is many things, and poor is not one of them.

Rosie and Boris have come into the main room now. As soon as I stand, Rosie slips into my seat. She waves a quick hello to me before depressing the hold button. The phone rings right away. Rosie pulls on her headset and smiles.

'Good Listeners, can I help?'

Sally and I follow Simeon through to the kitchenette.

The kitchenette is equipped with a microwave and a well-used kettle. The walls are a knocked-about cream, same as in the main room. In one corner, there is a table and chairs. The table's cheap veneer is already peeling away. Someone has brought in a bunch of dahlias and they look incongruous among the beige. Shocking pink, fiery scarlet, a boisterous, happy yellow.

'Tea?' Simeon asks. 'Coffee?'

Sally laughs. 'I've drunk my fill.'

She's eternally jolly, Sally. She's in her mid-fifties, with work-toughened hands and red hair seamed with grey. Her kids arrived in her early twenties, which means they've left home and Sally has time to spare. Sally listens with a calm confidence and just about restrains herself from doling out brisk advice. She fits the same profile as a lot of the Good Listeners.

'Great,' says Simeon. 'Did it all go well? Any problems?'

Simeon has a habit of clasping his hands together whenever he speaks. The higher his hands, the more emphatic the point. He buzz cuts his hair once a year. At the moment, it's about three inches long all over, with an equally patchy dark blond beard.

'All fine.' I hand over my notes and Simeon puts them in his file, and smooths Sally's into place as well.

'Jackie's calling more often at the moment,' he says to me.

'Sometimes, I wish we could help a bit more,' I say. 'She sounds like she's having a rough time at the moment.'

'She'll get caught one day.' Simeon shakes his head. 'And then she'll really have a rough time.'

'Doesn't seem like anyone gets caught these days,' Sally mutters.

Simeon stands. We're done.

'Thanks for coming in, both of you,' he says. 'We couldn't do it without you.'

And that gives me a warm feeling, somewhere near my heart.

The Good Listeners were one of the first crisis help-lines set up in this country, for people struggling with depression and suicidal thoughts.

I like the word help-line. It makes me think of a lifeline thrown out into a raging sea. Of an exhausted figure reaching out and – just, *just* – being dragged back through the storm to safety.

'Have a nice evening, Simeon,' I say.

Sally and I sneak out through the main room. Both Boris and Rosie are on calls, and they'll want to concentrate.

As we let ourselves out, a cold wind whisks down the street. From the outside, this terraced house looks like all the others. White render, blue front door, windows that could do with a splash of paint. Only if you looked closely would you notice the small brushed steel name plate beside the door: Good Listeners.

Sally and I smile our goodbyes and I drive out of Exeter, which is an awkward city with medieval bones, not designed with cars in mind. I head west down the dual carriageway until Dartmoor looms up like a sleeping giant, then make my way through the scattering of small villages on the edge of the National Park.

Gradually, the houses thin out and the lanes narrow. At last here's Coraton: more of a hamlet than a village. Once there would have been a butcher, a baker, a candlestick-maker, but now there is only a pub and a shop.

Off the lane now, and up the bumpy track that leads only to my house. There are potholes and tractor ruts, and my teeth jar if I take it too fast. Round one last corner and there, quite suddenly, is my stone-built rented cottage.

I park the car and open the front door.

Inside the house, there is a complete silence.

I close the door and lean back against the ancient, solid oak.

And I scream.

I scream and I scream and I scream until there is nothing left.

My darling Lyra, I do not know how to live without you.

3

In the morning, I come back to life. I wish I could stay in bed and hide from everything, but instead I force myself into the shower. Then I walk down to the big house just outside the village.

With its dressed granite, mullioned windows and neatly clipped box hedges, Harepath House – pronounced Harr-p'r by everyone in Coraton – is very grand. The drive picks its way through ancient oak woods, rhododendrons sprawling everywhere.

I looked up the name out of curiosity once. It may have come from the path used by actual hares – apparently they use the same tracks again and again – but it probably refers to an Anglo-Saxon army road. No one knows for sure. I like these hints of a forgotten Devon history.

I work as a gardener at Harepath House three days a week. My employers – Gabriel and Victoria Blackslade – don't mind when I do the hours, which is helpful because it lets me fit around the Good Listeners. The grounds are so large that I can work without disturbing them, even during the weekends. The garden is beautiful and the money keeps me going. Gardening tires me out enough to sleep, mostly. Between Harepath and the Good Listeners, I am busy.

Sometimes, I think Harepath and the Good Listeners are the only things that keep me sane.

The next morning, I make my way back into Exeter.

Anjali is my partner this morning. She is hanging up her coat as I walk in, smiling brightly.

Mikey and Tomos are coming to the end of their overnight shift. I like Tomos. He doesn't take anything too seriously. I had to throw a pencil at him once because his jolly laugh kept interrupting my call.

'Sorry,' he said unrepentantly afterwards. 'But my gal was going to top herself when she first rang in and by the time she put the phone down, she was giggling her head off.'

We do a lot of training before we start taking calls. Months of role-play and in-depth conversations about how to handle this or how to manage that and what we feel about the other.

But we're not doctors. We're not psychiatrists or counsellors, psychologists or therapists. We are here to listen, and that's all.

All we can do is listen.

Once we have finished our training, we are trusted to handle calls more or less as we see fit. There are some rules, of course. And a lot of guidance. We don't give out advice, for example. We can't. We don't know enough.

We definitely don't give out relationship advice, because it's impossible to know what's going on in a relationship from one of these calls. Frankly, I've been in relationships where I haven't known what's going on.

But we are expected to make our own decisions about how to handle a call. So if Tomos decides that a few jokes are enough to steer a weeping girl back on track, that's up to him.

Still. He could do it a bit more quietly. My Caller's cat had just died, and bellows of laughter from Tomos didn't create quite the right mood.

Tomos looks tired after his overnight shift, but he grins up at me all the same. 'Hello Clara.' He pretends to flinch.

I roll my eyes. 'Anjali's much better behaved than you.'

'Anjali is better than me in every single way.' Tomos twirls his office chair towards her.

'So true.' Anjali sits down.

Anjali is working on some needlepoint. 'I like having something to do with my hands,' she always says. 'Helps me concentrate.'

This one is swirly writing, ruby red and sapphire blue: *A problem shared is a problem halved.*

Although I'm not sure that's always true.

Mikey is finishing his call. He's very kind, Mikey, but very, very slow. I've eavesdropped on him sometimes in quiet moments and he seems to hesitate over every single word. But that's probably quite comforting.

Simeon is hovering, waiting for Tomos and Mikey to follow him through to the kitchenette.

'See you soon, my lovelies!' Tomos disappears, clutching his notes. Mikey ambles behind him.

For a moment, Anjali and I sit in peace, Anjali's needle moving rhythmically.

This happens sometimes. No one rings, just for a few minutes. The Good Listeners are set up so that a call is usually answered by the nearest branch. If both of the local Listeners are already on the phones, the call cascades out into the national pool and can be answered by Listeners anywhere from Penzance to Inverness.

We don't have any way of tracing calls, which people don't always believe. In this age of CCTV and NSA and GCHQ, I think people assume that we must have a way of tracking calls.

But we don't. The phone displays remain blank.

During the Troubles, the IRA used the Good Listeners to phone in bomb threats. They had code words back then apparently, to create time for civilians to clear the area. Today's terrorists don't follow quite the same etiquette.

The phone rings and I move slightly quicker than Anjali. 'Good Listeners, can I help?'

A little red dot lights up on the phone's display but the line remains silent.

'Hello,' I say. 'Is there something you would like to talk to me about?'

More silence.

We do get a lot of silent calls. It takes courage to type in our number, and it takes courage to listen to the ringing tone, and it takes courage to hear the click as the call connects. And for a lot of people, that click is when their courage runs out.

Sometimes you can hear them breathing. You can tell a lot by how someone breathes, it turns out. Quick and fast: that's someone on the verge of a panic attack. Long, sobbing gasps: sometimes people just need to know that there is someone else out there. That they're not completely and utterly alone. There is another sort of panting phone call too. We're free, you see, and you have to pay for a sex line.

But this time, there is only silence.

I will stay on the line even when the silence runs on and on. Every so often, I might say a few words.

I'm sorry that you're feeling so sad.

Would you like to tell me a bit about how you're feeling?

Don't worry, I'm not going to hang up.

I'm here.

I'm here and I will stay with you.

Sometimes I wonder to myself: what secret are you keeping?

Once, a Caller started talking after an hour of quiet breathing. I could hear them start to speak and then stalling, over and over again. But I watched the little red light, and I knew they were still there.

This Caller is still here.

'He filmed me.' When the woman finally speaks, her jaw muscles are so tense that she can barely open her mouth. 'When we were together, he filmed me. He must have sent the recording to one of those porn sites when we broke up.' The woman's voice is almost inaudible. 'And now it's everywhere. I can't bear it. I'm so… *humiliated*.'

'I'm so sorry this has happened to you,' I say softly. 'And I'm really glad you've been able to call us. Do you want to tell me a bit more about that?'

'Every time someone looks at me, I feel *dirty*. Tainted. They've seen everything. And it's *forever*.'

'That sounds really hard for you. I am very sorry.'

'I'll never be able to escape it. Never. This is always.'

'Have you thought about reporting him to the police?' I ask carefully. 'Revenge porn is illegal now.'

'But how would I ever prove that he sent it?' I can tell from this woman's voice that she will not call the police, that she feels defiled, contaminated, and that talking to a cool-eyed police officer is quite impossible. 'How would I... Why would he do it? *Why*?'

Because he could, I think to myself. Because he's a misogynistic creep who enjoys hurting women with whichever weapon he has to hand.

'It's such a betrayal,' I say aloud. 'Please remember that you didn't do anything wrong.'

'I don't even know who else knows.' A gasp as a fresh flood of pain soaks through her. 'I can hardly ask, can I? I'm sure everyone knows. And every time they look at me...'

The tension breaks quite suddenly. She sounds almost animal, howling down the line. *I hate him. I hate him. I hate him.*

Thank you, she says at the end. Thank you so much for listening.

There's an immediacy to volunteering for the Good Listeners. Before Lyra died, I volunteered at other charities, and I hoped that my work would benefit someone at some point in the future. But at the Good Listeners, people's voices change as you speak with them. You hear the difference.

After that, I speak to Janet, whose grandson is very ill in hospital. And to Laurel, who is facing an employment tribunal. And to eighteen-year-old Freddie, who begins his call with a detailed description of his car breaking down, but then pivots seamlessly to his father cheating on his mother and Freddie finding out by accident and *Mum's going to be devastated. I don't know what to do.*

Janet says that talking is a comfort. Laurel is much more positive by the time she hangs up. Freddie sounds like a different person.

But then, five minutes before the end of my shift, it is a woman's voice, muffled, desperate.

'He's evil. He's purest evil. What he's done... No one knows. No one *knows*. He's... If anyone knew... If *anyone* knew...'

'What has he done?' I ask, and there is urgency in my voice. 'Are you okay? Would you like to talk about it?'

'If anyone *knew*...'

'I'm sorry that you're so upset. What would you—'

The call goes dead.

4

He's purest evil… What he's done… No one knows…

The words echo around my head the next day as I work in the garden at Harepath House. Victoria Blackslade has asked me to hack back a big beech hedge, which is good because it takes all my energy. I rake up leaves too. They are falling in a late September flurry.

Victoria is slim and blonde, with a pastel prettiness. She wears brands that I recognise but will never own: Le Chameau wellies, N.Peal cashmere, Holland Cooper coats. She used to be a barrister, but clearly doesn't need to work anymore. Her husband, Gabriel Blackslade, is a criminal KC, and a very successful one at that. The Blackslades used to live in London, but he's mostly on the Western Circuit these days, travelling between Bristol and Exeter and Winchester.

Their children are Caspar and Cecily. They go to a local private school, which runs to ribboned boaters and badge-laden blazers. They're not boarding yet, but I expect it isn't far off.

I keep raking up leaves. Up in her annex, Linda, the Blackslades' semi-retired nanny, is practising her singing. A keen member of the Coraton choir, Linda has a beautiful voice. Listening to her contralto part calms me.

Mid-afternoon, my phone buzzes.

Is there any chance you can possibly do the morning shift tomorrow? Simeon has typed. *Really sorry to ask, Clara, and I shouldn't because you do so much for us already. But Ginny's got the flu and we're so short at the moment.*

The Exeter branch is always struggling for volunteers. Technically, I'm supposed to do maybe four or five daytime shifts a month and one overnight. In practice, I regularly get an anxious text from Alys or Simeon asking if I can possibly cover a shift in a few hours.

All the volunteers do their best, but between cost of living and a particularly virulent wave of flu going around at the moment, things are stretched.

No problem, I message back. *I'll be in by 8 a.m. tomorrow.*

You're a lifesaver. Simeon messages straight away. *I don't know what we'd do without you, Clara.*

As I drive through Coraton early the next morning, I have to pull over at the village green to let a tractor negotiate a narrow section of lane. Next to the green, Ryan Dallyn is already up a ladder, painting the white wall of one of the thatched cottages. He's charming, Ryan, and unquestionably good-looking, with his hard, bright blue eyes and dark curling hair. He's a decorator, in his mid-thirties. I often see his little van here and there, busy as a bee.

Ryan and his wife, Amber, live in a cottage just outside Coraton, along with their two children. The cottage is small and sullen, its thatched roof tugged down in a frown. Amber works as the housekeeper at Harepath House, so I see her fairly often.

Ryan and I smile politely at each other, and then, just for an instant, Ryan's smile falters and I know that mine has too.

I stayed in Coraton after everything, which surprised people. But I couldn't bear to leave. I have to know what happened to her.

I *have* to.

Although no one thinks I will.

Not now. Not after two years.

But I stay. I stay and I watch.

And Ryan Dallyn is one of the people I watch.

Ryan Dallyn's alibi was thoroughly investigated after Lyra went missing. He definitely was at the folk festival at midday, because he was one of the crew singing raucous sea shanties on the makeshift stage. But he definitely wasn't there when my daughter went missing, despite repeated calls over the loudspeaker. The calls over the loudspeaker were because Ryan had the key to the shanty crew's van, and it was blocking a gate. By the time he reappeared with the key – hours after Lyra had disappeared – there were already mutters.

Ryan told the police he had only hurried down to the festival for an hour or so, and was actually supposed to be at Harepath House for the whole day. This checked out as true: Ryan was meant to be painting the sitting room of the Gardener's Cottage. Victoria confirmed – I imagine slightly snippily – that she had indeed paid Ryan to work all day.

Ryan said that he had passed his cottage – Rose Cottage is just a few yards from the lion-topped pillars of Harepath – on his way back to work. As he was passing, he realised that the garden gate was open and the family's puppy was missing.

Ryan said that he started looking for the dog. He went and found his best friends, Lawrence Wrenscott and Jordie Meldon, and they all spent time looking for the puppy, sometimes in a group, sometimes separately.

In that first brief conversation with the police – the focus was still very much on search and rescue at this point – Ryan said that he, Jordie and Lawrence had been searching for the puppy all over Harepath's land and the Meldons' land. Jordie Meldon's family farm abutted Harepath's acres. Jordie and Lawrence agreed with Ryan's story.

Alarm bells must have rung loudly for Jordie's father, one of those canny Dartmoor farmers who are far richer than their clapped-out tractors suggest. Old Mr Meldon immediately brought in expensive lawyers for all three of them. The expensive lawyers analysed the three phones' GPS data fast.

GPS data from an app on Ryan's phone showed that he had been in Abbot's Wood – a relatively small patch of the Meldons' land – at the time of the search. Neither Jordie nor Lawrence had their phones with them at the relevant time, so there was no trace of where they had been during their search. Lawrence's phone was at home. Jordie's phone was in a tractor out in a field.

People leave their phones lying around all the time in Coraton, Lawrence and Jordie pointed out when this was queried. No bloody reception, is there?

Ryan immediately 'clarified' his statement, saying he was in Abbot's Wood all along. All three of them – Ryan, Lawrence and Jordie – swore that they were together in the nine acres of Abbot's Wood.

Abbot's Wood, a jumble of oak and birch and pine and hazel.

Abbot's Wood, where a few weeks later they found my daughter.

There was, one of the police officers admitted to me, 'considerable anger internally' that the lawyers had been able to pull apart the GPS records before Ryan Dallyn had set out exactly where he had been when. That first conversation had been too hasty, when all the focus was still on finding Lyra.

It must have been an awkward moment for the expensive lawyers when they realised their swift work had actually placed Ryan close to a murder scene. Despite this, Ryan avoided arrest because the GPS showed that at all times he had been several hundred yards from where Lyra was actually found.

There were rumours for months, though. The convenience of Jordie Meldon and Lawrence Wrenscott being with Ryan at exactly the right moment to provide an alibi? And the three of them saying that they were all in Abbot's Wood? Which is big, but not that big. And insisting that they saw nothing, and heard nothing?

The puppy was never found either.

But there was nothing else to connect Ryan to Lyra's death. No DNA evidence, nothing. Jordie and Lawrence were never even anywhere near the festival.

The police couldn't do anything at all.

Now Ryan and I smile at each other again, slightly too brightly.

'Morning, Mrs Brennan.' Ryan looks down at me from his ladder, roller in one hand, determinedly friendly, which I suppose is kind, probably. 'Thought I'd get started early, while it's not raining.'

I manage to mutter something about seizing the day and then the tractor has passed and I am driving away and my palms are sweaty against the steering wheel.

When I arrive at the Good Listeners, the main room is very quiet. The only sound is Sally, who is murmuring into her headset. Jimmy has moved his office chair close to Sally's, so he must have put his phone on hold. Sally's fingers are propping up her forehead with her elbows on her desk. It's the end of an overnight shift, and she must be exhausted. Her shoulders are stiff with tension.

This happens sometimes. Sometimes our calls are… Well, 'challenging' is the word the Good Listeners use.

Alys is in the kitchenette. She has jammed the door open in case she's needed. Jimmy glances around as I walk in.

Pills, he mouths, clumsily patting Sally's back.

This sort of call doesn't happen often. But they do happen. Because people don't want to be alone at the end and there aren't many people you can tell. In fact, there isn't anyone you can tell in this country. Not without triggering all the alarms.

So they call us.

We always tell people that we don't know where they are. That we cannot trace the calls. We remind them over and over again.

All the same, I worry that people don't believe us. That they think they are making a cry for help, when really they are screaming into the void. I worry that they think we will send an ambulance to their door.

But we won't.

We can't.

All we can do is listen.

Austin, who is on the morning shift with me, arrives. As I head towards the kitchenette, I catch a glimpse of Sally's face.

Sally's eyes are swollen. Above her sensible woollen polo neck, her jaw is quilted with muscles.

'I'm here,' Sally is saying quietly into her mouthpiece. 'I'm still here, Lexie.'

Alys lets the kitchen door swing shut behind me and Austin.

'How long,' I ask Alys, 'has she been on the line?'

'The call came in just after 4 a.m.,' says Alys. 'But I don't think she's heard anything for almost an hour.'

'So they're gone,' says Austin matter-of-factly. 'It's over.'

Austin used to be a Royal Marine and he can be quite brisk with Callers. I have also heard him talking to people with enormous compassion.

I flinch. 'They might still be there.'

'Do you mind taking over the call, Clara?' Alys asks me. 'I think Sally's had as much as she can take now. Her sister's ill and she's got to go and see her too.'

'Of course.'

As I follow Alys through to the main room, Sally looks up with relief. We are able to hand over calls at the end of a shift. I'll usually stay on a call until the end, but people have children to pick up, work to get to, dogs to let out. So we can make a brief note summarising the situation and pass over the despair in a few sentences.

'Lexie, I'm going to hand you over to my colleague now. Her name is Clara.' To me, Sally speaks quietly but audibly. 'Lexie has told me that she's taken a lot of pills. I think Lexie's gone to sleep now. I've told Lexie,' Sally speaks more loudly for this part, 'that we can only listen from here. That if Lexie wants an ambulance to come, she'll have to dial 999 herself or give me her address in a nice, clear voice. Okay, I'm handing over now, Lexie. I really hope you're alright.'

Sally pulls off the headset and stands up. Stiff from hours in the chair, she stretches out her arms as I move into the seat.

'Lexie,' I say quietly as I pull the headset into place. 'My name is Clara. I will be here with you for as long as you need. I am very sorry that this is happening to you.'

I listen.

But there is nothing there. Not even the sound of breathing.

There is no way of knowing what is happening.

5

The next hour passes very slowly. Once or twice, I am sure I hear a sound that might be the faintest gasp. I press the heels of my hands into my eye sockets, all my focus on the tiny sounds coming from my headset.

As I shut my eyes, hearing becomes the dominant sense. Once, I am sure that I can hear a siren far in the background. I *will* it to be an ambulance. For the ambulance to screech to a stop, and for the paramedics to leap out and throw themselves into the fray.

But the siren disappears again, clanging away down the road, and everything is silent.

I wonder where Lexie is. Is she in Exeter? Is she further out in the Devon countryside? Or did her call cascade in from much further afield? She could be in the house next door for all I know, just a few inches away.

I'm still here, Lexie. You are not alone.

For a moment, I indulge myself with the idea that I might be able to work out her location. Guess it from some tiny clue and send an ambulance racing towards her.

If you want an ambulance to come to you, I remind Lexie, *you have to make sure the doors are unlocked. We can't get the paramedics to break down doors. They won't do that for a Good Listeners' call.*

But some people do not want to be saved. Not like that anyway.

I'm here, Lexie. I'm here with you.

* * *

I don't even know if her name is Lexie. People will change their names when they are talking to us. They will change dates, change events, change everything. It makes them feel safer, I think.

That's why Sally phrased it like that: 'Lexie has told me that she's taken a lot of pills.'

Because Sally doesn't know, not really, what Lexie has done.

I'm here if you want to talk, Lexie.

We only know what people will tell us.

Unwanted, the call from my last shift echoes around my head again.

He's evil… No one knows… If anyone knew…

If anyone knew *what*? I wonder.

He's purest evil.

Because they never found Lyra's murderer, and because there were only ever suspicions about Ryan Dallyn, I will always have that fizz of fear: *he* is out there. *He* is out there watching, waiting, in his lair.

Most of the time, I bury the worst fear deep, deep down. The fear that he will do it again. That one day…

If anyone knew…

Concentrate on Lexie.

I think of Ryan Dallyn, the charm draining from those blue eyes.

Purest evil.

If anyone knew *what*?

Lexie. Lexie is all that matters.

I stay on the line until the call goes dead. One moment, the line is open, the next it isn't. The red light goes dark. The ephemeral thread has snapped.

Lexie must have called the Good Listeners on her mobile, I tell myself, and her battery simply ran out.

Or maybe she woke up. Maybe she hadn't taken quite enough pills and came to in a blur of confusion and sadness. Or maybe a friend arrived and hung up.

Maybe Lexie was alright, after all.

Although, deep down, I know that's not what happened.

Because I know that I would have heard the sheets rustle as Lexie struggled back to consciousness.

Because I know that I would have heard a friend banging on the door, shouting, 'Lexie! Lexie! Wake up!'

Maybe Lexie will wake up anyway, I tell myself. Maybe as the light filters into her bedroom tomorrow morning, she will jump awake with a sore head and a stiff neck.

I will never know though. That's the thing about these phone calls. You don't get to know what happens next.

6

'I can't ask you.' Alys looks up from her keyboard as I hand over my notes.

'What?' Our shift is finished now. Mikey and Boris have taken over, hunched over the phones.

'It's against protocol.' Alys is fiddling with her sleeve. Her face is round and she has long curly brown hair. Her clothes are always undyed cotton and unbleached linen and there are complicated tattoos all over her arms. Now she is tracing the swallow shape on her wrist.

'I'll help if I can,' I add.

'Hamish can't make it in for the 6 p.m. shift this evening.'

I've never particularly made sense of the shift system at the Good Listeners, although there is a sort of logic. The morning slot is 8 a.m. to 1 p.m. Afternoons are 1 to 6 p.m. Then there is a strange little 6 to 9 p.m. shift. It's so that people who work 9–5 can still volunteer. Simeon and Alys rarely waste me on that slot because they're usually quite easy to fill, except for on Friday and Saturday nights.

That little early evening shift reduces the overnight to eleven hours, from 9 p.m. to 8 a.m., although that can feel like quite long enough if the insomniacs of Devon are on the rampage. Sally always swears that we are busier when there is a full moon.

Alys knows that I work as a gardener, but she also knows that my employers don't mind when I do my hours.

'I can cover the evening shift,' says Alys. 'If push comes to shove.'

'Don't worry,' I tell her. 'I can do it.'

'Are you sure?' Alys's pale brown eyes are hopeful. It's Friday and I wonder if she has a date. She is wearing mascara, which she doesn't usually. She'll never find anyone else to cover a Friday shift at this notice.

'It's no problem,' I say, and Alys's face lights up.

There's no point in driving all the way home and back again between the two shifts. I'm already spending too much on petrol as it is.

For an hour or so, I wander around the great cathedral in Exeter. I like reading the dedications on the old plaques. I wonder who they were, these long-departed grandees. I make up stories for them, imagine their faces.

But then I come across Susannah, who *died 21 April, 1798, aged twenty-two years and three months* and *also in the same grave lieth her only child, Joseph Pool Bealey, died 16 Sept, 1798, aged eighteen months*. Motherless for five months, and then dead anyway.

All of a sudden, my eyes are hot with tears and I have to be outside. I sprint down the aisle, my feet loud on the flagstones, ignoring the concerned looks.

Outside, I force myself to calm down. I will borrow a book from the library, I tell myself, and then I will head back to the Good Listeners' office and I will sit, drink tea and read.

The book is terrible. By 4 p.m., I am bored.

My phone rings. Lucas. My ex-husband. No, I definitely can't face him.

A few minutes later, my phone rings again. Rachel, a friend, but no, I can't face her either.

For distraction, I look over at the big red files. Every time we finish a shift, we hand over our notes and Simeon or Alys puts them in the file. When a file is full, it is put on the shelf. There are rows of files now.

The files are there so that they can be checked if absolutely necessary. It's also why calls are fed to the local centres, so there can be a sort of oversight.

I know there was a problem last year, for example, when a woman got obsessed with a male Listener. Noah, the Listener's name was. Kind, quite shy, a postgrad from the university.

The Caller's name was Tania, or so she said. When she became a problem, Simeon was able to go back through the files to work out how often she was calling. She was calling a lot, it transpired. She'd demand to speak to Noah, and scream hysterically when she was told he wasn't there and couldn't come to the phone. When she took to loitering around outside the centre, Simeon called the police.

Noah was baffled. 'I was just friendly to her,' he said plaintively. 'She kept saying that she had no friends and that she was so miserable. All I did was listen.'

The police took Tania away.

Noah quit a few weeks later. 'I don't know what to say to people anymore,' he said. 'I worry I'm getting it all wrong.'

Without thinking, I flick back through the most recent red file. Here are my notes on Lexie and Jackie. There are my notes on the dead cat and the revenge porn.

It is a file full of sadness. Call after call of sorrow and regret, of anger and despair.

Some of the Listeners write more detailed notes than others. Austin, it turns out, writes the bare minimum. *Brian: lost job, can't tell wife* or *Billy: was raped, but can't tell anyone* or *Natasha: may be pregnant by best friend's boyfriend.*

Poor Brian. Poor Billy. Poor best friend. Poor Natasha.

The first hour or so of my early evening shift is ordinary. I have a call from Mel, halfway through a psychotic break and needing so much more than me, just me.

It makes me laugh sometimes – very darkly – when you hear celebrities parroting those words: *you are loved, you are seen.*

Because during a mental breakdown, people are not obligingly fixable, and they are certainly not gratifyingly grateful. They are repetitive and cruel and boring and angry – so blazingly angry – and violent and there is no end to it. There is no tie-the-bow-on happy ever after. Mel is not loved and she is not seen. For over an hour, she rants and she raves and then she slams down the phone and she is gone.

I breathe out, make a cup of tea and sit down again.

The phone rings, and for a moment, I am overwhelmed with a surge of exhaustion, and sadness for all the Mels who will never be fixed. For all the Mels who crash through life, hurting and being hurt, in a furious swirl of misery.

'Good Listeners.' The words are automatic. 'Can I help?'

Silence on the line. After the whirlwind of Mel, it brings a certain sort of tranquillity. For a moment, the Caller and I sit together in silence. Two of us, tied together for a moment, listening to each other breathe.

Then I remember myself. 'Is there something you would like to talk about?'

Silence.

I can hear breathing: there is someone there. Every so often her – for some reason I am certain that this Caller is a her – breath shortens. But then it stabilises and carries on evenly.

'You can talk to me about whatever you want,' I say softly.

The Caller's breath quickens. She almost begins speaking this time. But at the last moment, she pulls back again.

'Take your time,' I say quietly. 'There isn't any rush.'

A sound that is almost a sob.

'It's alright,' I murmur. 'I'm not going anywhere.'

When the woman speaks, her voice is quiet but clear. 'My name is… Emma,' she says. 'My name is Emma.'

'Hello, Emma. Is there something in particular you would like to talk about?'

The silence stretches out again, but this time I don't break it. Silence is a tool to a Good Listener. Emma has started to talk. She can go at her own pace.

Her breath shortens again, and this time she makes a sound like a whimper.

'It's my husband…' she whispers. Another silence. 'My husband…' She tries again, but lets the sentence trail away.

‘What?’ I ask in the end. ‘What do you want to say about your husband?’

‘I can’t…’

‘It’s okay. You don’t have to say anything if you don’t want to.’

‘I…’

Pause.

‘There’s no rush. In your own time.’

Longer pause.

‘He…’ A deep breath. ‘He killed… My husband killed a little girl.’

7

I gasp.

I shouldn't. I know it. But I can't help it.

My husband killed a little girl.

The edges of the room darken. For a moment, I think I am going to faint.

My husband killed a little girl.

From somewhere, a long way away, I know that the Caller is waiting for me to say something. But I can't… I can't find the words. I can't find any words at all.

'My husband…'

I am frozen, my brain a blur of syllables that can't form into whole words.

It's nothing, I tell myself. *Nothing.*

This woman must be talking about something else. She must be talking about a car crash or a freak accident or a doctor who made one tiny mistake at the end of a long exhausting day. Or she must be one of the fantasists, spinning some small piece of madness into her excitement for the day.

It doesn't mean anything.

From somewhere – somewhere deep inside that I didn't even know existed – I force myself to speak. I hear those oh-so familiar words fall out of my mouth.

'I'm very sorry to hear that.' Robotic. 'Do you want to talk about it?'

'My husband… My husband… He killed a little girl.' The Caller is stuck on those words, can't get past them.

I scrabble for my own words. 'Can you tell me a bit more about what happened? Is there anyone you can go to? Anyone you trust?'

The woman gasps. 'No,' she says. 'No. No. No. No.'

And the phone line goes dead.

I do not sleep at all that night.

I lie in my bed, hearing those words over and over again.

My husband killed a little girl. My husband killed a little girl.

It's nothing, I tell myself. It is nothing to do with me at all.

She must be talking about some idiot getting into his car after too many drinks. Smashing into a pedestrian at the side of the road, some poor innocent little girl.

Or a farmer, working all hours, and making one small terrible mistake with a five-tonne tractor. One small mistake that can never be fixed.

Or it's the horror of a baby battered to death by those who should love her best.

Although surely the Caller would have said *our* little girl if that were the case.

The Caller.

My brain freezes at the memory of that voice: her voice. *My husband killed a little girl.*

And the sound of the phone slamming down.

My husband killed a little girl.

She is only a voice, I tell myself.

She is only a voice.

As the dawn breaks, I stare out of the window. The valley below the cottage is full of mist. The fog lies thick along the river here.

Of course it doesn't mean anything, I tell myself again.

A little girl doesn't mean *my* little girl.

Of course, she doesn't mean *my* little girl.

My husband killed a little girl.

It doesn't mean anything at all.

Although, of course, it might.

Because he is out there.

No matter who Emma is and whether that call meant anything at all, Lyra's murderer is out there. Right this moment, he is getting up and getting in his car and smiling at the postman and going to work.

Probably.

Although maybe he is coming home from a night shift and eating cold pizza and slumping in front of Netflix.

Or maybe he is climbing into his little van – a decorator's, emblazoned with his mobile number – and saying goodbye to his wife and trundling off down Coraton's lanes.

No one knows.

No one knows a thing about him.

Sometimes I lie awake in the darkness, and I think I hear his step on the stairs. I dream of his hands on my throat and I wake up screaming.

He must know who I am. It would be easy – so easy – to find out where Lyra's mother lives.

Out here, so far from the village. So far from everywhere. Up this dark track, where the leaves whisper in the darkness.

Lyra's mother.

Sitting duck.

Bait.

One day, he might come.

After a while, I get dressed, because that is what you do in the mornings. I stand in the kitchen, drinking coffee that burns my tongue. Who was she, that woman? What does she know? What does she want?

Who are you? It is the only question a Good Listener would never ask.

Who are you? It is the only question in my head.

Emma.

Although from the way she hesitated over the unfamiliar syllables, I don't think it is her name. *My name is… Emma.* No one hesitates over their real name, a sentence they've said a thousand times.

She could be an Emily though. An Emerald. An Emilia.

A wife. That's the only thing I know.
A murderer's wife.
Maybe.
Because she may not be a wife. And he may not be a murderer.
She might call back one day.

8

I find that I am quivering with nervous energy. Lucas and Rachel both call again, but I can't face it and I let their calls ring out. Rachel then messages. *Call me*. But I don't.

For something to do, I walk down to Harepath. It's Saturday morning but they won't mind. Brambles are creeping their way across the orchard and I attack them, slashing and hacking until the air is filled with bitter sap and my hands are scratched and bloody.

It is colder today, winter not far ahead. I can hear the Blackslade children playing in the woods to one side of the house. They have a tree-house there, not much smaller than my tweely named Damson Cottage.

Later, I move around the house to tidy up the flower-bed in the turning circle at the front of the house. Gabriel Blackslade is working in his study, which is at the front of the house, looking out towards the Meldons' farm. He often works weekends. Despite the cooler temperature, he has the French windows half-open.

He likes to play music while he works, and the notes of *Moonlight* Sonata are drifting across the garden. I find myself hovering in front of the French windows wanting to speak, but not sure what to say.

Since Lyra disappeared, Gabriel – 'you must call me Gabriel,' he has always insisted – has helped me with legal terminology and various aspects of the case.

He knows that I have carried on the search. The police's attention may have moved on, but I follow up every rumour and I read every

Reddit thread and I plead for information anywhere and everywhere. Even when the Facebook commenters insist that *it's always the dad* or *the mum looks dodgy as sin to me*, I keep reading. Now I want to tell Gabriel about Emma's call, but I don't know if I can.

The Callers' anonymity is sacrosanct. Good Listeners are not allowed to tell anyone what we hear on calls. During our training, we were told about one unfortunate woman who was overheard talking about a Caller in a queue at Asda. That Listener was banned from every centre in the country. Had to be, Alys said firmly. Never, ever.

Eventually, Gabriel glances up and notices me.

'How are you, Clara?' he calls out. Gabriel Blackslade has the right voice for a barrister, mellifluous and sonorous all at once. Victoria has the same public school accent as her husband, but her voice is shriller. She often sounds as if she is complaining, even when she isn't, which can be unnerving as an employee.

I scrabble for something to say that isn't about Emma.

'Still on the hunt!' I try to sound cheery. 'I drove all the way to Cornwall last week because someone's brother's mate's cousin saw "something weird" that day.' I make quote marks with my fingers. 'Turned out he saw strange lights while taking magic mushrooms up near Hay Tor that weekend.'

'Nothing helpful then?'

'Nope.' I shake my head.

'I'm sorry.'

Gabriel Blackslade is tall and broad, and must be in his mid-forties. He has dark brown hair, which is greying at the temple, and it is easy to imagine him as a judge one day. He always listens very carefully, his head on one side. I have noticed that Coraton's residents have got into the habit of coming to him when a decision needs to be made. If it's a decision that requires money – do we fix the slide in the children's tiny playground or not? – he inevitably puts his hand in his pocket. Even though the rent on my cottage is relatively low, I am starting to run out of money. I suspect Gabriel Blackslade has guessed as much and the gardening job is a benevolence.

Both the Blackslade children are mostly polite and well behaved, although like all children they have their moments. Last spring, Cecily asked me if she could sow some carrots in the vegetable patch and was sweetly thrilled when they grew. Caspar, on the other hand, put up a football net and drilled a series of goals into the roses, reducing them to a flurry of petals drifting across the grass. I knew that he was wondering if I would say anything. I didn't.

A lot of money has been spent on both the house and garden. The garden is divided into different sections, including a walled vegetable garden, an arboretum and the rose garden. The Gardener's Cottage, which Ryan Dallyn was supposed to be painting the day Lyra disappeared, is now a holiday cottage. There is a housekeeper's annex off the ground floor of the main house too, but that is unused. The semi-retired nanny, Linda, has her own sitting room and bedroom in one of the wings of the main house.

Gabriel goes back to work and I carry on pruning, working my way around the side of the house. The leaves are starting to fall now and the woods along the driveway are rusting in the thin sunshine. *My husband killed a little girl. My husband killed a little girl.* I am just pruning back an overgrown climbing rose when I hear it: a screech of tyres from the drive.

I jump to my feet and race round towards the front of the house. Gabriel comes out through the French windows.

It is Amber's car. Amber Dallyn, who is married to Ryan. I often see her car parked at Harepath because she works here nearly full-time, but this time it stops half-skewed across the drive. Amber jumps out of the car and almost sprints across to the French windows. Her children are still in the back of the car. I can see them peering out, their faces pale and worried.

Amber's eyes are red-rimmed and she is on the verge of tears. When she sees me peering around the corner, she takes a step back.

I am intruding. 'Sorry.' I turn away, walking back towards my pruning.

I am only just around the corner of the house when I hear Amber's desperate words. 'I'm sorry, Mr Blackslade, but you said… You said we could stay in the housekeeper's flat if we needed to. And now we need—'

I stop. I am out of sight now, but I can still hear Gabriel's calm tones. 'Of course, Amber, of course. Are you alright?'

'I… I…'

And last night's conversation echoes through my mind.

Is there anyone you can go to? Anyone you trust?

9

'He wants me to kill him.'

It has been almost three days since Emma called and I haven't stopped thinking about her. Now I am back at the Good Listeners' centre for another shift and it is a relief, almost, to talk to someone whose problems are straightforward.

'He really wants me to kill him,' the woman says again.

'That must be very hard,' I say calmly.

'I don't think I can bear it anymore. He so desperately wants to be dead. But I can't just *kill* him, can I? Can I?'

We're a modern-day confessional, I often think to myself. Back in the days when the church was something people believed in, you might talk to your vicar, your priest, take that precious confidentiality for granted.

The urge to confess: it is intrinsically human. But nowadays people are reduced to ranting anonymously on Reddit and Mumsnet and Tattle, the only places we can hurl our secrets safely.

Because there is no one left to *tell.* GPs barely have time to spot cancer, let alone hold your hand while you're going through a tough time. The vicar is for Christmas. Lots of the Callers should probably be in therapy. But the safety net is ever more threadbare.

Sometimes, we're all there is.

Sometimes, it's just me, crossing my fingers and hoping for the best.

* * *

'I know he wants to be dead. I c-can see it in his eyes. We'd talked about it in the past. Dignitas and all that. But he's left it too late. We've left it too late.'

'It sounds brutal, Ruth. I really am sorry.'

Ruth lives beside a busy bus stop. I can hear the reverberations of a heavy engine and the brief pause as the doors open and close. Then there is a judder as the bus pulls away again. At least three buses have stopped while I've been talking to Ruth. The constant noise would drive me crazy.

'He's only forty-five.' Ruth's voice is broken glass. 'This disease... This bloody disease. I love him, you know? I really love him.'

'Life can be so unfair. I'm so sorry.'

My husband killed a little girl.

Not now.

'I c-can't bear the idea of him being in pain.' Ruth stammers very occasionally. She was probably given speech therapy as a child, because it is barely noticeable now. 'And he is in pain, I can tell. And what's the point of it now? What is the point in any of it?'

'It's so hard,' I say. 'But it sounds as if you're doing everything you can.'

'I am,' she says fervently. 'I am.'

And then Ruth is gone.

I never rang up the Good Listeners. Their phone number was on one of the pamphlets that the police left behind. I looked at the flimsy paper, and almost laughed at the idea that calling a stranger might help.

But the thing is, we do help.

I can hear it in people's voices. Ruth's voice was lighter by the end of that call. Able to face another day of smiling at Tony.

We help some people, anyway.

My husband killed a little girl.

All we can do is listen.

* * *

The phone rings again and my heart leaps. Every time it rings, my first thought now is: will it be *her*?

Her.

Might she call back one day?

Will I ever speak to her again?

If *anyone* knew…

Purest evil.

It isn't Emma.

It is a woman's voice, but this woman is thrilled, excited. She is scurrying down the road, off to see her lover.

'I shouldn't,' she whispers. 'I know I shouldn't. But I can't *not*.' I can hear the woman's footsteps. She is hurrying, rushing, overtaking slower feet.

'Why do you think you feel like that?' I can tell from her voice that nothing will stop this woman. At one home, there is a husband. At another, there is a wife. And they are not enough, never enough. 'Why do you have to do it?'

'I need…' The woman hesitates, not quite sure what she needs. 'I need something that is just mine.'

This woman hasn't told me her name and I know that she won't.

I wonder why she has called the Good Listeners. Maybe her friends would disapprove. Maybe her friends would close ranks. Maybe she is meeting a friend's husband. This woman has probably called me because human beings simply aren't very good at keeping secrets. And if she doesn't tell me, she will tell someone she shouldn't.

'Don't you ever just feel invisible?' she asks. 'Don't you ever feel that if you have to unload the dishwasher again, that if you have to wipe down the kitchen surfaces just one more time, you might disintegrate into a million pieces? I love my family. Really, I love them, but sometimes I feel as if I am a hoovering, dusting, laundry-folding *nobody*.'

For a moment, I am back in our London flat. I am wiping those kitchen surfaces, and I am folding that laundry, and I am tidying away the bright primary colours of the Lego for the thousandth time. I remember pausing, a few months after Lyra had died, and looking around the holiday cottage kitchen and remembering all those tiny acts of devotion.

Let me wipe your face. I love you.

Let me pair those socks. I love you.

Let me brush your hair. I love you.

I looked back upon a mosaic of love.

'It is exhausting,' I agree. 'I know what you mean.'

'I hate myself for doing this,' she says. 'But—'

A bus judders to a halt beside the woman. For a second, all I can hear are the reverberations of a dawdling engine and the brief pause as the doors open and close.

And the echo of a memory.

Ruth.

The bus grumbles away.

I *know* this voice.

Half an hour ago, Ruth was telling me all about Tony.

He wants to die. I know he wants to die. I can see it in his eyes.

And now Ruth is rushing down the road, with the very same buses thundering by.

He's left it too late. We've left it too late.

This happens occasionally. Someone will ring in with one story and an hour later, they will ring in with a completely different tale. It's just pure chance if the same Listener happens to take both calls. We would never let the Caller know that they'd been recognised anyway. Every call is a new call.

'If anyone found out...' Ruth – second Ruth – is suddenly on the verge of tears. 'It would hurt so many people. My children. My *husband*.'

These are two halves of the same story, and both versions can be true. Although there is no way of fitting these two pieces together for a whole, no neat gold kintsugi for a shiny happy ending.

Because these are not two halves. These are only two tiny fragments of Ruth's story, two shards of the whole. A glimpse of a life, nothing more. A peep through the keyhole, a twist of the kaleidoscope.

Ruth is a loving wife. Ruth is a brazen adulteress.

Ruth is an angel. Ruth is a whore.

Ruth is a saint. Ruth is a bitch.

Ruth is all of these things and no one else in the world can see it, not even Ruth.

'I've got to go!' Ruth says suddenly. 'Hello, C-Caroline! How lovely to run into—'

And I wonder to myself, even if Emma calls back, will I ever be able to believe a word she says?

10

My mother rings me a few minutes after I come off the A30, just after I've driven through the first of the small villages. *Mum*, insists the phone on its hands-free display. *MUM*.

I tell myself that I'm too tired to speak to her. That it has already been a very long day.

I do know – somewhere, my brain is capable of acknowledging this fact – that there is a certain irony in that I've spent all day listening to other people's tragedies, and it has left me too tired to listen to my own mother's woes.

But I can't face her right now.

The phone stops ringing and then starts again. A few minutes later, I turn onto the bumpy track up to my house and – as I knew it would – the signal cuts out.

I park outside and walk into Damson Cottage. After the bustle of the centre, and the hours of conversation, and the sense of teamwork, the cottage feels very empty and very quiet. When the phone starts to ring again, I answer.

'Clara.' There is a relief in my mother's voice that she can't quite hide. 'How are you?'

'I'm fine, Mum.'

'How are things going?' There is a breathless quality to my mother's voice. She's had to gear herself up to make this call, I can tell.

'They're going fine.'

'I'm worried about you in that cottage over the winter.'

I stare at the cottage's pink and white wallpaper. This house was designed with light-hearted frivolity in mind. Here and there, the pink and white wallpaper is starting to peel.

'It'll be fine, Mum. You know that I've got lots of tins if I get snowed in. And plenty of logs for the fire. I was fine last winter.'

'But still,' my mother goes on. 'What if you fall over and break your leg or something like that?'

'That would be sub-optimal even if I was living in a cul-de-sac just outside Swindon, wouldn't it?'

My mother, who does live in a cul-de-sac just outside Swindon, falls silent.

I've been mean. 'How are you?' I ask apologetically.

'I'm fine.' Snappy.

I don't think I ever made sense to my mother. I was the only child from a marriage that was already in free fall by the time I was born. Mum was an office cleaner, working awkward hours, and there was no money, ever.

It was a teacher – Mrs Sylvester, an English teacher at a very ordinary school in an unexciting patch of Wiltshire – who changed my life, which was the sort of cliché she would abhor.

'Speaking English is the most extraordinary privilege,' she would announce to a classful of children who had palpably never thought of themselves as privileged in any way whatsoever. 'Think of the *precision* of this glorious magpie language, with its magical pieces stolen from all over the world. Exactitude wrought from misrule. Think of – I don't know – the word *catenary*, the curve of a chain, hanging from two points. Tension and gravity, in perfect balance. From the Latin *catena*, chain. No other language is so deliciously *precise*.'

None of us had a clue what she was talking about, but her enthusiasm bounced several of that class to the best universities in the country.

'By the way…' My mother tries to sound as if the thought is only just occurring to her. 'Lucas is trying to get hold of you.'

'I know,' I say. 'I had some missed calls. Do you know what he wants?'

Our marriage had been bisected quite neatly in the end. Lucas went back to London. I stayed in this cottage. The End.

'No, sorry.'

My mother is lying, I can tell.

'You should give him a call,' my mother goes on. 'Rachel is trying to get hold of you too.'

'I'll call them,' I promise.

Although I think I know what Rachel wants.

And I can't bear it.

I have no idea what Lucas wants.

But I can't face him either.

11

The phone wakes me the next morning. *Lucas*, says the screen. For a moment, I think about ignoring it again. But I know Lucas. If I don't answer, he will eventually turn up.

'Hello.' I do not make the word friendly.

'Oh. Clara.' Even though Lucas was the one who called me, he sounds surprised by my voice. 'How are you?' he says, regrouping.

'I'm fine,' I say. 'How are you?'

'I'm well,' he says. The surprise in Lucas's voice is gone now. He sounds, once again, like the successful banking executive he is. 'I'm very well, Clara.'

The silence lengthens.

Do I tell him about Emma's call? *My husband killed a little girl.*

No, that's not exactly small talk.

'Did you want to talk about anything in particular?' I ask Lucas.

'Oh. Well. Actually, I was calling…' Lucas's voice fades away for a second and then carries on with a heavy dose on bonhomie. 'I wanted to talk to you about Ashley.'

Ashley is blonde and bright, glossy and American. Younger than me, but only by a few years, according to her busy Instagram page. I've never met her but I imagine her to be optimistic and enthusiastic and always smiling. I know Lucas is seeing her, but still there is something like the memory of pain at his words.

* * *

Lucas and I met at university, both bright, both ambitious. It was only later that I realised that being ambitious didn't automatically mean you had the same ambitions.

Lucas's ambitions took him to the City. One of the huge American banks that ate people's twenties and crapped out dollars. Sorry, that sounds crass.

My degree, meanwhile, was in English literature, in contrast to Lucas's rather more useful economics. Then I did an MPhil. Then I started my PhD. It was not clear if the world needed 100,000 words on *The Evolution of Metaphor in Shakespeare's Works: A Cognitive Linguistic Approach*, but that was what it was going to get.

Aside from academia, I painted a lot, covering our flat in oils and acrylics. I did a bit of freelance journalism. I wrote poetry and plays and things that might have been novels one day. Yes, I was *that* person.

Lucas liked having a leggy arty girlfriend who didn't mind if he was late home. He made me laugh too, with a wilder sense of humour than the suits and ties suggested. All the same, I am not sure if we would have lasted if it hadn't been for Lyra.

Lyra was an accident.

Four words, so blunt.

But she was.

I was about three quarters of the way through my PhD when I sat down in the toilets of our favourite bar and watched the two solid lines appear.

Shit.

Oh well.

I'll deal with it.

But then I – who had always been pro-choice, who had marched for women's rights – suddenly found that I couldn't do it. I went to the appointment, and sat on the table, and nodded and smiled as if everything was fine. I told myself that this foetus was just a collection of cells. An inconvenience, that's all.

But, still, I couldn't do it.

Lucas did the Right Thing, although we were too young to know what the Right Thing was back then.

We were married at twenty-five. Twenty-five! The first of our friends, by years. Such a great party, everyone agreed. Such a brilliant night.

I fell in love with Lyra as soon as I saw her. So tiny, squeaking, bewildered by the light. My body was ripped apart and I couldn't believe how much I loved her.

I remember how she calmed the moment they laid her on my chest. I was the only thing she knew in the whole world. I was safety. I was home.

But those long days and endless nights after Lyra was born pulled Lucas and I further and further apart.

After a while, it felt as if we were living in two separate worlds. In the morning, Lucas would put on his polished shoes and his neatly ironed shirt – he didn't trust me with his shirts; he would drop them off instead at the dry cleaners down the street – and his expensive Italian suit. He would kiss me distractedly on the forehead and disappear off to that office high up in the City sky. At night, he would return shattered. Climb into the spare room bed. Earplugs.

Lyra and I would drift through the day and the night, hardly aware of the shift from light to darkness to light. My world shrank to four walls, and my wailing, ravenous, delicious child.

Lucas tried. I think he did, at least. We would collide in the kitchen in the morning, him chomping Weetabix, me drinking coffee. He'd look at me and say that *the Treasury's money laundering plans are causing bloody mayhem* or *we should go and see that new play at the Almeida* and I'd look at him in bewilderment, trying to remember that these things used to matter.

I had taken a leave of absence from my PhD, but found that I couldn't face going back even after Lyra started at nursery. Instead, I fell into a receptionist job, smiling blandly a hundred times a day. At least my line manager didn't mind too much when I had to rush off because of yet another nursery bug. Lucas was always at work and none of my old friends had children yet, so I felt dislocated from everything. I kept meaning to go back to my PhD, back to my old life, but I couldn't seem to find my way.

We were all meant to be down in Devon together that last week, but some surprise takeover bid put paid to Lucas's week off.

I know that to his dying breath, Lucas will wonder if it would have been different if he'd been down here too.

'What do you need to tell me about Ashley?' I try to make my voice sunny, which isn't easy.

'She… err…' Lucas pauses long enough for me to guess. 'Ashley's pregnant, Clara.'

The world seems to quiver for a second. Lucas, having another baby. Lucas, moving on.

It's *normal*, I tell myself. *Don't be ridiculous.*

You're divorced. It's over. Of course he's moving on.

But a child.

A half-brother or a half-sister to my Lyra.

A child, running around, growing up: half-Lyra, alive.

'Clara?' Lucas sounds concerned. 'Are you there? Hello?'

'How lovely.' I wonder if my voice is giving away the truth. 'Really, Lucas, I'm pleased for you both.'

Because he is a decent man, Lucas.

'Thank you, Clara.' He exhales sharply. 'She's great, Ashley. Really. You'd like her.'

'I'm sure I would. When is the baby due?' It seems the right thing to ask.

'Next spring. Ashley's thrilled about it all.'

'That's nice.'

'Clara.' My name puts a full stop to the conversation. 'Are you alright?'

'I'm fine, Lucas.'

'Really?'

'Yes.'

'I worry about you. I worry about what you're going to do next.'

But I can't think about a *next*. I just can't. I can cope with one day at a time, just about. 'I'm fine.'

'You're not. I don't think it's… healthy. You, being down there. Alone.'

'It's where I want to be, Lucas.'

I can't bear the idea of leaving Dartmoor.

I remember the spring day when we arrived in Coraton towards the end of the Easter holidays. Lyra was so excited, thrilling at the daffodils and the crocuses and the lambs.

We were down for a week, Sunday to Sunday, and it seemed to stretch out forever. Sitting at the scrubbed pine table in the kitchen, we planned our walks and our picnics and our bicycle rides. Even the weather smiled down on us.

Coraton is a small village, but the day before we were due to leave, they hosted a big folk festival, which delighted Lyra. Held in big fields at the bottom end of the village, the festival was a chaos of music and dancing and laughter. Lyra was particularly fascinated by the broom dancing, which was the mania of all the small girls in the village at the time. They skipped to and fro over their broomsticks, tiny feet a blur. It certainly made a change from London kids being handed an iPad for brunch.

Then there were the morris dancers in their tattercoats, with bells on their heels and sticks clacking in unison. Then there were the sea shanties, bellowed over the head of the crowd with winks and salty nudges. At the end of the shanties, the crew leader let us know where to find them on Insta.

Lyra and I danced and sang and giggled.

Then she ran off to play games with all the other children, and it was all such fun. Such fun until I looked around – still laughing, still laughing…

And Lyra was gone.

12

It took me a few moments to realise. Those minutes that the police dissected later, second by second by second. The children had been playing hide-and-seek in the woods right next to the festival. They were within sight, giggling, a happy little mob. The parents all seemed relaxed about it. That was just what Coraton kids did during the folk festival, apparently.

But suddenly there was no Lyra among the little gang.

Perhaps she was playing in a tree-house somewhere. Maybe she was still hiding, and hadn't realised the game was over.

At first, I could speak to the other children calmly enough. 'Is Lyra having her face painted, Tabitha?'

Tabitha shook her head.

'Was Lyra with you when you were playing under that tree, Daisy? Did you see where she went?'

Daisy, two and tiny, only nodded and giggled regardless of the question.

'Can you keep an eye out for her please, girls?'

Nods.

I tried to push away the glimmer of fear.

Don't be silly. You're being hysterical.

But I found myself moving faster. I hurried around the craft tent and ran across to the carousel.

Have you seen a little girl?

I jogged past the hawk display and then I sprinted down to the classic cars with their belching, reeking smoke.

Have you seen a little girl? Have you seen a little girl?

It was the other mothers who reacted the fastest. The other women, who have also dressed their children in bright colours, all the easier to spot. The other women who have – once in the past – raced around a school fete searching for that red ponytail, those brown curls, that blonde bob.

The other women who understood and who rushed to my side.

But Lyra wasn't over by the roast pig. 'It's a whole pig!' my London daughter had shrieked in delighted horror as we arrived.

Lyra wasn't watching the ferret racing.

Lyra wasn't having her hair braided.

The fear was shards of terror slicing up through the bright colours of the afternoon.

Half the crowd is in fancy dress and face paint or masks, giving the whole festival a dreamlike quality, but Lyra wasn't having her face painted.

I found, almost to my surprise, that I was screaming. I was screaming to shatter the happy complacency of the festival. I was screaming because I needed everyone to search. I was screaming because I didn't know how to stop.

I became aware of a terrifying certainty: this is the moment that will define everything. If I chose right, I might still spot that small disappearing back. But if I turned the wrong way, that last chance would vanish forever.

It is those tiny decisions – those split-second choices, this way or that – that tear me apart afterwards.

I had a chance to get it right.

But then that chance was gone. And I could never get it back.

* * *

My panic rippled through the crowd.

The other women had their own children tight by the hand, and already their eyes were full of pity. The vicar's wife, her knuckles white on her daughter's wrist, had a message put out over the loudspeaker.

Over by the festival entrance, I heard a siren and I saw blue flashing lights. But I couldn't stop running, I couldn't stop screaming.

A police car crept across the grass. I don't remember how, but suddenly I was in the organisers' tent, and it was quiet and a police officer was looking at me with a compassionate professionalism.

Have you seen a little girl? Have you seen a little girl?

'Her name is Lyra,' I whispered. 'Her name is Lyra and she is six years old.'

13

Lyra is missing. The first week seems to last forever, but suddenly it is past.

Suddenly, Lyra has been missing for a whole week.

Day after day, people from villages all around turn out to cross the land inch by inch. On one of the worst days, the local reservoir is dredged.

Nothing.

Local mining enthusiasts appear and climb down into dark, unimaginable pits, because this is old mining country and the hillsides are still littered with gaping holes.

Nothing.

There are posters pinned up everywhere, Lyra grinning out.

Nothing.

Lucas is here. That was the worst phone call I'll ever have to make.

At first, Lucas can't understand. 'Clara, what? Darling, I can't hear what you're saying? What's happened to Lyra? What?'

Until eventually the policewoman – Leanne, her name is, I discover eventually – gently takes the phone from me. She speaks clearly and sympathetically down the phone until Lucas has understood. I hear his tinny voice as Leanne listens. I hear him start to cry.

Someone drives Lucas down to Devon. I remember him running towards me and I am astonished he is not furious with me.

'I'm sorry,' I say over and over again. 'I was watching her the whole time. I'm so desperately sorry.'

Lucas and I stay on in the holiday cottage. The owner, Mrs Ingram, tells us we must stay as long as we need. Cynically, later, I wonder whether all the other bookings have cancelled.

Because Lucas and I are *that* couple. The couple that the very worst has happened to. We are living everyone else's nightmare.

They don't find her.

For weeks, they don't find her.

The first flurry of panic is over and it is summer.

She must have been taken somewhere else, people start to say. Poor little girl. Poor little Lyra. She must have been taken somewhere far, far away. Kidnapped.

The police still chase down every lead, but there aren't many leads anymore. For all the appeals and the hundreds of phone calls to the help-line and the psychics saying confidently *she is here, she is there*, no one has seen Lyra since that afternoon at the folk festival.

He could do it again, I remind everyone, although we are not even sure that he is a he. No child is safe until he is caught. We have to keep looking. Have to.

I stare at one photograph in particular for hours every night. Bright, beaming, her hair in a complicated braid. Lyra is popping a puff of candy floss in her mouth, her little white teeth nipping at the pink sugar. She loved that jumper: emerald green with the embroidered red roses.

She *loves* that jumper.

There is nothing to suggest that this would be the last photograph. That this would be the last time my daughter would squint up at me, and roll her eyes, and pull a slightly forced smile.

I didn't know that this would be the photograph that would laugh up from a million front pages, that would peer out from a million televisions.

I didn't know.

* * *

‘This is hard terrain to search,’ one of the policemen tells me. ‘With the valleys and the woodland and the moor and the rivers.’

‘Yes,’ I say mechanically. ‘I’m sure it is.’

‘I remember one case in Scotland,’ the policeman went on. ‘The land was a bit like it is around here. This man lived on one of the big, old estates, with lots of woodland and so on. He disappeared one day, and they searched for years. *Years*. Trawling to and fro, the dogs out, everything. But there was no sign of him. Not even a hint. Until one day, fifteen years later, they found him propped up against a tree less than a mile from the house. He must have just had a heart attack, leaning against that tree, and no one ever spotted him. There was only a skeleton left by then, of course. They’d searched and searched. But you have to get lucky, really, sometimes.’

I stare at him, trying to work out if this story is meant to make me feel better.

I imagine searching for Lyra for years.

Because I will.

‘I’m fine, Lucas.’ I grip the telephone now. ‘Really, I am. This is where I want to be.’

‘I know,’ he says. ‘But I’m not sure that makes it the right place for you to be.’

‘There is no right place for me anymore.’ I can’t stop the words spilling out. ‘The only right place for me is with Lyra.’

After I have said goodbye to Lucas – with another unexpected pang – I wander over to the window. I stayed in Damson Cottage after everything, which surprised people.

I couldn’t think of anywhere to go, because when I stand at this window, I can see a patch of woodland far, far in the distance.

I can see the patch of woodland where they found her.

I can see Abbot’s Wood.

14

All the way through, there are worst moments. Calling Lucas to tell him our daughter had disappeared was the worst phone call. Watching the boats bob around on the dark water of the reservoir was terrible.

But nothing – nothing – will ever compare to the moment that they told me that my daughter was dead.

I saw the lights while I was getting ready for bed. A hot August evening, windows open for the breeze.

Arc lights in the far distance.

By now, I know these fields. They are a patchwork of green, criss-crossed by shaggy hedgerows. Sheep keep the grass short.

There isn't anything over there.

But there are arc lights shining in Abbot's Wood. I know Abbot's Wood. It's dense. Boggy. Wild. It's big, too. Covers several acres.

The police spent plenty of time in that wood during the search, especially after Ryan Dallyn's phone records showed he was in there on the day that Lyra disappeared. I'd been in it too, scrambling along, peering into crevices, tripping over fallen logs, desperate not to find anything. One of the villagers was hunting just a few feet away from me all day, and most of the time I couldn't see him at all.

The arc lights don't mean anything, I tell myself.

They don't mean anything at all.

Lucas wasn't there that night. He'd gone back to London after three months. Back to work, because that was the only place where things made sense to him. Interest rates and bonds and EBITDA: those follow rules and Lucas knew the rules.

'But we have to keep looking for her,' I insisted. 'We have to be here in case she comes back.'

'You think she's just going to walk in one day?' He had stared at me in disbelief. 'You really think she might just wander into the kitchen while we're drinking a cup of tea?'

'Yes,' I screamed. 'She has to. She *has* to.'

Lucas was lucky – if that is the word – that he had a cast-iron alibi. He was playing golf in Surrey with a group of people, all of whom could vouch for him from mid-morning until the moment I called him.

I found out later that Ashley was one of the group. Although I didn't care about that by then. I didn't care about anything.

I look out over the wood again. The arc lights are getting brighter, slicing up into the darkness of the night.

A moment later, I hear the rattle of a helicopter flying low over the land.

It's nothing, I tell myself. Nothing at all.

Then the doorbell rings.

It is Leanne. Leanne, the police officer, awkward on the granite step.

Leanne's presence is the only thing I take in as I sink to the ground.

I don't hear the words she says. I can't even hear my own screams as I collapse onto the cool of the flagstones.

Somehow it is later and somehow Lucas is there. A doctor appears and injects me with something, and I am falling into a swirling pit of darkness.

When I wake, it is morning, and the arc lights are gone.

15

They don't know much.

She has been dead, they conclude, for several weeks by the time they find her. And it has been a warm summer.

I am not asked to identify her.

They work it out for certain from her teeth. I stare at that photograph, that last photograph, again. Those little teeth, grinning as they nip at the candy floss. Those little teeth that she would clean only when I stood over her in the bathroom. *No story until they're done, Lyra.*

I wonder about all those mothers out there who have lost children. All those hours we have... Not invested, that is the wrong word. All those hours we have *devoted* to brushing hair and washing clothes and choosing shoes. It seems impossible that all those hours, all that care, all that love, can just disappear. Disappear into nothing.

That it can all vanish in one careless moment, as if it never was.

But it can.

Other than Ryan Dallyn, there are no other suspects. At first, there is even a suggestion that she might have wandered off by herself. Got lost and panicked and scrambled up to Abbot's Wood and then... had some sort of accident, maybe?

This theory is killed off when the post-mortem shows that Lyra's hyoid bone was fractured. By now, I am well versed in police process and jargon, and I know that a fractured hyoid bone means only one thing. Someone strangled her.

Someone strangled my daughter.

That night, I stare out at the woods and I do not think that I will survive.

I do not think it is possible for me to continue living in a world where my daughter is not.

After she is found, I spend days and nights in Abbot's Wood, as if I might somehow summon her back. Mr Meldon – Jordie's father, the rich old farmer – gave me permission.

Abbot's Wood is beautiful. A stream runs through the middle of the wood, not deep enough to attract the wild swimmers in their Dryrobes, but enough to fill the air with the whisper and trickle of water as the river splashes past rough hunks of granite.

It is *Sleeping Beauty* overgrown, buried in brambles and bracken and blackthorn. The trees are swaddled in moss, their branches fringed with ferns. Older trees have crashed to the ground and are slowly crumbling away, home to insects and worms and a thousand types of fungi. In places, the ground oozes and heaves beneath my feet.

A temperate rainforest, that's what an ecologist called Abbot's Wood during one of the hundreds and thousands of hours that the twenty-four-hour news channels dedicated to my daughter.

I had never heard of rainforests in England before, but it turns out that they were here all along, in small, forgotten patches. Atlantic woodlands, that's another name for them.

This wood covers nine acres, and I think the police are still surprised they found her at all.

The police keep hunting. It is a murder investigation now.

But the folk festival was a big happy chaos, which had sprawled over the years into cul-de-sacs of classic cars and ferret racing and a 10 km race. It wasn't ticketed, so there wasn't anything helpful like credit card data. Thousands of people visited from miles around. And there were dozens – maybe hundreds – of people staying in a pop-up campsite over in one of the fields.

'Some of these people are quite… itinerant,' says Leanne dubiously.

Not keen on helping the police with their enquiries, I deduce. Not keen on the police at all.

This may be a sparsely populated area, but there are still far too many people to pin down, to eliminate.

With no real evidence, it is an impossible task.

I stay on in the cottage. At first, during the search, the cottage was the only place I could be. *Lyra might come back. She might just walk in one day while I am drinking a cup of tea.*

Living there becomes a habit.

By the time I knew she was not coming back, I didn't know how to break the habit.

A few months after Lyra's body was found, Lucas stumblingly suggested that it was time for us to separate.

I stared at him in confusion. To me, it was so obvious that we were already separated. Lucas was back at work, managing to care what the dollar was up to in relation to the yen. I was in Devon.

The divorce was resolved quite easily. I was left with enough to rent the cottage and live for a few years, and that is all I could think about. The holiday cottage owner – Mrs Ingram, recently widowed, fed up with regulations – leased it to me lock, stock and barrel, right down to the seashell paintings and slightly incongruous anchor in the front garden.

I haven't changed a thing.

That bed: that is the last bed Lyra slept in. That Monopoly set, up there on that shelf: we played it together, squabbling over Mayfair and Whitechapel Road, bickering over the dog and the silver car.

That kitchen table: that is where she ate her last breakfast before we danced down the hill to the festival. Pancakes, her favourite, and I am so glad I made them for her.

Rents have soared around here, but mine has stayed the same on the unspoken agreement that I sort out plumbing glitches and turn a blind eye to damp.

But the money is running out now.

I can't bear to leave Coraton before I have found her killer. But I may have to.

By the time we had to decide what to do with Lyra's remains, I knew that I would never return to London. Burying her in Wiltshire, close to my mother, seemed impossible. Lucas's parents had retired to southern Spain and I didn't want her there either. Eventually, we decided she should be cremated.

Sweetly, Coraton's congregation raised money in her memory and awkwardly suggested a memorial stone. When I saw it, a weight lifted: a sense of *that is right*. Lyra's ashes are in the old churchyard now, next to an ancient yew hedge. The churchyard is a beautiful place, with its blanket of snowdrops in the spring, and its bright spatters of cyclamen in the autumn. On some days, that feels like a comfort.

Just under a year after Lyra died, I was wandering around Exeter – on my mother's advice: *Clara, you have to get out more* – and I saw the Good Listeners' sign. At first, I ignored it. But later on, standing at the window looking out over the woodland, it comes back to me.

Maybe I could help. Maybe I could help someone.

Because out here in the wilderness, up here in this cottage, I might as well be dead.

I sign up a few days later.

I sign up as Clara Winterson. Winterson is my maiden name, and I do it without thinking at first. All those appeals, all those despairing pleas, they were for Lyra Brennan. Lyra Brennan's name will be tattooed on the nation's consciousness for decades to come.

Clara Brennan is a weeping mother, staring out of the television screens. *Please keep looking. Please. She must be somewhere. She has to be.* Has *to.*

But Clara Winterson is no one.

I look different now. When Lyra disappeared, I was thirty-two years old. I had long hair, bleached out by the sun and the hairdresser. I wore long, floaty skirts and pretty shoes. I smiled a lot, I realise, in hindsight. Or more than I do now, because now I never smile.

My hair is different too. It got too long during the search, and irritated me when it snagged in brambles, tangled in branches. One night, I chopped it off, sawing away big clumps of hair and shoving them unceremoniously into a bin bag. The newspapers prefer the blonde pictures, though, so they have carried on using those whenever a child is murdered or lost. I try to avoid those articles, but sometimes, by accident, I come face to face with my old self.

These days, I wear jeans, shapeless jumpers, unremarkable shirts. I have aged far more than two years. I catch a glimpse of myself in the mirror every so often. Brown hair, brown eyes, fearful expression. Beyond Coraton, it would take someone who knew me well to recognise me now, and no one in Exeter knows me well.

Nobody knows me well at all.

There are questions during the Good Listeners' training.

What brought you here? Why do you want to do this?

It is easy to tell the truth I want to believe. A world where my daughter is alive, just about to turn nine. *She's a handful, alright. They grow up so fast, don't they?*

It is easy to make that the truth.

It takes me a long time to fall asleep that night, hours after my clipped goodbye to Lucas. My dreams are full of Lyra's half-brother or half-sister, and always underneath it all is the desperate hunger: I have to know. I have to know.

In the middle of the night, I sit up sharply.

My husband killed a little girl.

My husband killed a little girl.

And suddenly I know what I can do.

16

Nobody looks up when I walk into the Good Listeners' centre midway through the morning shift. Manon and Siobhan are already on calls, heads bowed over their phones. There are a dozen reasons that I might be here anyway: forgotten phone, lost wallet, half-read book. I am Clara, part of the furniture, and always, always here.

I head to the offices at the back of the building. Neither Simeon nor Alys are here. They tend to pop in at the beginning and end of shifts, and they would not be surprised to find me in here either.

All the same, my hands shake as I turn towards the red files.

My husband killed a little girl. I reach out briskly and grab a file.

I skip past my own notes and concentrate on all the other handwriting.

Emma: although that is probably not her name.

Emma: although she may call herself something different every time she calls. If she has ever called before or since, that is.

She may be in Exeter, but her call may have cascaded in from the national hub. She may have been calling from Scarborough or Dover or Hereford. If that is what happened, the chances of her ever cascading to the Exeter centre again are negligible.

Emma is a popular name, too, which doesn't help. An Emma has rung up distraught about an ill kitten. A different Emma called in about a bitchy colleague. Or they could both be the same Emma; it is impossible to tell.

I make myself a cup of tea and I flip through a few more pages.

Emma: has lost her engagement ring. Emma: fibromyalgia is really bad today. Emma: husband run off. (Austin's brevity, there.)

Manon pops into the back office with biscuits – people often bring biscuits into the centre – and finds me flipping through a paperback. In this quiet space, you can tell when someone is coming to the end of a call. I chat with Manon for a few moments, desperate to get back to my scarlet riddles. At last, Manon goes back to her seat.

I breathe out, grab a file, turn one more page and that's when I see it.

Emma: very upset. Inconsolable, to be honest. She says her husband killed a little girl.

A shiver goes down my spine.

She says her husband killed a little girl.

It was Rosie who took this call, I see, and it can't have been a long one, because Rosie doodles long, thoughtful notes as she talks and she didn't write much this time.

This Emma rang at 8.13 p.m. on Friday 11th August.

I stare at Rosie's scribbled note again.

It can't mean anything.

It can't.

It can.

I make a note of Emma's call. That's against the rules too. But I don't care. I flick on through the file.

Nothing. Nothing.

I go back another week.

And that's when I spot another call. 8.41 p.m. on 1st September.

Emma: claims her husband killed a little girl. Says she is scared of her husband.

It was Mikey who spoke to her this time. He's added a careful note, too. *I've got no way of knowing if this is true. Emma wouldn't give any further details and hung up when I asked her if she had thought about going to the police.*

Not a car crash then, I think to myself.

Not a freak accident.

Not an exhausted doctor slipping up at the end of a long shift.

I turn the pages faster now.

More Emmas. Emmas running out of money and Emmas being groped by friends' husbands and Emmas who can't stop drinking.

Stop. *There.*

8.01 p.m., 15th September.

That was yet another Friday, I note clinically. Emma seems to call during that evening shift, the time slot that I have almost never done.

This time Emma is *convinced her husband killed a young girl. Won't say why she thinks he killed her.*

No one has ever got much detail at all from Emma. This time it was Tomos who answered the phone.

Friday evening, I think to myself. Friday evening, again.

She says her husband killed a little girl.

It can't be my little girl.

It *could* be my little girl.

I know what I am going to do.

It is Wednesday today.

Which means there are two days to go.

17

Ginny sounds relieved when I ring up first thing on Friday morning and offer to take her shift that evening. We all have each other's numbers, because there's a WhatsApp group. Of course there's a WhatsApp group.

I gather the flu's really taken it out of her, I say. And I'm in Exeter, anyway, for a dentist appointment at 5 o'clock. It would be no problem to pop in after. No problem at all.

Ginny is very grateful indeed.

Simeon barely notices the changeover. People swap shifts all the time. As long as the shifts are covered, it doesn't matter.

I feel nervous as I drive towards Exeter, my hands tense on the steering wheel. I almost veer into another car on the A30 and curse aloud.

This woman doesn't ring every Friday night, I remind myself. Some Fridays, she doesn't choose to ring. Or maybe it's that she can't ring.

But she does ring most Fridays, shouts a voice in my head. She rang last Friday. And the Friday before.

As I sit down in my office chair, I feel a surge of adrenaline pour over me.

But it's luck of the draw whether or not I speak to her. Corin is my pair on this shift, and he could easily pick up the phone to Emma if I'm already on a call. And if we're both on the line, Emma's call will cascade out to the national pool.

Thinking about it, maybe Emma does call every single Friday night. But perhaps some of her calls have been diverted to Portsmouth or Shrewsbury or Hexham or any one of the dozens of Good Listeners' centres around the country.

I have no way of knowing.

It is difficult to concentrate. I have to force myself to answer each call in the same way that I would normally. And it is hard to watch Corin calmly answer his telephone as it rings, and not snatch the phone from his hand.

Jackie rings up to tell me about a pair of stolen Russell & Bromley mules and some bergamot and mandarin candles purloined from L'Occitane. But I don't care, I can't care. Not tonight, Jackie.

As I hang up on Jackie, I ask Corin – very casually – if he's spoken to anyone interesting so far tonight.

'The usual sort of thing.' He smiles sadly. 'That was a lady who's been given notice by her landlord and can't find anywhere for her family to live. Sounds like she's in a total panic, poor thing. It'll just end up being another wretched holiday home, too.'

That's when the phone rings.

Corin moves to answer, but I move faster.

I hit the button and the red light comes on.

'Good Listeners,' I almost sing. 'Can I help?'

Nothing. Nothing at all. The phone line is silent. But then I hear it: breathing, very quiet. There is someone there.

Can you recognise someone's breathing? Of course not, you're going mad.

But maybe you can.

Just then the breathing tightens: a burst of emotion perhaps, of sadness.

'Take your time,' I murmur. 'You don't need to rush.'

More breathing, almost a gasp.

And then I hear a shaky voice. 'Hello,' a woman says quietly. 'Hello. My name is… Emma.'

18

'Thank you for calling us,' I say after a short pause. 'Is there anything in particular that you would like to talk about tonight?'

'It's my husband,' she says quietly. 'I'm calling about my husband.'

'Okay. What would you like to tell me about him?'

A pause. 'I don't… I don't really know.'

I want to scream at her. I want to scream at the top of my voice: *Tell me. Tell me what you know. You have to tell me, because I* have *to know.*

But I can't do that. If this woman puts down the phone, if she cuts this frail connection between us, I have no way of speaking to her again.

'Don't worry,' I say gently. 'I'm here whenever you want to talk.'

'I think… I think that my husband killed someone.' Emma's voice is jerky. She has spoken these words before, over and over again, but still they shock her. 'I think that he killed a little girl.'

Those words have been echoing around my head for days. But all the same, I have to crush down my gasp of horror.

'That's very sad,' I force myself to say. 'Would you like to tell me more about that?'

I have read Emma's notes again and again. I know that she has clammed up and disappeared every time someone asks for specific details. She talked the most when she was speaking to slow, gentle Mikey. She wants – needs – to talk about it. But she will not be trapped into a confession.

'I think that my husband killed a little girl.' Emma says it mechanically, as if trying to erase the horror by stripping the words of any drama.

Why? I scream in my head. *Why do you think that?*

'That must be incredibly difficult to live with. Do you want to talk a bit more about that?'

'I don't think… I don't think that I can.'

'Why don't you tell me about your husband then?' I ask. 'What is he like?'

'Oh, I don't know.' She sounds uncertain, all at once. I hold my breath, waiting for the dial tone. But then she breathes out raggedly. 'I never should have married him in the first place,' she speaks in a rush. 'It was a mistake.'

'Why do you say that?'

'I don't know… We weren't well suited,' she said. 'Right from the off…'

'In what way?'

'He could be mean. Put people down.'

This woman has a West Country accent. It's not a strong accent, but it is definitely there. Every generation dilutes the old inflections a bit more.

I would guess that this woman is roughly the same age as me. Mid-thirties. Maybe through to early forties. There isn't that hint of croakiness, the slight breathlessness of age that I can hear in some voices. As we get older, our vocal cords become thinner and the cartilage of the larynx hardens. Oddly, men's voices can get higher as they age while women's voices get lower. This voice is neither young nor old.

'What sort of thing does he do?' I ask.

'Sometimes it feels as if he hates me. The things he says…'

'What does he say?'

'He'll tell me someone doesn't like me. That they think I'm an idiot. And I find it so easy to believe. And then I avoid that person and feel more and more alone. He always knows how to hurt me. You get lonelier and lonelier and sadder and sadder.'

'That must be very hard,' I say.

'We live in quite a small village,' she says. 'The sort of place where everyone knows everyone else.'

A village. Although, of course, there are thousands of villages everywhere.

'I know what that's like.' I try to sound friendly. 'It can be tricky.'

I don't want to be talking about villages.

'He could be fun, before we got married,' she says. 'He might put people down occasionally, say the odd nasty thing, but he was clever and interesting. I thought we'd go places together. I thought we'd see the world. When I look back, I can't believe all the dreams I had.'

'In what way was he interesting?'

'He was always quite aloof,' she said. 'But it made him seem intriguing. Not like all the other boys. It was as if he didn't want to give everything away. Back then, I didn't realise it was hiding this rotten, rotten core.'

I wait for a second, in case she is going to say anything else, and then I nudge her. 'And you think he killed a little girl?'

'Yes,' she breathes.

'Why do you think that?'

Emma's breathing shortens immediately. She doesn't say anything, and I am sure she is going to put the phone down. I lose my nerve.

'Why do you think you didn't end it with him?' I ask quickly. 'All the way back then?'

Emma's breathing slows. This is something she is prepared to talk about.

'He wanted to get married,' she said bluntly. 'He wanted children. And I wanted the same thing. He seemed like a good man, back then. And I've never been… good with men.'

'That doesn't matter. It doesn't matter at all.' And for a moment, I've almost forgotten why this woman is calling. 'How long have you been together?'

She hesitates, and for a moment I think I've lost her. 'Over ten years,' she says. 'We've been married a long time now.'

'Does he ever physically hurt you?'

Emma is clearly taken aback by the bluntness of the question. Again, there is a pause. 'Yes,' she says very quietly. 'Yes, he does.'

'Do you want to tell me about that?'

'He gets in moods,' she says. 'I don't think life… Nothing is ever enough for him. When he gets into one of his moods, I can't do anything. I can feel his anger boiling up. I try to get out of the house, but I can't always. I can't stay away forever, anyway. And I just know… I can feel it coming… At some point, something will send him over the edge. He loses it, you know? Loses it completely. I can see him screaming, his face all distorted. I don't know… I don't know what to do.'

'Do you ever think about leaving him?'

'Oh, I do,' she says hopelessly. 'All the time. But I can't.'

And I am just about to ask why she can't leave when she lets out a gasp.

'I have to go,' she whispers. 'I have to go.'

And the phone goes dead.

19

I put my phone on hold. Corin is talking to someone, his voice calm and comforting. He is paying no attention to me whatsoever.

I bought a notepad earlier and now I read back through my notes.

Not much, I think, with a thud of disappointment. Not much there at all. I have wasted this precious chance.

Then I force myself to sit up and concentrate on every precious word.

Emma has been married for more than ten years.

Emma is probably roughly the same age as me.

Emma grew up in the south-west of England.

Emma lives in a village.

But I know something else, already. From what Alys and Simeon have said, the Good Listeners' areas are divided up geographically. The fact that Emma has connected to the Exeter centre several times suggests that she is closer to Exeter than she is to the Good Listeners' centre in Taunton, thirty miles up the M5 towards London, or the one in Plymouth, which is forty-something miles to the south-west of here.

I search for a map on my phone, and draw rough lines in my head.

It is still an impossibly vast area.

Did Emma put down the phone because her husband was arriving outside? Did she hear a key in the lock or a crunch on the gravel? I have no way of knowing.

I still don't think her name is Emma, although she said it more fluently this time. I suppose Emma is a usefully generic name: there are a lot of them out there, and they don't belong to any particular class.

I don't have any other name for her either, so she will have to be Emma to me.

At the end of the session, I hand in my notes to Simeon in the usual way. My note on Emma is brief but accurate.

Emma: claims her husband killed a little girl. Says he is physically violent towards her.

As I leave the centre, my notepad is buried deep in my bag.

The next week crawls.

It is easy to swap onto the Friday evening shift again. On Monday morning, there is a message in the WhatsApp group from Tarek. *Can someone* pleaaaaase *take the Friday evening slot? My wife wants to go to a school reunion (no, I have no idea why either) so I need to be home with the kids.*

I answer straight away. *No problem.*

Clara, you're an angel, Tarek writes back. *I owe you!!*

On Tuesday afternoon, I am startled by a hammering on the front door. No one ever knocks at my door and it unnerves me. Then I hear a shout. 'Clara! I know you're sodding in there! Open up!'

Rachel. Even so, for a moment I don't want to open the door. I want to crouch down out of sight and wait for her to give up and go away.

But I can't. I mustn't.

Rachel was – is – my best friend, although, like everything else in my life, our friendship is a ghost of what once was. Nevertheless, Rachel has heroically maintained our friendship, despite the fact that at times it has been entirely one-sided. She has never taken offence as I've silenced her calls and stared blankly at the wall. She came down for weeks after Lyra went missing. She spent hundreds of hours searching, stuck up a thousand posters, made untold cups of tea.

Rachel and I met while we were doing our degrees and we carried on together in lockstep through our MPhils and onto our PhDs.

Since then, Rachel has gone on to become one of the world's foremost experts on the metaphysical poets.

I open the door and she drags me into a huge hug. With her wild black curls, dark brown skin, and smile that is both easy and knowing, Rachel is comfortingly familiar. I realise I am very pleased to see her.

'Hello,' I say.

'I didn't want you coming up with an excuse.'

Despite myself, I smile. I have been avoiding Rachel's calls and she knows it.

'Sorry.'

'I'd almost forgotten the sound of your voice, you idiot!'

'I know.'

'Doesn't matter. You've spoken to Lucas?' I've always enjoyed the contrast between Rachel's bluntness and the swirling sideways glances of her favourite poets. Rachel never hesitates, and we were once well matched in that.

'Yes. I have spoken to him.'

'And are you okay about him having another kid?'

'Yes. No. I don't know.' Rachel has swerved around me and is now switching on the kettle.

'It's okay if you feel like shit about it,' she says.

'It just feels like he's moving on with his life.'

'And that feels like a betrayal. And it also reminds you that while he is moving on, you,' Rachel glances around the room, 'are definitely not.'

I change the subject. 'What are you doing down in Devon?' I ask. Rachel is a Londoner to her core and even during the bleakest moments of the search, her nails remained perfect, her hair immaculate.

'My uni's doing an event with Exeter Uni.' Rachel waves a casual hand. 'And there was an exhibition of abstract art at Exeter Cathedral that I wanted to see. Amazing use of colour. Thought I'd come and see them and it and you all at once. Anyway...' She pauses for effect. 'I've had a stroke of genius.'

'It's always terrifying when you say that.'

'Josh Aarons has wildly underestimated how much work his next bestselling tome is going to require, and he urgently needs a top-notch researcher to do a lot of legwork in various libraries. I've told him he needs you.'

I haven't heard that name for years. Josh Aarons – Professor Aarons, to be precise – surprised everyone, including himself, when his 500-page book on Shakespeare's sex life hit the bestsellers list. It is very kind of Rachel to suggest me to help out with his research crisis. But the thought of leaving Coraton sends a wave of panic through me.

'Rachel,' I mutter. 'Rachel, I can't…'

'The pay will be peanuts,' Rachel says cheerfully. 'But it will be interesting and it could open a lot of doors. And Josh is very nice and decent.'

Rachel knows that I am running out of money. She knows that soon I will not be able to pay the rent on my damp lonely cottage.

'I am really grateful,' I say. 'But I can't… Rachel, you know that I can't…'

'Clara.' Rachel and Lucas are not united on much, but they agree that isolation in Coraton is a mistake. 'Clara—'

'You know that I can't leave Coraton.'

'I know you don't *want* to leave,' Rachel says gently. 'I really do get it, Clara. But the reality is that you can't afford to stay here for long on your gardening salary. I suppose you could do something at Exeter Uni, but, Clara, I really think it would be better for you to come back to London. Healthier.'

'I know you think that. But I can't, Rachel. I just can't.'

Even the thought of leaving sends a searing panic through my throat. I can't face the chaos and colour of London. I can't imagine leaving my memories. And I can't imagine not knowing, forever.

'You may have to, Clara.' Rachel may be generous, but an academic's salary doesn't go far in London and she won't be able to help me financially. 'You should have got more from Lucas when you split.'

She is probably right. I didn't ask for much.

'Are you sure?' my lawyer asked over and over again. 'You're entitled to more than that.'

'But I don't want anything more.' I'd had to put it in writing in the end, because my voice couldn't be trusted. 'I understand what you're saying – thank you very much – but this is all that I want.'

I wonder if perhaps subconsciously I was creating a deadline for myself. There would be enough for a few years in Coraton, but not forever. I could never ask Lucas for more. Not now. Not with children on his horizon.

'I'll think about it,' I lie to Rachel.

I find that I am not telling Rachel about Emma, even though Rachel does know that I am volunteering for the Good Listeners. She was my referee.

We wander out to the garden. This autumn is a beautiful one. Up on the moor, the bracken is copper. Under the big chestnut tree, I pick up a conker. It is fresh out of its shell, and so shiny that it seems to glow.

Lyra loved conkers. It was something about their glossiness, the way they sit so perfectly in a small child's hand. She used to gather them up and put them in our big fruit bowl, running her hands through them so that they whispered together. I remember her playing with them as a toddler while I tidied up around her.

'What doing, Mummy?' she would ask when she had tired of conkers. 'Oo dat one?' when she saw something she didn't understand.

The lawn is covered in leaves now. The autumn when she was five, Lyra used to try and catch the leaves as they twirled to the ground.

I look across the beauty of the valley and I think how much Lyra would have loved this autumn, the autumn when she should have been eight.

I don't know how long I have remained silent. Rachel is picking the last sharp blackberries from the hedge.

'I can't leave,' I say to her. 'I can't leave until I know what happened to Lyra.'

'Clara, you may never know,' Rachel says quietly. 'You may have to accept that one day you will have to leave without knowing.'

'But I can't,' I whisper. 'I won't.'

'But how?' she asks. 'How are you going to find out now?'

20

By Friday, I have to force myself to wait before driving into Exeter for the evening shift.

There are two of you on duty, I remind myself, so it's 50:50 if you pick up Emma's call or not. Although, admittedly, you can tilt those odds by snatching up the phone every time it rings.

Emma may not even call this week, I tell myself.

He may have a headache and decide to stay home.

She may be out with her friends.

Or she may just decide that she doesn't feel like speaking to the Good Listeners today.

The phone rings and I snatch it up. But it's not Emma. It's Bill.

People need to believe in their own anonymity. It's the founding principle of the Good Listeners.

But it is hard on a call like this.

I hate calls like this.

Hate them.

Bill, he says his name is. He tells me his name right at the start of the conversation, too, as if to remind himself. He doesn't quite spell it out, but he's not far off either.

He can't stop himself, he says. At first, he looked just out of… well, curiosity. That was all it was. Curiosity. But now… now he can't stop.

It's only photographs though, isn't it?

I know… I know I *mustn't*.

But I can't… I can't seem to *stop*.

Bill has no one else he can talk to, I remind myself as his voice whispers in my ear. If he told anyone else the truth, he'd be in jail. He could try therapy, of course. But he would have to lie to the therapist, otherwise the therapist might report him. And lying is not a great starting point for breakthroughs in therapy.

Bill has a cold. He coughs a lot. Although everyone is coughing a lot at the moment. He has a West Country accent, too.

We have rules about safeguarding children, of course. If we are told that a child is at risk, we have to report it.

But our ability to report depends on the people providing identifying information. And all I have to go on is that this man has a cold and he is not called Bill.

So I take a deep breath.

'Those children are hurt by those photographs, Bill. You know that and I know that.'

I'm not supposed to speak to a Caller like this. But Austin is deep on another call, and it is up to me to decide how to handle this.

There is a long silence. 'I do know that,' Bill says in the end.

'Every time you look at these photographs, more children are hurt, more children have their lives ruined.'

Another long silence. 'I know.'

'And you'll get caught in the end, Bill. You'll get caught and you know what will happen to you then.'

'I know.'

'Why?' I let my voice soften just a fraction. 'Do you know why you do this, Bill?'

That's when it all comes pouring out.

Because it happened to him. Every single time I speak to someone like this, it turns out that the same thing happened to them back when they were young. Back when *they* were children.

I believe them.

I believe Bill.

It's the only time his voice changes and I know that he is not lying.

Bill tells me about the footsteps on the stairs. About the dark figure in the door. About the terror. And the horror. And the strange, revolting excitement. Because he can admit all this to me, and only to me.

'My mother's boyfriend... Well, some bloke she was seeing. He would... He would come into my room... And I... I don't want to be like this. I would do anything not to be... *Anything*. I was – what? Seven? Eight maybe. And he... How am I meant to be normal after that? I just want to be *normal*.'

'I am sorry,' I say quietly. 'I am so sorry that this happened to you.'

'Why did it have to happen? *Why*?'

'I am sorry.' I feel a pity that is halfway to anger. 'It isn't fair.'

'If anyone knew what was going on inside my head, they would hate me. Hate me.'

'I'm sure there is good in you, Bill. And none of that was your fault. None of it.'

'She should have... She should have kept me safe.'

'I know. And I am sorry.'

These stories are always the same. The name changes. The date changes. But one thing stays the same: the destruction of a small child's innocence.

And Bill cries, red raw sobs ripping at his throat.

After a few more minutes, not-Bill hangs up.

I'm not naive. I don't for one second think that Bill will change what he does – who he *is* – because of one phone call.

But there is a chance, a very small chance, that this conversation makes him pause. That it makes him think. That something somewhere changes.

I think that's the only thing that gives me hope.

Of course, it could all be complete fantasy.

We get that too, a lot. People will give you extraordinarily detailed descriptions of their trauma – the plane crash, the mugging, the stabbing – and it is only slowly that you realise it's all a complete fiction.

Nowadays, I actually find it easier to tell if people are lying or not when I can only hear their voices. Facial expressions, body language: they are the things that create uncertainty. They are easier to disguise.

There's one woman who rings up every week to tell us that she's David Bowie's wife, but that no one will believe her.

Every. Single. Week.

Tomos once reminded her that David Bowie is – tragically – no longer with us, and she cried and cried.

The next week she rang up again. Still married to David Bowie.

People lie. They lie all the time.

After all, we all decide to whom we will tell our stories. And we all decide how to tell those stories.

When I saw those two solid lines in that bar bathroom, I went to Becky – lovely Catholic Becky – to ask her for her advice on having an abortion.

When, years ago, my friend Andi was wondering about bunking a day off work for a saucy weekend in Paris, she came to me.

You only live once, babe. Do it! Do it! And tell me everything!

I knew exactly what Becky's advice would be.

Andi knew exactly what my advice would be.

We decide to whom we tell our stories. And when you ring the Good Listeners, you get to decide the story, too.

I do find it odd that people will bother to ring up a total stranger just to tell them a lie. But they do. You can hear it in their voices. Prosody, it's called: the stresses and intonations in a language. Prosody changes when someone is lying and I've listened for long enough now that I can hear it.

Sometimes, they don't even know that they're lying.

And we only know what they tell us.

They'll ring up to confess, too. But gradually you start to sense that they're not really confessing. Instead, they are fantasising about something they would like to do at some blurry point in the future.

So some Callers reject the truth, and others confess to fiction.

And there is another thought that I cannot quite allow to penetrate my mind. The thought that Bill didn't just lie about his name. But that Bill lied about all the important details.

That when he said *little boys* he meant *little girls.*

And that he didn't just look at photographs.

But I will never know.

I will never know the truth.

When Bill hangs up, I have to go and sit in the kitchenette.

But then I jump to my feet. *Emma.* It is Friday night. It is Emma's time to call.

I hurry back to my seat.

21

I stare at the phone, willing Emma to call. I am glad I didn't rush Bill off the phone. But I can't bear the thought that I might have missed Emma's call.

More calls. No Emma. But just when I am giving up hope, my phone rings. I snatch it up.

'My name is Emma.' I know it is her before she has groped for the name.

'Hello,' I say. 'Thank you for calling us. Do you have something in particular you would like to talk about?'

I hold my breath. Will she recognise my voice? Does it matter if she does? I have an ordinary voice – although I suppose everybody's voice is ordinary to themselves. I have no particular regional accent, nothing to remark upon. I did wonder – madly – over the course of the week whether I should try a different accent. But then I realised that, at the very least, my duty partner would think I had gone mad.

So I speak like I normally do.

'I hate my husband,' Emma says sharply. 'Hate him.'

She sounds angrier than last week. Last week, Emma sounded scared, uncertain. This week, the husband has done something to make her furious.

Maybe, I think. Maybe this will help me.

'Why?' I ask calmly. 'What has he done?'

'He's a bastard.' Her voice quivers and suddenly she sounds close to tears. There is no mention of a murdered child this time.

'I'm sorry.' I don't say anything else. Silence is a useful tool. After a moment, Emma takes the bait.

'He's really upset my daughter.'

My daughter. The thought is a punch. This woman has a daughter. Somehow, this had not occurred to me.

Then I am felled by another realisation. Worse.

He has a daughter.

He has a daughter.

'I'm really sorry to hear that he's upset your daughter.' Somehow, my voice stays calm. 'What has he done?'

'She broke one of his trains,' Emma almost shouts. 'One of his stupid trains!'

'His *trains*?' I hope my probing sounds like confusion. 'What trains?'

'His Kimlock trains!' Emma spits. 'He's obsessed with them. He's collected them all his life. Spends a bloody fortune on them. It's insane. My daughter and my niece found the set-up in the attic and started playing with them. They didn't realise that they were special. How would they? They're only young. And of course, they managed to break one. He went crazy when he saw that they had broken it. Absolutely mad.'

'That's awful. How old is your daughter?'

The question triggers caution. 'She's seven.' And I can't tell whether Emma is lying or not.

'It sounds very upsetting.'

'My daughter couldn't stop crying all that evening. He's a bastard. He's an utter bastard.'

'Did he hit her?'

A long pause. Then a sob. 'No. But I thought he was going to. She thought he was going to.'

'Has he ever done anything like this before?'

Emma dodges the question, or doesn't hear it through her tears. 'How could anyone behave like that towards a little girl? I don't understand how anyone could do that to my little…'

She was going to say the daughter's name there, I thought. Interesting that despite not mentioning the murder of a child, Emma remains extremely secretive.

'Do you think you and your daughter are safe?' The question is blunt and it brings Emma to a juddering halt.

'He wouldn't hurt her,' Emma says eventually. But she doesn't sound certain.

'Has he ever hurt you?' It is crucial not to reveal that we have spoken before, that I already know the answer to this question. Emma is so cautious. I think she would slam down the phone at the smallest coincidence.

Again, Emma stalls. 'Yes,' she says quietly in the end. 'Yes, he has.'

'Have you thought about speaking to the police about that?' I ask. To me, my voice sounds oddly strained, but Emma doesn't seem to notice. I suppose she doesn't know what my voice is supposed to sound like.

'I can't...' says Emma. 'I can't. My children... I don't know where we'd go...'

'Was your daughter alright afterwards? Or as alright as she could be.'

'The next morning...' Emma chokes up at the memory. 'She was crying when we were walking to the school bus. She really had to pull it together to get onto the bus. And no child... No child should have to do that.'

'Are you worried that your children might be in danger?' I ask.

Emma is quiet for so long that I panic that she might have put the phone down.

'I don't think...' She speaks so quietly that I have to press the earpiece hard to my head. 'I don't think that he would hurt them.'

Neither of us believe her. And I think she is about to say more when I hear the patter of feet on a staircase.

Emma's voice changes instantly, half-tender, half-impatient. 'I thought you were asleep—'

She puts down the phone without another word.

22

I feel exhilarated as I race back down the dual carriageway towards Coraton. The rest of the session was busy. There was a teacher defeated by the demands of the week. A schoolboy – thirteen-ish from the up-and-down hoarseness of his voice – with a crush on his friend Ethan. And Jackie.

As soon as I reach the cottage, I run up the stairs. There is a little desk in Lyra's room – in my head, it is still Lyra's room; it will always be Lyra's room – and I hurry to it, gripping my notepad and my laptop.

A seven-year-old girl. Although I am not sure that the daughter is seven. There was a hesitation when she said that.

What else? I flip through my notes again. I notice that Emma has never called before 8 p.m. Maybe that is because her daughter goes to bed at 8 p.m., and if she rang before that, there might be a risk that the daughter could overhear something. That would suggest that the daughter is still quite a young child. So maybe seven isn't too far off after all.

I remember, too, that the footsteps pattered down the steps, quickly and confidently. Does that also indicate a slightly older child? At three, Lyra still took the stairs slowly, her chubby hand reaching up for the bannisters.

I check myself. I only *think* that the footsteps pattered down the stairs. I am not absolutely sure if I remember precisely. I feel a wave of frustration.

There is something else, too. It seems as if Emma is fairly confident she cannot be overheard speaking on the phone once the daughter is safely tucked up in bed. To me, that suggests that Emma lives in a fairly substantial house.

In Damson Cottage, for example, you would be able to hear someone on the phone downstairs. Even with both the bedroom and the kitchen doors closed, you would still have a good chance of catching some of the conversation. But Emma speaks freely, not at all concerned about being overheard.

So that suggests a larger house, the bedrooms safely out of earshot.

But even if the daughter is not seven, there was an important clue in Emma's story.

The school bus.

Okehampton is the nearest secondary school to Coraton, for example, and a large bus drops all the older children off at a stop down on the main road. The older children never look especially delighted at the prospect of the trek up the hill to the village. Parents don't need to meet the secondary school buses.

The Devon primary school buses are different. Parents meet younger children off the smaller primary school buses earlier in the afternoon, because those children are too young to be allowed to walk home alone. If Emma is taking her daughter to the bus, the daughter is still quite young.

The key thing about the primary bus – and here I turn to my laptop, pulling up the county council's website – is that not everyone qualifies for it. You have to live at least two miles from the school to be entitled to take the bus.

So maybe that means that Emma also lives at least two miles from one of the schools in one of the towns somewhere in Devon. Around my part of the moor, circles with four-mile diameters would block out a lot of the area.

You're making too many assumptions, I warn myself. The private schools also – more googling now – have different buses, different times, different systems.

I'll have to think in terms of probabilities, I tell myself. It is *probable* that Emma lives more than two miles from any of the primary schools.

* * *

Emma mentioned an attic. That also suggests this family wasn't living in a cramped flat in Exeter. But still. Useful to have it confirmed. And this attic is big enough for a train set.

Most importantly, she mentioned something else. She mentioned the Kimlock trains.

I know the Kimlock trains. Lyra had a few of them.

They're compatible with BRIO. All the toy train brands are: Bigjigs, Melissa & Doug, omnipotent Thomas.

But the Kimlock trains are different.

Some of them are ordinary children's toys. I can still remember a few of Lyra's. There was a bright red steam engine with pretty yellow twirls painted on it. And an emerald-green express train.

But some of the Kimlock trains aren't destined for knockabout childhood fun. The older ones, the antique ones, they're collectibles. Like *Star Wars* action figures and *My Little Pony*, Hornby trains and Pokémon cards. People hoard them, stashing them away, immaculate in their original boxes. These are toys that will never be played with. Someone paid over $300,000 for a Barbie, I read once.

To each their own.

And there are people out there who collect Kimlock trains with a feverish obsession.

Kimlock, I think cautiously. Kimlock.

It doesn't take me long to learn all about the Kimlock trains. The vintage ones are made of maple, I learn, and they are all hand-painted in a workshop in Lincolnshire. They are beautiful – even I can see that – with their tiny names painted in gold leaf.

That's the Kimlock USP: the names.

Bluebell. Dahlia. Buttercup. Cornflower.

No one seems to find the flower names incongruous.

I scroll on. Some of the Kimlock accessories are charming. A Tower Bridge that can be raised or lowered. A long-lost London Bridge. A Ponte Vecchio: the train-track set within a Florentine jumble.

I discover dedicated chat rooms and eBay sellers and specialised restorers. There are several self-appointed experts. There are tours of the Kimlock factory. Much excitement, I read, is being generated by the Sotheby's auction next spring.

Next spring: too far away for me.

I scroll through eBay sellers. There is an *Amaryllis* for sale for a mere £15,000. *Amaryllis* gleams up at me, a brilliant vermillion. A *Carnation*, one of the very first Kimlock trains ever produced, costs even more.

He's collected them all his life.

Spends a bloody fortune on them. It's insane.

I think of Ryan Dallyn's battered van bouncing from one decorating job to the next. Surely he wouldn't spend thousands on a toy train? But once again, it's all a matter of perspective.

A coral-coloured *Marigold* is £80. Ryan Dallyn could be just as furious at the destruction of an £80 *Marigold* as the owner of a ruined £15,000 *Amaryllis*.

I look through the listings again.

And then I start researching Kimlock collectors.

23

My research takes a long time. The night turns to day as I hunt. I set up a burner Facebook account and join all the Kimlock appreciation groups on Facebook.

There is an annual Kimlock conference, I discover. It's in February, which I assume was chosen because Kimlock trains are an indoor passion, and there isn't much else to do in February. Again, far too long to wait for the next piece of the jigsaw puzzle.

The next conference – organised by the Kimlock Society, no less – will be held in Middlesbrough. The last conference was in Royal Leamington Spa. The year before, Bury St Edmunds hosted.

I scroll through the photographs: men standing proudly beside highly polished *Daffodils* or *Azaleas* or *Camellias*.

I peer at the faces. But I have no idea what I am looking for.

Five years ago, the event was held at Launceston, I realise with a jolt, thirty miles along the A30, just the other side of the Cornish border.

But again, the faces tell me nothing. Certainly, there is no shock of recognition. No, oh *him*. I know *him*.

I trawl through the frequent commenters on the Kimlock Superfans group.

None of them have any visible links to Devon.

Or murder.

I find myself googling the chairman of the Kimlock Society. He lives near Brockenhurst in the New Forest, I discover. A Mr Francis Fenton-Brown Esq, married to the charming Maria.

I look at their photographs for a moment or two, at the greying hair and the contented expressions. Frank and Maria are major players at the Rotary Club, by the looks of things, and serious golfers to boot. There's a snap of Maria on the gate at the local show, one of a dozen smiling, Day-Glo stewards. Frank's onions cleaned up that day, and Maria's sweet peas took second prize among some very hot competition.

Some days, I wish I was Frank and Maria.

Frank's mobile number is on the Kimlock Society's stone-age website. It takes me a moment to realise that I am calling it.

'Frank Fenton-Brown!' the man himself announces after one ring. I freeze. 'Hello!' Fenton-Brown bellows. 'I can't hear you! Must be a bad line!'

I unfreeze. 'Hello, Mr Fenton-Brown,' I say smoothly. 'I'm terribly sorry to bother you, but my name is Clara Winterson and I am researching an article about Kimlock trains. I have been told that *you* are the man to speak to.'

'Kimlock trains!' I can tell straight away from the warmth in his voice that Frank Fenton-Brown will happily spend the rest of the week talking about Kimlock trains. 'Of course! Of *course*! What do you want to know?'

'Actually,' I say quickly. 'Do you live in the New Forest? I am going to be in the area this afternoon, and I was wondering if I could possibly drop by?'

'Of course!' Frank is delighted. 'We're about all afternoon. Stop by whenever suits. I can show you my *precioussss*.'

I laugh obediently. 'Two o'clock?'

'We'll have the kettle on!'

I'm in my car within minutes. Just before I reach the main road, I see Amber Dallyn, Ryan's wife. She is hurrying towards Nell Turner's house, her head down. Nell Turner is the barmaid at the Ring of Bells, the only pub in Coraton. She is usually fairly jolly, with lots of curly light-brown hair. Nell and Amber have been best friends all their lives, Amber told me once, as she helped me put up Caspar's bird box out in the orchard.

As I slow the car, Nell's front door opens and she comes running out. I brake sharply. Nell is moving too fast to notice a car, too fast to notice me. She races towards Amber. Amber is crying, I realise. That is why her head is down.

Nell throws her arms around Amber. But it is only as I am edging past them that I see Amber's face over Nell's shoulder. I gasp.

Amber has a very painful-looking black eye.

24

The drive to Hampshire takes three hours. I spend the first half of the journey worrying about Amber. At the Good Listeners, I have spoken to so many women trapped in the cycle of escaping a violent man only to slide back into the nightmare over and over again.

Poor Amber. Poor, poor Amber.

I feel desperately sorry for her children, too – that little boy and girl. Growing up thinking that it is normal for men to rage with violence. Growing up to think that love looks like anger.

At least Amber has Nell. I don't know Nell at all really, but she looks as if there is toughness mixed in with the jolliness. She probably has to be tough. Pauly, her husband, is regarded as amiably useless by Coraton. Pauly was a builder, but went bust. The Turners live in a permanently half-built house close to the main road. Pauly now works as a delivery driver, the house serving as a shrine to his incompetence.

Amber has the Blackslades, too, I remind myself. There is a safe place she can flee to, even if she is lured home afterwards. As a criminal barrister, Gabriel Blackslade will know more than most about domestic violence.

I push away the idea that Amber could be Emma. Amber. Emma. Perhaps.

I think I would recognise Amber's voice, but it's hard to be sure. I recognise Amber's voice at Harepath because I am expecting to speak to Amber. I've never heard Amber's disembodied voice, and I can't think of a way of achieving that.

Another complicating factor is that phones can distort voices slightly. Phone microphones and speakers vary in quality, and they don't transmit a full range of frequencies, so elements of a voice can be lost in transmission. Digital compression of a phone call can also affect audio quality. Some people use very different mannerisms and voices when they are talking on the phone.

So I think I would recognise Amber's voice. But I am not sure.

Amber could certainly call on Friday nights, the time that Emma calls. Ryan and his friends are always in the pub on a Friday night. Although most of the locals are, to be fair.

I wonder how often Amber has a black eye on a Saturday morning.

Has he ever hurt you?

Yes, he has.

Emma *could* be Amber.

Emma could be anyone.

Is there anything I can do to help Amber? Probably not. For all I know, it is the cloud of suspicion around Ryan that has put their marriage under intolerable stress. Amber quite possibly blames me for everything. She has always been polite to me at Harepath, but we have rarely exchanged more than a few words.

I couldn't talk to Nell about Amber either. Nell would – quite reasonably – think it was none of my business. Despite her jolliness, Nell has always been cool towards me, and I can't blame her. Pauly never had an alibi for the day Lyra went missing. He told the police he was busy working on the half-finished house, but no one saw him there. No one saw him at all that day. Of course there were whispers.

Not only did Pauly Turner not have an alibi, but the Turners' daughter, Tabitha, was one of the children who was playing with Lyra just before she disappeared.

Poor Tabitha, not her fault. Never her fault. Tabitha – little Tabitha – her glittery butterfly face paint smeared with tears.

Five minutes after I realised Lyra was gone, I saw Tabitha in the middle of a circle of adults. *Who did you speak to, Tabitha? What did you see, Tabitha? Where is she, Tabitha? Where is she?*

I remember Nell snapping in the end, driving away desperate questions. *She doesn't know anything. Leave her alone. For god's sake, she's just a child.*

It is always a shock when I see Tabitha around Coraton now: Tabitha, growing up pretty. Tabitha, eleven now – eleven! – while my daughter stays frozen in time.

In another world, I wonder if my daughter and Tabitha are friends.

Or in a parallel universe, maybe it was Tabitha who was snatched and, in that universe, I am happy. I'd sacrifice Tabitha in a heartbeat.

As I drive past Honiton, I realise it has been ages since I made this drive east. I have let my world become so narrow.

I think ahead to the Fenton-Browns. I have to make a plan. I put my foot down and roar along the A303.

And it is a relief, in a way, to escape Coraton. To escape the looming mists of Dartmoor.

The Fenton-Brown residence is charming. Double-fronted, Victorian, solid old brick: Brock House.

I looked up Brock House on Zoopla as I waited to pay for petrol at the Hazel Grove services. I concluded that the Fenton-Browns must have retired down to the New Forest ten years ago. Before that, Frank was a managing director at one of the big City banks. Not the very top, but an extremely comfortable existence all the same. Facebook introduced me to three children and a blur of grandchildren.

Maria and Frank definitely aren't Emma and her husband, and that is the only thing that matters.

Frank Fenton-Brown opens the door with a fizz of energy that defies his just over seventy years.

'Come in!' he declares. 'Come in, come in, come in.'

Frank doesn't bother with the drawing room – an elegant eau-de-nil-coloured room to the left – but leads me straight into the kitchen at the back of the house. This is big, with lots of pine and a scarlet Aga.

'My wife, Maria,' Frank declares.

Both Frank and Maria give off an air of happy fulfilment. Retired, affluent, happy. I sense an awareness that they may not have unlimited years to enjoy their good fortune, so jolly well *carpe diem*.

'You're here about Kimlock trains.' Maria rolls her eyes good-naturedly. 'Those wretched things.'

Despite the complicated coffee machine on the quartz countertop, Maria is pouring boiling water into a big Emma Bridgewater teapot.

'Maria's a Kimlock widow,' Frank announces.

'We gang up and take ourselves off to a spa.' Maria plonks the teapot lid back into place.

'Now.' Frank rubs his hands together. 'What would you like to know, young lady?'

I smile brightly. 'Do tell me, Mr Fenton-Brown, when did you start collecting?'

'Frank! Call me Frank! Well, my great uncle Peter gave me my first Kimlock train for my fourth birthday…'

The intertwined history of Frank and Kimlock trains takes a good half an hour. Maria resignedly hands round a plate of millionaire's shortbread that tastes homemade.

'Would you like to see them?' Frank comes to the end of his monologue.

'I'd love to!' I enthuse. 'Your silver jubilee *Aster* sounds wonderful!'

'Come on, then!'

It is only when we reach the attics that I understand Brock House's key selling point for the Fenton-Browns.

Frank's collection takes up a whole floor, the Kimlock train lines running from one side of the house to the other.

'She likes it.' Frank is watching my face closely.

'Everyone likes it,' Maria says. 'Especially if they don't have to live with it.'

'It's wonderful.' Despite myself, I can feel a smile spreading over my face. 'Magical.'

The attention to detail is extraordinary. Over by a big brick chimney stack, there is a town, complete with passengers waiting on the platform for their train. Under a big Velux window is the industrial zone, a sprawling port spiky with gantry cranes waiting to unload the miniature trains.

I realise Frank has asked me something and I did not hear the question.

'Are there lots of collectors with this number of trains?' I ask hastily.

'Quite a few.' Frank nods approvingly, back on track.

'Not many with this sort of set-up though.' Maria, proud despite her eye-rolling.

'No,' says Frank quickly. 'Not many.'

'Do you know each other?' I ask. 'All the collectors?'

'I know some of them quite well.' Frank purses his lips. 'We meet up at the conferences, of course. And if you see someone once a year, well, after a while it builds up, doesn't it?'

'Yes,' I agree. 'I'm from near Okehampton in Devon. Not far from Exeter. There isn't a big collector round there, is there? It would be so helpful to talk to them for this article.'

'Can't think of one.' Frank was shaking his head. 'There's Bob Carlyon. He's got a blue *Primrose*,' he added wistfully.

'Bob's much further west than that,' Maria interjects at once. 'He's the other side of Truro.'

I sense that Maria has spent enough time at Kimlock conferences to know the main characters.

'I'm interested in anyone in Devon really.'

Maria is looking at me more closely now.

'Nobody jumps out.' Frank picks up a small green steam engine and strokes it unselfconsciously. 'I know a couple of big collectors in Dorset.'

'You're sure?' I ask, an edge of desperation creeping in. 'Quite sure? I suppose there might be someone who doesn't come along to the conferences.'

'It could be.' Frank replaces the small green steam engine. 'The conferences aren't everyone's cup of tea.' He laughs as if the idea was unimaginable.

'Would it be possible to find out?' I ask. 'If there was a big collector around me?'

'I'm not sure.' Frank ponders.

'It would be so helpful,' I say again. 'Would there be any way of looking them up?'

'Um...'

Maria is nobody's fool. 'People can be quite safety-conscious,' she says coolly. 'Some of the rarer Kimlocks are quite valuable, you know. People might want to keep a low profile.'

Frank straightens up sharply.

'They certainly are valuable.' He looks around his cherished attic. 'And I suppose they would be very easy to move around, and crooks like that sort of thing, don't they?'

They are both staring at me now, suddenly aware that they know nothing about me, that they may have invited absolutely anyone into their home. Frank moves in front of Maria.

'What did you say your name was?' Maria asks.

Maria is tougher than her Cath Kidston apron implies, I realise. Frank may have moved in front of her, but it is Maria who would defend her home and her husband to the bitter end.

'I'm sorry,' I speak rapidly. 'It's not what you think.'

'I think,' Maria's voice is pure ice, 'that you had better explain.'

25

Maria puts on a pair of bifocals and reads the article quickly. She glances up at me and then looks back to her laptop screen. She must be looking at an old photograph of me, I think. From one of those endless desperate, fruitless appeals. Then she nods briskly.

'I am terribly sorry for your loss,' she says. 'I do not know how anyone endures that level of grief.'

Maria's voice is calm and compassionate. I feel a sudden urge to weep into her shoulder.

But I am not here to cry.

We are back in the Fenton-Brown kitchen, their fears now assuaged.

'How can we help?' Frank is a couple of beats behind Maria, as I suspect he often is. 'I don't quite understand what we can do… But if there is anything…?'

'Absolutely.' Maria looks at me expectantly. 'What can we do?' A moment later, Maria answers her own question. 'Frank, you've got addresses for most of the members of the Kimlock Society, don't you?'

'I… Yes.' Frank agrees. 'But there are rules, darling… Data protection… That sort of thing.'

'Don't be ridiculous, Frank. No one will ever know.' Maria looks at me to confirm and I nod swiftly.

'Well. Um. I suppose…'

* * *

Maria and I follow Frank into his study. This is clearly a man's domain. The desk is walnut, the lightshade Tiffany's. There is a Stubbs-esque racehorse painting on the racing-green wall behind the desk.

Frank sits down at his desk and powers up his computer. The Society's addresses, it soon becomes clear, are held in a spreadsheet in a way that I suspect does not, in fact, fulfil the requirements of the Data Protection Act.

'Layla comes in two mornings a week,' Frank says vaguely, and I see the old man he will be not many years from now. 'She helps with the running of things.'

'We can manage,' Maria says firmly. 'Now, Clara, which postcodes should I search for? Where should I start?'

By the end of the afternoon, I have addresses all over Devon and up towards Somerset. There are Kimlock enthusiasts in Exmouth and Tiverton, in Hittisleigh and Great Torrington, in Budleigh Salterton and Zeal Monachorum.

I feel my fingers itch at the urge to start trawling these names and addresses. To find out who these people are and what they do and whether they have a seven-year-old daughter.

Maria is watching me shrewdly. I have shied away from explaining how I have created my suspect's profile, but I think Maria has guessed that I have not acquired it by reasonable means.

'Do you think he's in there?'

'I don't know. Not yet.'

'None of these names are leaping out, though.'

'No,' I admit. 'Not exactly.'

From their birthdates, a lot of the Kimlock Society members are too old to fit my profile of Emma's husband, although there are a few younger associates scattered around Hackney where Kimlock appreciation apparently has a certain kitsch coolness.

'What if this man doesn't live at any of these addresses?' Maria asks. 'What will you do next?'

'I haven't got that far ahead,' I confess.

The three of us sit in silence for a few seconds. Maria gets up and puts the kettle on the Aga again.

'The manufacturer might know,' said Frank slowly. 'This man might be one of their most regular customers.'

'The manufacturers won't just give out addresses,' said Maria. 'They're not like us.'

'No.'

'The Kimlock Society could send out an email?' Maria suggests. 'Although I am not quite sure what you are looking for?'

'Thank you,' I say. 'But I'm not sure what we would say.'

'Let us know,' Maria urges me.

'It may well be one of those addresses.' It is me who is trying to cheer the two of them up now. 'I'll have to go through them slowly, work it out.'

It is a long shot, I know. The Kimlock Society is friendly, cheerful, faintly ironic. None of these are qualities I associate with Emma's husband. It is a chance.

Maria folds her hands together and presses her thumbs to her mouth.

'There must be a way,' she says. 'There has to be. We've got all these trains upstairs. There must be a way of using them.'

'As bait, I suppose,' I say carefully.

Frank looks nervous at the thought of his precious trains being used as bait.

'It *is* a historic collection,' he admits. 'If there were a way…'

'I need to trap him,' I say delicately. 'I need him to come to me.'

'Exactly…' Frank hmms and ahhs again.

'Frank.' I sound wheedling. 'Could I possibly take some photographs of your trains?'

It doesn't take long to set up my brand-new eBay account. Hampshirelass143 has a wide range of Kimlock trains available at a variety of price points. She has inherited them, she says, and she'll be sad to see them go, but granddad's trains deserve a home where they will be properly appreciated.

Frank enjoys writing my blurbs and setting the minimum bids. Maria copy-edits.

'A mint-condition *Azalea* is worth at least £8,000,' Frank tells her firmly. 'And that golden *Petunia* is one of only ten ever made.'

'Well, why don't we really eBay it?' snaps Maria. 'We could take all the grandchildren to Barbados for Christmas.'

As they bicker, I photograph the Kimlock royal train. It is crucial, I know, that these photographs do not appear elsewhere on the internet. This has to be believable.

We set up auctions, and a few listings with a Buy-It-Now option. I don't make any of the auctions live yet. I want to comb through the Kimlock Society addresses first. And I want more from Emma.

'Stay the night,' Maria urges me. 'It's such a long drive.'

But I am on the rota tomorrow, and with all this driving I really need the Harepath hours. 'That's very kind,' I say. 'But I really must be getting home.'

'Let us know if there is anything more we can do to help. And come and see us again.'

I feel an odd pang as I steer my way out of the New Forest.

At the Good Listeners, I am surrounded by a professional sort of kindness. A benevolence doled out from beyond the safety of a phone line. But Frank and Maria have welcomed me into their home and tried to help. This was not an anonymous cordiality. This was not the professional sympathy of the police. This was something else. This was a humanity that I had almost forgotten existed.

I am exhausted by the time I make my way through Coraton. At my postbox at the bottom of the bumpy track, I stop. There is just one letter.

The envelope is plain and white and gives no hint of the chaos it will unleash in my life.

26

Mrs Ingram has died, the letter informs me dispassionately. None of the inheritors can or wish to buy out the others. The house will have to be sold. This is a formal notice. I have two months to leave.

For a moment, I can't move.

At the Good Listeners, I have spoken to so many people who are losing their homes, their most basic security. I have listened to the shock and the despair and the grief.

I wasn't prepared for it though. I didn't even know Mrs Ingram had died. I had vaguely sensed that Damson Cottage had been her husband's indulgence, becoming something of a millstone after his death. There seems to be no affection for the house among her heirs either. Simplest to sell.

There is no way that I can buy it. House prices have soared in Devon. A pretty cottage at the top of a track: it will be someone's dream, despite the damp.

Rents have soared locally too. The Gardener's Cottage is a holiday home costing hundreds of pounds a week. So is the Olde Dairy and the Olde Granary and the Olde School. The Ring of Bells's chef lives in a caravan behind the pub.

I can't leave Coraton. But I can't stay either. Two months. *Two months.* I feel desperation start to burn.

Lyra's room. That bed: that is the last bed she slept in. That kitchen table: that is where she ate her last breakfast. I imagine peeling myself off the walls like one of Lyra's old Disney stickers, tearing and disintegrating, taking the paint with me.

I can't leave.

Even though it is late, I find that I have called Rachel and the words are flooding out.

'I am sorry,' she says. 'I am so sorry. I know how much that house means to you.'

For a moment, madly, I wonder if I could borrow the deposit from someone. But I can't ask Lucas. Our lives are too far apart now. Rachel rents anyway. And my mother… She scrapes by on her pension. She doesn't have anything to spare.

'I can't leave without knowing what happened,' I whisper to Rachel. 'Without *justice*.'

'Come back to London, Clara,' Rachel says gently. 'There is a way back, I promise you.'

Rachel does not expect the killer to be found. Not now. No one does.

'But I can't.' My eyes burn. 'I can't.'

'I'm hectic this week,' Rachel says. 'But I can come back down this weekend. I can even be there by Friday lunchtime if you want.'

'I've got to be at the Good Listeners on Friday night,' I say apologetically. Emma may call.

'You spend all your time at that place,' Rachel says. 'But don't worry, I can hang out at yours while you're busy. Mark some essays.'

'It would be nice to see you, Rachel. I'm sorry about this.'

'Clara,' Rachel says softly. 'Don't be stupid.'

'Thank you though.'

I can't sleep that night. I read the Ingrams' lawyer's letter again and again. I can't leave Coraton. I can't.

I think of the graveyard, and Lyra's memorial. I can't leave here.

And I have to find Emma.

27

'It's medieval,' Rachel whispers in delight. 'Properly Olde.'

At teatime on a Friday afternoon, the pub is already busy. The Ring of Bells is picturesque and thatched, with age-blackened beams low enough to concuss the clientele. Most of the time, I can't face the pub. The chit-chat, the well-worn jokes, the smoky fire. But seen through Rachel's eyes, it is charming.

Rachel arrived just after lunch on Friday and dragged me straight out for a walk up to Coraton Tor. On the way back to the cottage, she diverted me into the pub.

'I can only stay for an hour,' I remind her. 'And I'll have to have a lemonade or something.'

'Fine!' Rachel rolls her eyes. 'Fine!'

The first person I see is Ryan Dallyn, Amber's husband. He is standing among the crowd at the bar and as we walk in, his pint freezes halfway to his mouth. Jordie Meldon – Ryan's friend and alibi – spins around too, pint slopping. Awkward smiles and I wish I hadn't come.

Rachel hums the *Deliverance* theme tune under her breath, but smiles at everyone as she makes her way to the bar. I find a small table and sit down.

Behind the bar, I can see from her body language that Nell Turner is being glacial to Ryan and Jordie. It must be difficult in a place like Coraton – where there is only one pub – to avoid people.

I look around the rest of the cosy room. The bell-ringers are in one corner. They practise on Friday afternoons and retire to the pub fairly swiftly. Gabriel Blackslade is with them. Bell-ringing is the sort of thing he thinks is important for the community. In another corner, some members of the choir are having a quick drink before their session in the church.

Rachel reappears with a lemonade and a gin and tonic. 'Who is that?' There is a glint of appreciation in her eye.

I look around to see who has come in, then twist back towards Rachel.

Rachel realises she has said the wrong thing. 'Don't worry,' she adds quickly.

'No, it's fine,' I say. 'That's Lawrence Wrenscott.'

Lawrence Wrenscott is the good-looking and charming son of Ferdinand and Georgia Wrenscott. Until a decade ago, generations of Wrenscotts had lived in the splendour of Harepath House. Unfortunately for everyone, Ferdie Wrenscott enjoyed both a flutter at the races and a drink, habits which eventually spiralled into full-blown addictions. In the end, Ferdie and Georgia Wrenscott had to sell Harepath to the Blackslades and retreat to a crumbling farmhouse across the fields from the manor.

I wonder what it's like for Lawrence now, watching Caspar rollerskate up and down the drive and Cecily trot by on her pony.

At the bar, Jordie and Ryan greet Lawrence noisily. Gabriel, who is buying a round, gives them a thin smile. Nell glowers at all of them.

I've never thought Gabriel liked Lawrence much. Gabriel, I suspect, quite enjoys the 'lord of the manor' role that possession of Harepath imparts. But while people don't quite doff their caps to Lawrence, everyone still defers to him.

'Those three have been friends all their lives,' I explain to Rachel. 'Jordie's from a big local farming family. Lawrence's family are faded grandees. Ryan's a decorator. They've been best friends since they were at the local baby group together, from what I've heard.'

'The barmaid's not a fan though,' Rachel observes.

'That's because Ryan is a violent creep,' I say simply. 'Nell is best friends with Amber, Ryan's wife. Nell spends a lot of time picking up the pieces.'

'Yuck,' says Rachel. Then she remembers. 'Isn't Ryan the one who...'

'Yes,' I say. 'He was the one in Abbot's Wood that day. Those three all gave each other alibis. They said they were together the whole time.'

'Village life.' Rachel shudders. 'I don't know how anyone does it.'

'A lot of the other people are nice,' I say quickly. 'And Jordie Meldon came up with his big tractor to cut the hedge up to my house last winter. He brought a jar of strawberry jam that his wife had made.'

As I say this, I am aware of how ludicrous it sounds if Jordie lied to give Ryan an alibi. But Jordie has always been the friendliest of the three. He has straw-like blond hair that is usually trapped under a tweed flat cap, and his trousers always look as if they are held up by baling twine. All the Meldons have the same narrow faces, which taper to a pointy chin. I don't know Jordie's wife. She works flat out on the farm, from what Amber has said.

'What does Lawrence do?' Rachel's eyes are still on Lawrence's russet good looks. Lawrence is running his hand through his hair, leaving it artfully dishevelled.

'Not much.' I know I sound dismissive. 'He peaked about a decade ago. Went to Sherborne – very expensively – and then got a job in the City and married a woman called something like Arabella or Araminta. But then he lost his job, and Arabella or Araminta ran off with someone else, and he ended up back with his parents.'

Like Ryan and Jordie, Lawrence is in his mid-thirties now. 'I can't imagine living with my parents,' says Rachel. 'We'd all kill each other.'

'Tell me about it.'

'I've left Mum trying to do a roast on the Aga,' Lawrence is saying loudly. 'But the Aga's so buggered that it's already taken bloody hours. Dad's renamed it the Aga Khan-t.'

Jordie and Ryan laugh.

I can vividly imagine the three of them getting stoned behind a hay bale as teens, and never quite leaving behind that adolescence of surfing and drink-driving and wild camping on Dartmoor. Although

Jordie will inherit hundreds of acres and Coraton instinctively defers to Lawrence, I reckon Ryan has always been the leader of that pack. The leader, and the poorest.

It is at that moment that Amber Dallyn walks into the pub. I watch Nell look up, horrified. *Not again*. But Amber just smiles blandly. She is wearing a lot of make-up, I notice, and the black eye must have faded a bit.

Amber walks across to Ryan and greets him affectionately. Behind them, Nell shakes her head and slaps up a beer tap with an unnecessary force.

'Ryan and Amber must be back together,' I say. 'They had a fight the other day.'

'She's very pretty,' says Rachel.

Amber is beautiful, certainly. She has long tangled dark brown hair and very bright blue eyes. She got together with Ryan when she was only twenty-two, she told me wistfully once, on one of the few occasions we spoke properly; Victoria Blackslade had asked us to put up a trampoline for Caspar and Cecily and it took us hours.

'It was too young to settle down,' Amber had said. 'I wish I'd done more living before having the kids. We never go out. We never do *anything*. I don't want to spend the rest of my life as a glorified cleaner.'

She must have got someone to babysit tonight.

Rachel watches me watching Ryan. 'Have you thought about that job with Professor Aarons?' she asks me carefully. 'Now that you may have to leave Coraton anyway.'

'I can't leave Coraton.' It is a refrain.

'Clara, you may have to.' Rachel glances across at Ryan too. 'And, to be quite honest, it may be the best thing for you.'

'I know.'

'You do need to let Josh Aarons know one way or another as soon as possible,' Rachel says. 'There are plenty of other starving English students out there.'

I don't want to talk about the future. 'Tell me about that guy you went out with last week,' I say.

'He seemed great at first.' Rachel plunges into one of her favourite topics of conversation. 'But then…'

Over Rachel's shoulder, I watch Jordie and I watch Lawrence and I watch Ryan. And I think of the electronic trail Ryan left that day, with his phone in his pocket, as he walked up to Abbot's Wood. The beautiful wood, where they found my daughter.

Nell clatters past, picking up empty glasses. She is still scowling.

As she picks up Rachel's empty glass, Nell mutters crossly.

'I can't stand that man.' She isn't speaking to me, but she knows I can hear. 'I can't stand any of them. And I can't understand why Amber keeps going back to Ryan.' Nell meets my eye. 'She knows what he can do.'

28

I have to drive straight from the pub to the Good Listeners.

Friday night. Emma may call.

My first Caller is busy masturbating and I cut him off without hesitation. This time, these hours, they are far, far too precious.

Luckily, Tomos then gets stuck into a long call, leaving me to deal with every other call that comes into the centre, while simultaneously hoping he is not talking to Emma. I have to force myself to handle each call correctly, to give every Caller the proper amount of time and not rush them off the line.

It wouldn't be too bad if Emma got redirected to another centre tonight, I tell myself. She might get suspicious if she comes through to me yet again.

But I can't help the surge of elation when the phone goes at 8.24 p.m. Only a few seconds of breathing and then: 'Hello?' she says timidly. 'Hello?'

I know Emma's voice straight away. It is almost familiar to me now. It is incredibly hard to disguise a voice convincingly anyway. But, of course, I won't tell her that I know who is calling.

Not that I do know who is calling.

'Hello,' I say gently. 'How are you this evening?'

I have never been fishing. Or angling, is that what it's called? But Lucas liked it. While we were still married, he would occasionally head off to spend the day on some soggy riverbank in the rain, apparently quite happy. Afterwards, he would tell me about the battle to reel in a fish, edging it towards the riverbank. At any wrong move, it might slip off the line and escape back into the wilderness.

This phone call feels like the same dance. I am coaxing Emma forward, drawing her in. But at any moment, she can slip the line.

Emma can't even know there *is* a line.

'I'm…' Emma's voice trails away.

'It's alright,' I say. 'We can just sit here quietly until you know what you want to say. It can take time to find the words.'

'I hate my husband.' The words spill out of her. 'I can't stand him. I hate him so much.'

'Why do you hate him?'

'He's cruel,' she says. 'There's something wrong with him. He's… There is something evil about him.'

I feel a shiver travel down my spine.

'Do you want to tell me more about him?'

'He's clever,' she says. 'Too clever, really. He should be… He should be doing something else with his life. Not…'

I wait, but she doesn't say. 'In what way?' I ask.

'He's calculating. Manipulative. He likes setting traps. Setting people up. Playing tricks on people, but not nice ones. Not fun ones. He likes getting people excited and then pretending they had misunderstood. That it's their fault that they got excited.'

'Can you give me an example?'

In the background, behind Emma's voice, I hear the chime of church bells. Very dim, but there: half past eight.

'I don't know…' She thinks. 'One of my children found an abandoned puppy one day. A little terrier. They heard it crying, and found it tied up. I can't believe that someone would do that to a puppy, but our kids were so thrilled. They've always, always wanted a dog, but he's never let us have one. They were so excited. Saying it was a sign that we should have a dog. And he was happy for once – he can be like that sometimes, weird mood swings – and saying we could keep it and call it Linnet – of all names – and we would train it to bring us our slippers. Everyone was so overexcited. Giddy. And then all of a sudden, he turned and said, of course we couldn't keep it and he would take it off to the vet or something to have its microchip scanned. The kids were so upset.'

'That's really mean,' I say. 'To raise their hopes like that.'

'It was so cruel!'

'Do you ever think about leaving him?'

'All the time.' Emma sounds as if she is on the verge of hysterics. 'I pack up my stuff and I get my children's clothes together, and then I sit there and I can't think of anywhere to go.'

'There are women's refuges,' I say. 'There are people who can help you.'

I don't want Emma to leave her husband. I want her to stay and flip out and call the police. But this is a woman in distress – real distress, I can tell from her voice – and I can't possibly try and convince her to stay.

'I know,' she says. 'I know there are people who can help, I just don't feel as if they can help *me*.' Emma is silent for a moment, but then she goes on, sounding almost apologetic. 'I don't have many friends, you see. My husband, he never got on with my sister, with any of my family. I don't really talk to them anymore. I don't have anyone.'

'I am sorry. That must be very hard.'

'I went to my sister's once. Ran away. Told her a bit about what was going on. But then he turned up, and he was so angry and confused. He couldn't believe I would leave him. People know him where we live, you see? It would be embarrassing if I left. Embarrassing…' The word faded into a bleak laugh. 'My sister thinks I'm an idiot. All this drama, all this nonsense, and then I go running straight back.'

'I'm sure she doesn't think that.'

'She doesn't know what to believe. One minute, I'm telling her he's the worst man on earth, the next moment I'm back in his house.'

His house.

'Your sister would understand. I'm sure she would.'

'I can't do anything,' she says desperately. 'If I left him… I'm so out of practice. I haven't done anything interesting for years, and I never got far even then. I don't know what I could do. Where I could go. And I have my children… I have to think about what is best for them.'

'There will be things you can do,' I say, and I find that I am genuinely trying to comfort her, even though this woman holds the answer I so desperately need. 'There will be a way. There is always a way.'

Emma bursts into tears. For a few moments, I let her cry.

Then, ever so delicately, I start to speak again. 'Is there someone you get on well with? Someone you could talk to?'

Dully: 'No.'

'How about your family? Your mum or your dad?'

'My father's always been… difficult. And my mother's frail. She would never be able to stand up to him.'

'Are there people around you in the community who could help you? Or, you know what? Are there people that *you* could help? It might help you to meet new people, get you out of the house a bit more. Some people like to volunteer at food banks or help out with the church flowers. The PTFAs always need help too.'

'My husband doesn't like me to leave the house much.'

I register the irony that we – two such different women – have spent years trapped in our houses by the very same man. Because I too have locked myself away. I too have cut myself off from the rest of the world.

'Can you sing? How about joining a choir?'

'No,' she almost yelps. 'No. I couldn't do that.'

'You said you have children,' I say – children, I note again, not just the one daughter – cautiously. 'Round where I live, the schools are always asking for people to help out with reading and play leaders and that sort of thing.'

'Yes.' A gulp. 'I suppose I could do something like that.'

'Or do you have any hobbies?' I ask. 'Are there any local groups you could join? Feeling isolated is so miserable and soul-destroying. What do you like to do? What would you enjoy? Something you could focus on just for yourself?'

'I loved playing the piano.' Again, the distress is shimmering in her voice. 'I like painting, although I'm no good.'

'Why don't you try an art class? It doesn't matter how good you are. It's whether you enjoy it. What did you enjoy doing as a child?'

'My mother used to take my sister and me to art exhibitions,' Emma says suddenly. 'I loved that. My father… He could be horrible to us all. But my mother used to get lots of books about art and art history out of the library and from charity shops – she loved a charity shop – and read them all. And then she would take us to the art exhibitions and tell us everything she knew.'

'She sounds great. Is that the sort of thing you could do with your kids?'

'Yes.' Emma's voice has lifted.

'I went to a great exhibition the other day,' I say chattily. We are not supposed to talk about our own personal experiences, but Emma won't know that and Tomos is concentrating on his own call. 'In Exeter Cathedral, of all places. A group of abstract artists. Amazing use of colour.'

'That sounds wonderful.' For the first time, Emma has come alive. 'Maybe I could take my children to see that. I really could.'

She sounds decisive. Certain.

'You should!' And my voice sounds so cheery. So enthused. 'I know you can do it. You can give your children those happy memories, too. Golden moments for them to hold on to.'

'Golden moments…' She sounds wistful.

'They'll remember them,' I promise. 'Your children will remember these days for the rest of their lives.'

'I could tell them about the times I spent with my mother,' she says. 'Tell them about the paintings she loved.'

'Yes,' I say. 'That exhibition is really beautiful. You should go.'

'I will!' she says. 'I really will.'

29

First thing on Saturday morning, I am sitting in the cathedral.

My hastily set ambush is well positioned, it turns out. Anyone can sit in silence in a church for as long as they want, head bowed virtuously. Rachel has taken herself off to do some research at the university.

The exhibition has been hung in one of the chapels off the nave. I try not to jump every time someone walks in, but a surge of adrenalin floods through me whenever footsteps approach the exhibition.

Emma did sound excited at the end of our call. Determined, buoyed up. But it is possible that the moment she put down the handset, all that conviction leached away.

I have no way of knowing what Emma will or won't do. All the information flows only one way, and the tap can be switched off at any moment. She has all the power, although it isn't really power.

As I wait, I sit in my pew and read through my notes and try to make sense of who Emma is.

The more I think about it, the more I have convinced myself that Emma lives in a detached house, possibly at a fair distance from any other house, but within earshot of a church. She was not concerned about being overheard by her child, and neither does she seem worried about the eavesdropping of a nosy neighbour. When I mentioned Exeter, it seemed to be her default big city too.

I have checked the big red file again and as far as I can tell, Emma has never called except for on a Friday night.

To me, this suggests that despite her loneliness, solitude is not something Emma takes for granted.

There has been a surge of people working from home around here ever since the pandemic. But there are other jobs, too, where people drop in and out of their houses. Farming, where the cow sheds and the hay barns and the tractors ring the old farmhouses with a muddle of corrugated iron and concrete blocks. Decorating, where the self-employed worker goes from one job to the next, popping home whenever suits.

I have been keeping an eye out for Amber, as I sit in the church. Just in case. There are several differences between Amber's life and the story that Emma has told. But I still can't shake the thought.

Amber was in the pub looking buoyant when I left at 5 p.m.; Emma called at 8.24 p.m. sounding sad. But there are plenty of reasons why Amber might have been home and sad by 8.24 p.m.

One of the kids could have been too much for the babysitter, so Amber was summoned home. Or Ryan and Amber could have had a fight, which they so often do.

Anything.

I wish I had asked Rachel to stay and take a note of what time Amber left.

That is the problem with having to be at the Good Listeners every Friday. I can't work out who is where and when at the time that Emma calls. Unless I recruit a spy, and I don't know who I can trust.

What else? Emma mentioned a puppy. Linnet. It's a fairly unusual name. Linnets are small finches, according to Wikipedia.

Amber and Ryan had a puppy, although I have no idea what its name was.

That puppy was lost the day that Lyra went missing. Ryan said he was out hunting for the puppy in Abbot's Wood when the search for Lyra began.

That doesn't align with Emma's story at all.

* * *

On the other hand, people don't tell Good Listeners neat, linear narratives. Stories sprawl and ramble, often with peculiar, deliberate distortions. A woman once told me all about her son dying. That was a hard telephone call to listen to until the woman let slip that she was actually talking about a dead guinea pig. I think she thought she would get less sympathy for a guinea pig. Or maybe she truly felt as if the guinea pig was just as important as any child and it was the only way to make me understand her grief.

Maybe the guinea pig *was* as important as any child to her.

People tell stories about pets all the time, using them as symbols, as avatars, as metaphors.

The wider public does not know that Ryan claimed he was out searching for his puppy.

The media was very careful about what it reported in relation to the search for Lyra. Several newspapers had recently been punished in court for naming a murder suspect who was subsequently cleared of any wrongdoing. As a result, the media never reported much about Ryan at all, and they never mentioned the puppy.

I'm sure they would have done if he had been arrested and charged, but he never was.

Everyone in Coraton must know about the Dallyns' puppy though.

I have not eliminated the possibility that Emma is talking about the murder of a completely different child. Child murders are rare, but they do happen.

Nor can I eliminate the possibility that the whole thing is complete nonsense and Emma is not connected to me in any way at all.

Nor can I eliminate the possibility that I am slowly going mad, trying to fit these different stories together.

I cannot eliminate that possibility at all.

The organ starts to play, running through a deafening cascade of scales. A rehearsal.

I look around the cathedral again. Since I've been sitting here, a steady stream of people have come in to see the exhibition. There are students from the university, noisy in the quiet. There is a gang of pensioners who have come in from Broadclyst in a minibus. There is an intense man, in his thirties maybe, who is muttering to himself as he paces between the paintings. A curator watches him suspiciously.

But there is no Emma. Right now, there is no one who could possibly be Emma.

I concentrate on my notes. What else do I know? Emma's voice. What is it telling me? There have been hundreds of studies done on the voice and communication. I search through some of them on my phone as I sit and wait.

One study found that 55 per cent of human communication comes from body language, 38 per cent from tone of voice and only 7 per cent from the words. Good Listeners, of course, get none of the body language cues.

Apparently women's voices change when they ovulate. They become slightly more high-pitched, sounding younger, sexier.

Apparently, human beings are surprisingly good at working out a person's height merely from listening to their voice.

Apparently, we're all attracted to deeper voices.

And your voice softens when you're speaking to someone you find attractive.

And someone once made a documentary called *Do I Sound Gay?*

Weirdly, it turns out that we are much better at recognising voices once we know what someone looks like. Thanks to a bit of the brain called the fusiform gyrus, voice recognition and facial recognition work together.

So it's a catch-22. Once I know what Emma looks like, I will be better at recognising her voice. If I ever know, that is.

I know from personal experience that before I started volunteering for the Good Listeners, my voice got rusty. Vocal cords can and will atrophy from lack of use.

I know, too, that every generation has its own emphasis, its own slang, its own inflections. Sometimes, during a Good Listeners' call,

I can tell that someone's been watching a lot of the Kardashians. Vocal fry. A croaky *whateverrr*. That age group often sounds slightly surprised to find themselves on an actual phone call, the verbal interaction a novelty.

We all make split-second decisions as soon as we hear a voice, but Emma's voice? What is *Emma's* voice telling me? I stare up at the stained-glass windows and force myself to think. Sometimes she sounds strangulated, as if her voice is being crushed, as if her voice is reflecting her constraints: Little Mermaid, losing her words.

Emma will sometimes hesitate on a word, as if she is not quite sure of her right to say it. Not quite a stammer, but a noticeable delay. If I had to guess, I would say these uncertainties are a habit that date back to childhood, not just to an unhappy marriage.

Although an uncertain, unhappy childhood might well lead to a miserable marriage, too.

Sometimes the voice and the words will tell us different stories.

Emma, I think. Who are you?

'Emma!' someone calls out, and I whip around.

I find myself sidling closer to this Emma, towards blonde hair cut in an unforgiving bob. But this is not my Emma. There is a hint of Brum in this voice. And I'm fairly sure I am not looking for an Emma anyway.

I sit down in my pew again and close my eyes. The moment I do, the voices around me become clearer. I listen to someone who thinks *my niece could paint better than that* and two genteel ladies debating which National Trust house to visit next and a couple squabbling over whose turn it is to take the dog to the vet.

Emma's voice is not among the babble.

As I wait, I make myself think about all the things I need to do this week, to follow up on my suggestions to Emma. Visit the food banks. Find a way of approaching the PTFAs. Volunteer to help out with the church flowers. Maybe at one of these places, there will be a new volunteer. Maybe she will be Emma.

Completely by accident, I appear to have created the busy timetable of a Dartmoor housewife for myself as I try to hunt down Emma.

Church bells: those were another clue. I am always surprised by how far the sound of bells travels. But it is cold now, the nights drawing in; I would be surprised if Emma was sitting with the windows open. So if I could hear the bells chiming down the phone line, Emma must be fairly close to a church.

Not all the village bells ring every quarter of an hour, either. Newcomers grumble about farm smells and church bells: perennial bones of contention. People have come to blows over cockerels on dawn patrol. Many church bells fall silent at dusk now.

It must be possible to find out which bells still chime every fifteen minutes.

They still chime at Coraton.

Behind me, I hear the high-pitched chatter of two children. I turn around. Two girls and a pram.

Their mother looks anxious and exhausted. Late thirties, wearing the Exeter mum's uniform: Blundstone boots and ME+EM trousers.

I jump to my feet.

It could be her.

30

Several women could have been Emma this morning.

I have chatted to Sian, who was pacifying Coral – eight years old and cheeky – with a flapjack. I helped Kath after Jojo (seven) dropped her cardigan. I have drifted closer to Beth, who was trying to convince six-year-old Wilma and eight-year-old Boris to take an interest in a particular brushstroke technique.

Sian turned out to be going through a nasty divorce. Beth's husband works on an oil rig, and I managed to ascertain that he was in the North Sea when Lyra disappeared. Kath is married to Antonia.

None of them could possibly be Emma.

This woman in the Blundstone boots really could be Emma though.

She has two small children – both girls – with her. Seven and five, I would guess. Peering, I see that the baby in the pram is asleep.

I watch as the woman makes her way into the exhibition and then I come up behind her.

'Excuse me,' I say cheerfully. 'Did you drop this? Is it yours?'

It's the guide to the exhibition, as useful a prop as any.

'No!' the woman says equally cheerfully. 'I didn't actually buy one. I probably should have.'

'Oh, you might as well have this one then!' I say merrily. 'I'm about to leave.'

'Thank you very much!' The woman has brunette hair cut into a messy bob. She pushes the pram over towards me. 'Say thank you, children!'

'Thank you,' they chorus. They all have very faint West Country accents.

Just then – helpfully – the baby wakes up and starts to cry. The woman looks flustered. 'Do you need a hand?' I ask. 'Have you heard of any of these artists?' I ask the children.

While the mother picks up the baby, I tell the little girls all about the nearest painting, reciting the guide. Slightly unexpectedly, they listen agog. *Thank you*, the mother mouths at me.

No problem.

By the time the baby has been appeased, we are all friends.

'They have such great exhibitions in here,' I say. 'Have you been to many before?'

'We're just visiting my parents-in-law actually,' she says. 'Down from London for a long weekend.'

'How nice.' I hide my disappointment.

'I needed to get the girls out. They were trashing Pam's house!'

'But they're beautifully behaved!' I laugh and protest.

'They are now. Not like that little monster we saw as we were coming in!' The woman is smiling down fondly at her children.

'Oh dear,' I say. 'Someone didn't fancy the exhibition?'

'This kid was throwing an absolute mega-tantrum, wasn't he? Being really nasty to his mum.'

'Oh dear.' I'm not quite listening. I am trying to work out who to approach next. 'Kids! It's so hard when they do that.'

'He was being so rude.' The woman isn't laughing anymore. 'It was quite upsetting, really. You know when a child's obviously seen someone being really horrible to their mum. They've picked up that contempt. That sneering.'

Suddenly, I realise what the woman is saying. 'When did you see this?' I ask quickly.

The woman shrugs. 'As we were coming in? A few minutes ago.'

'What did she look like, this woman?'

'I'm not sure.' The woman is confused by my interest. 'Ordinary, really. Couple of kids with her. Boy and girl, I think. She was wearing a really nice dress… I noticed that. Wiggy Kit, I think?'

But already I am running.

I sprint out of the cathedral. But there is no tantruming child, no maybe-Emma.

Just outside the cathedral, a man is selling coffee from a van. 'Was there a mother here?' I call to him. 'A couple of minutes ago? With a couple of children – one of them having a tantrum?'

He laughs. 'That kid was going bloody mental!'

'Which way did they go?' I beg.

The man points across the cathedral green to where a narrow lane leads to the high street.

I race across the green, running as fast as I can.

But already I know I am too late. I shoulder my way down the lane, moving as fast as possible, trying to peer into the little shops as I pass. By the time I reach the high street, I am desperate. Everywhere I look, there are women with children. There are mothers watching children as they try on trainers in Sports Direct. There are mothers helping children buy birthday cards in the newsagent. There is a whole crowd clustered around a busker. There are families everywhere I look. It is impossible.

'Emma,' I whisper, clenching my fists with frustration. 'Where are you?'

31

I spend as much of the week as possible in the cathedral, but no likely-Emma appears. I am haunted by the thought that I just missed her on Saturday morning.

I went back to the coffee man, who clearly thought I was very strange, but he couldn't remember anything about the woman, or her tantruming child.

On top of that, the next Friday, I miss Emma's call. She rings while I am talking to Asmaan, who fled Kabul and now finds herself on the soggy outskirts of Cullompton with a suicidal husband and three traumatised small children.

Asmaan's English keeps breaking up as she speaks. It's her sister, I understand slowly. Back in Afghanistan, Asmaan's sister has been killed. It was the Taliban, of course. Asmaan always dreamed of seeing her sister again, one day. They were so close when they were growing up, always. They loved each other so very much. Through all the misery and the despair and the loneliness and the racism, that dream was the one thing keeping Asmaan going. The thought that one day they would be reunited.

Now it will never be.

Nageenah is gone forever. Murdered by the Taliban for daring to hope for something better.

'I will not see her again,' says Asmaan slowly. 'I will never see her again.'

* * *

Sally picks up the phone while I am speaking to Asmaan. Even though I am deep in conversation, I guess that it is Emma. It is her time to call, after all.

When Asmaan rings off, I casually ask Sally who has called.

'Some woman called Emma,' Sally reads from her notes. 'Says her husband hit her. Didn't sound like it was the first time it had happened either. Poor woman.'

'Poor woman,' I echo her. And I tell myself that it is fine that I missed the call. That if Emma had reached me yet again, of all the Good Listeners in the country, she might become suspicious.

'She didn't stay on the line for long.' Sally shrugs. And she is about to say something else when the phone rings again and Sally answers it before I can.

I have casually let it slip to Alys that I have a regular physiotherapy session in Exeter at 4.30 p.m. on a Friday and that it is convenient for me to carry on to the Good Listeners' centre when that is finished.

By the next rota, I am on every Friday evening shift. Alys is not one to look a gift horse in the mouth.

As well as staking out the cathedral, I have spent much of the last week trawling through what I know – or think I know – of Emma.

I have found out as much as I can about every single Kimlock Society member in Devon. None of them appear to be Emma's husband.

I have also tried to plot out my conversations with Emma in advance. What can I ask her? How can I get her to talk about her husband? How can I piece together more clues about who she is? About where she is?

Maybe I could ask her to describe the view from her bedroom window? Although I can't think how I would phrase that question. And if she lives in the countryside, what distinguishing features would she be able to see anyway? A few fields. A hedge. Maybe the granite of a church steeple.

Useless.

* * *

What else do I know about Emma?

She has a Devon accent.

She likes painting.

He likes Kimlock trains.

The family probably lives at least two miles from a primary school.

They probably live within range of church bells that chime every fifteen minutes until at least 9 o'clock at night.

Emma probably has a sister.

She probably has a niece, although I suppose this could be her husband's niece.

Emma loves playing the piano, although that could mean anything from 'Chopsticks' to the *Hammerklavier*.

I have never heard any traffic sounds behind Emma's voice. Good Listeners' calls are often interspersed with the sound of an engine accelerating, the toot of a horn, the scream of a siren. There is barely any background noise at her house at all, in fact. She appears to live in what should be an enviable peace.

Emma and my daughter's killer have probably been married for over ten years.

Back at my cottage, because it is still mine, although not – that acid tang of panic – for much longer, I stare at my notes.

I wonder if I have now accumulated enough information that a trained investigator could identify Emma. There might just about be enough clues that access to the right databases could narrow the group of possible Emmas to three or four candidates.

Three or four women married to three or four potential killers.

My mind flickers to Leanne, the policewoman who managed me during the hunt for Lyra.

Managed: it was the only word.

But she was kind, Leanne. She was doing her best.

Maybe I could speak to her about all this. I still have her number somewhere.

But I cannot think of any plausible, legitimate way that I might have put together this strange pen portrait of Emma.

And that means I have no way of giving Leanne these clues without triggering a spiral of scrutiny that would be impossible to control.

The first thing that would happen is that I would be banned from the Good Listeners for breaching confidentiality. I've lied too much, as well. Clara Winterson is Clara Brennan. And Clara Brennan would never have been allowed to join the Good Listeners in the first place. You can't volunteer at the Good Listeners if you're in the middle of your own crisis.

Poor Clara Brennan. I'm sure there is something else she could do to get her out of the house. Maybe she could volunteer at a food bank? Or help out with the church flowers? But not the Good Listeners. No. Certainly not.

It is not that being banned from the Good Listeners would be the end of the world. It is only a voluntary role, after all. But if the police failed to find Emma – if one too many of my oddly gathered clues proved to be too inaccurate, too disorienting – then the whole inquiry would collapse.

And there would be no way of ever gathering any more information.

I do not know if I am breaking any laws by speaking to Emma like this, but I don't want to find out. Lucas's banker phrases float up from somewhere. Breach of confidence. Non-disclosure agreements. I don't know what applies to this situation.

I am not sure if anyone knows what applies to this situation.

That's if there was an inquiry, anyway. That's if Leanne didn't calmly and politely usher me off to the nearest mental health unit.

Would a private investigator be able to do something? But I am already running out of money and that would be hugely expensive.

Although Lucas shares my rage and earns a lot.

But a private investigator might get me shut out of the Good Listeners.

I have no choice.

I have to do this alone.

* * *

What else do I know? I concentrate on my notes again.

Piano. Sister. Devon accent. Church bells. Remote house.

Loneliness.

Loneliness and isolation.

It is possible that Emma knows very few people at all.

It is possible that Emma could leave her husband any moment.

It is possible that Emma could pack up a few belongings and flee to her sister, and, if she does that, I may never hear from her again.

It is possible that every conversation may be our last.

32

On the Saturday morning after I miss Emma's call, I make my way down to the church.

Coraton's church is beautiful. Ancient granite shaped in a rudimentary cross, surrounded by venerable yew trees. As you drive west up the narrow road into Coraton, you come to the village green first, which is big and lined with oaks. Beyond the green is the church, on its rough east-west axis. Behind the church, the moor rises up.

Walking around the village, you come across the same names again and again. On the war memorial, on the gravestones, in the farm names themselves. Five Meldons died in the Great War. A whole corner of the graveyard is taken up by Dallyns. A Major Cyril Ferdinand Wrenscott died at Arnhem.

Harepath House is off down a road on the right just before the church. Ryan and Amber live in the cottage a few yards before the lion-topped Harepath pillars. If you carry on down the road beyond Harepath, you reach the Meldons' farm.

Last night, I dreamed that I was out in Abbot's Wood again, and the dream hasn't quite let go of me. I was scrambling through a bog, but at every step I sank deeper. Above me there was a latticework of trees, the moon shining peacefully. But the mud sucked me down and I was screaming, scrabbling at anything solid. As the mud filled my throat, I jumped awake.

I feel guilt in a way that almost no other human being can. It is a guilt that sears my throat at night, that fills my head with a silent scream. It is a guilt that will never go away.

I remember Lyra bobbing around in that pack of small children, her long blonde hair catching the breeze. She was so happy, so delighted to be one of the crowd and I thought – I *assumed* – that she would be safe. I deliberately pushed away my concerns. Look how happy she is. You have to let them explore the world. You have to let them *go*.

Now, looking up at the granite of the church, I remember my daughter's hand in mine, and I scream at the thought that I could have let her go for even a minute.

Lyra, I would do anything – *anything* – to hold your hand again for just a few minutes.

Georgia Wrenscott is waiting for me in the churchyard. Her husband, Ferdie Wrenscott, is the one-time squire who had to sell Harepath House after losing everything. Georgia must be in her sixties now, but she has excellent bone structure and an easy gracefulness.

I always think there is a profound sadness in Georgia's eyes. I imagine that losing Harepath must have been devastating, not least because Georgia has always struck me as being very well suited to the role of squire's wife. She is constantly organising bring-and-buy sales or raising funds for a defibrillator.

Even though her son Lawrence was one of the people looked at closely by the police, Georgia has always been friendly to me on the rare occasions we have interacted.

She was actually one of the first people I ever spoke to in Coraton. It was during the week that Lyra and I were down for our holiday. May Day wasn't far ahead and Georgia had organised a rehearsal. All the little girls of the village – including Nell Turner's Tabitha, Amber and Ryan's Aimee, and Victoria and Gabriel's daughter Cecily – were practising the dance around the maypole on the village green. Georgia invited Lyra to join in the rehearsal and Lyra was ecstatic.

That was how she got to know some of the little girls.
That was why she ran off to play with them at the festival.

'Good morning,' Georgia says pleasantly as I arrive. But I see her eyes flicker to Lyra's memorial stone and I hear the split second of uncertainty in her voice. The uneasiness is glossed over almost instantaneously. 'Thank you *so* much for helping out, Clara!'

Talking to Emma has renewed my determination to turn over every stone, to ask every question, to pry into every corner. Georgia, seeped in Coraton's ways, will know more than most. If Emma has taken up flower-arranging or helping out at one of the local food banks, Georgia may know.

'It's a pleasure to help!' I match Georgia's jolly tones. 'What should I do?'

At Georgia's feet are prosaic plastic buckets filled with the brightness of dahlias. Church flowers; there's a rota.

'I'll get the key!' Georgia takes a few steps to the left of the church's porch and sticks her hand into a crevice between two chunks of granite. 'Typical bit of Dartmoor security, isn't it?'

I know this by now. If you ever need to break into a Dartmoor house, check under the flowerpot to the left of the doorway or under the boot-jack to the right. That's if the door's been locked in the first place. The key to the church is six inches long. Georgia puts the key in the ornate lock and it turns with a screech.

Inside the church, it is chilly. The heating is only turned on grudgingly for the Sunday service. I drag in the buckets of dahlias while Georgia sets out the vases.

Hefty granite plaques have been put up in honour of long-dead local squires. At the back of the church, there are various registers and leather-bound books. The gold-painted list of vicars dates back to 1307.

'It's fascinating, isn't it?' says Georgia as she hands me a tray of vases. 'A time capsule of Coraton.'

Although, it's not really. Time capsules are a frozen moment and this is scrolling centuries of history, crystallised.

'Did you grow up here?'

'Yes.' Georgia nodded. 'I moved away for a bit, but I had to come back.' From the way she speaks, I can't work out if she was forced back by duty, or simply couldn't bear to live anywhere else.

'And you're Lawrence's mother?' I ask.

'Yes!' Georgia says merrily, but there is a flicker of something in her eyes that isn't quite happiness.

'He seems very nice,' I say. 'I saw him in the pub the other night.'

'He spends rather too much time in the pub! Now you just run wild with those.' Georgia gestures to the buckets. 'October's not a great time of year for any of the gardens. One frost and those'll be done too. Next week, I think I'll bring in some autumn leaves.'

The holly berries are coming now too, a promise of Christmas to come. I've volunteered to cover the Good Listeners on Christmas Day. It's a busy time – people hysterical over everything from incinerated turkey to 'I'm not being racist, but' brawls – and I don't have anything better to do.

'Have you had any new volunteers recently?' I ask. 'Apart from me?'

'No.' Georgia is certain, as I suspect she usually is. 'People are so busy.'

'Do you volunteer anywhere else? There must be a lot of projects that need support at the moment.'

'Oh, there are.' Georgia nods. 'I'm the treasurer for the local WI, which is more work than you'd think. I'm in the local choir, too. And I'm leading the fundraising for the village hall. That roof is going to collapse right on top of the Scouts if we're not careful.'

'And have you had many new joiners for those?' I feel a sort of desperation. 'Any new people?'

'No.' Georgia compresses her lips. 'It's the same old faces. But that's village life for you! Oh, yes, I'm part of the Spreyton am-dram too, up in bandit country.'

'Bandit country?' I ask.

'North of the A30,' Georgia explains.

As I stick dahlias into vases, I wonder if there is any way of coaxing Emma into using extremely local slang to identify her village.

I have been reading about Antarctica research stations, where they've developed their own colloquialisms, their own tiny linguistic microcosms. To American researchers, for example, newcomers were 'fingies', from FNGs, which in turn came from the military's 'Fucking New Guy'. To British researchers, on the other hand, newcomers were 'fidlets', a diminutive of 'FID', from Falkland Island Dependencies. Antarctica, according to my book, is an ICE environment – isolated, confined and extreme. Perhaps it is not impossible that the smaller Devon villages have ended up with equally eccentric linguistic cul-de-sacs?

Maybe.

Or perhaps I could get Emma talking about her local history somehow.

'Moretonhampstead and Chagford have always hated each other,' an old farmer told me chattily once about two villages not far from Coraton.

'Why?' I wondered if there had been some dubious umpiring in a football match.

'Moreton was Roundhead during the Civil War, Chagford was Cavalier.' This in tones that made it clear that a four-hundred-year vendetta was perfectly reasonable.

Georgia is still talking about Spreyton's version of *Lady Windermere's Fan*. Evidently two of the main actors declared undying love to each other the day before opening night, which was inconvenient for everyone – but entertaining for most – because both were married to other people.

I don't think Emma is having an affair. But any gossip might be helpful.

'Do you get a lot of that sort of thing round here?' I ask casually.

Georgia positions another dahlia. 'Oh lord, yes. Last year, Minty Searle came home to find her very rich husband in bed with Jemima Venn. Apparently Jemima walked slowly down the stairs, stood in front of the Aga stark naked and announced, "It's my house now, Minty."'

'Coraton seems to have a lot of secrets!' I say.

It is meant as a joke, but Georgia's smile falters. 'I suppose so,' she says. 'I suppose there have always been a lot of secrets around here.'

33

The days are getting shorter now. Every day, the sun rises a little further to the south. Coraton Tor, high above the village, is often lost in the mist. The leaves have fallen from the trees, leaving only starkness behind.

The bleakness feels apt. On Dartmoor, summer only ever feels as if it has been borrowed. Summer is a skirt begged for a party. Winter is her soul.

It is so beautiful here. But the weeks are ticking away on my time in Damson Cottage. Every time I think of leaving, I feel a choke of panic.

When I drive home through the village in the evenings, the lane smells of wood smoke, and the windows are bright and cheerful. Sometimes, often, I peer in through the leaded panes. I would like to prise these houses open, as if they were doll's houses and I were some ruthless ogre. I would like to claw apart these pretty cottages and rip out every last secret.

On Tuesday night, I am driving home in the dark after a shift. I am not far from Nell and Pauly Turner's half-built house, and only half concentrating on the road and going too fast.

I think I see a small shape. A *child*. I spin the steering wheel desperately. My wheels lock. I skid sideways and everything is a blur. Then the car has stopped and I haven't hit anything and the world is still again.

But… That was a child, wasn't it?

Wasn't it? For a moment, I am not sure. For a moment, I am seeing little lost girls everywhere I look.

No, that was definitely a child. I switch off the engine and climb out of the car.

'Hello?' I call into the darkness. Silence. 'Is there someone there?'

More silence. Then a sob and I know that it is real. This wasn't a ghost, a glint of madness.

'It's okay,' I call out. 'You're okay.'

Another sob. I pull my phone out of my pocket and switch on the torch.

Eyes gleam in the light. A girl ducks her head, twisting away from the glare.

I realise it is Tabitha, pretty Tabitha. Tabitha, eleven now – eleven!

She isn't hurt, I realise with a thud of relief, and her clothes are untorn. Not that, thank god.

Then I see the tear marks and I already know this story. Eleven and starting the swoop into the agonising world of adolescence. Running off into the darkness, *I hate you all, I* hate *you.*

I did it to my mother, I remember.

Lyra, I am sure, would have done it to me.

Even at six, there were glimpses of this wild future. The dress that wasn't exactly right, the sparks of cattiness at school. *Lily said* this, *Willa said* that. God, how I wish I was facing the drama and the hormones and the spots.

'Are you okay, Tabitha?'

Tabitha is wearing only the grey skirt and white polo shirt of her school uniform. She must be freezing out here, painfully vulnerable.

'Tabitha?'

'I *hate* them,' she spits. In the darkness, I can't read her eyes. 'No one knows what they're like.'

'Who?'

'My parents. I *hate* them.'

'Everyone hates their parents when they're your age.'

'Not like this. Not like this.'

Yes, I don't say aloud. *Exactly like this.*

'Your parents will be worried about you,' I say gently. 'Can I give you a lift home? Or can I lend you a coat, either way?'

A pulse of pain, sharp, sudden. Here I am, such a good Samaritan. Here I am, helping someone else's child. Why was there no one there to help *my* child? What vicious quirk of fate led her to walk out of that festival, unnoticed, unremarked? *Why*?

But that is not a question for right now. Right now, I can be helpful. Right now, I can be kind.

Tabitha is shivering, the cold biting deep. I am getting cold, even in my coat, warm from the car.

'I *hate* them,' she says again. But I see defeat in the angle of Tabitha's head now.

We drive towards the half-built house in silence.

The front door is thrown open as soon as the car stops, a bright rectangle cast across the half-finished garden. Tabitha's little brother Reuben stands in the doorway, charged with keeping watch.

'Daddy's out looking for you, Tab!' The little boy is alive with disapproving excitement. 'Mummy's—'

Nell is dashing forward. She throws herself on her daughter, her words inaudible.

For the briefest instant, I allow myself to imagine sprinting towards my daughter. Because she was only watching the dog agility. Because she was only having her face painted. Because it was only five minutes of terror, after all. 'Lyra! Where were you – I was so *scared* – you *mustn't...*' I allow myself the briefest instant of the purest happiness, and then it dissolves in the darkness of the garden.

Nell's eyes meet mine over her daughter's head. 'Thank you,' she says. 'Thank you so much.'

'No problem.'

I am turning away when Nell calls out. 'Would you like a cup of tea?'

I look back, surprised. Nell has only ever kept just this side of rude. But as I turn, she opens the door wider.

And I think: Nell knows everything that goes on in Coraton. I think: Nell knows Amber.

I smile. 'That would be lovely.'

34

As I step into the house, Tabitha and her little brother are disappearing off to the TV room.

I am surprised to find that the kitchen is filled with cake-making equipment and that the air is heavy with the scent of chocolate and ginger. In contrast to the rest of the house, the kitchen is immaculate, only a few traces of flour and icing sugar on the kitchen table.

'Amber and I have a stand at the farmers' market on Wednesday morning.' Nell wipes away the icing sugar and the flour. 'We sell cakes. I'd better crack on now that Tabitha has reappeared.'

'I didn't know you had a stall.' The farmers' market is always busy. I know that Victoria Blackslade sells honey from the Harepath bees at one stand, although it is Linda, the nanny, who actually mans that stall.

'We do quite well,' says Nell.

'Your cakes smell delicious.'

Nell gives me a quick sideways smile. 'Have a bit of brownie.' She slices off a sticky chunk, plonks it on a plate and waves me towards the table.

As she peers into the oven to check on a cake's progress, Nell is making a call. *She's home, panic over.*

'He's going to the pub.' Nell rolls her eyes as she hangs up. Then, half-forgiving: 'It's been a difficult evening. My mum's done her hip, so I've been over at hers most of the day. Tabitha's been a right little madam all week. The teen years are going to be so much fun.'

On cue, a squabble breaks out next door.

'Siblings!' Nell rolls her eyes after she has resolved the spat.

'Do you have brothers or sisters?' I ask.

'One sister.' Nell pulls a face. 'We don't get on at all. Although she does remind me how I might look with a decent skincare routine.' Nell scowls at herself in a mirror: she has lots of freckles. 'How about you?'

'I'm an only,' I say. 'What was Tabitha upset about?'

'Oh.' Nell cracks a smile. 'She wants to go and live over at her cousins' house. Because they've got *everything*. The cool shoes, the brand-new bikes, the ponies. I could tell her they don't have it easy either, but she won't have it.'

'She'll learn.' I roll my eyes and now we are laughing together.

'Were you coming home from anywhere interesting?' Nell asks.

I don't want to mention the Good Listeners. As Listeners, we are discouraged from telling people that we volunteer, so that no one is put off from calling. We are not Lorna next door who enjoys Zumba on Tuesdays. We are not Victoria down the road who disapproves of people who say *toilet*.

We are blank sheets of paper.

We are bland white walls onto which a Caller can project anything they want.

We are magnolia spattered with blood.

It still surprises me that within two minutes some people will tell a Caller things that they would never be able to tell their best friends in a lifetime. But they do.

And there is something else now, too. Although the chances must be tiny, I won't let there be even the smallest chance that Emma could find out that Lyra Brennan's mother is a Good Listener.

Nell is waiting for my answer. 'Just a yoga class in Exeter,' I say.

'Nice.'

We talk for a while about yoga. Nell pulls an orange and ginger cake out of the oven.

'By the way, Nell,' I begin cautiously. 'Is Amber okay? I've seen her...'

Nell sighs heavily, but she obviously wants to talk about it.

'I don't know,' she says. 'She seems okay right now. Ryan's a twat, though.'

'I saw them in the pub ten days ago,' I say. 'They looked as if they were settling in for a session! Were they there all night?'

It's an awkward question, I know. But I left the pub at 5 p.m. that evening and Emma called at 8.24 p.m. I want to know if Amber could possibly have made that call.

Nell looks slightly surprised, but she does think before she answers. She always thinks before she speaks, I have noticed.

'Amber went home fairly early that night,' she says. 'She was grumbling to me because the babysitter called and said her own daughter had got sick while on a sleepover. So the babysitter needed to go and pick her up. The boys stayed until closing, though. Of course, it wouldn't be Ryan who went home early. They may even have stayed on for a lock-in with Terence. I don't know.'

Terence is the rotund owner of the Ring of Bells. He was helping to run the temporary bar at the folk festival that day: highly visible throughout.

I hate that I know the alibis for most of the men in this village on that day. It is the first thing I think of when I see many of their faces.

Old Mr Meldon: lambing.

Coraton's plumber: selling raffle tickets at the festival.

Gabriel Blackslade: drafting a skeleton argument at his desk.

Ryan Dallyn: searching for a lost dog (perhaps).

Pauly Turner: working on the half-built house (perhaps).

Given she was summoned home by the babysitter, Amber could have been calling the Good Listeners at 8.24 p.m. that Friday night.

'I saw her the other day,' I go on cautiously. 'She had a black eye. Is she okay?'

Nell shakes her head. 'No, not really. They've always been up and down, those two. But they've been a lot worse the last few months. I don't know what's changed.'

'I wonder what happened,' I say idly.

I am thinking: a few months ago, Emma called the Good Listeners for the first time.

'I've got no idea,' says Nell. 'But I am really worried about Amber. And I know that Ryan—'

Nell stops talking abruptly. She bends her head over a recipe for a chocolate torte and moves the conversation on.

We chat for another half an hour, and all the time, I am screaming inside: *What is it? What is it that you know about Ryan?*

35

'He killed a little girl.'

Three days later, I am back in the centre. On one hand, it is a relief to hear Emma's voice again. On the other hand, those words will always cut me to the very core.

'That's terrible.' I force out the words. 'Do you want to talk about it?'

'I don't know… I don't know…'

'What makes you think that he killed her?'

Six weeks ago, Emma would have put down the phone at this point. But Emma is getting into the habit of speaking now, and once you start, it can be hard to stop. People will ring up who have never ever spoken about bullying or childhood abuse, and once they get talking, a call can last for hours.

There is silence.

'Why?' I make my voice as persuasive as possible. 'Why do you think he killed someone?'

'Because I helped him,' she whispers.

'Okay.'

How? I want to scream. *Tell me. Tell me everything you know. Tell me at once before I* choke *with rage.*

I am desperate to hear Emma's words, but if she tells me she is talking about Lyra, if she makes it real, I am not sure that I can bear it. I want to scream at her. I want to claw her face – whatever it looks like – and rip the words from her one by one.

But I can't.

I can't.

Emma is a victim, I tell myself again. Emma is a victim.

And besides, I can't get my hands on her.

Emma is only a voice.

But she is not the only one whose life has been eviscerated by this man. And if she is talking about Lyra, there is only one true victim anyway. My beloved daughter.

'Do you want to tell me more about that?' I ask.

'I helped him…' Emma says again.

'How?' I ask quietly. 'How did you help him?'

I can't hear this. I *can't*. There will be no way back.

'How did you help him?' I ask again.

'I can't…' Emma lets out one sob. 'I can't tell anyone…'

I force my jaw to unlock. I force myself to straighten up ever so slightly in my seat. And then I lie through my teeth.

'You can trust me,' I murmur. 'Everything you tell the Good Listeners is completely confidential.'

Another sob.

My nails are digging into my palms now. I feel a prickle of sweat down my back.

'I told them…' she says. 'I lied to them that he…'

'Lied to who? About what?'

She gasps. 'I've got to go.' And I know that I am going to lose her. I know that I have pushed her too hard.

I smile at the beige wall. I smile at Anjali's needlepoint. I smile because it makes my voice sound friendly.

'You don't have to talk about anything you don't want to,' I say calmly. 'What would you like to talk about?' There is a pause. But Emma is still there and I can hear her sobs turning back into breaths. 'What do you enjoy doing?'

A long expiration. 'I feel useless,' she says quietly. 'I love my children, really I do. They're my whole world. But they take up *everything*. All my time, all my energy, all my brain. I've lost everything. I used to enjoy my job. It wasn't a very important job, but I was good at it. I used to have everything ahead of me. But now I just… I don't have the confidence to go back to anything proper. He's… chipped away at everything. I can't imagine going to an interview, *getting* an interview even. I used to laugh with my friends. I used to have fun. It seems impossible now. Impossible.'

'What can you change?' I ask. 'What would make you happier?'

'I don't know…' But she sounds as if she is contemplating her options. 'I don't know if it's possible to be happy married to someone like that.'

'What could you do about that?'

'I could leave him.' She sounds decisive all at once. 'I could do it. Really I could do something interesting. I could build back—' She stalls again.

'What do you do to let off steam?' I ask carefully. 'Is there a walk you like to do? Somewhere close to your house?'

'It's beautiful where we live.' And all at once Emma sounds almost dreamy. 'So beautiful. Sometimes, I think it's the only reason that I stay.'

'What's it like? Around where you live?'

'We live close to the moor,' she says. 'Sometimes I go all the way up there and I stand in the middle of nowhere and I scream.'

For a moment, I can't think. I can't breathe.

'It's so gorgeous, the moor,' I hear my voice saying. 'I've always loved Exmoor.'

'Oh no,' Emma corrects me before she can stop herself. 'We're on Dartmoor. We're right up on the edge of the moor.'

36

Dartmoor.

And Emma has told me during another call that she lives in a village.

A village on the edge of Dartmoor.

There are quite a few villages on Dartmoor that are closer to Exeter than Plymouth.

But there aren't that many.

And Coraton is one of them.

'It is very beautiful up there, too.' Somehow my voice stays calm. 'So remote. So peaceful.'

'It is.' Emma's voice is wobbly. I'm not sure if this is because she is worried she has said too much.

'How long have you lived there?' I try to make this sound like an ordinary question.

'Years,' she replies unhelpfully.

I decide to push on. 'How do you know?' The words are hard to say. 'How do you know he killed a little girl?'

'I don't… I wasn't *there*.' She sounds defensive.

'No, no, of course not.' I back-pedal. 'So how can you be sure? Could he have made it up to frighten you?'

'He lied about where he was,' she says simply. 'On the day that little girl was killed.'

'You said you helped him, lied for him. Can you tell me more about that?'

'I… I backed up his story.'

'Did you talk to the police?' I am asking too many questions. But I can't seem to stop myself.

'I lied to the police. I hate myself so much for doing that.'

For an instant, I hate her too.

'When did all this happen?' I ask.

I have to know if Emma is talking about Lyra. I have to.

'Two years ago.'

It is as if a lump of ice is stuck in my throat. I can't speak. I have to speak.

'Two years ago…' I try so hard to make myself sound merely curious. 'Isn't that when that little girl was killed in Coraton?'

Emma doesn't say a word. I stare at the red light. I stare so hard that it jumps and skips, a little dot of madness. But I have to know.

'Lyra Brennan, that's the one,' I say. I have to sound as if the name has just sprung into my mind. I can't sound desperate. I can't beg. Lyra Brennan. Four syllables, an eternity of sadness.

At Lyra's name, I hear a gasp. It is as if Emma can't quite control her despair.

But I am not sure yet. I still don't know.

Emma doesn't say anything. But the red light is still on. Pulses of rage jolt through me like electricity.

'It must,' somehow I speak so gently, 'be very hard living with a secret like that. Very hard to bear it. Is that who he killed? Lyra Brennan?'

And at that, Emma breathes out very slowly. 'Yes,' she says. 'Lyra Brennan. My husband killed Lyra Brennan.'

37

My daughter's name in Emma's mouth sounds impossible. I want to tear the syllables out of the air. My fists are so tight that the skin could split over my knucklebones.

'It must be horrible to live with that knowledge.' I manage to choke out the words.

'It is.' She dissolves into tears. 'It's unbearable.'

Emma can't speak for quite a while after that. She keeps almost speaking and then breaking down again. I ask a few more questions, but it is hopeless.

'What could you change?' I ask in the end. 'What would make you happier about your life?'

'I could leave him.' Emma manages to answer that question. 'I could—' But suddenly, her voice changes. 'I've got to go.'

The phone slams down, and the red light goes out.

With numb fingers, I manage to put my phone on hold.

I stumble through to the kitchenette. Tomos is still speaking to his Caller, his voice a soothing mumble.

I sit down at the scuffed table and put my face in my hands.

My husband killed Lyra Brennan.

I have suspected for weeks that Emma was talking about Lyra. There aren't many child murders, and certainly – bleakly – very few where the child is not known to the adult.

But all the same, the words are agonising.

Agonising, but they also send judders of anger through my body. I find that I am shaking.

I helped him.

Dazedly, I think back to the investigation. I try to remember who was given an alibi by their wives.

The police spoke to hundreds of people during their investigation. But, still, it narrows the group significantly.

Amber Dallyn, for example, insisted that her husband had been searching for that puppy.

Dartmoor. The area that Emma may live in is still huge. I stare at the map.

Dartmoor is the biggest wilderness in England, almost twenty miles across from north to south and the same again from east to west, nearly four hundred square miles. The Dartmoor Way, the walking path that roughly follows the National Park's boundary, is over a hundred miles long. Around half of that is closer to Exeter than Plymouth. There are dozens of towns and villages and hamlets that could be called villages.

But, still, my search area is much smaller than it was.

'Emma,' I murmur. 'Where are you?'

The following day, back at home – not my home, not for much longer – I return to the Fenton-Browns' list of Kimlock train fans.

There are no obvious addresses in Dartmoor villages closeish to Exeter. There is an address in South Zeal, but the man who lives there is eighty-three and registered blind, receiving Braille versions of the Kimlock Society's newsletter. I find a five-year-old obituary notice for his wife, too.

There is a member who lives in Ivybridge, but if Emma were calling from there, she would be connecting to Plymouth. The same goes for an address in Sheepstor.

As far as I can tell, Emma's husband is not a member of the Kimlock Society.

All the same, I text Frank Fenton-Brown to ask if he could possibly email people to the north and east of Dartmoor asking them if they knew of any major Kimlock collectors local to them. *Maybe you could say that someone rang you up, but you took down their number wrong? But they were very keen to be in touch with the Society and you're feeling guilty about it – does anyone have an idea about who that might be?*

On it, Frank messages me back.

I log onto eBay and make some of the auctions live. If Emma's husband buys one of the trains, eBay will generate a packaging label, and I will get an address. If it is in one of the villages on the Coraton side of the moor…

While I wait, I find out more about databases.

I find out that I can go and look at the electoral roll if I want, and I may even be able to buy a copy of it if I can come up with a convincing reason why I need it.

Then there is Companies House.

There is Ancestry.com.

In fact, the volume of available information is almost overwhelming.

With the clues Emma may or may not have given me, I could spend a lifetime searching and never find anything. Because if just one fact turns out to be wrong – if they have been married for nine years, not eleven – I could spend months searching the wrong haystack altogether.

I think Emma is clever. I guess that she has misled me at times, scattering breadcrumbs with deliberate abandon.

I know that I don't know enough.

I force myself to wait for a couple of hours and then I log in again; eBay has been busy.

A lot of people are interested in the gilded *Sunflower*, but she had a low starting price.

Someone else has already snapped up a saffron-yellow *Zinnia*, and sent through the payment; eBay has created a packing label and I click on it with a surge of hope.

A Capt J. McCarthy of Ellesmere Port, Cheshire, expects to receive *Zinnia* in three to five working days.

Capt J. McCarthy of Ellesmere Port can't possibly be Emma's husband.

Damn.

As I wait some more, I think about Emma's last call. She is changing. Her voice is more confident now. She is becoming bolder.

Questions that would have had her slamming the phone down a few weeks ago are answered with a certain self-assurance.

Maybe she will escape. Maybe she will take her children's hands and run.

Maybe there will be no more phone calls and it will be because she has fled.

Maybe that would be a good thing for both of us.

I have no idea if Emma knows she is speaking to the same person over and over again. No idea if she has even the faintest clue that this is a subtle dance between two people, or if Emma simply thinks she is talking into a vacuum.

As she should be.

While I am waiting for eBay, I read more about linguistics. Accents used to change roughly every twenty-five miles across the UK, although each isolated village might have its own slang, its own tics, its own idiosyncrasies. The distinctions of those old accents are mostly gone now, of course. Swept away by modern life. Henry Higgins, forgotten.

After another half an hour, I check eBay again.

A Ms N. Heyworth has bought the pink *Peony*. Ms N. Heyworth lives in Craven Arms, Shropshire.

Not Ms N. Heyworth.

Frank Fenton-Brown texts me in a panic: he has accidentally bid on one of his own trains.

Don't worry! I message back. *I'm sure you'll be outbid soon.*

Yes, but please *don't tell Maria – she'll have my guts for garters! I've sworn blind that I won't buy anymore!*

* * *

The calm mechanics of my hunt calm me, but every time I think of Emma, I burn with anger again.

I helped him.

What exactly did you mean by that, Emma?

And what did you do?

38

Four days later and I am back at the Good Listeners, and Liam is near a motorway. I know Liam is near a motorway because when he opened his car door briefly, I could hear the whoosh whoosh of cars racing past.

I think Liam may be an HGV driver. He has a gentle Devon accent and sounds middle-aged. The vehicle door was heavy when he closed it.

Liam is sitting in a peaceful cocoon.

Liam is dying.

He has been swallowing pills, one at a time, for quite a long time.

If someone walked past, they would just see a man knocking back a pill and washing it down with a gulp of some drink. They'd assume he was taking an aspirin, a statin, a vitamin, maybe? Something to stave off the aches and pains of an ordinary Wednesday morning.

But Liam's ordinary Wednesday pills are paracetamol. And this number will kill him.

'Do you want to tell me a bit about yourself, Liam?' I ask softly. 'Do you want to talk to me about why you're doing this?'

I've told Liam that I cannot call 999 on his behalf. I've told him again and again.

'What I've done…' Liam is sounding sleepy. 'No one could forgive me. No one.'

'People can be very forgiving, Liam. Why do you think they wouldn't be able to forgive you?'

'I tried to talk to my wife about it all.' There is a rustle. Another gulp of water. 'But the way she looked at me... Her eyes. I don't know... She looked at me as if I was shit on her shoe. The contempt on her face...'

'I am sorry.'

'The thing is that I couldn't... I couldn't stop myself. People who see me from the outside, they'd think I was a nice guy. One of the good ones... But to the people who know me... I'm a horrible human being.'

'Why do you say that?'

'It's a terrible thing, isn't it?' He sounds almost dreamy. 'When the more that people know you, the more they think you're a horrible human being.'

'You might be surprised, you know. It can be hard to know how other people perceive you.'

'Every day, I have to wake up and be *me*. It's like a prison that I can never escape. A prison that I carry around everywhere I go. I hate myself so much. The other day, I passed someone who had lost a leg. And I thought, I wish I could be like that instead. I would so much prefer to not have a leg than be like this inside. All broken. All fucked up. I wish... I wish I could be someone else.'

'It's never too late,' I say soothingly. Although it may be too late for Liam, depending on how many pills he's taken. 'It's never too late to try again.'

'She'd be better off without me. My kids... They'd all be better off without me. I'm toxic. Poisonous. It would be better for everyone if I was dead.'

'Why do you think that?'

'Do you believe in forgiveness?' Liam asks the question abruptly, and I lie the way I always do.

'Yes,' I say to Liam. 'Yes, I believe in forgiveness.'

'But I'm evil. I'm *evil*. What I did... And I'm scared I might hurt someone else...'

'I believe that there is good in everyone,' I say gently. 'I think life can change and it can get better. Some days you might think you will never be happy again. But then you see the snowdrops coming up or a daffodil flowering, and you realise you will find a way to be happy again one day.'

'Do you really think that?'

'I think there is beauty everywhere.' I think I am trying to convince myself, too. 'And you can find happiness in unexpected places and in unexpected ways.'

'It hurts,' he says suddenly. 'Everything hurts.'

'Do you want an ambulance?' I ask again. 'You have to tell me where you are.'

Austin is beside me, although there isn't much he can do either.

Because now Liam is lapsing into silence and I am speaking into a void.

I'm not going to hang up, I keep murmuring down the phone.

I'm here.

I'm here and I will stay with you.

'I deserve to die.' Liam sounds very hazy now. 'My wife thinks I deserve to die. Do you?' He sounds more awake suddenly. 'Do you think I deserve to die?'

'Of course not,' I say urgently. 'Please, Liam, if you want me to call an ambulance, you have to tell me where you are.'

There is a long silence then. A snoring sound.

I look across at Austin, who shrugs resignedly.

I'm here.

I'm here and I will stay with you.

'I'm in Cullompton Services!' Liam's shout jolts me upright. 'I'm in the car park. Please send an ambulance. Please! Please help me! I don't want to die! I'm sorry. I'm scared—'

Austin is on the case with military efficiency.

'Keep talking to me, Liam,' I say. 'They'll be there as soon as possible. Stay awake.'

I can hear vomiting. I think he is making himself sick. 'I don't want to die,' he says again. 'Please… I don't want to…'

The police get there astonishingly fast. Or it's an ambulance. I don't know.

I only hear the car door opening. Someone grabs the phone. It is a man, hurrying, but not panicking. 'That the Good Listeners? We've got him, okay? Cheers.'

The phone goes dead.

I stare at the phone. I feel a strange sort of euphoria. I need to stand up for a moment. I need to breathe. I put my phone on hold.

Through to the kitchenette.

I have been speaking to Liam for just over an hour and I feel dazed.

Austin has followed me. 'You alright?' he asks, biting into a custard cream and switching on the kettle all at once.

'I'm fine,' I say automatically. 'I hope he'll be okay.'

Of course, we'll never know if Liam was okay or not.

'You probably saved his life,' Austin says cheerfully. 'You heroine, you.'

'Shut up.'

'It's true. He'd be dead without you. Now he's got a chance. Not every day you get to save a life.'

Austin is already heading back to the call room. I wait for a few seconds and then I hear him answering the phone. 'Good Listeners. Can I help?'

In the peace of the kitchenette, I stand at the sink and grip a dish-cloth. I usually manage to compartmentalise everything, but Liam's call, on top of everything else, is not easy to tuck away.

It has been a difficult few days. I had high hopes for my eBay trap, but several of the auctions have ended now and none of the purchasers have been closer than Bristol.

My time in Damson Cottage is still ticking down. I was given two months to leave three weeks ago, and I have no idea what to do or where to go.

It feels as if everywhere I look, doors are slamming shut.

I force myself to straighten up. I can still be a Good Listener.

After Liam, I speak to a woman who is watching her child die – so slowly, by agonising degrees – of leukaemia. To Meredith, who can't stop eating and hates herself a little bit more every time she opens another packet of digestives. To Jed, who has chronic pulmonary disease and a tracheostomy, and has to put a finger over the opening in his throat every time he wants to speak. Jed sounds muffled and very, very sad.

The phone rings, time for one last call in this shift, and I almost let Austin pick it up although it's my turn. He won't mind. But no. I should.

'Good afternoon,' I say. 'Good Listeners. Can I help?'

'It's not his fault…' The voice sounds almost dreamy. 'Not his fault.'

'Okay,' I say. 'Do you want to tell me a bit more about that?'

'That little girl…' It is a woman speaking, a Devon accent. 'That poor little girl…'

It can't be.

But it is.

I *know* this voice.

Even half-slurred, half-dreamy, I know this voice. But… But it's not long after midday on a Wednesday. This is not her time.

But it is.

It is Emma.

39

Say something, I order myself. Come *on*.

'Do you want to talk about a little girl?' I ask soothingly. 'Do you want to tell me what happened to her?'

'He killed her. The poor little girl… She died. And it ruined everything.'

It *is* Emma.

I know her voice. I *know* Emma's voice.

'What happened to the little girl?' I try to keep the desperation out of my voice. 'How did it ruin everything?'

'Everything… Everything was wrong from that moment…'

Lyra? I want to ask directly. Are you talking about Lyra?

But I can't. I mustn't. Every call is a new call. 'Do you want to tell me what happened to the little girl?' I ask as gently as I can.

'Yes,' she says vaguely. 'No. Her name was Elizabeth Rose.'

'*Elizabeth Rose*?'

'Yes. Elizabeth Rose.'

It doesn't make sense. My mind spins. Emma sounds drunk. Could she be drunk? I glance at the clock again. Just before 1 p.m. on a Wednesday afternoon. She could be. Anything is possible.

Come on, I order myself. Pull yourself together. Treat this call as you would all the others.

I force myself to sit upright, to loosen my shoulders.

'That is very sad,' I try to sound sympathetic. 'How old was this little girl?'

'She was six,' says Emma. 'Six years and seven months.'

For just one sentence, Emma doesn't sound drunk. Instead, she sounds oddly precise.

I do the terrible maths. Lyra was six years and two months old when she died. So that's… a mistake? Or a different child altogether?

'That's not very old. How very sad.'

'Yes,' Emma agrees pleasantly, as if she was talking about the weather. 'Very sad. Very sad indeed.'

'Do you want to tell me more about it?'

'Hmm? Yes. *Yes.*'

'Someone killed this little girl? Elizabeth Rose?'

'He strangled her.' Quite suddenly, Emma speaks with clarity again. 'He strangled her to death. And it sent the father mad.'

'The *father*?'

'Yes.'

I hear a clink of glass on glass, and the glug of liquid flowing into a glass. Emma takes a big swig of whatever it is and I hear her swallow.

'Are you alone?' I ask.

'You can hear the bottle, can't you?' There is almost a giggle in her voice. 'I've drunk a lot. A lot, a lot, a lot. "Never drink alone," that's what my mother always said. But sometimes… Sometimes you have to.'

The glass clinks again. Another glug of liquid.

'Are you okay, drinking alone?' I ask.

'No.' Emma almost sings the syllable. 'No, I am not.'

'When did this happen?' I ask. 'When did this little girl die? Have you told the police?'

'What?' Emma is sounding hazy again. 'Hmm?'

For a moment, in the swirl of madness, I wonder if this is Emma's daughter ringing in. Emma's daughter, who has somehow discovered her father's sins and rung up with a whole new smokescreen of names.

But, no, this is not a young girl's voice. This is Emma herself.

'Did you know this little girl?' I ask. 'Elizabeth Rose? Was she someone known to you?'

'No.' Emma is certain. 'I never knew her.'

'What do you—'

'I need to go.' Emma's voice sounds wobbly and I wonder if she has been flooded by a sudden wave of nausea. 'I have to—'

The phone goes dead.

I stare at the phone. I press the hold button with numb fingers.

Elizabeth Rose. *Elizabeth Rose*?

What the hell is Emma talking about? It sent the *father* mad? Is she talking about some strange coded version of Lyra's death?

I have no idea.

Elizabeth Rose.

Lyra did have a middle name, but it was Selene, for the goddess of the moon.

Emma was strangely precise about Elizabeth Rose's age, too.

I stare at Anjali's framed needlepoint and I don't have any answers at all.

I hadn't guessed that Emma was a drinker. She's never slurred her words before. Never lost her train of thought. She might shy away from a question, but she always sounded quite sharp. On the ball.

She usually calls on a Friday evening, too, and – without wishing to sound judgemental – that is a time that I would expect most drinkers to be drinking. We get a lot of slurred sad calls on Friday nights.

She doesn't *sound* like an alcoholic. You can often hear it in their voices. Because if someone drinks enough, their vocal cords get dry and inflamed. Through the bleariness, there is a hoarseness too, and I have never heard that in Emma's voice.

Why is she calling now? Why is she calling at lunchtime on a random Wednesday?

I itch to find the red file. To dig through and discover whether Emma has taken to calling more frequently in the last few days. Once the floodgates are opened, they can be hard to close.

Maybe she has called because she is drunk and out of her routine?
Maybe he is away and she has seized her opportunity?
Elizabeth Rose.
Elizabeth Rose.
Who are you, Emma? Who are you, Elizabeth Rose?

40

I am home and I can't find an Elizabeth Rose.

Or – correction – I cannot find *the* Elizabeth Rose.

There are hundreds of Elizabeth Roses – not least because Rose can be a first name and a surname – but I can't find a murdered one. I ponder over an Elizabeth T. J. Rose, born in Orpington on the eve of the Golden Jubilee, and an Elizabeth Rose Jenkins, born in Harrogate to a Tudor devotee, but both of these Elizabeth Roses are alive.

Frank Fenton-Brown enthusiastically informs me that there is no Kimlock train called Elizabeth Rose, 'although there *was* a limited run of *Damask Roses* created in 1978. I have a magenta *Damask*, but I thought it best not to list that on eBay because only two magenta ones were ever made.'

There is even an actual Elizabeth Rose – 'a majestic rose bearing clusters of large, crisp apple blossom pink rosettes' – that takes up several pages of Google rankings. It is a whole new haystack to search, and once again I am lost.

I try cross-referencing Elizabeth Rose, but in my confusion of trying to make sense of Emma's new story, my scribbled notes make no sense. Who was the father? Why was he sent mad?

More precious clues lost to the ether.

* * *

The red file had revealed nothing. Apart from my Friday night entries, no Emmas have called up about the death of a little girl. No one has called up about the death of a little girl at all.

This afternoon does seem to have been a one-off.

Another thought strikes and I reach for my laptop and google. I've talked to several women whose husbands have drunk their way to dementia. Several women who have watched their husbands' memories flow away down the drain.

The bleak prognosis pops up on my screen: Korsakoff syndrome. Even in the cruel world of dementia, Korsakoff syndrome is one of the most brutal paths. It is the consequence of years of alcoholism that slowly – so slowly – destroy the brain.

I read Korsakoff's symptoms defeatedly because there it is, one of the main indicators for Korsakoff's: confabulation.

Confabulations, I read, *refer to the emergence of memories of experiences and events that are incorrect in place and time, or never took place at all.*

I sigh and rub my eyes. *Confabulating individuals are not intentionally being deceptive, and sincerely believe the information they are communicating to be genuine and accurate.*

The symptoms can start in middle age. Middle age: Emma's age?

I scour the local news for events that morning.

There was a lecture on 'Dartmoor Through the Ages' at the Bovey Tracey Methodist Church Hall.

There was an auction in Sticklepath, the contents of an old manor house sold off piecemeal.

Or there might have been a dentist's appointment, a haircut, a hike.

All the usual ways to spend a wet morning on Dartmoor.

Why would she drink on a Wednesday morning, but not on a Friday night?

Too many questions and only guesses for answers.

Every minute of the next day, the thought hammers away in my head. Emma is not reliable. Emma is inconstant. Emma cannot be trusted.

I knew that, of course.

I did.

I didn't.

Deep down, I trusted her.

Deep down, I put weight on her every word.

Piano playing.

Linnet.

Kimlock trains.

That school bus.

I added up the words one by one. Letting myself believe that in the end, they would equal the truth.

But Emma is not ringing up to tell me the truth.

Emma is searching for her own truth, not mine.

For all I know, I have been rambling around in her imagination for weeks.

And she doesn't even know I exist.

Lying in bed that night, I know one thing that I can do. It is a gross abuse of trust. It is unforgivable. But I don't care anymore.

Amazon helps me out. Earbuds: small ones, wireless. I can hide them in my ear and an app on my mobile will record any telephone conversation at the touch of a button.

The earbuds arrive on Friday morning – probably dumped in my postbox by Nell's delivery driver husband, Pauly. I read the instruction manual cover to cover and then call Rachel for a sound check.

A few seconds later, I listen back to the recording on my phone. *You need to make up your mind about that Josh Aarons job, Clara. He needs someone, like, yesterday.*

The sound of the recording is perfectly clear, and I should not be doing this.

But I do not give a damn anymore.

If I had started recording Emma's words earlier, I might be able to convince the police to take my suspicions seriously. Instead, I am left with only rambling notes.

* * *

You are being dragged into a madness that isn't even yours, I tell myself. This is a borrowed hysteria, an adopted lunacy.

Anything not to face your own tragedy.

And maybe I should have stopped.

Maybe I should have given up on it all.

But I didn't.

41

'Hello. My name is Emma.'

'I'm very glad you've called the Good Listeners, Emma. Can I help?'

As I answer the phone, I press the record button. The earbud is almost invisible under my headset. There is no way that my partner could spot it, even if he was looking at me, which he isn't.

For a moment, Emma sits in silence. She starts to speak before stopping herself. She does this three or four times.

'Has anything upset you recently?' I ask.

'I don't know... I don't know...'

Emma sounds exhausted today. There is no flame of anger.

Who are you? The question roars in my ears. *Who are you?*

'Is there anything you'd like to talk about?' I ask instead.

'Do you think it's possible,' the words come slowly, 'to hate and pity someone all at the same time?'

'I suppose almost any combination of emotions is possible,' I say.

'Yes.' Emma likes this response, I can tell. She is turning the thought over in her mind.

'Is there someone in particular that you feel hate and pity towards?' I ask.

Pause. 'My husband.'

'Do you want to tell me a bit about him?'

'He's pathetic, he really is.' The anger crackles sharply, briefly.

'Why do you say that?'

'You wouldn't know to look at him.' Back to the apathy. 'From the outside, he looks… I don't know. *Decent.*' She makes the word sound like a curse.

'How does he look decent,' my voice acknowledges the awkwardness of the grammar, and tries to hide my desperation, 'from the outside?'

'We look normal.' Her voice reverberates with cynicism. 'We've got it all.'

'In what way?'

'We're a *nice* family. Proper.' Devonians say proper in a distinctive way. Prah-perrr.

'But not at home?'

'No.' Defeatedly. 'Not at home.'

'Is there a reason for his behaviour?'

'I don't know. I… I don't know if… He's… illegitimate.'

For a second, I think I've misheard. Then, wildly, I try to work out how old this makes her husband. For Georgia's generation, illegitimacy would have been an irrevocable stain. For Lyra's generation, it would be entirely unremarkable. This man must be somewhere between the two, so it is interesting that from her inflection of the word, Emma – or perhaps she is echoing him? – infuses it with such shame. Perhaps at the end of the long, winding lanes, the stigma endures longer?

'And you think illegitimacy still affects him?' I try to make sense of what she means.

'I *know* it affects him.' Her voice changes. 'It's not really the illegitimacy, I suppose. It's his mother…'

'What about his mother?'

'He calls her horrible names. Horrible words.'

'What sort of names?'

'Slag. Slut. Whore.' The roll-call of misogyny. For a moment, the words echo between us. 'He thinks she's so far beneath him.'

'Does he speak to her like that often?'

'They don't see each other often.'

'And how does he speak to you?'

A sob, compressed. 'He needs me to behave *right*. He thinks that because everyone knows that his mother's a *whore*, we need to be the opposite. Or seen to be the opposite, anyway.'

'It sounds very difficult. I'm sorry. Is there anyone you can talk to about this?'

'He'd kill me.' The words are bleak, not an exaggeration. 'He'd kill me if I spoke to anyone at all.'

42

Illegitimacy should be another clue for me. But it isn't. Because the identity of a child's father can be hidden, even from the father himself.

After Lyra was born, I felt something close to awe that some women bury that particular secret. I would stare so intently at Lyra. Those miniature feet, with the unusually small little toe: *mine*. The shell shape of those tiny pink ears: *Lucas*.

As Lyra grew, there were more shocks of familiarity. As her legs lengthened, I recognised my shins, long and narrow. She would fiddle with her ears as she fell asleep, self-soothing. I had forgotten that I used to do that, but as I watched her, the memory came flooding back.

She was kind, Lyra. Caring. If another child fell over in the playground, she would rush over, hugging the startled four-year-old close.

She was always taking care of things. A fledgling, fallen from its nest. Her smallest teddy, tucked in every night. When she was five, I would hear clinking from the kitchen early – painfully early – on a Saturday. After a busy half an hour, she would appear at the bedroom door. A tray, with heavily jammed bread and a note, *I love yew sow sow sow much*.

Back to illegitimacy.

I am home now, sitting at the kitchen table, disentangling Emma's most recent call.

The problem is that Emma believing that her family looks like a nice family from the outside could mean almost anything. I don't know what she means by *nice*.

Although it does mean something.

I don't know if Nell, with their half-built house and their broken dreams, would describe her family as *nice*. But maybe she would.

Would Amber? If she studiously leaves out her husband's violence, perhaps. Ryan is good-looking, healthily employed, charming. Their children are apple-cheeked, delightful.

Perspective is everything.

But Emma has told me something. *We look normal. We've got it all.*

The husband's illegitimacy must be known about, for him to feel shame. Although it is possible that only very close family members know, which is inconvenient from my point of view. I decide to ask around about Ryan's relationship with his mother.

Illegitimacy may well not be documented either. No paper trail to follow.

Emma's voice. For the millionth time, I try to work out what it is telling me. All the voices around me have become an obsession now, even the ones I only hear fleetingly.

Nell Turner: light Devon accent, rapid-fire speech.

Tabitha Turner: can't get through a sentence without something being *salty* or *low-key* or *lit*.

Lucas: transatlantic cadences picked up from Ashley; long, soft vowels and flapped Ts: *budder* not butter.

Ryan Dallyn: resonant bass and oddly monotone at times, which makes me wonder if he might be very slightly deaf.

Victoria Blackslade: crisp enunciation, every consonant clear.

Gabriel Blackslade: golden.

Linda, the Blackslades' nanny: strong Devon accent. She'd told me she never shouts or whispers the day before a choral performance, to protect her voice; interestingly, a speaking voice gives very little indication of whether someone can sing well or not.

Georgia Wrenscott: plummy, harmonious.
Ferdie Wrenscott: gin-soaked, with smoke-toasted vocal chords.
Lawrence Wrenscott: yo-yoing between Sherborne and Ryan's West Country.

I've even started concentrating on Good Listeners' voices.
Anjali: lived briefly in Newcastle as a child, and you can still hear a hint of Geordie in a few of her words.
Manon: has a French mother. No French accent, but despite having spoken English since babyhood, her voice is distinctive. Different languages use different facial muscles, creating specific movements of the jaw and the cheeks and the tongue. Manon doesn't use the muscles at the top of her cheeks in the same way as a typical English speaker, and you can hear it in her voice.
It's endless.
But what does Emma's voice tell me?
What?
I still don't know.

I pace around the house. I prowl from one end of the kitchen-diner to the other, and back again and back again.
It's not enough. I feel claustrophobic. There is not enough air in the house. I pull on my coat, yank open the front door.
It is raining. Coming in sideways. Up on the high moor, it will be wild.
Down towards the village then?
Lyra, I think. I will go and see Lyra's memorial.

43

The rain-darkened granite of the church looms up as I make my way to Lyra's memorial. I find myself here often, almost without realising it.

It is simple, her plaque. Just her name, a few words, the year that she was born, and the year that she died.

They are so close together, those two dates. So painfully, horribly close.

I pull up a weed which has sprung up since I was last here and then I sit down. Not long now until her birthday, the birthday when she should have been nine.

'Darling Lyra,' I whisper. 'Darling, darling Lyra.'

After a while, I start to shiver. I stand up and wander around the graveyard. Through the row of beech trees, I catch glimpses of the moor in all its chilly beauty.

I pass the same names over and over again, the weeds diligently kept away.

And that's when I see it.

Tucked away in a corner, near the darkness of the yew. Close to the dell where the snowdrops grow in January, in defiance of the cruel winter frosts.

Elizabeth Rose Wrenscott.

Elizabeth Rose.

The shock is stunning. I stand in front of the grave, unable to move.

It doesn't make sense.

None of it makes sense.

Elizabeth Rose Wrenscott
Beloved daughter
19 April 1985 – 28 November 1991

The words blur. I am reading them, but they don't seem to sink in. My mind won't let them penetrate.

A shake begins in my knees and spreads through my body until I think I might fall down. This grave is nearly forty years old.

Who is Elizabeth Rose Wrenscott? And what is she to Emma?

It doesn't make sense. It doesn't make sense at all. A flash of horror that is almost painful: did Emma make everything up?

Was it all a lie?

I imagine Emma in this very same graveyard, reading the inscriptions one by one. I remember wandering around Exeter Cathedral, reading the dusty inscriptions, imagining stories for those long-dead people. To Emma, are Lyra Selene Brennan and Elizabeth Rose Wrenscott just words chiselled into unforgiving granite?

Has Emma, in her sad madness, been rambling around this very same churchyard, inventing tragic stories for these girls?

Have all my hopes been for nothing?

Six years and seven months. I can hear Emma's voice in my head.

Six years and seven months.

I start to shiver.

Emma, slurring. Emma, delirious.

Elizabeth Rose.

I walk between the two gravestones. They are less than a hundred yards apart. Patches of lichen have grown over the writing on Elizabeth's grave.

Elizabeth Rose Wrenscott
Beloved daughter

Lyra Selene Brennan
Forever loved, darling girl

Beloved daughter.
Beloved daughter.
Because that's all you can be, dying so young.
Not a wife, not a mother.
Only a beloved daughter.
Only.

Lyra's story, easy to learn.
The whole world knows Lyra's story; I took care of that.
And Elizabeth Wrenscott… Well, who knows?
Almost certainly not Emma.

I think of the desperate sadness in Georgia Wrenscott's eyes. I assumed it was the loss of Harepath. But maybe I misjudged everything. The loss of a house would be a triviality next to this sadness.

I have been trailing in Emma's wake, hunting for truth where there is only tragedy.

I have picked up the shards of Emma's delusions, and built my own wild stories, my own strange interpretations.

Who are you, Emma?

Who am I?

And what have I become?

44

'Are you quite alright, Clara?' Victoria Blackslade stops, mobile in one hand, halfway through a phone conversation.

Her question feels less like an inquiry into the state of my health, and more a hint that I am not working hard enough. Which I am not. Instead my thoughts keep slipping back to Elizabeth Rose Wrenscott. Who are you? How did you die? What *happened*?

It is Thursday morning and I have spent every moment since I saw that grave trying to make sense of Elizabeth's story.

Elizabeth Rose Wrenscott is indeed the daughter of Ferdinand and Georgia Wrenscott, Ancestry.com informed me. Elizabeth died when her brother Lawrence was only three years old.

The death certificate gave only dates. Google had no detail either. I suppose Elizabeth died years before the internet took over.

I am going to go to the local newspaper's offices as soon as possible, to rummage through their microfiches. But both the local library and the local newspaper operate on skeleton hours these days, it turns out.

I suppose Ferdinand's drinking and gambling make a painful sense now. It drove the father mad…

The Father. I had even reached the point of suspecting the vicar.

Lawrence's aimlessness – which I had scoffed at – is also easy to understand. A small boy, growing up in a house of grief and whisky.

Poor Lawrence.

* * *

'Yes. Sorry. I'm fine, Mrs Blackslade. I was just about to put up Cecily's bug hotel. Is there anything else you'd like me to get done this morning?'

'Those sweet peas need to be cleared. Can you put the bamboo poles in the shed once they're disentangled? Please.'

Victoria Blackslade marches off down the garden. She has already gone back to the conversation on her mobile. 'For heaven's sake, Penelope, it's your turn to do it. I'm busy.'

She doesn't look busy and her voice grates on my ears. I don't know where Victoria Blackslade went to school, but it must have been somewhere smart. She disappears towards the river.

A few minutes later, Gabriel Blackslade appears with a cup of tea. Gabriel knows how I take my tea. Milk, no sugar, and it looks like an apology. There is a slice of Amber's chocolate cake too. I smelled that cooking earlier.

'Victoria's mother isn't well,' he says. 'She and her sister are trying to co-ordinate her care.'

'She does seem quite stressed.'

'I don't think Victoria's happy down here,' Gabriel admits. 'She's never loved Dartmoor, especially not over winter.'

'It can be tough.' I try for cheeriness. 'Sorry that I got distracted. I've just got a lot on my mind at the moment.'

'Anything I can help with?'

For a moment, wildly, I wonder if I could ask to stay in the Gardener's Cottage for a few months. But I know it's impossible. I've looked it up on a holiday home website before, and I couldn't afford even one night in the Gardener's Cottage.

'Ryan Dallyn,' I say instead, impulsively.

'What about him?' Gabriel raises an eyebrow.

'You remember that the police looked closely at him? Back then.'

Gabriel knows what I am talking about. 'Yes. His phone records showed that he was in Abbot's Wood on the day that Lyra disappeared.' Gabriel always presents facts with unflinching precision, as if he is trying to ensure that a jury has fully understood his case. 'Jordie Meldon and Lawrence Wrenscott both also said that they were in Abbot's Wood at about the time that Lyra died.'

'Yes. What did you make of Ryan's story?'

Gabriel sits down on a bench next to the study's French windows. The Harepath gardens are full of scenic places to sit, and the view from that bench – across towards the Meldons' farm – is particularly beautiful. He folds his arms and ponders. The day is unusually warm for early November. He is only wearing a light gilet over his shirt.

'I wouldn't like it much if I were Dallyn's defence barrister. There was confusion between what the three of them said when they first spoke to the police, and what they said the second time. I'd be concerned about what the prosecution would do to Jordie Meldon and Lawrence Wrenscott on the stand.'

I always get the impression that Gabriel Blackslade enjoys these legal questions. He cheerfully refers to himself as a legal geek. I remember him once telling me that his barristers' chambers had brought out a new document management system to ensure client confidentiality while working from home and he looked genuinely thrilled about it. That management system also showed that he had been working at his desk when Lyra died.

'Ryan's phone data definitely showed that he was in Abbot's Wood, up by the folly,' I say. 'Lawrence's phone data suggested that Lawrence's phone never left his house. Jordie's phone was in one of his fields the whole time.'

Both Gabriel and I know Jordie's and Lawrence's explanation of this. 'Lawrence said he left his phone in his coat pocket at home.' Gabriel nods. 'Jordie said he forgot his phone on the dashboard of his tractor.'

It was warmish when Lyra went missing. Lots of people were in shirtsleeves. It was perfectly plausible that Lawrence went out in only his jumper and that Jordie had abandoned his phone in the tractor.

'If there had been any forensic evidence,' Gabriel still looks serene, 'it would have been very different. As it was…'

'They gave each other alibis,' I say quietly. 'But now Ryan and Amber have obviously had a falling-out. I wonder what it is that Amber knows.'

I am watching Gabriel's face closely. I sense that he knows more than he is saying – Amber must have given him some sort of explanation for arriving in tears the other day – but I can't tell a thing from his face.

Frustrated, I throw caution to the wind. 'Do you know if Amber has a sister?' I ask.

'What?' Gabriel looks confused.

'Someone mentioned something,' I say. 'I was just wondering.'

'I don't know.' He shakes his head at me. 'Anything else?'

'Actually,' I make it a sort of joke, 'do you have any idea if Ryan Dallyn collects Kimlock trains? You know? The toy ones.'

'Kimlock trains?' There is mystification in Gabriel's voice. 'Not as far as I know, no.'

'And do you know if anyone around here has a puppy called Linnet?'

'Linnet?' Gabriel looks bewildered. 'What are you talking about, Clara? I don't think so?'

I plough on. 'And this is a really weird one. Do you happen to know if Ryan Dallyn is illegitimate?'

The smile slips off Gabriel's face altogether. 'No, I have no idea. Why? Such a peculiar question, Clara!'

I've gone too far. Gabriel is looking at me in uneasy confusion.

'I just heard a rumour about it,' I say hastily. 'And wondered if it was something that Amber had mentioned to you.'

Gabriel is looking worried. 'Amber definitely didn't mention anything like that. Has anything happened, Clara? I know you've kept looking for new evidence. Have you discovered something new?'

For an instant, I do think about telling him. But I don't know my legal position in relation to the Good Listeners, and I think that I might put him in a very awkward position.

'No, nothing's happened.' I smile brightly.

There is a crease between Gabriel's eyebrows as he looks at me. 'Are you sure?'

'Yes, I'm just… asking questions.'

'Okay. Of course I'd tell you anything that might help… But do be careful, won't you? Coraton… It's not a big place. The people here, their lives are entwined. Tangled up. Nothing is secret and everything is secret all at once. And people like Ryan Dallyn… They know everyone around here. Everyone.'

'I'm aware.'

'Clara… People like Ryan Dallyn don't like prying. And that man, he can be…'

I gaze down the garden, to where Victoria Blackslade has disappeared around the corner. 'I need to know what happened to my daughter. I have to know.'

'Clara.' Gabriel Blackslade sounds very concerned now. 'Please promise me that you will be careful?'

45

I go back to gardening, but even after working late into the afternoon, I find that I am still twitching with nervous energy.

Emma. Can I trust a word she says?

After the Elizabeth Rose call, I just don't know anymore.

She could be insane. She could be a drunk. She could be a complete fantasist.

But there is a little voice in my head: Emma is the only new information you have. There is nothing else.

As I walk home from Harepath, I pass Ryan and Amber Dallyn's house. The kitchen window is open. Half hidden by the sprawling hedge, I can hear voices. Before I realise it, I have stopped.

Although their home is called Rose Cottage, there are no roses in the overgrown garden. The house sign is peeling, almost illegible, and the thatch is greenish. Ryan's van is in front of the house. There is no parking space, so he just stops the van on the verge. The grass has given up now, swallowed by mud. The garden gate – the one the puppy escaped through that terrible day – is half off its hinges.

They both have Devon accents, Amber and Ryan. As I listen to them, scraps of my old linguistics research come back to me. The rhotic R: luv-errr, not lov-ah. And this accent has a retroflex, the tongue curling up.

I focus on Amber. But her voice is quieter, almost inaudible. She could be Emma, whoever Emma is. Perhaps.

As I listen, I can hear that Ryan is angry about something and getting angrier. I know that I should leave, but my feet won't move. I feel as if I am glued to the spot, desperate for any clue. What are they saying? I can't quite make out the words… Just then, Ryan must have turned towards the window, because his words are suddenly clearer.

'It's all fucking Jordie's fault!' Ryan shouts. 'He needs to keep his fucking mouth shut!'

As he shouts, Ryan throws open the door and storms out of the house. I have no way of getting away before he sees me. Ryan stops dead and I try to look startled, as if I just happen to be passing. It doesn't work.

'You!' The rage is too intense to disguise. Ryan's anger is a physical force, pouring down the lane towards me. 'What the hell are you doing here?'

46

I race off down the road towards the village, leaving a flurry of words behind me that make no sense and must be inaudible to Ryan Dallyn anyway.

I don't look back, but I am sure he is watching me.

After a few seconds, I hear the van door slam and the engine roar. He's coming. The van accelerates towards me, travelling at speed. He is going to—

I throw myself into the hedge, flattening myself into the bank. The van screeches past, scarily close, deliberately close. I shout out – no words, just panic. But then the van is gone, the engine screaming away, and I am left in the quiet of the lane.

I find that I am shaking.

All fucking Jordie… All fucking Jordie's fault…

What was Jordie's fault?

I start walking back towards my house again. As I walk, I realise where I can go. Nell has lived in Coraton all her life. Nell will know what happened to Elizabeth.

Nell is out in her garden, filling pots with bulbs.

'I've always liked planting bulbs,' she says as she spots me. 'It's something to look forward to when winter finally retreats. Even,' she looks wearily around the scruffy garden, 'if the rest of this place is a disaster.'

'What are they?'

'Daffodils, tulips. Those are hyacinths.'

'Gorgeous.'

I think of the promise of spring, still so far away. In the frosts of winter, I always find it hard to remember that summer even exists.

Nell looks at me shrewdly. 'Cup of tea?'

'Yes, please.'

I follow Nell into the half-built house.

'What are you after, then?'

'Oh—'

'It's alright. Spit it out.'

'Do you know anything about,' I ask slowly, 'a girl called Elizabeth Wrenscott? Elizabeth Rose Wrenscott?'

Nell freezes.

'Why?' Nell sounds very old all of a sudden. 'Why do you want to know about Elizabeth?'

47

Nell takes a long time making tea, but eventually we are sitting down in the unpainted sitting room.

'Now,' Nell says apprehensively. 'What do you need to know, Clara?'

'Elizabeth Wrenscott died when she was six years old, didn't she?'

'Yes.' Nell looks very tired, suddenly. Wary, too. 'She did.'

'I saw her grave up by the church,' I say hastily.

'I guessed you must have done.'

'What happened to her, Nell?'

Nell looks me straight in the eye.

'She was murdered, Clara.'

'Oh god.' The fire crackles in the wood burner. I stare blankly at a row of art history books on a bookshelf. 'That's horrendous.'

'I know that it was terrible at the time. Truly awful for everyone. I don't have to tell you that, of course.'

'No. Her poor parents. Poor Georgia. Poor Ferdinand.' I hesitate. 'Nell, how did she die?'

Another long silence. It is long enough that I know that Emma's description of little Elizabeth Wrenscott's death was correct.

'She was strangled, I'm afraid. I am so sorry, Clara.'

My throat closes up. Emma was right. 'You don't have to be sorry, Nell,' I manage to say. 'There's nothing for you to be sorry about.'

'I know.' Nell curls her feet up into the old armchair. 'But I didn't want to upset you.'

'No one's ever mentioned her to me.'

'They didn't want to upset you any further, I expect.'

'Yes, but…'

'And it all happened a very long time ago, Clara. Before I was born. The boys' – I know she is referring to Lawrence, Jordie and Ryan – 'were only three when she died.'

'It wasn't that long ago,' I protest. 'I couldn't see anything about it online, but it must have been a big story at the time, surely?'

'Things were different in Coraton then, I guess. It was still so remote up here. It wasn't the same as when your daughter went missing. There would have been interest at the time, but there wouldn't have been weeks of journalists everywhere. Georgia and Ferdinand… They didn't, well, bring in all the journalists…'

Nell's voice trails off, although I am not offended. When I was searching, I was desperate for everyone to be searching too. I didn't know it was already too late.

Once Lyra was found, and everything was lost, I craved silence.

The journalists left me alone after a while. Only so much you can write once someone's dead anyway. There is a magic in the missing. I suppose it's called hope.

I wonder, too, if Coraton had preferred the quiet around Elizabeth's death. People hold their secrets close here: *least said, soonest mended.*

I always knew that Lyra – pretty, white, middle-class Lyra – took up more airtime than most. One child a week is murdered, according to the NSPCC, and many of them go almost unremarked.

I think of Elizabeth's little gravestone by the old yew tree and I am hit by a sudden realisation. Forty years from now, Lyra's history will be just a few words on a bleak lump of stone.

Unknown eyes will flick over her: oh look, only six, shame.

Because who will tell the story of Lyra? I can't imagine that Tabitha will be regaling her children with tales about that time at the folk festival when…

No. Lyra's story will be forgotten. Lyra's story will be lost.

'Who killed her?' I ask Nell quietly. 'Who killed Elizabeth?'

'I don't know.' Nell's eyes are dark. 'No one knows.'

Nell looks at the fire. I guess that she is trying to decide whether to tell me something or not. I stay silent. The longer Nell stays silent, the more she is acknowledging that there is something about Elizabeth's death that I ought to know. The silence is its own admission, and we both know it.

'Elizabeth was found dead in the woods,' Nell says in the end. 'She was found out in Abbot's Wood.'

'In Abbot's Wood?' For a moment, I can't breathe. Abbot's Wood, where Lyra was found. *Abbot's Wood.*

'Yes.' Nell nods.

'You should have told me.' I feel betrayed, as if something has been stolen from me. 'The police should have been told about that.'

'Clara, this was decades ago. None of the people… Most of the people involved are old. Elizabeth's parents… They're old now.' There is a pleading note in Nell's voice.

'But no one said anything.' I realise how silent the village has been.

'Elizabeth's been dead for years. The killer? He'd be old by now, too. He might even be dead—'

'So what?' I say stubbornly. 'Copycat murders… You hear about them all the time.'

There has been a wall of silence around the Wrenscotts, I realise. No one mentioned a word to the police about Lawrence's tragic sister. Anyone in Coraton over the age of forty had to have a memory of a little girl found strangled in Abbot's Wood. And not one of them told.

'Not all the time. But I suppose… Clara, it's just that it was a very long time ago. Georgia… She can't bear anyone to speak about it. She's so nice, you know? But she just shuts down at any mention of Elizabeth. She always has, my mother said.'

Ferdinand Wrenscott may have collapsed after Elizabeth's death, I think. But Georgia is respected and liked. I can easily imagine that everyone got into the habit of silence about Elizabeth's death, if Georgia was destroyed by any passing mention.

'Everyone would remember something like that, though.'

Nell looks at her hands, folded in her lap. Her eyes are veiled. 'Of course people remember, Clara.'

I am being unfair and I know it. 'Sorry, Nell. I don't mean to… Did the police investigate? Back then?'

'Of course they did. But I know that there wasn't much to go on. There wasn't…'

'There wasn't what?'

'Elizabeth wasn't found straight away. There wasn't much… Well, there wasn't much evidence.'

Nell's words take my breath away. I know what she means. I know that if twenty-first-century technology struggled with Lyra's death, decades-old science must have been utterly defeated by Elizabeth's.

'Were there suspicions?' My voice sounds as if it is coming from a long way away. 'Do you have any idea who killed her?'

'No.' Nell is certain.

'And the Wrenscotts were still living up at Harepath when Elizabeth died?'

'Yes. My mother said that she was adorable, Elizabeth. A real little darling.'

'And you said Lawrence was only three years old when she died?'

'My mother said he was the only thing that broke the silence at Harepath.'

I try to imagine what it must have been like for Lawrence, growing up in that silenced house. I think of the blustery bravado in the pub, the too loud laugh, and Arabella or Araminta giving up on a hopeless task. I imagine a small boy trying to comfort his shattered parents. And, later, saying goodbye to his childhood home, and walking away from the ghost.

Or trying to, anyway.

Lyra didn't leave broken siblings behind.

Where is Arabella or Araminta now? I wonder to myself. What happened to her? I don't think she could possibly be Emma?

Could Lawrence potentially be illegitimate, for example? Perhaps. It doesn't seem likely, and I can hardly imagine asking Georgia such a question, which she would regard as unacceptably impudent.

I realise that Nell is still talking. '… That's how Lawrence and Ryan ended up such good friends.'

'What?' I ask. 'Sorry.'

'Only that Ryan's dad was the gardener at Harepath House, and the Dallyns lived at the cottage there.'

'They lived at the Gardener's Cottage?'

'Yes,' said Nell. 'While his father was still working there. When Ryan's father retired, they moved out to Rose Cottage, all of a few hundred yards. Those boys grew up together, with Jordie Meldon in the farm right next door. They were all inseparable.'

'What was Ryan's mother like? Is she still alive?'

Nell's face is blank. 'Chrissie Dallyn. She was just a mum, you know?'

'Are they close? Ryan and his mother?'

'I don't know, to be honest.'

'By the way, what was the name of the puppy?' I ask. 'The one that went missing on the same day that Lyra did? The one that Ryan was out looking for.'

Nell looks baffled. 'Ziggy, I think? The kids named him.'

'And I know it's odd, but does Amber play the piano?'

Nell is on the verge of impatience. 'Clara, what is all this about? You're not making any sense!'

'Does she?'

Nell sighs. 'Yes, a bit. There was a lady in Coraton who taught all of us the piano back when we were kids. She taught me and my sister. My sister was a lot better than me.'

The door opens and Pauly walks in. He is skinny, Pauly, apart from a paunch. He has thinning brown hair and unusually large ears. He looks tired and that awkwardness between us is still there.

'Evening,' says Pauly, and I start to say goodbye.

It is late now, and the night is dark. I start walking back up the track to my cottage. I can't imagine this not being my walk home. I can't imagine living anywhere else. Where will I go? What will I do?

I don't know what it means, this discovery of Elizabeth Rose's grave.

It could mean that Emma is completely delusional. That she can't be trusted at all.

Or perhaps her husband really did kill Lyra, and she has developed a strange obsession with Elizabeth's death, almost as a sort of diversion.

Or is it also possible that Emma really does know something about Elizabeth Rose's death?

Is there a chance that my daughter's death is linked to a murder that happened almost forty years ago?

I tell myself that this is impossible. Vanishingly unlikely.

But as I walk up the dark track, my mind keeps spinning. Ryan Dallyn was a toddler back then, but…

Old Mr Meldon? The rich farmer, Jordie's father. Physically tough, wiry. He was lambing the day that Lyra went missing, working flat out as the Meldons' Texel population trebled within a month. Nobody was with him, out in the sheep barn.

Or Ferdinand Wrenscott? With his whisky-rusted face, thin strands of hair and his air of pompous inadequacy? I remember Ferdie sitting toad-like on a folding chair as Lyra danced around the maypole. But the police must have looked very closely at his alibi when Elizabeth died. And she only died a few decades ago, long after anyone would have looked the other way for the squire. *It's always the dad.* I shudder. Ferdie Wrenscott was at the folk festival that day; lots of people saw him. But could he have slipped away?

I have asked around about Ryan's father, but he died long ago. It must have been shortly after he retired to Rose Cottage. A stroke, nothing suspicious. Although everything is suspicious to me now.

I am nearly at the gate to Damson Cottage when behind me there is a sound which might be a fox or it might be a scream.

I spin around.

There is nothing there, I tell myself. Nothing there at all.

But just then there is a rustle. A scuffle.

A stick snaps, very close by.

'Who's there?' I hate my voice for sounding quavery. 'Who is it?'

Silence. The wind blows, stirring the ragged beech leaves.

There is nothing there, I tell myself again. Nothing at all.

But was that the patter of feet? Is that the sound of breathing?

'Who is that?' I shout. 'Go away!'

Another rustle, closer this time. 'Stop it!' I scream. 'Leave me alone!'

There is no one to hear me. The village is a few pinpricks of light in the far distance. There is no one. And that... Those were definitely footsteps. And the sound of someone forcing themself through a hedge.

All at once, there is a dark shape in the lane, just a few feet away from me. It is so dark that I can't make out anything more.

'Stop it!' The words are hoarse. I can't breathe. I can't move. My feet are solid lumps of cold flesh and the rest of me is scorching fear. 'Stop it!'

The shape pounces, but suddenly I can move. Suddenly I can turn away and sprint, racing up the track towards Damson Cottage.

And behind me, I hear those long jeery vowels. *Woooooo. Woooooooo.*

At least two voices, men's voices, and then, clear through the darkness, I hear the words of contempt.

'Fucking nutter.'

Snigger.

Silence.

48

The next evening, I am ruthless. Friday night, Emma's time.

Jackie calls at 8 p.m. I have to pick up the call because Austin is on the other line. Two minutes into the saga of the swiped Molton Brown hand soap – wild mint and lavandin, this time – and I can't stand it for a second longer.

'Sorry,' I say. 'You're breaking up… Hello? Sorry…'

I press the red button and cut her off.

Jackie tries again straight away.

'Sorry!' I almost scream. 'I can't hear you!'

Jackie does not try again.

Good.

Because this is not a help-line anymore. And I am not throwing out a lifeline. I am throwing out a fishing line and my bait is full of hooks. Swallow it down. For I will tear out your stomach to get to the truth.

A few feet away, Austin is still absorbed in his conversation. The telephone rings. For a couple of seconds, I listen to the jingle of the phone. Then I take a deep breath and press the answer button.

'Hello?' says a tense voice. 'Hello?'

'Good Listeners,' I say. 'Can I help?'

Emma sounds the same as she always did. Her words are clear and precise. There is no slurring. This is Friday evening Emma: sober, coherent. I press record.

'My name is Emma,' she begins. 'It's my husband,' she says. 'I need to talk to someone about him.'

'That's why we're here,' I say gently. 'You can tell me anything you want.'

'He... He...'

'What,' I ask calmly, 'would you like to talk about?'

'My husband hit my daughter.' Emma sounds as if she is struggling to make sense of her own words. 'My husband... he hit my daughter.'

Emma's daughter.

Emma's little girl.

I think of this small child – of this nameless, faceless, voiceless girl – and my anger shatters into sadness.

'I am so sorry to hear that,' I say. 'That must have been terrible for your daughter. And very difficult for you.'

'I can't believe he actually hit her,' she murmurs. 'I always thought...' Her voice trails away.

'What?' I mustn't let myself be too desperate. 'What did you always think?'

'I always promised myself that I would leave if he hit one of the children,' she whispers. 'I promised...'

'But you haven't left?' I guess.

'No,' she says. 'I'm still here. I'm still bloody here.'

'What happened?' I ask. 'Have you taken her to the doctor? Is there anyone else you can speak to?'

'I...' Emma won't tell me. I hope intensely that this is not guilt. Guilt that she knows her daughter needs medical attention, but can't bring herself to take her to the GP.

I can't let the silence go on too long. I ask a different question. 'Do you want to tell me why he hit her?'

'Oh, it was so stupid,' says Emma. 'He's—'

'Clara!' Austin hisses to me.

I shove my hand over my mouthpiece. We don't usually use each other's names, just in case. I turn around, irritated. Austin has knocked his tea over and it is spreading everywhere, trickling over the edge of the desk.

I point wildly at my headset. *Sorry*, he gestures, *didn't realise you were on a call.* The cooling tea is pooling on the lino. Frantic to concentrate on Emma's words, I grab a notepad and lob it at Austin. But the notepad just spreads the tea around, it doesn't absorb anything.

Emma is still talking in my ear. 'He's a manipulative bastard.' Her sobs echo tinnily. 'He always has been. Always.'

'I'm really sorry.'

'He slapped her across the face.' Emma is crying. 'He really hit her too. He meant to hurt her. If my niece had been here...'

'That's terrible,' I say again. 'I am so sorry to hear that. Violence against children, it's so terrible.'

'I don't know what to do,' Emma sobs. 'I need to get my children away, don't I? I have to. I can't subject them to this. Oh Christ...' Her voice changes. 'I've got to go.'

Without another word, she puts the phone down. I stop the recording, and ease the earpiece out of my ear and try to reassure myself. Emma could have put the phone down for any reason.

It could be her daughter, wandering downstairs again.

It could be a pot boiling over on the stove.

It could be her mother, dropping by for a gossip.

It could be anything.

The shift continues calmly. I am not rushing people off the phone now, but it is a quiet evening all the same. Austin's call continues. I get a tea cloth and wipe up the spill.

So I am completely thrown when I answer the phone and it is Emma again.

'I'm Emma,' she snaps without preamble.

'You're through to the Good—'

I am scrambling to get my earpiece into place, hurrying to press record. Hopeless. I glance at the clock. 8.47 p.m. Later than usual. *Recording*, announces the app.

'My husband killed Lyra Brennan,' Emma almost shouts the words. 'He murdered little Lyra Brennan.'

And for the first time, I think that Emma wants to tell someone what really happened.

49

'Lyra Brennan?' I say. The adrenaline is a wave breaking over me. I can't think. I can barely breathe. 'That is terrible. Do you want to tell me a bit about what happened?'

'He's a monster!' she spits. 'I have to get my children away from him. I have to.'

'That sounds like the only thing to do.' My words sound as if they are coming from a long way off. 'You must do whatever it takes to keep your children safe. That's the most important thing. Have you told the police?'

But Emma ignores my question. 'I don't know why I stayed so long.' She is almost speaking to herself. 'I don't know *how* I did. Why didn't I get away from him years ago?'

'If you haven't told the police yet, you might want to,' I say. 'If you and your children are living with a killer, that puts you all at risk.'

'My children...'

'Go to the police,' I urge her. 'For your children's sake.'

'He hit me,' she murmurs. 'He hit my daughter. I need to get away from him. Why am I still here?'

'Women can find it incredibly difficult to leave domestic abusers.' Everything has gone numb now and I am speaking by rote. 'Abusers isolate women and destroy their self-confidence, and that makes it harder and harder for them to actually leave.'

'You're right,' she breathes. 'You're *right*.'

'How?' I am struggling for the right note of horror in my voice. 'How do you know he killed that poor little girl?'

There is a sharp intake of breath. I stare at the red light, pleading for it to stay lit up. Praying for this delicate line of communication to stay open.

'Something must have happened,' I say, as persuasively, as kindly as I can, 'for you to be sure that he did something like that?'

'I… don't know if I…' Her voice trails off.

Silence. Emma is still there though. She is listening to me. She is listening to every word.

'This man is controlling you,' I say firmly. 'And he is controlling your whole family. You have to do what is right for your children.'

'I…'

'This man has made you scared to tell anyone anything about him. He has made you scared to leave him, scared of everything. But you can make the choice to speak out. Break the silence, Emma.'

'You're right… I know you're right.'

I wait. I wait until I can't stand the silence a moment longer, and then I speak. I speak with a voice of honey. 'You can tell me,' I murmur down the phone, 'what happened.'

There is a gasp, which might be assent.

'Come on, Emma.'

'I don't know how to—'

'Just by speaking, you diminish his power.' My voice is louder now, edged with anger. 'His power depends on your silence, Emma.'

I have no right to do this.

This is a woman who is in intense distress, who has been brave enough to reach out for help. And I am exploiting her despair.

'I guessed right from the start.' The words spill out of Emma all of a sudden, a dam bursting. 'The moment I heard that that little girl had gone missing, I *knew* it was him. He's always been… evil. He said that he was going to walk down to the folk festival, but when he got home, there was something about him. I don't know… He was *quivering* with excitement. He's never been like that. I asked him where he'd been and he just ignored me. But when the police investigation started properly, he told me to tell them that he'd been working the whole time. And when I said, "What do you mean? Where the hell were you?", he said he'd been out in the woods the whole time, but that wasn't an alibi, was it? He said he'd just fancied a walk. And I *knew*—'

There is a smashing sound behind her. It sounds as if someone has kicked in a door. Emma screams.

'Who the fuck are you talking to?' It is a man's voice. 'What the fuck are you *doing*?'

Emma screams again. Now there are footsteps marching across the floor, getting louder.

'What the *hell*?' the man shouts again. 'Who the fuck are you talking to?'

Emma drops the phone. I hear the crack as it hits the floor.

'Don't!' she screams. 'Don't touch me.'

I can hear scuffling. A sharp grunt of pain.

'What are you *doing*?' the man shouts again. There is another noise: it sounds like a punch and Emma howls with pain.

'Let me go!' Emma's voice is breathless now, terrified.

'You crazy *bitch*.'

'No!' Emma tries again. 'Don't!'

'Stop!' I shout down the phone. 'Stop it! Please!'

Austin has spun his chair around. 'What's going on, Clara?'

'Stop it!' I scream again. 'Let her go!'

I can still hear Emma screaming, but then it abruptly changes to a choking sound.

'Emma!' I shout. 'Emma!'

It sounds as if Emma is fighting for her life, frantic, desperate. There is the thump of feet on the floor. Gasping sounds. Scrabbles.

Then there is silence.

'Emma!' I shout again. 'Emma!'

I hear steps, and a rustling sound as the phone is picked up. 'Shit,' says a man's voice. 'Shit. Who the fuck is this?'

The phone goes dead. The little red light goes out.

For a moment, I can't move. Austin is beside me now. Simeon has appeared from somewhere, and has his hand on my shoulder. I still have my headset on.

'DV?' Simeon murmurs.

I nod. I can't say anything else.

Austin and Simeon mustn't see the earbud, I think blearily to myself.

'What happened?' asks Simeon. 'What's going on?'

'Clara, are you okay?' Austin has his hand on mine. 'Are you alright? You look very shocked.'

'I'm fine,' I manage. 'I'm okay.'

'What was going on?' asks Simeon.

'I'm not sure.' My voice trembles. 'It sounded like a woman...' There is a hot feeling in my throat and I know I am going to cry. 'It sounded like someone was killing a woman.'

'Oh Clara,' says Austin.

It is at that moment that my telephone rings again. I stare at it for a second, befuddled. Austin has abandoned his phone, but I forgot to put my line on hold.

'Don't answer it,' says Austin. 'You're in no state. Whoever it is, they'll call back.'

But there is a thought at the back of my mind. A thought that I cannot shut down.

I reach forward and I push the green button.

'Don't—' says Simeon, but it is too late.

'Who is this?' It is the same man as before. His voice is deep and rough and his strong Devon accent sounds like a snarl. As soon as I hear it, I know that this man will continue to press the redial number until he finds out who his wife was speaking to.

Eventually, someone will have to pick up. Eventually, someone will have to say those well-worn words.

'Good Listeners,' I say. 'Can I help?'

50

The man crashes the handset down with a curse.

Simeon reaches past me and puts my phone on hold.

'Let Plymouth take the slack for a bit,' he says. 'Idle buggers they are anyway.' He tries to smile encouragingly at me, but the smile wobbles.

'Tea,' he decides. 'And I think Alys has some Bourbons somewhere for times of emergency. I'd say this counts.'

No protocol for murder, I think. I feel shivery, almost nauseous. Despite his attempt at a smile, Simeon's hands are shaking too.

'It's going to be okay, Clara.' I think Simeon is trying to reassure both of us. I must look haunted. I touch my face and realise I am crying.

'I'll be fine in a moment, Simeon.' I try to reassure him, too.

As Simeon disappears towards the kitchenette, I slide off my headset, catching the earbud in my hand as I do. As soon as I've shoved the earbud into my pocket, I pretend to check my phone and manage to stop the recording. I don't think Austin notices anything. He is gazing out of the window onto the dark Exeter street, biting hard at a thumbnail.

The adrenaline is ebbing away now. I force myself to breathe slowly, deeply. I have to be careful – very careful – about what I say now.

'Right, Clara.' Simeon walks back into the main room with three cups of tea on a tray. 'Hot sweet tea. That's what people always drink in a crisis, don't they?'

'Thank you, Simeon.'

'Do you want to talk about what happened? It sounds really terrible. I am very sorry you had to go through that.'

I find that I do want to talk about it. 'It was a woman called Emma,' I say. 'And she was upset about something.'

I pause. I have to pick my words carefully. This has all happened so fast that I can't think straight. Emma may not be dead, I tell myself. She may have been knocked out and be swimming back to consciousness even now.

If I tell Simeon the whole story, I will never be allowed back into the Good Listeners' offices. And there is a chance that Emma will ring back at some point. There is a chance that there may be more to learn.

Somewhere in my mind, a small voice whispers that this is not likely, that there was an appalling ferocity to that struggle. And then a terrible silence.

But you never know, I tell myself. She might still be alive. She may have survived.

Simeon is waiting patiently. Good Listeners learn patience.

'This woman was upset about something?' he echoes me.

'Yes,' I say. 'She was interrupted while she was speaking. I think the man overheard her conversation and attacked her.'

Guilt begins to pierce the shock. Emma was talking to me, I realise. And I was encouraging her to talk. And because she was talking… Because she was talking to me…

Because she was talking to me, she may very well be dead.

Guilt burns like acid.

'Then what happened?' Simeon is taking notes.

'The man came into the room.' I find that I am struggling to remember the sequence of events. Emma's screams are echoing in my head, but her words are blurring. 'I think I heard the door crash open. He was very angry. Emma dropped the phone, I think.'

'And then?'

'He hit her, several times I think. She was screaming at him to stop. And then…' My throat closes up. 'Then I think he strangled her.'

'You were shouting her name.' Austin nods in agreement.

'It was horrible,' I say. 'The poor woman. My god…' I hear those gasping sounds again. The desperate pleas.

'Do you think she's…' Simeon stops.

'Dead?' I struggle to say the word aloud. 'Yes, I think she may well have been killed.'

Outside, the wind moans down the street.

'That poor woman,' says Simeon gently. 'The poor thing.'

'It's not just her,' I say. 'It's her children… She has children there.'

'Oh no.'

'What do you think I should do?' My mind is working slowly. I can't think straight. I feel as if I need Simeon to think for me.

Simeon glances at his watch.

'The new team should be coming in to take over any minute. We'll leave the phones on hold for now.'

Blearily, I wonder if the man is screaming at the Plymouth office as we speak. But Plymouth will have no way of knowing who he spoke to. It's useful, in a way, that siloing of information.

'And then what?' I ask.

'Was this woman alone when she called?' Austin asks sharply. 'Were there any kids actually in the room?'

'She didn't mention any children being present,' I say. 'But she said that he had been violent towards her children.'

Austin swears under his breath.

I can't bear to think of Emma's children. I imagine them walking into the room, and into that terrible silence. No child should… No child.

'You don't have any idea where she is?' asks Austin. 'She didn't say?'

I can't lie, but I can't speak either. I stare at him mutely. 'Not in that call, no.'

'We need to tell the police,' Simeon decides. 'There are children involved, and that's a serious safeguarding issue. I've never heard of anything like this happening before, but we will need to get the police involved. And Head Office.'

I nod. We all stare at the silenced phones.

'Clara, can you make a note of everything you remember right away?' says Simeon. 'Time, length of phone call, any names mentioned. If the police get a report of a murder – a strangulation – in the right time frame, you could be in a position to provide evidence.'

Simeon is having to work out how to handle this. There are procedures for terrorism and safeguarding and confidentiality and hoaxes, but there is nothing to cover anything like this. At the Good Listeners, we always say – slightly smugly – that we've heard everything. But there is always more, it turns out. There is always something worse.

Austin checks his own watch. 'That call came in at 8.45ish. If someone was strangled at that time in Devon this evening, or anywhere in the UK, the police should be able to check their phone records and see if this Emma woman was calling the Good Listeners' number at the time she was killed.' Austin sounds dispassionate now, the trained soldier showing through. 'At least the man wouldn't be able to run any sort of "she loved it" defence.'

I shiver. We get plenty of women who ring up after being brutalised halfway through what started out as consensual sex.

'I can take you to the police station,' says Simeon. 'It's not far from here.'

I am on the verge of agreeing when I remember: every officer in the Devon & Cornwall Police will know me as Clara Brennan. And Simeon has only ever known me as Clara Winterson. There is no way that Simeon can come to the police station with me.

'Don't worry.' My assurance is forced, but just about believable. 'I can manage on my own. You don't want to ruin your Friday night, Simeon!'

'Are you sure? I'll have to call Head Office and let them know what's happened, but I can come with you after that? I don't think you should be alone.'

'I'll ask a friend to come and meet me,' I lie. I can't let Simeon come to the police station with me. 'They'll stay with me. I'll be fine, I promise!'

I do want to tell the police, I realise. I need a record of this somewhere.

Because Emma's children are out there somewhere.

Because Emma's children are all alone with a murderer.

51

Detective Constable Tremayne is concentrating on me with that fierce intensity that suggests she recognises me from somewhere but hasn't quite remembered where yet.

'So you're saying you want to report a murder?' she is saying with an edge of incredulity. 'But you're not sure where it happened?'

'Yes,' I say. 'Sorry.'

'Start again,' she says. 'Sorry, it's been a long day.'

Detective Tremayne's hair is scraped back in a bun. It has been highlighted, but not for at least six months. Her nails are bitten, but her eyes are a glowing chestnut, bright with intelligence. She is looking down at her notes, trying to make sense of my story.

I fold my hands in my lap and sit up. 'I volunteer for a help-line,' I say. 'The Good Listeners. You may have heard of them?'

'I have. Yes.'

'A woman rang up this evening.' Already, at my third repetition of the story, the event is taking on a more manageable quality.

'You said her name was Emma.' Detective Tremayne consults her notepad. 'But she didn't give her surname.'

'She *said* her name was Emma. If I had to guess, I would say it's probably not her name. People lie about that sort of thing.'

For a second, Detective Tremayne catches my eye. 'Yes.' She almost smiles. 'We know a bit about that round here.'

'I'm sure you do.'

'And you think she would have been somewhere close to Exeter?'

'Probably. I think she said she was close to Dartmoor, but it's all a bit of a blur, I'm afraid.'

I have explained the Good Listeners' overflow system, but I haven't told Detective Tremayne that this was not the first time I have spoken to Emma. The moment I admit that, she will be on the phone to Simeon to find out everything about the pattern of Emma's calls. Simeon will realise, and I will be locked out of the Good Listeners forever. And it is still possible that Emma is alive. It is still possible that I may speak to her again. I am clinging desperately to that thought.

'Can you remember anything else about this man's voice?'

'He had quite a strong Devon accent. They both did.'

'And you say this person—'

'This man.'

'This man came into the room and attacked her. He hit her and strangled her.'

'That's what it sounded like.' I pause. 'It was horrible.'

'I'm sure it was.' There is compassion in her voice. 'And you think the woman died?'

'I don't know,' I say honestly. 'It is possible that she blacked out. Lack of oxygen.'

Please let that be the case, I think to myself. Please. I can't bear the alternative.

'What were you talking about before she was attacked?' As I hesitate, Detective Tremayne looks up and I watch her recognise me.

'Oh.' She is caught off guard. 'You're—'

'Yes. Yes, I'm Lyra Brennan's mother.' I try to strip the words of all emotion. 'I go by my maiden name now. Clara Winterson.'

I gave my full name and address when I arrived, but the sergeant handed me over to Detective Tremayne as just Clara.

'I see.' Detective Tremayne consults her notepad again. 'This must have been very difficult for you, Clara. Very difficult indeed. I am sorry.'

I force myself not to cry. 'Can you find her?' I ask. 'This woman?'

Detective Tremayne compresses her lips and stares at her notes. 'I can certainly try,' she says. 'The problem, as you know, is that the Good Listeners don't store their phone data. Even if we demand it, they can't actually hand it over. It's just not there.'

'I know,' I say bleakly.

'If this woman is dead,' Detective Tremayne says, 'her body will be found and an investigation will be opened. I can make sure your statement is linked to that. If there are any suspicious deaths in this time frame, I promise you that I will make the relevant officers aware.'

'Okay,' I say. 'Thank you.'

The statement takes a long time. Detective Tremayne is scrupulous, checking all the facts over and over again. I wonder if she would have done all this for someone who wasn't Lyra Brennan's mother. I wonder if she would have sat late into the night with Austin or Anjali or Manon. I know it haunts the officers who worked on the case that they have not been able to bring Lyra's killer to justice.

At the end of it all, Detective Tremayne sits back in her chair. 'And that's everything?' she asks diligently, and I must hesitate because her eyes fly to mine.

I haven't told Detective Tremayne that Emma claimed her husband killed Lyra. I can't think of any way of saying those words to this tough-eyed professional in a way that won't sound insane. I am in too deep, and I still don't know anything.

I think if I even mention Lyra's death in relation to Emma, Detective Tremayne will decide that I am delusional. Paranoid. Poor Clara, she's been through so much. On to the next actual crime.

I need Detective Tremayne to be hunting for Emma and her killer. Any other admission from me will only muddy the waters.

'It's all I can remember at the moment,' I say.

Detective Tremayne gives me a long look. 'Come back to me if you remember anything else, Clara.'

And I think of Emma, somewhere out there. I think of Emma, and I think about her children.

Could Emma possibly still be alive? I have to find her. I have to find her children. But how?

52

The next few days are a blur. I ricochet between hoping that Emma survived and that she will ring up as usual on Friday and that everything will be as it was before.

And knowing, deep down, that Emma will not ring on Friday. That she did not survive.

That Emma is dead.

I scour the news for any mention of a death near Exeter on Friday night.

On Monday afternoon, after a shift at the Good Listeners, I ring Detective Tremayne. She still sounds tired, but her voice sharpens at the sound of my name.

'No,' she says. 'There haven't been any reports of any murders that match up.' She is checking her computer as she speaks; I can hear the rattle of her fingers on the keyboard. 'A man was arrested for stabbing his wife to death in a village near Dawlish on Friday night, but she was dead by 7 p.m. The police attended at 7.11 p.m. after a concerned neighbour rang in.'

'Not Emma,' I say. 'Emma was still alive at 8 p.m.'

'Exactly. A woman was brought into the RD&E – that's the local hospital – with serious head injuries on Friday night. She'd been attacked just outside Crediton. But that lady only speaks Cantonese and her attack was caught on CCTV. She wasn't on her phone at the time of the attack. I'm keeping an eye on other forces, too.'

I feel a surge of gratitude to Detective Tremayne that she has taken me seriously, that she is checking up on these women.

All these woman, beaten and killed.

All these women, beaten and killed so regularly that their attacks don't even make the local news anymore.

'I've sent a report out more widely on our systems,' says Detective Tremayne. 'People are aware, Clara. If anything comes in, I will make sure that the facts are linked up.'

'Thank you,' I say. 'I do appreciate it.'

Emma couldn't just disappear, I tell myself after I've hung up. People don't just disappear. Not nowadays.

Although people do just disappear, and nobody knows that better than me. Lyra disappeared.

But other people *notice* when you disappear, I insist to myself.

People would *notice* Emma disappearing.

I didn't think I could feel more guilt than I did already. But I do. Because I was the one who encouraged Emma to speak out. I was the one who encouraged her to stand up for herself. And I had my motives for both those things and it was not simply: this is the right thing for Emma.

At Emma's lowest point, I tried to take advantage of her for my own purposes.

Emma, a woman abused and exploited.

And I did the same thing all over again.

And it may have killed her.

People *would* notice.

But Emma said she didn't have friends, I remind myself. She may well have been very isolated. A nanny could be brought in. A rumour put round that a wife had bolted.

And there are many places around here where a body could lie unnoticed. Where a body might lie forgotten forever.

I know that better than anyone.

Emma's children would talk, I tell myself. They'd tell their friends, 'Mummy's gone!' and ears would prick up. Aren't teachers trained to listen out for issues at home nowadays?

But what if these are small children who have grown up to the sound of Mummy and Daddy fighting? What if they have listened to the thuds and the screams and the silences? What if these are small children who have been taught to keep their mouths shut? Who never talk about what happens at home?

A little girl who has already been attacked at least once by her father…

And now that child – those children – are all alone with a murderer. And I may be the only person who knows.

Emma couldn't just disappear, I tell myself again.

But there is a small voice in the back of my mind: Emma could very well disappear.

Emma could be gone.

53

I head to Harepath on Tuesday morning. It is November now, and the rain is turning to sleet. When I pass them walking down the drive, Caspar and Cecily are smothered in coats and scarves and woolly hats.

Amber isn't at Harepath today. Amber wasn't here yesterday either. A cold feeling starts in my stomach.

I did an hour of weeding in the garden yesterday afternoon, hoping to bump into her. This morning, I spend quite a lot of time mulching outside the kitchen window, hoping she will appear. She doesn't. My hands get numb in the cold.

Gabriel is working in his study and comes out to say hello.

'Is Amber about?' I ask him. 'I was wondering if she wanted anything specific planted in the vegetable patch.'

'Amber's off for some reason.' He shrugs. 'I know that Victoria wants more beetroot. And winter kale, I think? Whatever that is. It sounds terrifyingly healthy.'

'It is.' I try to make it a joke.

'Oh god.'

'So Amber definitely isn't about?'

'No,' says Gabriel. 'She texted Victoria saying she needed to get away for a week or so. Not sure where she's gone. The household is already in a downward spiral.'

'Victoria hasn't spoken to her then?' My voice is sharper than I meant it to be and Gabriel looks surprised. 'Amber only texted her, I mean?'

'I can check with Victoria, but I'm pretty sure she said Amber texted.'

'Could you…' I hesitate. 'Would you mind checking with Victoria as soon as you can?'

'Sure.' Gabriel can't quite hide his confusion. 'She's in London today, but she should be back this evening.'

Victoria spends a lot of time in London. Amber once told me that she doesn't trust the Coraton hairdresser with her highlights, for starters. Mind you, the Coraton hairdresser doubles as the local sheep shearer, so this is probably wise.

'Why are you asking?' Gabriel asks.

'I'm worried about Amber,' I say bluntly. 'The last time I saw her, she looked very upset. And her husband is… Well, you know what I think about him.'

'I do.'

I cast around for something else to talk about.

'What's Victoria up to in London?' I ask.

Suddenly there is sadness in Gabriel's face. 'She wants to move back up there, actually.'

'Really? All of you, back up to London?'

'Yes, unfortunately.' Gabriel looks up at the old copper beech that looms over this part of the garden. 'You know how much I love it here. But she's never loved it, I don't think.'

'I suppose so.'

'She's already house-hunting.' He sounds tired. 'She's been going for job interviews. Looking for new schools for the kids.'

I should be house-hunting too. I feel that clutch of panic again.

'Could you keep Harepath?' I ask, hoping I am not being rude. 'Come down for holidays and the weekends?'

I wonder – madly – if I could offer to house-sit.

'Maybe.' He sighs. He starts moving back towards the house.

Although it will mean more change, I find myself thinking of Victoria – spiky and strained – with a new sort of respect. Well done, I think. For saying: no, this is not making me happy. This is not enough. I will change my life.

'Can you let me know if you see Amber?' I ask as he opens the French windows. 'Or speak to her?'

'Of course,' Gabriel says over his shoulder. 'Of course I will.'

54

That night, I jump awake; Emma's voice is as clear in my head as if she were standing in my small bedroom.

He said that he was going to walk down to the folk festival.

He said he was going to *walk.*

I find that I have leaped out of bed. My feet are cold on the floorboards.

In the chaos of that call, I missed it. *He said he was going to* walk.

Emma and her husband live within walking distance of the folk festival.

Not just one of the villages on the edge of Dartmoor.

They live within *walking* distance of Coraton.

I scramble down the stairs, unable to stay in my bedroom. I don't need to look at a map, but I do anyway.

Apart from Coraton, the nearest village to the folk festival is two miles away. Walking distance, certainly. Especially if someone was intending to get stuck into the cider. But it must – surely – hugely increase the chances that Emma and her husband live right here. Or in one of the houses and cottages scattered randomly across the countryside. Or in one of the farms.

It is 3 o'clock in the morning and I feel as if I am fizzing all over.

Coraton is largish, but it isn't that big. There aren't that many families in the area at all. The local primary school is over three miles away and it has just over a hundred children on the roll.

There aren't many children around here and there aren't many potential Emmas in Coraton.

And there is… Amber. Where is she?

I need to know where Amber is.

Because no matter how many distortions there are, no matter how many differences between Amber's story and Emma's story, there are many, many similarities. I have to see Amber. I need to lay eyes on her and be sure that she is alive. And most of all, I need to know her children are alright.

It is very early on Wednesday morning, I think slowly, and the farmers' market is on a Wednesday, and Amber and Nell sell cakes at the farmers' market. So Amber will be there.

Amber *has* to be there.

The market is held in the Coraton parish hall and it starts at 9 a.m. I can't go back to sleep. I pace around the kitchen, drinking black coffee, unable to sit down.

I fight the urge to go and hammer on Amber's door, and to go and hammer on Nell's door, and to wake up everyone in Coraton and scream until they give me the answers I need.

But I can't do that. If Emma's husband is in Coraton, I may need Nell's knowledge to track him down. Unless it is Ryan Dallyn, in which case…

I am outside the parish hall well before 9. Linda is there with her neat pots of honey. The cheese man is still setting out his strong-smelling Bries and his pungent Stiltons. I head to the back of the hall, where Nell and Amber usually set up their bunting-festooned stand.

Only Nell is there.

Only Nell, unwrapping cake and setting them out on flower-painted cake stands.

'Is Amber here?' I speak too urgently for politeness. 'Nell, where is Amber?'

Nell looks up at me, and there is apprehension in her eyes.

'I don't know,' she says. 'I haven't seen Amber at all.'

55

'When did you last see her?' I ask Nell.

I've waited painful hours until Nell's cakes sold out. Now we are back at her house, in her neat kitchen.

'I…' Nell works it out. 'I haven't seen her since last week. Last Thursday, I think.'

'I saw her last Thursday too,' I say, 'when I was working at Harepath. Six days ago.'

I think back to when I was walking past Rose Cottage that evening.

Ryan, furious: *It's all fucking Jordie's fault*.

Although, could I absolutely swear that was Amber's voice if it came to it? She was talking quietly, and I just assumed it was her.

But she was definitely in Harepath that Thursday. She made that chocolate cake and I saw her cleaning the windows. She was there last Thursday. She was alive last Thursday.

'Is it like her to disappear?' I ask.

At this question, Nell's face relaxes fractionally. 'It's not totally unlike her,' she says. 'She's disappeared with the kids before.'

'Has she got the kids with her this time?'

'I've been over to her house,' says Nell. 'Only Ryan was there, and he wasn't chatty, to put it mildly. I am pretty sure the kids weren't there. I can ask Tabitha when she gets home whether they've been at school.'

'Where did Amber go last time?'

'She went to her sister's.'

I went to my sister's once. Ran away. Told her a bit about what was going on.

'Where does her sister live?' I ask urgently.

'Over towards Plymouth, I think,' says Nell. 'She's moved around a bit and I never knew her as well as I knew Amber.'

'I'll see if I can find an address for her.'

'Clara.' Nell is really worried now. 'What's going on? Why are you asking all these questions about Amber?'

I can't tell Nell. I just can't. It is Wednesday afternoon now. If Emma is still alive, she may call on Friday evening.

And if I hear her voice, I will be freed of this crushing sense of guilt. Because if Emma really is dead…

I can't live with any more guilt. I can't.

I also don't know Nell well enough to know how she might respond if I tell her the truth. She might rant and rage. She might tell Ryan everything. She might ring the Good Listeners Head Office. I just don't know.

The other thing is that – and it is only deep down that I can admit this – there is a small part of my brain that has tried to fit Emma into Nell's life.

It doesn't quite fit, of course. But Nell has a sister. Nell plays the piano. Nell has an eleven-year-old daughter, so there is a good chance she has been married for at least ten years.

Nell has a row of art history books, which look slightly out of place in her unpainted sitting room. Emma's mother collected them from charity shops.

And there is Pauly: inadequate, unhappy Pauly. Pauly told the police he was working on their house when Lyra went missing, but no one saw him. No one was with him at all that day.

There is Tabitha, too: *I hate them. No one knows what they're like. My parents. I hate them…* That could be melodrama from an overwrought eleven-year-old. But it could be something else, too.

I can't bear to think it, but Tabitha was one of the last people to see Lyra alive, and I think of Nell driving away the desperate questions.

She doesn't know anything. Leave her alone. For god's sake, she's just a child.

If it was Pauly who...

What if these are small children who have been taught to keep their mouths shut?

No. Don't even think it.

So it may be paranoia. It may even be insanity. But I still can't bring myself to tell Nell everything. I don't trust anyone anymore.

So I lie.

'Last Friday evening,' I begin, 'five days ago, I got a strange call.'

'Oh yes?' Nell is stirring her tea.

'A woman called me on my mobile phone,' I say. 'She withheld her number.'

'Okay. What did she want?'

I pause. Nell looks up.

'This woman said she lived locally. Nell, this woman said that her husband was the man who killed Lyra.'

Nell stops stirring her tea, her eyes wide with shock. 'Clara, I – *What?* What on *earth*?'

'She was crying,' I say. 'Completely hysterical. And just as she was talking to me, her husband walked in and... he attacked her, Nell.'

'How badly?' Straight to the point. She's tough, Nell.

'I think he strangled her.'

'What?' Nell won't believe it. 'I don't understand...'

'I think this woman may have been killed, Nell,' I mutter. 'I think that man may actually have killed her.'

Nell realises what I am saying. Horror comes into her eyes. 'And you think there is a chance that it was *Amber* who called you? And this call came into your phone last Friday?'

'I don't know,' I say. 'I just don't know. It sounds crazy, I know. But...'

'But I don't understand. Did you recognise the woman's voice at all? Or not? Did it sound like Amber?'

'She was crying and sort of whispering at times,' I ad-lib. 'It was hard to work out how she would have sounded normally.'

'Have you spoken to the police about this?'

'I have.' Again, not quite the truth. 'But I'm worried that they think I'm completely mad. And it may all be complete nonsense anyway.'

'But you think it might have been *Amber* who called you?' Nell says again, as if she is trying to make the words sink in. 'And you think it might have been Ryan who attacked her?'

'I don't know. I know it sounds mental, Nell. But if I could just *see* Amber, then I'd know she was okay.'

'But *Amber*…' Nell sounds shocked. She grabs her phone and dials a number. No answer. Redial. No answer again. Voicemail. 'Amber, it's Nell. I need to speak to you right now. Stop fucking about and call me.'

Nell hangs up.

'It might not have been Amber,' I say. 'It could have been anyone. It could have been a crank call. She may have been calling from the local psych ward, for all I know.'

'But you don't think that she was.' Nell is watching me closely.

'No,' I say firmly. 'There was something in her voice. It was as if she had been frantic to tell me for years, and now the dam was bursting.'

'You're not sure it's Amber though?' asked Nell.

'No. The woman did have a Devon accent. Is Amber usually in the pub on a Friday night?'

If she is a regular on a Friday, she can't be Emma. But Nell shakes her head. 'It's too expensive to get a babysitter every Friday. Ryan's usually out on the Friday. Amber sometimes goes out on the Saturday.'

I can't imagine Emma going out regularly on a Saturday night, but I just don't know. 'Okay,' I say. 'And I know that this is a really weird question, but does Ryan collect Kimlock trains?'

'What? The toy trains?' Nell stares at me, as if she is trying to work out if I've gone insane. 'I don't think so? Why? Lawrence Wrenscott was into them for a while, I think?'

'Never mind,' I say hastily. 'Don't worry about it.'

A thought hits Nell. 'How did this person get your number?'

'I have no idea,' I say. 'But I gave hundreds of people my number during the search and I've never changed it. Someone could probably get it if they wanted to.'

'If it was Amber, and she hid her number, would the police be able to track it?' she asks. She is quick, Nell.

'I don't know.'

'This call,' says Nell, and there is the faintest hint of wariness in her voice. 'This call came after you started asking questions about Elizabeth Wrenscott, didn't it?'

Nell knows there is something I am not telling her.

'Yes, it did.'

'So what do you think happened?' There is still an edge of disbelief in Nell's voice now, but it is spliced with fear. 'You think Ryan killed his own wife and got rid of her body somehow? That's insane.'

'I know, Nell. I know. But we do know that it is possible to do that around here.'

For a moment, the wilderness seems to wrap itself tighter around Nell's house. There are a thousand places to hide a body in just one acre of woodland. And there are miles of empty moorland just a few minutes' walk from Coraton. I think of silage pits and reservoirs and huge diggers that could carve out a grave within seconds. No wonder the police looked exhausted by the end of the search for Lyra.

Nell breathes in sharply. 'What do you want me to do?' she asks.

'There are two things.' I try to make it sound normal. 'Can you ask the police to do a welfare check on Amber? Say that the last time you saw her, she had a black eye. I've seen her with a black eye before.'

'Yes.' Nell doesn't need to think. 'What's the other thing?'

Nell is embedded in this community. These people have known each other their whole lives. They are entwined together by decades of memories and secrets. In five minutes, Nell can find out information that would take the police weeks to unravel.

'It could be anyone who called me,' I say. 'Not necessarily Amber. Her going missing could just be a coincidence. So can you tap into the local mum's network and find out who hasn't been seen… Well, for a while? Not just since last Friday.'

Emma has talked about being isolated. If she isn't Amber, she could be someone who has stayed at home for weeks already. Emma may not have been seen for months, even.

'The school group WhatsApp,' I add. 'That sort of thing.'

'Yes.' Nell's eyes are steely. 'I can find that out.'

Nell picks up her phone and starts tapping. As her phone starts to buzz in response, I think of ripples in dark, dark pools and of my little house at the end of that long, dark lane.

The fear starts to trickle through my body.

He moves fast.

Him.

Yes, him.

He moves faster than I ever could have imagined.

56

I barely sleep that night. I lock every door, check every window and leap at every creak of a floorboard.

In the brief time that I am asleep, I dream of Lyra. In my dream, I am searching for her. And there is still some sort of hope that she might be alive. But I know the hope is ebbing away every moment, and soon all that will be left is despair. In the far distance, I can hear Lyra's voice. She is laughing and chattering, but it is like chasing a rainbow. Every time I scramble to the last place that I heard her voice, she is somewhere else, and she is always just out of sight.

I wake up screaming.

The next morning is Thursday, not long until Friday night. I walk down to Harepath and hack back some apple trees.

I am on a Good Listeners' shift in the afternoon and as I drive out of the village, I feel a surge of relief. All morning, I have thought of Nell's questions, bullets ricocheting around the village.

But in Exeter, life is too normal for terror. My sense of danger is crushed underfoot by the crowds on the high street as they plough from Starbucks to Primark to Lush. It is hard to be scared of someone who is elbowing their way into YO! Sushi.

Complacency, though, is lethal.

Exeter is dense with fog today. It is often like this: the city inhabiting quite a different season to blue skies on Dartmoor. Sometimes, it is the other way around. In March, I can leave a Dartmoor winter and find daffodils flowering in Exeter.

My shift is ordinary, if any shift can be ordinary. Mo is being bullied at work. Carla is terrified by her daughter's anorexia. Sonny can't get it up.

There is no Emma. Of course, there is no call from Emma.

There might be a call from Emma, I tell myself. There might be a call from her tomorrow night.

It happens just as I am being screamed at by Finn. *You fucking stupid bitch. You shitty piece of trash. What is the fucking point in you, anyway?*

These calls come in sometimes. When a man's anger is so intense that it will boil over for the smallest of reasons, no matter what you say. You can hear it in their voices from the moment you answer the phone. And you know that this is a rage just looking for a target, for a human punchbag. The bomb will go off, no matter what you do or say.

Who the fuck do you think you are?

Volunteering for the Good Listeners doesn't make you especially enthusiastic about the male sex. Women, weeping in pain and shame after being forced into anal sex that they didn't want, because they think it is just what everyone does now. Teenage girls crying because they're *boring* and *lame* and *basic* if they don't send nudes at the drop of a hat.

You fucking cow.

At least, I am telling myself, Finn is safely at the other end of the phone line. At least he does not know who I am. At least I will never have to deal with Finn again.

You smug bitch.

That is when it happens.

I am just telling myself that there is no point in listening to Finn anymore, and that I would be justified in terminating the call – which we can do in certain circumstances.

But I let Finn run on for just a few more seconds because maybe – just maybe – Finn needs to be heard? He called in the first place because he wanted to talk about his daughter, to speak about his little girl. He misses her so much. So very much. His darling little girl. Because his fucking bitch ex Lizzie won't let him see Gigi. The stupid cow won't let him anywhere near her. And the courts just let her get away with it. Can you believe it? Can you fucking believe it?

After less than a minute of Finn, I can see precisely why Lizzie won't let him anywhere near Gigi. I can see why Lizzie would go to the ends of the earth to ensure that Finn is never allowed any contact with Gigi ever again.

But I have a sneaking suspicion that if I put down the phone on Finn, he will call Lizzie yet again. And the thought of this abuse being poured over her head – Finn knows where she lives, she has been dealing with this for months – is enough to keep me on the line.

The anger has to go somewhere.

So I am not really concentrating when I hear the front door buzzer go. The Good Listeners' buzzer goes off fairly frequently anyway. There are deliveries, and there are Listeners who have forgotten the entrance code for this week, and there are potential Listeners visiting to get a sense of the place.

It is Simeon who opens the door. I listen vaguely to his welcome. I don't really feel like giving Finn my full attention, to be honest, so the new arrival is a useful distraction.

You fucking whore. I bet you make up shitty lies about men too, don't you? Sluts like you deserve everything you get.

Simeon is fussing. He often does that. 'Yes, do hang up your coat there. Grizzly day, isn't it? Why don't you come through to the back office? Then we can have a proper chat?'

'Great.'

The voice sends ice down my spine.

That voice… I *know* that voice.

Deep and rough. It sounds like a snarl.

I know that *voice*.

'Just through here!' Simeon says cheerily. 'As you can see, there are a couple of Listeners taking calls right this minute!'

'Yes, I see.'

I know that voice.

That is the voice of Emma's killer.

That is the man who murdered my daughter.

57

I can't move.

Turn around, I scream inside my head. Turn around and look at his face.

But I can't do it. My brain is a chaos of panicked thoughts.

Why is he here?

Through the blur of Finn's abuse, I realise that this man must have come to the centre because he knows that Emma was speaking to the Good Listeners just before he killed her.

He must have come here to find out who knows what.

Maybe he has been rattled by Nell's questions blasting around the village. Perhaps he planned this recce days ago.

Either way, Simeon was expecting him. Simeon is showing this man around in the same way that I have heard Simeon show around countless potential Listeners... So this man must have rung up and enquired about Good Listeners' training.

Fucking Lizzie. Fucking bitch.

But that's impossible.

Surely.

Turn around, I tell myself again. *Look* at him.

We had a good thing going, you know? And then that fucking slag had to go and ruin everything.

But if I turn around at this precise moment, Emma's husband may recognise me.

This is the man who killed Lyra Brennan: of course he will know Clara Brennan's face.

If this man realises that Emma was speaking to Clara Brennan – of all people – just before she died, his rage may reach boiling point instantly. He murdered his wife without hesitation.

There are panic buttons in this office, I know that much. They were installed after the drama with that stalker. And some other incident at one of the London centres, which was only discussed in hushed tones. But he may have a knife, a gun. We are the softest of targets, after all.

I can't turn around.

Call Detective Tremayne, I tell myself. Call her right now. Tell her to come and arrest this man.

But on what grounds would she be able to arrest him?

Because I recognised a snarling bass voice? No one would believe in that.

And if Emma is not dead – and that remains a possibility – Detective Tremayne could storm into their house and find Emma busily baking a cake or diligently doing the laundry.

I'm going to kill her. I'm going to kill that fucking slag.

Sure, Emma might have yet another black eye. But she could deny everything, promise faithfully that she walked into a door like all the other women.

And what would the police have to go on then?

The investigation would end within minutes and the police would never take anything I said seriously again.

I lean forward, resting my elbows on the desk and my forehead on my hands. I can't even put the phone down on Finn because it would attract attention.

Women like that, they don't deserve to fucking live.

If I end this call, Simeon will expect me to turn around, say hello, smile politely. *This is Clara.* I can almost hear Simeon's voice. *One of our very keenest volunteers.*

No, I have to stay on the line. I don't even want to say a word, in case this man recognises my voice in turn. I have to sit here, with my head down, and stay silent.

I just want to see my little girl. I just want to see my little Gigi.

From the rear, I must be completely anonymous, I tell myself. Dark tufty hair, navy blue sweatshirt, the silver of the headset. Hamish, to my left, is in a forest-green fleece, with exactly the same headset clamped to his head. From where that man is standing, we must be completely indistinguishable.

I cannot bear the idea that I am sharing the same space with this man. I cannot bear the thought that we are breathing the same air.

They'll move through to the back office in a second, I tell myself. Simeon loves showing people around the centre; he's got his special tour. Then you can work out what to do next.

Fucking women, you think you're all so clever, don't you? Whore.

Maybe I could get my phone out and use that to photograph this man surreptitiously over my shoulder. No, he might be looking straight at me. And my face would be bright on the screen. And Simeon would be horrified by me apparently taking selfies while on a call.

You fucking women deserve everything you fucking get.

I'll wait until he goes into the office with Simeon and then I'll try and position my phone with the camera running. Hide it somehow. Maybe I can film him on his way out?

Fucking cow.

My eyes fall on Anjali's needlepoint: *A problem shared is a problem halved.* Anjali had her embroidery framed and glazed. She must clean it regularly, because the glass is bright. Maybe...

I pretend to reach down for my handbag. As I lean down, I inch my chair to the left. Now I am opposite the needlepoint. Very casually, I shift about until Simeon and the man are in the reflection.

Fucking whores.

Simeon is blocking my view of the man. I almost cry out with frustration. Maybe if I shuffle to the right?

No. Nothing.

I force myself to breathe in and out, slowly, calmly.

You will think of something.
Slags.
There will be a way through this.
There will be.
Fucking sluts.
There has to be.
Cunt.

58

The moment the door to the back office closes, I put the phone down on Finn.

Not today, Finn. Not today.

I put my phone on hold and work out what to do next.

This man will have supplied contact details to Simeon. If he has handed over his real name and address, I could be a few minutes away from finding out who he is.

It is a shattering thought. After all these years, after all the burning rage, I may be on the verge of identifying my daughter's killer.

For a second, I can't breathe.

I can hear the men's voices through the door. Simeon's voice is higher-pitched, trying too hard. The other man's voice is deeper. It reverberates through the wood of the door, making my skin crawl.

It is impossible that Emma's husband is here. It is impossible that he is in this special space, laughing and joking with Simeon.

I imagine ripping the door open. I imagine leaping on him and clawing at his throat and his eyes. I imagine the blood trickling down his face.

I could kill him. I know that much. Rage this visceral, no one could stop me.

Don't, I whisper to myself. Not now. Not here.

Hamish is chatting away to a Caller. I force myself to concentrate on Hamish's voice.

The world is not full of Finns. It is not full of nameless killers.

The world is better than that.

It has to be.

I pick up my phone and my handbag and assess their potential.

If I prop the camera phone against the wall and then use the handbag to hide the camera, so the lens is just peeking out over the bag… Then I can use my scarf to disguise it a bit more…

Maybe…

Maybe.

I can hear Simeon's chit-chat coming to an end, but all the same, I jump as the kitchenette door flies open. Simeon is still babbling away – *here's your coat, so great to meet you, do let me know when you'd like to start your training.*

I keep out of the way of the camera.

'Thank you for your time,' the man is saying. 'I'm really keen to get started. You do such important work here.'

The man is parroting Simeon's exact words back to him. He's clever, I realise.

I must not underestimate him.

There is, too, a small voice at the back of my mind: does this visit mean that Emma *must* be dead?

This man wouldn't bother coming here – surely – if I had overheard 'only' a bit of domestic violence.

No. He must be trying to work out if someone here at the Good Listeners knows what happened that night. He must be trying to work out if there is a way he could be identified.

He missed the start of Emma's conversation with me, so he does not know exactly what was said. He doesn't know who knows what. And he is the sort of man who needs to control everything.

Emma may still be alive. I am still clinging on to this hope.

But her husband's visit to the Good Listeners makes it even less likely.

* * *

Is it Ryan Dallyn? I can't tell. I try to remember Ryan's voice. Because I'm sure there is something familiar about this man's voice…

It could be Ryan.

This man has charm. I can tell from Simeon's reaction to him.

But I am still not sure.

I need to get this man's name and address. I need to find out if Emma is still alive, and who she is, or was. I need to gather every possible piece of evidence, and only then can I go to Detective Tremayne and bring this to an end.

Only then will I have hunted down my daughter's killer.

59

The moment Simeon has disappeared into the kitchenette, I grab my phone. Hamish, luckily, has been on the same call for over half an hour now.

I stop the recording and cross my fingers. I stare fixedly as the still life of the kitchenette door spools out.

A flash of movement. Simeon opens the door.

For a second, Simeon stands there, talking to someone over his shoulder. *Let's get your coat, so great to meet you.*

Then there is more movement, Simeon laughing, and then a second or two of a man following Simeon out of the kitchenette. I scroll back and freeze-frame the footage.

Bugger.

The man has his head down and he is wearing a baseball hat.

Damn.

He is also wearing an unremarkable hoodie and what looks like jeans. From his body language, I am even more convinced that this man has not come to the centre as a potential volunteer. This is a man who anticipated the possibility of CCTV.

From the man's hands and a few inches of neck, I can see that he is white. I scroll back and assess Simeon's height against the door frame. Then I scroll forward again. This man is perhaps two inches taller than Simeon's 5 ft 8. Ryan is about 5 ft 10. Millions of men are 5 ft 10.

I slump in my seat, too shattered to take my phone off hold.

* * *

I sit like that for almost an hour. I feel guilty about the calls that must be cascading to other centres, but there will be Listeners available. And I can't speak to anyone right now.

Just a few more minutes left of this shift. Jojo and Tomos are coming on duty, and soon I hear them laughing in the lobby. Just then, a thought occurs to me. I pick up my notes and make my way into the kitchenette.

'Is this someone's scarf?' I wave my own scarf around.

Simeon looks up vaguely. 'Not mine. Might be Hamish's?'

'Not mine.' Hamish has followed me into the kitchenette.

'It must belong to that new volunteer,' I say. 'What was his name?'

'Will,' says Simeon. 'Err…Will Harper.'

Will Harper. The words burn themselves into my brain.

Will Harper. Is that his name?

I don't recognise the surname, I don't think. I mentally run through the Coraton residents, but Harper doesn't come up. I can check the gravestones, I think with a certain icy humour. I can check the war memorial, too.

'Does Will Harper live nearby?' I ask casually. 'I could drop it off on my way home.'

I pick up a pen and a piece of paper, look nonchalantly at Simeon. I am helpful Clara. I am nothing-is-too-much-trouble Clara. Simeon shrugs and taps at his keyboard.

'He doesn't live too far away from here,' he says. '14 Lapwing Terrace, Exeter.'

I don't know Lapwing Terrace, but already it doesn't sound right. An Exeter address doesn't line up with what I think I know of Emma or her husband. My stomach tenses.

'I'll look it up when we're done,' I say indifferently. 'If it's close, I can just post it through the door.'

'Sure.' Simeon forgets about the scarf. 'Did your shift go okay, Hamish?'

Hamish starts telling Simeon about Olena, who fled Ukraine and is still horrifically lonely and finding it impossible to make sense of life in England.

14 Lapwing Terrace. 14 Lapwing Terrace.

'How about you, Clara?' Simeon interrupts my thoughts.

Speaking quickly, I tell Simeon about Finn and Lizzie and Gigi, although that conversation seems a lifetime ago. Simeon smiles sympathetically, makes a note, clips the papers into the big red file.

'Do you think he's going to sign up with the Good Listeners?' I ask. 'That Will Harper person?'

'He emailed practically as soon as he left the centre to say that he's keen,' Simeon says, nodding.

I imagine Will Harper sitting solemnly in the Good Listeners' training room and I shudder.

I pick up the scarf again. 'See you soon!' I try to hide the tremor in my voice.

'See you soon,' they chorus.

It is only a ten-minute walk from the Good Listeners' centre to Lapwing Terrace.

Night has fallen and it is cold. I wrap my scarf around my neck. I don't need a prop anymore.

In the darkness, the street lights are pools of orange, and a brisk wind follows me down the street. All at once, every gap between parked cars is a hiding place. Every alleyway, a trap. That man has tracked me down to the Good Listeners' centre and he could easily be lying in wait outside. He could be behind every corner, he could be watching from a doorway. He could be…

The fear is a wave washing over me. This man is a killer. And he could be anywhere.

Stop it, I tell myself. Fourteen Lapwing Terrace. Get on with it.

But Lapwing Terrace could be an ambush.

Stop it.

I force myself to keep going. As I walk, it occurs to me that only Simeon knows where I am and where I'm going at this precise moment, and that nobody in the world knows why. It's another similarity between me and Emma. No one would immediately notice my disappearance either.

Simeon would notice, eventually, probably, when he had a gap in his schedule, a non-appearance for a shift. Nell would notice, I think. But our last conversation was so strange that she might just think I'd fled Coraton.

'Out of character.' That's the phrase that the police use when people go missing, isn't it? For me, disappearing would not be out of character. Losing Lyra has become who I am. To people like Alys and Simeon, who have no idea what happened, I have no character at all.

I come to a halt under one of the orange pools of light. I will have to tell Rachel, even though I have been avoiding her calls because I know she will ask me about the job with the professor, and Damson Cottage, and I can't face thinking about any of it.

I am going to visit a Will Harper at 14 Lapwing Terrace, Exeter. I type. *It is possible that he may know something about Lyra's death. I'll let you know as soon as I leave.*

Rachel calls me back straight away. I let the phone ring out.

Call me. The message blips in as soon as the phone stops ringing. *Please.*

But there is nothing more that Rachel can do from two hundred miles away.

I ignore her message. Then I tighten my scarf around my neck and I turn into Lapwing Terrace.

60

Lapwing Terrace feels wrong.

I remember again those conversations with Emma, the ones when she spoke freely, with a ringing voice, confident that no one would overhear her.

Lapwing Terrace is modern, probably built in the eighties. The front of the houses is part-brick, part-wood cladding, and the design does not speak of robust construction. These houses look as if you could sit in your kitchen and listen to the neighbours' television and the neighbours' dog and the neighbours' rows.

You could not sit in 14 Lapwing Terrace and talk about your husband's murderous habits without 12 Lapwing Terrace and 16 Lapwing Terrace calling the police.

I walk slowly along the pavement, looking in through the front windows whenever it is possible. The front rooms are cramped. These houses are family homes, but they are not large. They will have two, maybe three, bedrooms upstairs.

I have started at the wrong end of Lapwing Terrace and the house numbers this end are up in the fifties. As I walk along the pavement, my heart begins to sink. I recalculate quickly.

No, I am right.

I reach number 14 and stare up despondently. Number 14, it is immediately clear, has suffered a fairly disastrous fire and the blaze must have happened some time ago. Number 14's windows are boarded up with those anti-squatter barriers. Above the boards, I can still see scorch marks, as if the house has put on too much eye make-up. The front garden is a jungle. A rose – still with a few late flowers – is cascading over the wall, sending spiky tentacles out over the pavement.

Will Harper, whoever he is, does not live here.

That's if his name even is Will Harper, which it almost certainly isn't.

'Who are you?' I whisper. 'Where are you?'

The street is silent.

I feel the precious surge of hope dying away. There will not be justice for Lyra. Not today.

I text Rachel. *Sorry – false alarm. Ignore.*

Rachel has texted five times since I messaged her. As soon as I send my message, her response pops up immediately.

Clara, what the hell are you doing? Where are you? What are you doing? Call me. Please.

I do owe Rachel some sort of explanation. *I'll call you when I get home*, I message. *Getting in the car now.*

I'm not getting into the car now. I trail back along the streets of Exeter, shivering.

It's partly because of the cold, partly because of a growing sense of nausea.

If I had called Detective Tremayne and told her confidently that Will Harper of 14 Lapwing Terrace had killed my daughter, this investigation would already be over.

Open and shut in a matter of seconds.

The police would glance at a made-up name and a burnt-out house: poor Clara. Poor crazy Clara. By now, I would be banned from the Good Listeners, but at the same time, no one would be any closer to knowing who killed Lyra.

I need to be absolutely sure. I need conclusive proof that this is the man who killed Lyra. And above all else, I have to be in the Good Listeners' office on Friday evening – tomorrow evening – to be there if Emma calls.

There is no room for error.

I'm really keen to get started. You do such important work.

Simeon: dissolving in a pool of delight.

This man is clever and he is ruthless and he is determined.

He has taken a risk here, giving a burnt-out house as an address. But it is a calculated risk, one that is unlikely to backfire. I don't think I've ever received a letter from the Good Listeners. Everything is done by email, and they didn't get round to checking my references – Rachel and my mother, who thought I needed to get out of the house – until I was training.

And if anyone ever queried the address, Will Harper could say that whoever took his details had just misheard. 'Oh, did they write down fourteen? No, sorry, it's number forty.'

It has only taken Will Harper a few days to work out how to access the Good Listeners' office. He is moving with speed and boldness. Even though I am not sure what Will Harper intends to do at the centre, I know that I need to stop him.

I will have to find clear evidence. I say this confidently in my head, as if by thinking it, I can achieve it. I will need concrete proof that this man killed Lyra and, probably, that he killed Emma too. The proof can't be: 'I heard his voice and I knew it was him.' Because even though this is true, it sounds ludicrous.

I curl my hands into fists and march into the cold wind.

I will do this.

I will.

I have to.

This man may be clever and ruthless and determined.

But I will do anything.

My phone bleeps twice. Two messages from Nell, both brief and to the point.

Clara, call me.

Clara, it's urgent.

61

'I don't know...' Nell speaks in a rush. 'This all seems... Well, it all seems mad, to be honest.'

I am back at Nell's house, in her spotless kitchen. By the time I drove back from Exeter it was already 8 p.m., but she insisted I come over whenever I got back. Now she is jittery, unable to sit down. 'What is it, Nell?'

'It's just that they're a nice family,' she says. 'They would never... But, given what's going on with Ryan and Amber... I just thought...'

A *nice* family.

'I really appreciate what you're doing, Nell,' I murmur. 'I know it's hard, all this.'

'I still haven't heard a word from Amber.' Nell twists her fingers together. 'Tabitha says that the kids aren't at school.'

'I'm sorry, Nell.'

'And now people are talking.'

'Talking about who?'

Nell twists her fingers even tighter. 'I hadn't realised that no one has seen her for such a long time. And people... Well, they're starting to worry... And he... Well, he won't talk about her at all. It's weird.'

'Who won't talk about who? Who hasn't been seen for ages?'

'I don't like to... It's only because I know what you've been through...'

'Who?' I ask again, more forcefully. 'Who are you talking about?'

'Jordie Meldon,' the words fall out of Nell's mouth almost by accident.

'Jordie *Meldon*? Ryan Dallyn's best friend?' It feels as if the floor of the kitchen is shifting.

Nell plaits her fingers together, avoiding my eye. 'It's just that no one's seen Hailey Meldon for a long time. But I'm sure there's a perfectly good reason.' Nell is nodding her head, trying to convince herself, me, everyone. 'I mean, the Meldons, they're lovely…'

I have stopped listening.

'No one's seen Hailey Meldon?' I ask blankly.

Jordie Meldon, one of the close-knit gang: Lawrence Wrenscott, Ryan Dallyn, Jordie Meldon, best friends since they were kids. Jordie, the rich farmer's son, the one I have thought about the least.

All fucking Jordie's fault…

'Jordie told the police that he was in Abbot's Wood the day Lyra went missing,' I say slowly. 'He and Lawrence both said that Ryan came and found them and then they all went to look for the puppy.'

'That,' Nell looks at the floor, 'is what I heard too.'

I wait for Nell to look up at me. 'But neither Jordie nor Lawrence's phones were in Abbot's Wood that day,' I say coolly. 'Both of them said there was no point in carting their phones about, because there's no phone reception anyway.'

'That is what they said,' Nell agrees.

'Jordie said he left his phone in his tractor while he was off searching,' I say. 'But he could have been anywhere. No one would have seen him in the Meldon fields; they're in the middle of nowhere.'

'But *Jordie…*'

I look at the wariness on Nell's face and know I am about to lose her. So I smile. I make myself sound brisk, efficient, normal.

'When did you last see Hailey?' I ask Nell, as if this is quite an ordinary question to ask, and watch as her eyes focus.

'Not for ages.' Nell bites her lower lip. 'I don't think I've seen her since Christmas last year. I'm sure she came to the carol service. But other people have seen her more recently.'

I think back to Christmas. It's almost a year ago now.

'Has anyone seen her in the last week?' I ask. 'Jordie and Hailey live in one of the farm cottages, don't they?'

'No one has seen her in the last week,' says Nell. 'Hailey and Jordie will inherit the whole farm one day, I guess. But his father still rules the roost for now.'

'And no one's been out to their cottage for a long time?'

'Some of the girls have been texting and calling,' says Nell. 'But they haven't had any response. Jordie's down the pub, same as usual. But Jordie… He won't tell you anything unless he wants you to know it.'

'What's she like? Hailey?' I ask. 'How long have they been married? Do they have kids?'

Nell is more relaxed talking about these details. 'Hailey and Jordie have been married for years,' she says. 'They've got two kids. Georgie and Rowan. Hailey's quiet. Shy. Amber knew her better, but…' Nell shrugs: Amber's not here to tell. 'They must have got married when Hailey was in her early twenties. Young. Jordie's a bit older, but not by much. Five years, maybe? They've got a couple of kids. Ryan's the loud one of that gang, the charmer. Jordie's quieter. Nicer,' Nell concludes determinedly. 'Jordie would never…'

Nell's voice trails away.

'Could you go and see them?' I ask. 'Just check if Hailey's around? Pop in?'

'If I went up now…' Nell makes an awkward gesture. 'People are talking. The WhatsApp groups, all that… You know what gossip's like round here. Jordie and Hailey might guess why I'm there.'

I wonder, briefly, what on earth is circulating on the local WhatsApp groups. I don't want to be responsible for a lynch mob. Unless this man killed my daughter, in which case I'll lead the crowd.

I wonder if part of the reason that Nell has come to me is so that the rumour about Hailey Meldon can be quashed one way or another.

Jordie Meldon. I try the name on for size.

Will Harper. Neither of these names tell me anything.

Ryan Dallyn.

'Georgie's a girl?' I ask. 'And Rowan's a…'

'Boy,' says Nell. 'Georgie's sevenish and then there was a gap down to Rowan. He's only two.'

The kitchen seems to get darker. 'Does Hailey have a sister?'

Nell looks curiously at me, but she shakes her head. It's uncertainty, though, rather than a definite no.

'What's he like?' I ask Nell. 'Jordie Meldon?'

Nell bridles. 'He's nice. I don't know him very well. He's a farmer, you know?'

This description could apply to hundreds of men on Dartmoor alone. I guess that Nell – chatty and sure of herself – has little in common with Hailey and Jordie.

'Does Hailey have any hobbies?' I ask. 'Does she play the piano?'

Nell doesn't know. 'Hailey wasn't at school with us.' She shakes her head again. 'She grew up over near Ivybridge. She might have played the piano or something like that, but I don't know.'

Jordie and Hailey Meldon seem as anonymous as a Good Listener.

'When was the last time that you heard of anyone seeing Hailey?' I ask.

'Well, that's the thing,' says Nell. 'Hailey used to meet the kids off the school bus. But she stopped doing that quite recently. It's Jordie who meets the kids off the bus now.'

'He meets the kids off the bus…' My voice trails away.

And then I think of something else, a thought that makes my throat close up.

The Meldons' farm.

Abbot's Wood is part of the Meldons' farm.

Abbot's Wood, where they found my daughter's body.

I stand up and walk out of Nell's house, leaving a silence behind me.

And then I turn. I turn and walk down the lane towards Jordie and Hailey Meldon's home.

I walk towards that house because Jordie Meldon gave Ryan Dallyn his alibi.

But if Ryan's story is a lie, then Jordie Meldon does not have an alibi at all.

62

I am above the Meldons' cottage. It is dark, and a cold November rain is falling relentlessly.

I texted Rachel just after I left Nell. *I'm going to check out Rossiter Cottage, just along from Harepath. A man called Jordie Meldon lives there.*

Clara, please don't.

My phone starts buzzing with texts and calls, but I don't answer.

Rossiter Cottage is about a quarter of a mile from the main farmhouse, where Jordie's parents still live. The cottage is a Dartmoor longhouse, one of the ancient medieval farmsteads that dot this landscape. The longhouses are narrow buildings, one room leading to another without the convenience of a corridor. Deathtrap spiral staircases twist their way up to the bedrooms. Although they are picturesque, they do not adapt especially well to twenty-first-century life. The ceilings are hobbit-low and the windows are pinched.

For me, however, the meanness of Rossiter Cottage's windows is helpful. Perhaps because the house already feels enclosed, no one has bothered to close the curtains in the kitchen.

I am watching from the darkness just beyond a narrow strip of garden.

Yes, I am obsessed. Yes, I am maddened.

But I *have* to know.

For years, I have lived with the belief that there was no real way of finding out what happened to my daughter. I had to tell myself that

I would never know, and that this mystery would hang over every single day of the rest of my life, and I just had to endure that.

Now that it seems as if I might discover who killed Lyra, there is nothing I would not do to find out.

Nothing.

But I have no way of knowing if I am trespassing on the privacy of an innocent man and his family.

Or if I am gazing down at Lyra's killer.

Jordie Meldon is sitting in his brightly lit kitchen. There are two children in the kitchen. The girl – Georgie, I guess – is sitting at the other end of the kitchen table. She has her head bent over what looks like homework.

The boy, Rowan, is on the floor. He is playing with something, possibly a few trains. Possibly a few Kimlock trains.

There is only one thing missing to make it a family scene ready to be stitched into a sampler.

Only one thing.

There is no mother. There is no wife. There is no Hailey.

It is not just the cold that is making me shiver.

Rowan is sitting with his back to me. He could be singing happily, he could be crying. I have no way of knowing. From this dumb show, it is impossible to know what is happening in Rossiter Cottage.

At the Good Listeners, I am told everything and I see nothing. Here, I see everything and I am told nothing.

Here, I am blind.

You're going mad, I tell myself. You're slipping off the edge.

The dog barks suddenly. Jordie Meldon looks up. The dog disappears from my sight line and Jordie jumps to his feet. It takes him only a couple of seconds to throw open the door and drag on his boots. Taken by surprise, I can only throw myself to the ground. The light from the kitchen spills across the garden and splinters through the hedge.

The dog is barking wildly.

'What is it, Tam?' Jordie asks. 'What's the matter?'

Do I know this voice? Through the dog's barking, it is impossible to tell. I try to edge deeper into the shadows. I can't turn and sprint across the fields. I'd be seen at once. Running uphill through mud, I would move pathetically slowly. Jordie, hardened by years of physical work, his quad bike parked by the farm gate, would catch me in seconds.

The dog's barks increase.

'What's going on, Tam? Go on then.'

Why did I come here? What was I *thinking*? Jordie's steps crunch along the garden path. My house is so far away, across fields and hedges and acres of mud. Why did I come here? I should never…

'What is it, Daddy?' asks a small girl's voice.

The dog is skittering across the grass now, yapping with excitement. A nose snuffles excitedly at the hedge, just inches from me, and then the dog turns away, moving fast. It must be bounding to the garden gate, ready to spring round the corner… It can probably jump straight over the gate.

I have only seconds…

Where can I go…

Where can I run…

There is the sound of a car from the farmyard.

Jordie's footsteps stop abruptly. There is a pause, and then I think I hear him turn on the gravel path. I hold my breath.

'It's Beverley,' says the small girl's voice.

'She's early,' Jordie replies. 'Stupid dog barking up the wrong tree, as usual.'

But he has stopped walking towards me. The dog, too, has paused. I force myself to stay still. Jordie is looking towards the farmyard now. The dog races that way.

Beverley? I wonder. Has Emma already been replaced by a Beverley?

Jordie Meldon glances up at the garden hedge one more time. I feel his eyes sweep over me, my whole body rigid with fear, but then his eyes move on. He turns towards the farmyard and the sound of a car door slamming.

Get away, I tell myself.

This may be your only chance. While the focus is on this new arrival.

Hurry.

But I can't move. I have to know.

'Evening, Jordie.' Beverley's voice is bright and jolly. 'How are you today?'

'I'm alright…' Jordie's voice fades as he walks towards her.

Come on, I scream inside my head. Get out of here.

But I can't.

Two shapes are heading back towards the house now. The dog skitters ahead of them.

I have to *see*…

Jordie Meldon and Beverley walk into the pool of light that is spilling out of the kitchen and I know that uniform at once. In this light, the navy blue uniform is black. But I recognise the collar, white on blue. I recognise that sensible hemline below Beverley's pragmatic coat.

Beverley is a Macmillan nurse.

Palliative care, that's what this is. These nurses come out when the cancer is too far gone, when there is nothing else to be done and it is only a matter of easing the journey from life into death. That is when women like Beverley – kind, practical Beverley – make their way out to these houses.

I look at Rossiter Cottage again. There is a light on upstairs, behind curtains, faint, almost invisible. It is only when I look at the house again that I notice it.

I watch as Beverley and Jordie make their way into the kitchen. Rowan is pleased to see Beverley, it is painfully clear. He scuttles over to her, holding up his little toy, *Look*. Beverley dumps her bag on the table as Jordie puts on the kettle.

I look away then.

Because upstairs, somewhere in Rossiter Cottage, Georgie's mother is dying. Rowan's mother is dying. Jordie's wife is dying. The faint light is fading.

I have no right to this.

I have no right.

* * *

I turn away and start plodding up the hill through the mud.

Everyone will know. Have you heard? Have you *heard*? Hailey Meldon's *dying* and that madwoman at the top of the track…

A wave of shame sweeps over me. Who am I? What have I become?

I am almost at the gate at the top of the field when I hear it: the roar of a quad bike. I feel a fizz of fear. Jordie Meldon. It must be Jordie Meldon, out to get any trespassers. Jordie Meldon, furious.

Quad bikes speed across muddy fields, bouncing over ruts. I have no way of getting away. No hope of escaping.

I try to run, all the same. I try to sprint the last few steps to the gate. But it is hopeless. With every step, I skid and slide and almost fall over. A second later, I am caught in the bright headlights, and the quad bike's engine roars even louder.

If I can only make it to the gate…

If I can only…

But there is no escape.

63

Jordie Meldon catches me easily. The quad bike roars up behind me. I am exhausted by the mud and the rain, sliding around in the mud. When Jordie is a few yards away, he leaps to the ground and catches me in a few strides, knocking me to the ground.

'Jesus.' He realises it is me. 'You crazy bloody bitch. What the fuck are you doing out here?'

'Sorry.' I am struggling for breath. 'I know… It's not you…'

Jordie lets me get to my feet. I am panting so hard I can barely speak. We stand in the headlights of the quad bike.

'You're mental,' he says concisely. He straightens his tweed cap.

'I'm sorry,' I say. 'I should never have come up here.'

'No,' he says. 'You really fucking shouldn't have. What the hell are you doing?'

'I'm sorry…'

'I know you're obsessed with Ryan. But why the fuck have you come up here?' he asks. 'It's so bloody… *weird*. What are you doing creeping around like this?'

There isn't any way of hiding it. Gasping for breath, I tell him what I told Nell: a woman phoned me up to tell me her husband killed Lyra, and was then attacked.

'Someone said that Hailey hasn't been seen for ages,' I finish lamely. 'And I thought… I thought…'

'What?' Jordie is horrified. 'You thought that *Hailey*… She's *dying*, for fuck's sake. How could you? Don't you have any decency at all?'

'I am really sorry.' In the cold rain, it sounds pathetic.

'How could you possibly think that I… Jesus Christ, why are you so mad?'

And suddenly, I've had enough. 'You know why I've been driven almost mad,' I scream. 'Because my daughter was killed and I still don't know who did it. But I know that it was probably someone in Coraton and there's a good chance you know damn well who it is. So yes, Jordie, I will do whatever it bloody takes to find out who killed my daughter.'

My outburst catches Jordie off guard. His mouth drops open. Somehow, his silence only increases my anger.

'You weren't with Ryan Dallyn the day my daughter died!' I bellow at him. 'Were you? He was on his own and you were on your own, too. That means that either of you could have killed Lyra, but you gave each other an alibi, didn't you? Didn't you?'

'I didn't—' Jordie hasn't denied it fast enough. He's used to dealing with misbehaving livestock, not raving women halfway up a rain-sodden hill.

'You lied to the police!' I shout at him. 'Fuck you, you lying bastard. Don't you dare tell me I'm mad.'

'We didn't…' Jordie tries. 'I didn't…'

'I know that Ryan lied to the police,' I shouted. 'I know it. He said you were all in Abbot's Wood, but you—' Tears choke my words.

'The phone records…' Jordie stops.

'The phone records don't prove anything,' I scream. 'You fucking know that. They never showed where you were and they never showed where Lawrence Wrenscott was, either.'

'I—'

'Was Ryan with you?' The anger has gone out of my voice. I am pleading now. 'For god's sake, Jordie. We're talking about my daughter. Was Ryan with you that day?'

'He was searching with us for some of the time,' Jordie insists.

'But not all of the time?' I am a maddened dog on the attack now. 'He wasn't with you all the time, was he?'

I watch loyalty and sadness and guilt chase each other round Jordie's face. He looks exhausted. Defeated, almost.

'What if it was one of your kids?' I ask him, speaking more softly now. 'What if it was Hailey?' Jordie's head jerks up. 'Please, Jordie, I have to know. Was he with you or not?'

Jordie rubs his face hard with his hands. There are no expensive lawyers to think for him up here. He breathes out slowly and comes to a decision. 'No,' he says in the end. 'No, he wasn't.'

I want to leap at Jordie, to tear at his face.

'Why did you lie?' I ask. 'Why did you lie for *him*?'

'Because he didn't do it.' Jordie looks broken. 'And we were all bloody suspects, weren't we? You've got no idea what that was like. What would happen to my children if I went to jail? With Hailey… We hadn't *done* anything. You don't know what it's like for men these days. The police wanted someone – anyone – to go to jail and you know damn well that it would have been Ryan if we hadn't stuck together every step of the way.'

'But how can you possibly know that Ryan didn't do it? How?'

'Because I've known Ryan all my life.' Jordie sounds pitifully naive. 'He just wouldn't.'

'He's hit Amber though, hasn't he? Everyone in Coraton knows that. Everyone knows he's a violent little shit. You have no idea what Ryan could and couldn't do.'

'No.' Jordie looks away. 'I don't know. Those two… I don't know what goes on in their house. And neither do you,' he ends stubbornly.

'You can't possibly justify that sort of behaviour,' I shout in disbelief.

'No, I know…' Jordie's words are lost in the wind.

We are no longer fighting each other, though. The anger has focused on others and the sheer nightmare of both our situations. Jordie sits down sideways on the quad and contemplates me over folded arms.

'It wasn't Ryan,' he says again, but more quietly now.

'You don't know that,' I insist. 'Not for sure. No one knows what happened for sure.'

'I'm not going to change my story,' says Jordie. 'All that would happen is that Ryan would go to jail, and it would be the wrong person.'

There is no point in arguing that point out here.

I remember something else.

'What happened a week ago?' I ask. 'Ryan Dallyn was shouting about something being all your fault.'

It's all fucking Jordie's fault. He needs to keep his fucking mouth shut.

'When did he say that to you?' Jordie is wary, all of a sudden. This question has blindsided him. I don't want to tell Jordie I was eavesdropping outside Rose Cottage.

'I was just passing,' I say hastily, 'while Ryan was talking to Amber.' Jordie gives me a searching look. 'What was Ryan talking about?' I ask him again.

Jordie scratches at the mud with his rubber boot. 'I don't know...'

'You fucking do, Jordie.' My anger flares up again. 'Tell me what Ryan was talking about. Or I am going straight to the police and telling them that you've admitted you weren't with Ryan that day.'

'You can't prove that!' Jordie's head jerks up.

'I'm Lyra Brennan's mother,' I spit. 'The police are pretty quick to follow up things like that. I'll go to the media if I have to.'

Jordie kicks at the quad's tyre. 'It's not what you think...'

'Tell me, Jordie. Tell me right now.'

Jordie looks up at me. 'Someone else told Amber that they knew I wasn't with Ryan that day,' he says flatly. 'That I wasn't up in Abbot's Wood.'

'What?' I feel stunned. 'How did they know that? *Who* told Amber that?'

'I don't know.' Jordie realises belatedly that it matters who told Amber. He refolds his arms tighter and a stubborn look comes into his eyes.

'Who told Amber that you and Ryan weren't together that day?' I ask. 'Why on earth did they tell Amber after all this time? Why now?'

Jordie stares angrily at his wellingtons, then he looks up at me with something close to defiance. 'I don't bloody know, Clara. For god's sake, I know this is all you think about, and I do get it, really I do. But I've got Hailey and the kids, and it's all been a fucking shitshow, if I'm honest.'

'I'm sorry, Jordie. But it might be important,' I tell him. 'Please. Can you ask Ryan exactly what happened a week ago?'

Because Ryan wouldn't tell me the day of the week, I know that already.

Jordie writhes. 'Ryan hates any talk about the day your daughter died,' he says. 'Can't you just ask Amber instead?'

'But I don't know where Amber is to ask.' My voice rises sharply.

'What do you mean?' Jordie looks startled.

'No one has seen Amber.' The wind whips my words away. 'No one has seen Amber for a week. That's the whole point. Where the hell is she?'

'I didn't know that.' Jordie has the grace to look sheepish. 'I didn't… What's going on?'

'When did you last see her?'

'I have no idea.'

'Try and remember,' I say between my teeth. 'Because it's important, Jordie.'

Jordie is trying, I can tell. But I don't think he can work it out off the top of his head.

'I don't know,' he says in the end. 'Last week, maybe?'

'Don't you think it's a bit odd, Jordie?' There is spite in my voice. 'Last week, Amber asked her husband about his involvement in a murder case. Last week, she asked about your involvement in a murder case. And nobody has seen her since.'

64

I wake up very early on Friday morning. There is still a whole day to get through before my evening shift tonight. I check eBay. After getting home last night, I texted Rachel – *home safe, sorry sorry* – and then I made all Frank Fenton-Brown's auctions live. I have to try everything.

Please let Emma call tonight, the refrain rattles through my head as I make coffee. Please let her call tonight.

And please let someone find out where Amber is.

I yoyo between being certain that Amber is Emma, and that finding Amber will solve everything – and thinking that Emma is someone completely different and I am nowhere near knowing who killed Lyra.

The local newspaper office is open today, though. It has taken several days and a lot of pleading for the right combination of people to be present to let me into the old microfiche room at the back of the small offices.

'We keep meaning to bin all that junk,' the deputy editor told me cheerfully. 'You're lucky it's all still there.'

When I arrive, the newspaper office looks dusty and unloved. The editor – there only appear to be three members of staff – unlocks the back room with some ceremony. 'Took us ages to find the key, to be honest.'

He shows me how to use the microfiche machine and then points at rows and rows of storage units. 'Good luck!' he says merrily. 'We'll come and excavate you if we hear the shelves give way.'

I have the date of Elizabeth's murder, but it takes a long time to make sense of the newspaper's filing system and longer still to find the right pages.

Eventually, I find several articles about her death. The stories are piteous – *mystery surrounds young girl's disappearance* – and accompanied by smudged-looking photographs of police officers searching moorland, of a desperate-looking Georgia and Ferdinand.

After a few weeks, Elizabeth's body is found in Abbot's Wood and then *mystery surrounds young girl's death*. Slowly, devastatingly, the number of articles tail off and Elizabeth's tragedy is superseded by the cost of beef and a record number of foals being rounded up off the moor.

There is nothing useful that I can see in any of these articles.

I sit down on the newspaper's mothy carpet. What else can I look up? There are various key events in the Coraton calendar, and I doubt they have changed much over the last few decades.

There is the Coraton show: pony club, vast roses, suspiciously shaped vegetables.

There is the folk festival.

And there is May Day.

I think of Georgia Wrenscott teaching the little girls of Coraton the maypole dances. They still parade around the village every year, little girls in white dresses, holding posies and singing their pretty songs. May: when the glory of summer is all promise.

Highly photogenic, apart from anything else. A reporter will have been there.

I go back to the microfiches and search for these Coraton showpieces.

There is something eerie about spotting a two-year-old Ryan Dallyn at the Coraton show the summer before Elizabeth died. Already a beautiful child, he is smiling in the arms of his mother.

Chrissie Dallyn – according to the photograph caption – triumphed in best Victoria sponge.

I peer at Chrissie Dallyn and think about Emma's husband's names for his mother.

Slag. Slut. Whore.

In the photograph, Chrissie is beaming merrily with her red rosette, but I can't tell much from a photograph.

I flip through a few more microfiches and spot Paul Turner, smiling in delight as he plays his violin at the folk festival. He looks quite different to the sad-eyed man I saw at Nell's house.

Then I turn to the May Day celebrations, and at once Elizabeth's name snags my eye. Elizabeth is dancing around the maypole, ribbons flying and so pretty in her lovely white dress. She is twirling and grinning, her white socks pulled up. And Elizabeth… Elizabeth could be Lyra. They have the same blonde hair, the same happy vitality.

Elizabeth. Elizabeth and Lyra.

I stare at the fly-blown ceiling and force myself not to cry.

I don't know how Georgia bears it.

I don't know how anyone bears it.

Back to the microfiches.

There aren't any more clues from the May Day coverage though, not from that year.

Wearily, I turn back a few more months. Back to the Coraton show, which is held every August.

Elizabeth, again, smiling up at the camera. In this photograph, she has a dog on a leash, a well-behaved Labrador. The Labrador has a red rosette clipped to its collar. In the background, I can make out Georgia and Ferdinand Wrenscott, smiling with heart-breaking pride. Georgia is holding a very small Lawrence. I read the caption, and for a moment I can't breathe.

'Best in Show!' runs the caption. 'Elizabeth Wrenscott and Linnet.'

Linnet.

65

By the time I reach the Good Listeners that evening, I am struggling to sit still. Linnet.

Linnet, the puppy Emma's children brought home.

Linnet, Elizabeth Wrenscott's dog.

What does it mean?

It may mean nothing at all. Or it may be yet another distortion. A rambling deception that was never even meant to be a deception in the first place.

I think I may be going mad. I can't trust anything.

That thought snaked round my head as I drove towards the Good Listeners.

I cannot trust anything and I cannot trust myself.

I have been so desperate to believe in Emma that I swallowed every scrap of her story, twisting lies into truth. I picked up the fragments of her story and tried to create a whole truth.

It was always going to be impossible.

Emma could never, ever have imagined that she was talking to someone who would believe in her madness, who would trust in her delusions.

And now I am in the Good Listeners' office and I am praying that Emma will call and I have no idea what to say to her if she does.

Why on earth do I think I am qualified to listen to people like Ruth and Emma and Liam?

I am useless.

Useless.

I should not be here. I should not be answering these calls. But I can't bear to stay away when there is even the smallest chance Emma may call.

My shift starts and I nod to Sally and put on my headset.

Alys offered to move me off the Friday evening shift in case it brought back bad memories, but I promised them that I was fine.

I don't know if I am though.

I don't know anything at all.

After my first call, Alys reappears. 'All okay?'

'All fine,' I promise. 'A woman called Tazzy. Her life sounded chaotic.'

'Poor thing.'

'Have you spoken to anyone yet?' I ask Sally casually.

'One very quick call.' Sally looks at her notes. 'Mila. She got a breast cancer diagnosis this week, but the doorbell went and she rang off.'

A couple of minutes, I think. There have been a couple of minutes when Emma could have rung in and been cascaded out to Cardiff or Norwich or Thirsk.

You're mad, I tell myself. She's dead.

The phone rings again.

It's not Emma.

By the end of the shift, neither I nor Sally have spoken to Emma. I have watched the clock tick down, my heart sinking deeper and deeper.

It has not been an especially busy evening. Over almost three hours, there were probably forty minutes when Emma's call might have been diverted elsewhere. So she definitely could have called.

Or he may have stayed home tonight.

Or she may be in hospital, battered, bruised but somehow unspotted by Detective Tremayne.

Or Emma may be Amber, staying with her sister somewhere in Plymouth's orbit.

Or Emma may be someone completely different, and has fled to Truro, or Bristol, or Aberdeen.

Or he may have confiscated her phone.

Or she may not want to call the Good Listeners ever again.

Or she may be dead.

I cannot trust myself.

The phone rings and now Adrian's voice is in my ear.

'She's dead.' Adrian can't believe the words. 'My wife is dead.'

'Oh, I'm so sorry to hear that, Adrian.' Automatic. 'That must be so sad for you.'

'She killed herself. I can't believe it. She actually killed herself.'

'What was she like?' I ask mechanically. 'Do you want to talk about her?'

A sigh. 'She was… I don't know… I love her. Loved her. She was complicated.'

'In what way?'

'Her name was Jacqueline,' he said slowly. 'She was kind and beautiful. Really beautiful. Even after nearly twenty years of marriage, she still made me catch my breath. So many people loved her.'

'She sounds wonderful.'

'She was… She really was… And yesterday, I came home to find her *dead*.'

'I'm so sorry. Had something happened to her recently?' There's never one reason, but Adrian needs to talk. 'Was she upset by something?'

'She… She was complicated.'

'How?'

There is a long pause. Then he carries on, almost apologetically. 'Jacqueline… She… Well, she shoplifted.'

As the admission erupts out of Adrian, I hear my own gasp.

Jacqueline: Jackie.

Jackie, who rang the Good Listeners again and again. Jackie, with her wild mint and lavandin hand soap and her bergamot and mandarin candles. *Jackie*.

Jackie killed herself.

* * *

A second later the realisation hits me. I spoke to Jackie just a few days ago. But that time, I didn't listen to her stories. I didn't give her time. Instead, I hurried her off the line. Because I was desperate to speak to Emma and I couldn't bear to listen to Jackie talk about some stolen Marks and Spencer pyjamas.

And now Jackie is *dead*.

Did I do that? Was Jackie clinging on for dear life when she rang up with her elocuted vowels? And did I coolly peel away her fingers one by one? *Sorry, you're breaking up, sorry, I can't hear you*?

Sorry, sorry, sorry.

Adrian is waiting for me to speak. 'Why do you think she shoplifted?' I scrape the words from somewhere. 'What do you think caused that compulsion?'

And all the while that Adrian is telling me about his beautiful girl – his wonderful wife with the terrible flaw – my mind is pounding down the tracks again and again.

Jackie is dead. Jackie is dead.

Jackie is dead because I was hunting Emma.

But then Adrian speaks again.

'Jackie called the Good Listeners a lot,' Adrian says. 'She said that you kept her going.'

'Jackie said that?' The surge of relief knocks the air out of me. 'She said that we helped?'

'She said it the night before she died.' Adrian lets out a sob. 'She was always so grateful to the Good Listeners. I suppose I just wanted to say thank you.'

After Adrian has put down the phone, I put my line on hold. I look at the little red light bulb, dark again now.

As I stare at it, I realise Sally has put her phone on hold, and is watching me. She must have heard my gasp when Adrian told me Jackie was dead. Must have heard the strain in my voice.

'Are you alright, Clara?' she asks gently.

There is no judgement in Sally's voice. But my eyes meet hers and, just like that, I know that she knows.

We sit there for a moment. Two Listeners, trained in silence.

'How did you guess?' I ask, and it is an admission. 'How did you know?'

Sally breathes out through her nose, the quietest of laughs. 'It was the radio,' she says. 'I never watch TV, you see. Never got in the habit of it. But I heard you on the radio once.'

It must have been during one of those hundreds of interviews. *Keep looking, please. Please keep looking.*

Sally listened.

'One day we were on duty together,' Sally goes on. 'And you were talking to someone whose daughter was killed in a crash on the A38.'

I remember that call. A carful of teenagers, giggling, shrieking, drinking: every parents' nightmare. He was only eighteen, the driver.

'I remember that call,' I say.

We remember that call. We remember all the calls.

'I had my back to you, so I couldn't see you. All I could hear was your voice,' says Sally. 'I recognised it.'

'Oh.' Of course.

'I wasn't on a call myself,' Sally adds hastily, because she is as conscientious as they come.

'I shouldn't be volunteering here,' I say slowly.

The silence lengthens. 'I'd have told you to stop if I thought you needed to,' Sally says in the end. 'The way you handled that call… No one else could have done it, Clara. You've helped so many people.'

We both hear it in the silence: *but maybe it is time to stop now.*

I drink my tea. Sally drinks hers. I think of all Sally's kindnesses to me. The way in which we were paired on shifts so often. I thought it was a coincidence. It wasn't.

I know that she won't say anything to the Good Listeners, but I also know my time here is over.

Even if Emma is alive, I will not be here to answer her call.

'Thank you,' I say. 'Thank you so much, Sally.'

* * *

I drive home slowly. It's now been a week since Emma was attacked. No one has seen Amber for a week.

I need to tell Detective Tremayne everything.

I won't get anything else from the Good Listeners anyway.

I bump up the drive towards my house, which won't be my house for much longer. And I don't know where I will go. I don't know what I will do.

I climb out of the car and walk up the narrow path to the front door.

A dark shape moves towards me.

And I scream.

66

It is Nell.

'Shit, sorry, Clara. I didn't mean to scare you… My eyes had got used to the darkness. I didn't realise that you—'

'It's fine.' I breathe out slowly and walk to the front door. 'What's going on?'

'No one has seen Amber.' Nell blinks as I turn on the light in the kitchen. There is panic in her voice. 'I've asked practically everyone in the village. No one's seen her for at least a week. Amber's not been at Harepath at all. Ryan is fucking furious with me. Jordie Meldon is spitting tacks. I haven't heard back from that police welfare check – I suppose I wouldn't – but I have left one more message on Amber's phone telling her that if she doesn't contact me by tomorrow morning, I am reporting her as missing to the police.'

'What did Ryan say to you?' I ask. 'Did you see him face to face?'

'He came over to our house. He'd spoken to Jordie – apparently you went up to their cottage?' I nod. 'And he'd told Ryan. Ryan went absolutely mental at me, saying it was his children missing too and how could I possibly think that he would ever hurt his kids?'

I sit down and breathe out slowly. 'I'll come with you to the police,' I say.

'She is okay, isn't she?' Nell's hands are shaking. 'Amber, I mean. I can't bear it if she's not okay.'

A text buzzes into her phone. Nell reads it and rolls her eyes. 'Who was that?' I ask.

'My sister. I asked her if she'd seen Amber, or if she had any idea where Amber's sister is living at the moment, and all she has to say is "I have had the bare minimum to do with Amber's family for years". My sister is such a fucking snob.'

'Does she not like Ryan either?' I ask.

'No, although I suppose she's not wrong there. But still. She doesn't like Pauly either, and that's because he's a mere delivery driver.' Nell puts on a posh accent for the last few words.

'I'll try and track down Amber's sister,' I say, for something to do. 'What's her name?'

'Lauren Dunn,' says Nell. 'She's a potter. Moves around a lot. Bit of a hippy.'

I send Lauren's name to Rachel, who has several journalist friends in London, and ask her if she can find any contact details. I send it to Lucas, too, because he's got a couple of researchers on his team and there's every chance they're all still in the office.

Who the hell is Lauren Dunn? Rachel texts me straight back. *Clara, what's going on?*

Please, I text back. *It's really important to find her.*

Together, Nell and I trawl 192.com and LinkedIn and everything else we can think of. Nell texts everyone who might have Lauren's mobile number.

There are several dead ends, but at last Rachel works out that Lauren's in a relationship with a farmer called Pete, and Lucas finds Pete's farm, just west of Plymouth, and I spot a Facebook post about missing sheep and someone identifying them as Pete's sheep and 'give Lauren a call, her number's…'

'I'll call Lauren,' Nell decides. 'I know her a bit.'

Neither of us say aloud the thing we both know: that Amber may be escaping me just as much as she is escaping Ryan.

'Lauren? Hi, babe. It's Nell Turner. Don't know if you remember me… Amber's friend. Look, I know things are tricky, but I just want to know that Amber is okay… Have you seen her in the last week?' Silence. 'It's all gone a bit mad here. I don't need to speak to her or anything. You don't even need to say if she's there. But can you just tell me if you've seen her or spoken to her.' Another silence. Nell shakes her head at me, eyes dark with frustration. 'Look, Lauren, I know you're completely loyal to Amber, but I'd never say anything to anyone about where Amber is, either. I need to know that Amber and the kids are okay.' Longer silence. 'Lauren, I don't want to do this, and I don't want to cause any trouble, okay? But I am going to have to go to the police first thing in the morning, alright? I'm just too worried about her. I need to be sure that Amber is okay. A text message isn't enough. One of us has to speak to her or see her.' Nell slams the phone down with a curse. 'Lauren hung up on me.'

'Do you think Amber was there? Do you think Lauren has seen her?'

'I don't know.' Nell is on her feet. 'I don't bloody know.' Nell can't sit down.

'Maybe Lauren wants to talk to Amber before she talks to you?' I suggest. 'Maybe we caught her off guard and she needs to check what Amber wants. Maybe she'll call back.'

'Maybe.' Nell glances at her watch. 'Fuck it, I'm going down there. You stay here,' she says bluntly. 'It's best if it's just me. You look knackered anyway.'

I don't try to dissuade her.

'Call me,' I say. 'If Amber is there.'

'Yes.'

'And make sure no one follows you.' Nell's head jerks up. But her eyes are serious.

'I won't,' she promises. 'I won't.'

After Nell has gone, I try to go to bed. It will take Nell at least an hour to drive to that farm and I am desperately tired. I lie down in the darkness. But I can't get to sleep.

I am just turning over for the tenth time, kicking the duvet with frustration, when my eyes fly open.

67

I have a recording of his voice.

In the chaotic aftermath of that conversation, as Austin and Simeon gathered around my chair, I shoved the earpiece and my phone deep into my bag. I couldn't bear to listen to it again. I couldn't bear to listen to Emma's voice choke into horror.

But I did record her, and that means that I recorded *his* voice too. And the recording is sitting right there in my bag.

I read an article, once, about voice analysis and voice recognition. I know it is a science, a real discipline. The police use it, although I am not entirely sure how.

There is no central database of voices, of course. But if I managed to record Ryan's voice somehow, and got someone to cross-reference it to the voice on the tape, this recording could be evidence.

His voice.

There might be something else on the recording too, I remind myself. Some clue I've missed.

After most of the calls with Emma, I looked back through my notes afterwards. I coolly considered any new details and evaluated how they related to what was already known. Or what might already be known, because all of it could be a lie.

Every call became another piece of the jigsaw puzzle.

But I do not want to listen to that recording. I recoil at the thought.

To hear his voice, I will have to.

I pick up my bag: battered denim, serviceable, not pretty.

I am not sure if I can bear the sound of Emma's voice echoing up from her grave, wherever that grave might be.

If she is dead, I remind myself automatically. If. *If*.

I don't think I can bear to listen to Emma telling her story when I know that any minute that door will smash open. I don't think I can listen to those faintest flickers of hope, when I know that any second he will throw her to the ground and clamp his hands around her neck.

No.

But I have to.

I don't have anything else right now.

Taking a breath, I pull out the phone. It sits innocently – comfortably – in my hand, a little block of secrets.

It only takes a few moments to upload the recordings onto my laptop. There are two recordings from that night. If Emma had called just once, after eight, as usual, maybe nothing would have happened.

But calling back half an hour later meant that she was on the phone when he returned home. Our second conversation killed her.

And I was one half of that conversation.

On the screen, the calls look like mountainous electronic peaks. I hold my breath and press play.

I listen to the second recording first. There may be a clue I missed, and I want to get it out of the way.

My husband killed Lyra Brennan. I know he killed her.

Emma, almost shouting.

I close my eyes, shut out everything. Amber, is that you?

I am not sure that it is.

I think I would know if it was.

I – who have spent so long listening to all these voices – would know if Amber and Emma were the same person.

* * *

I will have to make sure, though. When Nell gets back to Coraton, I will tell her everything and play it to her. Nell will know if that is Amber's voice.

I am out of the Good Listeners anyway. I have nothing to lose.

Lyra Brennan? I am so sorry to hear that. That must be incredibly hard to live with.

On the recording, my voice sounds impossibly calm. It is hard, almost, to be certain that it is me.

But somewhere, too, I feel something that is almost a burst of relief.

See. It is *real*. Emma *called*. I *spoke* to her.

I hadn't realised – until then – that I wasn't quite sure. That I wondered if my brain might be playing some mad game.

Deep down, I wondered whether I am so desperate to find my daughter's killer that I might have invented everything.

He's a monster. I have to get my children away from him. I have to.

Children whose mother has disappeared.

Children in terrible danger.

I remember that the first time that Emma spoke about her children, I felt a swirl of emotions. Was it jealousy? Your children are *alive*, Emma. *Alive*. What more could you possibly want? It could have been frustration, too, certainly: Emma, you are choosing to keep your children in the presence of a man whom you believe to be a murderer. How can a mother – any mother – do that?

There was anger.

I can admit that now.

There was a terrible, undeniable anger.

He's a monster.

But now Emma's children are out there somewhere, and I may be the only person who knows how desperately they need help.

Emma's voice rattles on.

He said that he was going to walk down to the folk festival… Quivering with excitement… What do you mean? Where the hell were you?

And then it happens.

Even now, even in the safety of my bedroom and even though I know it is coming, the sound of the door crashing open makes me jump.

Emma screams.

I find myself reaching out. It is only a convulsive instinct, because there is nothing to be done, nothing to be changed.

All I can do is listen.

I hear the thud as the phone smashes to the floor.

Don't touch me.

What are you doing?

Let me go.

You crazy bitch.

I force myself to listen to the recording twice.

You crazy *bitch.*

Once more, I note mechanically that this man has a Devon accent.

I stop the recording, then let it start again.

Let me go.

You crazy bitch.

Is it Ryan?

I am not sure that it is.

68

My husband hit my daughter. My husband… he hit my daughter.

I'm so sorry to hear that. That must have been terrible for your daughter. And very difficult for you.

It is easier listening to Emma's first call. Well, as easy as it can be, listening to a mother talk about her daughter being assaulted.

What happened? Do you want to tell me why he hit her?

Oh, it was so stupid. He's—

Clara!

Austin's voice. I had forgotten about that. The spreading tea stain, the liquid dripping from the desk. The shrugs. Oh well. That ancient lino will barely show a mark anyway.

But this time, I concentrate on Emma's voice gabbling on.

'He likes setting traps. He likes tricking people.'

'Mmm.' I can tell from my voice that I am not listening. I am filling the silence on the line as I cast around for something – anything – to lob into the flood of tea.

'He did it that day… He set one of his traps that day.'

'Yes.' Still not listening.

'He's making me lie for him. More and more lies. I hate it… He set him up. He set him up and he's forcing me to help him with his lies.'

'I see.' By now, Austin and I had given up on the tea and I am sitting down again. Concentrating on Emma's voice.

'He's a manipulative bastard.' Emma's sobs echo tinnily. 'He always has been. Always.'

I press pause.

He did it that day.

He set him up.

Set who up?

He's forcing me to help him with his lies.

Help him how?

I know now that Jordie and Lawrence and Ryan lied. Did one of them set up another somehow? Or is it something completely different?

I know Emma isn't Hailey Meldon. I don't think she is Amber Dallyn.

But what happened to Lawrence Wrenscott's wife? The one who ran off? Arabella or Araminta.

Nell said Lawrence used to like Kimlock trains, too. Maybe I could ask Frank Fenton-Brown if there are any Wrenscotts anywhere in the Kimlock Society systems.

But Lawrence doesn't have any children.

That I know of.

The thoughts spin around my head until nothing makes sense anymore.

I am so tired now. I get into bed again. But it is hopeless. It is as if there is an itch in my brain that won't let me sleep. Because there is something… Something in that conversation with Nell… Something Nell said. Something… But what was it?

I close my eyes and try to remember Nell's exact words.

Lauren Dunn. Does Lauren's name mean anything to me? I don't think so.

I've asked practically everyone in the village.

Ryan is fucking furious with me.

Go to sleep, I tell myself. Nell will call as soon as she knows anything about Amber, and in the meantime, I need sleep. I lie down in my bed.

But still Nell's voice rattles around in my head.

I've asked practically everyone in the village.

Stop it. Go to sleep.
Ryan is fucking furious with me.
I am nearly asleep.
Amber's not been at Harepath at all.
I jump awake with a terrible surge of realisation.
I think I know what happened.

69

Nell's voice echoes through my head. *Amber's not been at Harepath at all.*

Harepath House. Harepath.

The moment I am fully awake, I realise it is nonsense. Stop it, I tell myself. You're driving yourself mad.

That's impossible.

I lie down again.

Harepath.

You're being ridiculous, I tell myself.

Idiotic.

It can't be.

Harepath.

I sit up again. The twenty-four-hour eBay auctions will be finishing about now. To distract myself, I check in on Hampshirelass143.

The golden *Petunia* has sold for £18,287 to an H. Russell of Chalford St Giles, Buckinghamshire.

Useless.

Amber's not been at Harepath at all. Nell's voice is in my head again.

It's impossible, I tell myself.

Impossible.

Is it?

It's how Nell pronounces the word Harepath. That is what is sticking in my brain. She pronounces it in the same way that everyone in Coraton pronounces Harepath. Harepath House. Harepath. Harr-p'r.

I think again of that snarling voice that visited the Good Listeners.

Harr-p'r. There it is. Harepath. Harper. *Will Harper.*

Madness. It is madness.

Gabriel Blackslade is amiable, erudite, urbane.

Of course it's not him.

You're being completely insane.

But I find myself trying to remember when I last saw Victoria Blackslade.

I can check with Victoria, Gabriel told me when I asked after Amber, *but I'm pretty sure she said Amber texted.*

That was just over three days ago, the Tuesday after Emma was killed.

See? Victoria was alive then. Long after the attack.

A small voice in the back of my mind: Gabriel told me that he had spoken to Victoria. I didn't actually speak to Victoria myself.

She's in London today, but she should be back this evening.

I don't know that anyone has spoken to Victoria.

I haven't seen Victoria for quite a long time, I realise.

Between the house hunt and the job search in London, I haven't actually laid eyes on Victoria for days. At least a week, actually.

But Victoria's accent is cut-glass RP. She can't possibly be Emma.

Emma has a soft Devon accent. Of course she's not Victoria.

I reach out and play the recording again.

He's a manipulative bastard, Emma insists. *He always has been.*

Emma can't be Victoria Blackslade.

Can she?

70

I lie down again. There is something else, not quite a fully formed thought.

Nell's voice is in my head again.

Amber's not been at Harepath at all.

Stop it, I order myself.

It's not possible.

But there it is again. Nell: *Amber's not been at Harepath.*

What is it? Why am I focusing on that sentence?

Nell.

It can't be.

It could be.

Victoria has a sister. Emma has a sister.

Nell's voice is in my head again. *My sister is such a fucking snob.*

No.

My mum's done her hip, so I've been over at hers.

You're being insane.

I remember hearing Victoria talk to her sister on the phone, once. *For heaven's sake, Penelope, it's your turn.*

Gabriel cutting in smoothly. *Victoria's mother isn't well. She and her sister are trying to co-ordinate her care.*

Maybe it's pure coincidence that both Victoria's mother and Nell's mother are ill.

Nell said that her sister is well turned out. *She does remind me how I might look with a decent skincare routine.*

Victoria in her cashmere and smart boots.

They don't look very similar. Nell has curly light-brown hair and Victoria is an ironed blonde.

An ironed blonde who regularly goes to London to get her hair done.

Nell's sister, whoever she is, does know Ryan Dallyn well enough to dislike him.

She doesn't like Pauly either, Nell's voice echoes in my head again, *and that's because he's a mere delivery driver.*

That must mean that Nell's sister is at least familiar with Coraton.

Tabitha was sulking because her cousins have everything: *the cool shoes, the brand-new bikes, the ponies.*

Not that Nell was seduced by the cousins' luxurious existence: *I could tell her they don't have it easy either, but she won't have it.*

Victoria's sister is Penelope.

Penny is a nickname for Penelope. My brain is working slowly. While Nell…

Nell can be a nickname for all sorts of names. If I had thought about it, which I didn't, I would have guessed Eleanor, or Cornelia, or Helen, or Ellen.

But Penelope can become Penny or it can also become… Nell.

I think of Nell's Devon accent.

I think of Emma's Devon accent.

And for the first time, I wonder what Victoria sounded like, once, a long time ago?

71

No, this is madness. I lie back down again.

I *saw* Nell receive a text from her sister, just a few minutes ago.

I have had the bare minimum to do with Amber's family for years.

I am being hysterical. It's the lack of sleep, it's the endless suspicions. Enough to drive anyone over the edge.

That text message: *I have had the bare minimum to do with Amber's family for years.*

It definitely sounds like Victoria.

So Nell's sister is alive anyway.

Although once again, it was only a text. Nell didn't actually speak to anyone.

I am pacing the bedroom floor now.

Gabriel Blackslade divides his time between court and working from home. So Victoria couldn't rely on him being out of the house day-to-day. But she would know when he was going to be away. His court hearings in Bristol or Winchester would be scheduled in advance. Whenever he was safely in Taunton or one of the other courts, she could have called the Good Listeners. But why – if that was the case – did she almost only ever call on Fridays?

He was out of the house on Friday nights. Out with the bell-ringers, and then on to the pub.

And another thud of realisation: there was someone else in the house almost all of the time. Linda, the semi-retired nanny. Linda was semi-retired... but perhaps Blackslade asked her to stay on to keep an eye on his wife. Stay on to keep an eye on Victoria, who couldn't be trusted not to go out and buy alcohol – a lot of alcohol – when there was no one else about.

I think of Linda, running through her contralto part. Linda, in the choir. The choir that practises on a Friday evening. Linda, who is reliably out of the house every Friday evening.

Leaving Victoria all alone.

There is something else, too.

Nell and Amber run their cake stand on Wednesday mornings at the farmers' market. And Linda sells the Harepath honey there too. But perhaps one Wednesday morning, Gabriel Blackslade was called away urgently to a hearing.

Perhaps Victoria knew Amber and Linda would be at the farmers' market.

Perhaps Victoria knew she would have the house to herself.

And that was when Emma called in drunk.

That very first call all those weeks ago. *He's evil. He's purest evil. What he's done... No one knows. If anyone knew...*

That call came in on a Wednesday morning too.

I remember the notes of *Moonlight* Sonata drifting across the garden at Harepath.

I loved playing the piano.

Not a child practising.

Not a recording.

Victoria.

I sat in Nell's house and saw her row of art history books. Emma told me her mother loved buying art history books in charity shops.

But perhaps Emma's mother was Nell's mother too.

* * *

But Gabriel has an alibi for the time of Lyra's disappearance, I remind myself. He was drafting a skeleton argument at his desk. He was able to show the police that he had been logged in on that new document management system at the time of the murder. That brand-new system set up by his chambers to ensure client confidentiality while working from home.

I helped him...

I remember Emma's desperate words.

I lied to them that he...

Victoria used to work as a barrister too. Would she have the knowledge to work on Gabriel's cases? Could she have logged into Gabriel's system to carry out his more mundane tasks?

Maybe.

I dial Nell's number. I have to know. I have to know right now. Are they sisters, these two? Did they grow up together, and then grow apart?

No answer from Nell. My call goes straight to voicemail. I leave her a message, but there are lots of holes in the mobile coverage over the moor. I may not hear back from Nell for ages. Or she may already be at the farm in Plymouth, and there may be no phone reception there either.

This may all be madness. This may all be yet another wild splurge of imagination, useless, and hurtful.

But I have to know... I have to know more about how all these people intersect. I need to know who is related to who. I need to know.

And suddenly, I know where I can go.

I can go to the church, where Coraton's history is engraved on cold, hard stone.

72

In the daylight, Coraton Church is beautiful, with the russet bracken of the moor rising behind it. But tonight the church is lost in mist and darkness. Even from the lych-gate, the ancient entrance to the graveyard, nothing can be seen of the church's lichened walls.

I make my way to Lyra's memorial first, before anything else. I run my fingers over the engraving. *Forever loved, darling girl.*

You are, dearest Lyra, and you always will be.

I glance towards Elizabeth Wrenscott's grave, too. These two young girls, tied together despite the years, in a way that I can't quite understand.

Then I turn towards the church. It is beginning to freeze and the path is slippery. My breath clouds in the air.

Thanks to Georgia Wrenscott, I know where the key is hidden. In the small alcove, my fingers meet the cold of the key.

I hurry into the church, closing the huge oak door behind me. I brought a torch from my car and now I point it at the first of the big leather-bound registers stored in the back of the church.

Where to begin? For a moment I stare blankly at centuries of records. Then I think carefully. Nell and Pauly Turner. A Paul Turner may have got married in Coraton at some point in the last couple of decades. That will give me Nell's full name.

I reach for the marriage register, heavy with gold leaf.

There aren't that many weddings held at Coraton Church, so it doesn't take long to leaf through them.

It doesn't take long to find a Ryan Dallyn and an Amber Dunn.

And a Lawrence Ferdinand Wrenscott marrying an Ariadne Eugenie Cunningham-Palmer.

Then there is a Jordan Meldon and a Hailey Cox. Jordie and Hailey.

And then I turn a page and there is… There is a Paul Turner and a Penelope Anstey.

Penelope Anstey. Nell Turner.

I search back a decade, but there is no sign of Nell's sister, of another Miss Anstey, stepping up the Coraton aisle.

But maybe they didn't marry here.

Maybe they married elsewhere.

A registry office. An elopement. Who knows?

I go far enough back to find a Thomas Anstey marrying an Alice Pollock before I give up.

On to Births.

Another heavy book, this one bound in red leather.

Again, the familiar names.

Jordan Meldon and Hailey Meldon nee Cox register a Rowan. Further back, they register a Georgina.

Ryan and Amber Dallyn register a Lewis and an Aimee.

A long way further back, Thomas and Alice Anstey register a Penelope. That must be Nell with the gentle Dartmoor accent and those softly rolling syllables. Whose parents almost certainly had robust Devon accents, too, along with an enjoyment of frilly girls' names.

I race to read the next pages. Where… Where…

For a moment, I can't breathe. I stare at the faded writing.

Because perhaps Emma told the truth more than I realised.

Perhaps Emma told the truth almost all of the time.

Victoria, with the public school accent. Victoria, with not a hint of a Dartmoor accent in her day-to-day life: Victoria Emmeline Anstey's birth was registered in Coraton's parish church forty-two years ago.

And now Miss Victoria Anstey must be Mrs Victoria Blackslade. Mrs Blackslade who hides her real voice every single day, except for those precious moments when she is speaking to the Good Listeners.

Mrs Blackslade, who speaks the truth only when she thinks no one is listening.

Mrs Blackslade. Emmeline. Emma.

I race back through the pages, although I am not sure what I am looking for. But then I see it, and I can't stop the gasp.

Gabriel Ferdinand William Blackslade, born to Donna Blackslade, father unknown.

Gabriel Ferdinand William Blackslade.

Gabriel Blackslade of Harepath.

Will Harper.

Victoria Emmeline Anstey.

Victoria Blackslade.

Emmeline. Emma.

Emma.

Perhaps she was telling the truth all along.

73

I find myself sitting on the cold stone floor of the church.

I think of Gabriel's voice, flowing like honey.

And Victoria's voice, strained and shrill.

Gabriel, the barrister, for whom a beautiful speaking voice was all-important. Fighting to the top at the bar, a world where Eton still matters, even if they pretend it doesn't. Did they teach themselves, these two? A team until they weren't?

I am running through the things I think I know about Gabriel and Victoria Blackslade and Emma.

Is Harepath within earshot of the church bell? Yes, it must be, just about.

Illegitimate. Yes, he is.

Although I think I can guess at Gabriel Blackslade's parentage anyway. Major Cyril Ferdinand Wrenscott dying at Arnhem: Ferdinand, a family name that comes up again and again.

Gabriel Blackslade must be the son of Ferdinand Wrenscott.

Because why else would they have returned here, Victoria and Gabriel, when they had worked so hard to cover up their past? Why else would they come back to the place where everyone knows their truth even if it is never mentioned?

I always thought vaguely that Blackslade disliked Lawrence Wrenscott, but I never really wondered why. Lawrence, the prince across the water. Lawrence, the half-brother, beloved by their father.

Donna Blackslade didn't give her son the Wrenscott name, but Ferdie's name was enshrined all the same. Born ten years before Lawrence, and seven years before Elizabeth, Gabriel Blackslade probably arrived several years before Georgia and Ferdinand were married.

I wonder if he grew up somewhere in Coraton. Yes, I guess that he did. I can almost see him watching from afar as the Wrenscotts luxuriated in the enviable grandeur of Harepath House.

The Wrenscotts, representing everything that Gabriel ever wanted.

I think back to that photograph in the newspaper's back room.

Best in Show! Elizabeth Wrenscott and Linnet.

Perhaps, for a few glorious minutes, Blackslade even named the wretched puppy after the Wrenscotts' family dog.

I try not to think about what might have happened to Elizabeth Rose Wrenscott. To pretty little Elizabeth, beloved by Georgia and Ferdie Wrenscott. Beloved by everyone. The apple of Ferdie's eye.

As Gabriel – still a child, but a few years older than sweet little Elizabeth – watched so darkly from the wings.

If he was seven years older than Elizabeth, he would have been thirteen when she died.

I think he was thirteen when he killed her.

I lean back against the old oak pews.

I think about Victoria: aloof, unfriendly, cold.

But maybe she was only ever sad and lonely. Cut off from her past, living a strange half-lie that no one quite believed.

I think of Nell, tough and resilient, surrounded by friends.

Poor Victoria. Poor sad Victoria.

I feel as if I am dancing on the edge of madness. I feel as if I have tried to fit this costume of clues onto so many women now, pinning it into shape, hemming it to size. Making myself believe that it fits.

But on Victoria, perhaps, it does.

I ring Nell, but again her number goes through to voicemail.

I stare at my phone, frustration raging through me.

And just then, it rings. A number flashes up and for a moment I feel a surge of hope.

Amber. Amber is calling me.

74

'Amber! Are you alright? Are you okay? We've been so worried,' I babble. 'Where are you?'

'I'm fine.' Amber sounds exhausted, her voice devoid of emotion.

I close my eyes and try to recall Emma's voice. Amber's voice is so close to Emma's, but she is not Emma.

'Where are you?' I ask again.

'I'm back at Rose Cottage,' she says quietly. 'Don't worry. Everything is fine.'

I find my knees have gone shaky. Whatever else has happened, Amber is alive.

'Where have you been, Amber?' I ask.

'At my sister's.'

I tell myself that I don't need to see Amber in order to confirm she is alive. But I find that I do want to see her. There have been too many shifting parts. Too many uncertainties, for too long.

All this time, I have believed that Ryan killed my daughter. All this time, there has been impossible pressure on Amber and Ryan's marriage. I want to be sure, beyond any possible doubt, that Amber is okay.

'Have you seen Nell?' I ask. 'She's been—'

'We need to talk.' Amber cuts me off. 'Can you come over?'

If I go to Rose Cottage, I can see Amber with my own eyes. I can ask her the questions I need answered.

'Yes,' I say at once. 'Of course. I'll be there in five minutes.'

There is only one thing I want to do before leaving the church. I log into my emails.

The golden *Petunia* has sold for £18,287… I've already read that one.

Another auction has finished. The mint-condition *Azalea* has gone to a person who bid almost as soon as I set the auction live twenty-four hours ago. The mint-condition *Azalea* has gone to…

When I see the name, I feel a surge of something that is close to relief.

I have hunted for years now. Years.

I leap to my feet.

A Mr G. Blackslade bought the mint-condition *Azalea*.

A Mr G. Blackslade of Harepath House, Coraton, Devon.

75

I start down the track towards Rose Cottage. Rose Cottage, in the shadow of the Harepath gates. I think of Ryan, and fear returns like a habit. I should have asked Amber if he was there. He will be there, presumably. And I don't want to…

You don't have to fear Ryan anymore, I remind myself. All this time… At this thought, I feel a new flood of guilt: all this time, Ryan has been wrongfully accused. He has been living under that shroud of suspicion…

I think back to that terrible day again. Ryan's phone records. *I was in Abbot's Wood.*

I think about it all step by step, one more time.

Ryan said that his puppy went missing. He said he searched for his puppy all over the Harepath and Meldon land. Then his phone records showed that he was in Abbot's Wood. Then he said he was actually in Abbot's Wood. Then Lyra was found in Abbot's Wood.

I come to a halt. Ryan was working at Harepath that morning. He was meant to be painting the sitting room of the Gardener's Cottage, as confirmed by an unimpressed Victoria Blackslade. But he bunked off to go and sing at the folk festival.

I think of Ryan marching off down the drive, half-secretive, half-defiant. *It's a one-off. It's only for an hour or so.*

I think of Gabriel Blackslade, watching from his study. It was a warmish day, so perhaps Ryan was in his shirtsleeves.

People leave their phones lying around all the time in Coraton.

How calculating was he, this man who knows every aspect of the criminal law? Did he premeditate it all?

Did he ask Victoria to do some basic work for him – something too menial for the great King's Counsel? – and then wander out to the Gardener's Cottage? Did he look down at Ryan's abandoned coat? The abandoned coat with a phone in the pocket.

It is unbearable to think of such calculation. Of such terrible manipulation. But maybe that is what happened.

'Everyone knows he's a violent little shit,' I'd screamed at Jordie.

It would have been almost too easy to set him up.

I think of Blackslade starting out towards the folk festival. As he walked, he would have passed Rose Cottage. Was there anyone in? No. Amber and her children were down at the folk festival. Dozens of people said that they saw them there.

Maybe the puppy was in the front garden. Maybe Blackslade opened the front gate? And let the puppy wander out?

Or – worse – maybe he tempted the puppy towards the folk festival? Picked it up and started walking down the hill.

A thud of realisation. Because that is one thing my daughter would not have been able to resist. We'd had the stranger talk, of course. She knew to say no to sweets.

But a puppy?

And shortly after that, Ryan's phone made its way out to Abbot's Wood.

And maybe around that same time, Ryan – foolish, brutish Ryan – finished his sea shanties. He hung around for a bit – buzzing after the performance, maybe he had a quick pint – and then he started walking back up towards Harepath. That would have taken him past his own front gate, and maybe that was dangling open.

Ryan would have known that the gate was meant to keep the puppy in. So perhaps he investigated, and found that the puppy was missing and went out to search. Alone, because he didn't have his phone on him, because he'd forgotten it at Harepath. Alone, because the lack of phone meant that he couldn't call Lawrence and Jordie, who he would normally have called.

Ryan must have searched for quite a long time, round the fields, here and there. Eventually, he must have given up and walked back to the village.

Only then did he discover that Lyra was missing and that nothing in Coraton was ever going to be the same again.

I have no idea how Blackslade returned the phone to Ryan.

Perhaps he simply deposited the phone back in Rose Cottage's kitchen. Placed it on the kitchen table. In Dartmoor, where houses are left unlocked all the time. Ryan, a pawn, a game.

Ryan must have been terrified when he heard that Lyra was missing.

Every man in Coraton who wasn't visibly accounted for at the moment she disappeared must have felt a flash of horror. It wasn't me: that instinctive bleat.

I wonder if Jordie and Lawrence felt that same fear too.

Let's all say we were together, searching for the puppy. Plausible. Actually true, in Ryan's case.

Then Jordie's father, the canny farmer, learned of their naive plan. Brought in lawyers, fast.

And at first, that wasn't a disaster. Maybe Ryan wasn't sure what had happened to the phone and only knew reception beyond the village was patchy, unreliable, jumpy. Maybe he shrugged – slightly baffled, perhaps – and adapted his story. Hoped for the best.

It was only weeks later, when Lyra's body was found, that this small discrepancy became all-important.

Ryan was lucky, really, to have avoided charges.

He only got away with it because Jordie's father brought in expensive lawyers and they got ahead of the disaster. That and the fact that there was no further evidence. There was only ever the shadow of suspicion.

I wonder, now, if Ryan ever realised what had happened.

Probably not.

Not far now. I turn onto Harepath Lane. Rose Cottage is in near darkness. There are no lights from Harepath, beyond, either.

Ryan's van is parked on the muddy verge. Amber's car is there too. I knock and Amber opens the door at once.

The light of the kitchen is behind Amber, which dazzles me for a second, but then I can see that she has been crying and that her blue eyes are red-rimmed.

But it is her. It is Amber. She is alive.

'Come in.' She gestures feebly.

I walk into the room. Ryan is sitting at the kitchen table, his head bowed. I walk towards him. But as I move, the front door slams shut behind me. I jump and spin around.

It wasn't Amber who closed the door so sharply. There, smiling with a strange savage brightness, is Gabriel Blackslade.

76

'Hello, Clara.' Gabriel Blackslade's voice is silky.

Ryan Dallyn is still sitting at the kitchen table and he is not looking at me. Without saying a word, Amber steps past me to the table and sits down opposite Ryan.

Blackslade stays between me and the front door.

Flashes of awareness burn through my mind.

Amber summoned me here.

Amber hid Blackslade's presence from me.

And that means Amber is either complicit with Blackslade. Or she is completely terrified of him.

I look at Ryan. Ryan is sitting apparently calmly at the table. But his hands are in his lap and his fists are clenched.

I realise: Ryan and Amber's children are upstairs. Asleep, perhaps. But upstairs.

Amber and Ryan are paralyzed with fear.

Blackslade steps forward.

He is still smiling, but his smile is terrifying.

I know that there can be only one reason why we are all here tonight.

Blackslade must suspect that I have guessed what has happened to Victoria. I look at Blackslade's courteous smile and I know beyond any doubt that if his suspicions are confirmed, I will not escape this house alive tonight.

I have to convince him that I know nothing at all.

I have to convince him that he is safe.

The only thing that gives me the faintest hint of hope is the fact that he hasn't killed me already. Maybe I can survive tonight. Maybe.

I turn to Blackslade and smile with equal brightness. 'Gabriel! That's a surprise. What are you doing here?' I keep talking. I look back at the kitchen table. 'Amber, we've all been so worried about you! We didn't know where you were. Didn't know where the kids were either. I'm so glad you're back! Nell will be so relieved too.'

Amber picks up the baton. 'I just needed a few days away,' she says softly. 'I just needed…'

'I know,' I look disapprovingly at Ryan, 'that you've been having a tricky time.'

Ryan's fists clench even tighter, but he manages to look apologetic.

'Me and Amber,' he says heavily, 'need to… We just need to spend some proper time together. Work things out.'

'Good!' I say brightly. 'Great! Sorry, you must all be knackered. I'll head home.'

I turn towards the door, but imperceptibly Blackslade blocks my way. I stop. I don't want him to force me to stop.

'We know it's been a terrible time for you, Clara,' he says. 'But we just wanted to check if you're okay too.'

'I'm fine,' I say firmly. 'Completely fine.'

'It's just that you've been asking all sorts of weird and wonderful questions,' he says. 'People are worried about you.'

It must have been completely shocking to Blackslade when I suddenly started asking those odd questions the other day, I think. Does Amber have a sister? Do any of the locals have a puppy called Linnet? Does Ryan like Kimlock trains? And, by the way, he isn't illegitimate, is he? Blackslade must have felt like he was looking at a distorted simulation of his own life.

Blackslade is waiting for my response.

'I'd been listening to a podcast,' I say randomly. 'One of those true crime ones. It wasn't even anything to do with Lyra, but it just got me thinking and asking some questions, which must have sounded odd, now I think about it.'

Blackslade doesn't look convinced. 'Ryan also mentioned you'd been up to see Jordie Meldon last night? I gather the Meldons were rather upset about it all.'

Ryan squirms slightly. I guess that Blackslade has been using him to find out about me. And to find out that Amber was on her way back to Coraton, too. And to find out everything else. Ryan, the useful idiot. I feel a surge of disgust.

'I did go over to Rossiter Cottage.' I try to look apologetic. 'It was stupid of me to upset Jordie like that, and his family. But it's been a really horrible few years. You all know that I've been trying to find out what happened to' – at her name, I think I might start to cry, but force myself to carry on – 'Lyra. Sometimes I go too far. I'm sorry.' I turn towards Ryan. 'And can you please tell Jordie that I really am sorry for accusing him and upsetting his family?'

'What we didn't understand,' Blackslade's voice is still smooth, still controlled, 'was how you had reached the conclusion that it was Jordie who had killed your daughter?'

For a moment, I can't remember either. Everything is a churning madness.

Then I remember: it was Nell telling me that she hadn't seen Hailey Meldon since Christmas.

But the last thing I want to talk to Blackslade about is vanished wives. I realise that, like me, Blackslade has been picking up fragments. But while my fragments have been distorted by Emma's narration, his have been mangled by the Coraton rumour mill. Like me, he must be finding it hard to put it all together.

I guess that although Blackslade may have a network of informants around Coraton, Nell – his sister-in-law – is not one of his spies. He must have found out from someone that Nell was asking questions, but he hasn't yet worked out why.

Independently of Coraton gossip, he also knows that Victoria called the Good Listeners, because she was on the phone to them when she died. He must have gone to the Good Listeners' office to learn whatever he could there.

But I don't think he's joined the dots yet, because why on earth would he?

And he certainly hasn't been able to risk asking Nell – his wife's own sister – because then Nell would ask even more questions.

I realise how painstakingly Blackslade has been manoeuvring. He has so much to lose. And so much to cover up. Ever since Victoria died, Blackslade has been plotting how to escape the slow-closing noose.

She's already house-hunting. She's been going for job interviews. Looking for new schools for the kids.

I remember Blackslade's words with a new awareness. Because even though Victoria's relationship with her sister was frayed, Nell would have noticed her disappearance eventually. But on the other hand – given that Victoria had become so isolated over time – perhaps an alleged new job, new house, new everything would have been enough to explain the sudden departure of the Blackslades from Harepath.

Nell would have been left bruised and sad. Perhaps even angry, given their mother's needs. But not suspicious. Not for a long time.

Blackslade is calculating and ruthless, I am reminded again, and he has encyclopaedic legal knowledge on his side. He hasn't given up. He is just rewriting the story.

The children? Perhaps Caspar and Cecily will be told a different story altogether. *Mummy ran off*, spoken of with sadness, with shame. Not to be spoken of at all, soon enough.

We all decide how to tell our stories, after all.

Blackslade must be bewildered by how I am gathering my strange clues. But he has a brilliant analytical mind. Eventually, he will think about that phone call one more time.

And that redial.

'Good Listeners.' The words I'd said a thousand times. 'Can I help?'

He will work it out in the end.

And at that point, he will kill me.

Blackslade is still waiting for me to explain how I ended up at Jordie Meldon's house. I think quickly.

'I suddenly realised that it was possible that the three of them had acted together,' I say. 'I don't know why it hadn't occurred to me before.'

I don't want Blackslade to think that I have completely eliminated Ryan as a murder suspect. He has put in too much effort to incriminate Ryan to dismiss that possibility.

'And it was Jordie's father who brought in those lawyers,' I add too. 'You yourself said Ryan would have been charged if those lawyers hadn't been so sharp. What was Jordie's father so worried about? What did the Meldons have to hide?'

'Jordie and Lawrence and Ryan?' I think that Blackslade has relaxed very slightly. 'You thought they might have attacked Lyra together?'

'Yes.' I am trying not to babble. 'Maybe. I don't know… It's horrible living like this. With all these suspicions all the time. All these fears.' I have a moment of inspiration. 'It's living in Coraton that's making it worse, I think. You know that my house is being sold? My tenancy is coming to an end. I've realised that it might be a good thing, actually. It's time for me to leave.'

My phone starts to ring in my pocket. I ignore it.

'You're going to leave Coraton?' Blackslade asks.

My phone stops ringing.

'Yes. It is such a beautiful, wonderful place, and I will miss it,' I stammer slightly. 'But I need to move on with my life. Lyra will always be with me, no matter where I go. But living here, suspecting perfectly innocent people like this, it's not healthy.'

Amber's phone rings and then stops ringing.

Ryan and Amber are nodding now. 'A fresh start,' says Amber. 'Fresh starts can be really great.'

I start to move towards the door. My phone rings again. I keep moving. Blackslade smiles pleasantly. 'Someone really wants to speak to you, Clara.'

I shrug. We are all still pretending this is amiable, but I know we are on the brink of disaster. 'I'll check later.'

Blackslade smiles again, as if this is still all normal. 'Why don't you check now?'

I can't think of any way of saying no. I pull out my phone. *Missed call – Nell Turner*. Blackslade can see the screen. As I look at the phone, it starts ringing again.

'Why don't you answer it?' Blackslade's voice is friendly.

'That's okay. I'll call her back as I walk home.'

'She's obviously really keen to speak to you.' Still smiling, Blackslade reaches across and presses *answer* and then before I can jerk the phone away, he has put the call on speakerphone.

'Amber's bloody gone back to Rose Cottage, after all that!' Nell's voice, bright and purposeful, rings out of the phone. 'She'd left Lauren's before I even got here. I'm on my way back to Coraton now.'

'That's great news, Nell,' I say hastily. 'See you tomorrow?'

'And Lauren's physically seen Amber.' Nell sounds triumphant. It's not a good line. Her car engine is noisy in the background. 'Amber's definitely alive.'

'Great!' I say. 'Let's catch up tomorrow.'

'It does mean that it definitely wasn't Amber who called you the other night,' says Nell. 'So who the hell was it?'

Blackslade's eyes narrow.

'No idea!' I try to sound cheerful. 'Maybe it was all nonsense. Some madwoman making a fuss. Anyway, you're breaking up!'

I reach out to end the call, but Blackslade moves the handset just very slightly and Nell's voice carries on, loud in the silent room. 'Why did you ask me about Victoria, by the way?' she asks. 'Yes, she is my sister.'

I shudder. Blackslade's eyes burn into mine. My voice sticks in my throat and I can't say anything and I can't stop Nell speaking. I can't…

'Vic lives her lah-di-dah life in Harepath.' Nell's voice echoes out of the phone. 'We barely see each other these days. Amber sees a lot more of Vic than I do, to be honest.'

Behind me, I hear Amber make a sound like a cough.

'I see,' I say cheerfully. 'Cool, well, let's talk tomor—'

'You know what?' To my horror, Nell is sounding doubtful. 'Now that I come to think of it, I haven't seen Vic for quite a long time. You're at Harepath all the time. When was the last time you saw her—'

'The line's breaking up!' I shout. I reach across and hit the end button.

Nell is silenced.

Blackslade is quite still. Then he puts my phone in his pocket and looks past me, to where Amber and Ryan are sitting at the table. Behind me, I hear the screech of a chair as someone stands up.

Blackslade nods decisively. 'Kill her, Ryan.'

77

I look towards the table. Ryan is standing there, almost embarrassed. He moves towards a cupboard and when he turns back, he has a knife in his hands. The knife glitters sharp and pointed and lethal.

'No!' I hear myself scream.

'Shh.' There is pure desperation in Amber's whisper. Her eyes are pleading, and I realise why she is so desperate.

Amber's children are asleep upstairs. Sleeping, but in terrible danger. Amber must have been forced to call me. Forced to summon me to my death.

But her children are too small to promise silence, too young to trust. If they wake up, they become witnesses.

'Go on.' Blackslade sounds weirdly calm. 'Go on, Ryan.'

'No,' I gasp. 'Please, Ryan, don't do it.'

'He says you've got something on me.' Ryan's voice whines with indignation. 'Something really bad. I don't even know what it fucking is. You can't have anything on your daughter, because I didn't—'

'There isn't anything,' I promise him. 'There isn't anything at all. You're lying,' I say to Blackslade.

'No.' Blackslade is undisturbed. 'I am not.'

'What is it then?' Ryan demands to know.

Blackstade stares levelly at him, and I have the uncomfortable feeling that he is deciding exactly which of the many weapons in his armory he is going to use.

'There isn't anything—' I begin desperately.

'I certainly don't know if she's going to be able to prove that you killed Lyra,' Blackslade interrupts me smoothly. 'But Clara certainly did tell Victoria that she was going to, and I quote, "see you in jail, whatever it takes".'

'That's not true,' I insist.

'I'm afraid it is,' Blackslade tells Ryan almost sympathetically. 'She's been pursuing you for months.'

'So what?' Ryan snaps, but he looks uneasy. 'I haven't done anything.'

'She filmed you attacking Amber.' Blackslade sounds almost apologetic. 'There was significant violence in the attack. Clara told my wife that the footage was more than enough to merit a long jail sentence in its own right.'

Amber gasps.

'What?' Blindsided, I spin round. 'That's a lie!' I say hotly. But Blackslade just watches me coolly, lab technician to a rat, and even though I know he is lying, I wouldn't know it from his face. I turn back towards Ryan. 'He's lying, Ryan,' I say desperately. 'Don't listen to him. It's total nonsense.'

'What do you mean?' Ryan looks stunned, and even though I can't stand Ryan, I have the feeling that we are both sliding further and further into Blackslade's trap.

'Clara must have been walking back to her cottage one evening after work,' Blackslade explains, 'and she must have looked in through the window.'

Blackslade gestures almost casually out to the lane.

'I never…' But Ryan's face is flushing a dark red and we all know that he is lying. 'I didn't…'

Almost carelessly, Blackslade pulls his phone out of his pocket and waves it at Ryan. 'Clara sent the footage to Victoria. I've got it here. You can watch it if you want.'

Ryan stares at the phone with horror, but he makes no attempt to take it. We all know the footage could exist.

'I didn't film you, Ryan!' I promise him. 'It wasn't me.'

But Ryan isn't listening to me.

'I'm afraid you're looking at several years in jail, Ryan.' Blackslade sounds strangely regretful. 'Even if Amber refuses to testify.'

I don't know if this is true – and looking at Ryan's face, I can tell that he doesn't either – but it sounds plausible.

I imagine Blackslade lingering outside this cottage, slowly, patiently building his traps for me, for Ryan. Unhurriedly gathering the evidence for whatever outcome was required in the end. I suppose it must have been easy: wait for Ryan to totter home from the pub on Friday night and then film whatever happened next from the darkness of the lane. Blackslade probably managed to convince himself it was the right thing to do, anyway. Maybe I should have done it.

'You bitch!' Ryan's eyes glaze with rage. He takes another step towards me. 'You stalking, manipulative *bitch*.'

'Please, Ryan. Don't—'

'Clara's absolutely determined to see you in jail, Ryan.' Behind me, Blackslade's composure is almost as terrifying as Ryan's rage. Blackslade sounds as if he is chatting about the weather. 'You know she's obsessive. You know she's mad. Even if she has to fabricate the evidence, I think you'll face charges for Lyra's death in the end. You'll never be safe as long as she is around. And she'll never, ever leave. You need to finish this now.'

Ryan takes another step forward.

If Ryan stabs me to death, I realise, they will tell everyone that it was self-defence. Ryan will tell the police that I broke into his cottage in the middle of the night. He will say that it was dark, and that he didn't know what was going on. He will say that I attacked him and maybe everyone will believe him.

Because some people will agree that I've got increasingly obsessive. *She even accused the Meldons. It was stalking, basically. Poor Hailey. Poor Clara, really. It's enough to drive anyone mad, what happened to her.*

And Blackslade… Blackslade will have flitted away through the night long before the police arrive. I bet there will be nothing to show he was ever here. He hasn't touched anything, I notice. He knows exactly how the police operate. There will be nothing whatsoever, I am sure of it, to link him to this crime scene.

Or maybe he will even be the first to arrive on the scene, the hero of the hour. *I heard screams. But there was nothing anyone could do.*

'I'm sorry.' Tears are tracking down Amber's face. 'I'm so sorry, Clara. But my children… My children.'

'I won't say anything about any of this.' I turn towards Blackslade. I am begging him, but I don't care. 'I've got no proof about Lyra… About anything… I don't know what happened.'

'I know you've got no proof,' Blackslade sneers at me. 'Everyone will conclude that you just went mad. You're the madwoman at the top of the drover's track, after all. Going around, accusing innocent people. Rossiter Cottage one day, and the next moment you're breaking into the Dallyns' house… Terrifying them… And with their children upstairs.'

Behind me, I hear Ryan step closer. I spin around.

'Stop, Ryan. Please.'

Ryan ignores me and takes another step towards me. His face is blank. I have stood in silent accusation for years. Ryan doesn't owe me anything, and Blackslade is threatening his children.

'I'm sorry,' Amber whispers again.

'Ryan will go to jail,' I say to her. 'He won't get away with this. Your children will grow up knowing that their father killed someone.'

For a moment, Amber's face contorts. 'They've basically grown up with that anyway,' she says. 'Thanks to you.'

I turn back to Ryan. 'I didn't film you, Ryan.' I force my voice to sound calm. 'Blackslade must have filmed it. He's setting you up, and it isn't the first time, either. He's done it before and if he needs to, he'll do it again.'

The faintest hint of confusion enters Ryan's eyes. 'What do you mean, he's set me up?'

'Ignore her, Ryan.' Blackslade speaks from behind me. 'She's just trying to manipulate you.'

'He set you up for Lyra's murder,' I say. 'But Gabriel Blackslade is the one who killed Lyra.'

'What the—' Ryan's knife wavers.

'I told you she was insane, Ryan.' Blackslade still sounds calm. 'Don't listen to a word she says. It's all lies.'

'Gabriel Blackslade murdered Lyra and he made sure he was carrying your phone when he did it.' I try to match Blackslade's mild tones. 'He meant you to be caught instead of him all the way back then.'

'What?' Ryan shakes his head. 'He never—'

'Did you have your phone on you every moment of that day?' I am an interrogator now. 'Were you really up in Abbot's Wood that day?'

'No. Yes.' Ryan has told his lies so many times that he is stumbling over the truth. 'Shut up, you mad cow.'

'Blackslade might get away with this,' I say. 'But if he doesn't – if there's even a hint of danger to him – there will be a plan, Ryan. And you're going to be the fall guy.'

Again, Ryan hesitates.

'What story has Gabriel Blackslade told you about Victoria?' I soften my voice now. 'That she's had some terrible, tragic accident? That I've gone mad and accused Blackslade of her murder? That I've got to be silenced for both your sakes?'

Amber looks up sharply.

'No.' Ryan still sounds mulish.

'What was it then?'

Behind me, I hear Blackslade start to speak, but at a glower from Ryan, he stops sharply. I guess that Blackslade has learned that Ryan's pride is easily bruised. Blackslade needs Ryan, and he knows that Ryan's temper is on a hair-trigger. If Blackslade is staying silent, it must be because he believes he can still keep things on track.

'Blackslade says that Victoria's buggered off with someone else.' The admission spills out of Ryan. 'And that he's got no idea where she's gone. And after you heard that she'd left, you went to Harepath and told him you'd been in love with him for ages. And when he told you he wasn't interested, you went mental, and said you were going to tell everyone he'd murdered Victoria.'

'That's insane.' Despite everything, I am stunned by Blackslade's audacity. 'That's all lies. Victoria is dead!'

'That's exactly what he said you'd say!' Ryan says, almost triumphant.

'But Victoria hasn't gone anywhere!' I say. 'He's killed her.'

Ryan shrugs, and in my desperation, I can't think how to prove him wrong. How will I ever be able to prove that Victoria isn't just missing when there is no body? Especially when Blackslade may have been planning this for weeks.

'I told you.' Blackslade sounds almost rueful. 'I told you she was obsessed with Victoria leaving. And Victoria was losing the plot, too. You know how much she drank.'

This is directed at Amber. Amber looks up sharply and I see that it is the truth, and again I think: how long has Blackslade been planning this?

'You're all mental.' There is a self-pitying note in Ryan's voice. 'All fucking crazy.'

'I don't think Victoria was thinking straight.' Blackslade sounds rueful. 'She had been struggling for a long time.'

'It's all a lie.' I can't keep the rage out of my voice. 'Blackslade killed my daughter. And he killed Victoria too. And now he's tying up all the loose threads by getting you to kill me. He's using you, Ryan! He's playing you for a fool.'

'I'm not an idiot!' Even now, Ryan manages to look affronted. I remind myself that – like Blackslade – I have to tread carefully. I have to persuade Ryan.

'He's setting you up, Ryan,' I say again, softly. 'You'll end up in jail for the rest of your life.'

Ryan is shaking his head. He looks like a confused bullock being dragged into the abattoir, not sure where the true danger lies.

'Get on with it, Ryan.' There is anger in Blackslade's voice too now, his vocal cords starting to tense. 'I warned you that she'd try to manipulate you. I said this is exactly what she'd do.'

'There'll be something on you for Victoria's murder too, Ryan.' My voice is pure menace now. 'Victoria is dead and no matter what Blackslade tries, he won't be able to cover that up forever. It'll all come out in the end. And when it does, Blackslade will have set a trap for you. Whether it's a blood-stained knife somewhere in your cottage or a few of your tools and a clump of your hair buried in Victoria's grave, there will be something.'

'Shut up.' Blackslade is losing control. He shoves me hard in the back, and I cry out. 'Shut up, you psychopath. Get on with it, Ryan.

Don't let her get inside your head. It's what she does. She's absolutely insane.'

'Ryan…'

'She's come into this village…' There is something hypnotic about Blackslade's voice. 'We all know she's had a terrible time, but she's tearing our community apart now. Turning us all against each other. She's paranoid and obsessed and she wants to take you down.'

This hits a nerve. Ryan lifts the knife higher. I twist back towards Blackslade, tensing my back against an attack from Ryan.

'Where is your wife?' I hiss up at him. 'Where is your wife right now, Gabriel Blackslade? Nell will be on the hunt for her by now. And I'm sure you know Nell well enough to know exactly how relentless she is.'

Blackslade's jaw clenches. Nell's phone call was a shock to him, not something he had factored in. And it will be hard, I think, to put off Nell when she is searching for her sister. When she is already starting to suspect. She is ruthless, Nell. Tough and determined.

'Nell will get you,' I whisper. 'Even if I am dead. Especially if I am dead.'

I can see that Blackslade is thinking. That clever mind is working fast, racing through all the options. For the briefest of moments, I think he might give in. I let myself hope that I might somehow escape. But this is a man who will never give in, and as I turn away from him, looking back towards Ryan, Amber screams.

I whip back towards Blackslade and my brain can't take in what I am seeing. I can't think at all. Blackslade is holding a gun.

My terror is so total that all I can see is the black ugliness of the gun. The Dallyns' kitchen blurs to nothing.

Blackslade raises the gun. He points at me and I can't breathe, I can't move. I hate him with every fibre of my being.

But then Blackslade steps to one side and aims the gun. He aims at Ryan.

'Kill her,' he says, 'or I will kill you and Amber.' He gestures, almost casually, up the stairs. 'And then I'll kill both of them, too.'

78

'No,' Amber yelps. 'No.'

'Please.' My eyes are fixed on Ryan's. 'Please don't do this.'

Ryan is still hesitating. He can't do it, I realise. This man, who I've loathed for so long, can't bring himself to stab a knife into my flesh.

'I mean it, Ryan.' Blackslade is icy. 'I will kill your whole fucking family and then I will find a way of hanging it on you.'

'Don't do it, Ryan,' I beg him. 'You'll go to jail for the rest of your life.'

'What am I meant to do?' Ryan is panicking. 'He's going to kill my children!'

The knife is shivering in Ryan's hands. Blackslade cocks the gun.

'He won't!' I try to convince myself. 'He knows he'll never get away with it. There'll be forensic evidence, there'll be something.'

'But he knows the law and everything!' Ryan looks pathetic all at once. 'He'll know how to get off.'

'Please,' I say. 'You can't let him get away with this.'

'This is your last chance, Ryan.' Blackslade's voice slices through the air. 'You want your children to survive, don't you?'

Ryan's shiver has turned to a shake. I am not sure he would have the co-ordination to stab me. But it is Amber who moves. She leaps forward, snatches the knife off Ryan and in one fluid motion, she has turned on me. Her eyes are bitterly cold.

'I'm sorry,' Amber says to me, almost conversationally. 'I really am sorry.'

And even in that moment, I think: no, I would do the same, Amber. I would kill for my child without missing a beat.

Because now I know what is coming. I will not be able to stare down Amber Dallyn. Amber will do whatever it takes to keep her family safe. She steps towards me. I spin round, with a last desperate plea.

'Victoria told me everything!' I shout at Blackslade. 'We spoke over and over again. She told me all about you murdering Lyra. And I've left the proof in a safe place. Nell will be able to work it out.'

A spark of confusion enters Blackslade's eyes. I sense that Amber is just inches away from me now. Any second that knife will plunge into my back.

But Blackslade has to know what I am talking about. He can't bear not to know. And he can't risk not knowing.

He gestures sharply at Amber. *Stop*. 'How?' he says to me. 'Why the fuck would Victoria tell someone like you anything at all?'

But even as his contempt pours over me, I think I see the first flicker of comprehension.

'Because I'm a Good Listener,' I spit. 'I've been there for months. Victoria called them. She called them again and again. She called whenever she had the house to herself. On Friday nights, when you were in the pub and Linda was at choir practice and the kids were asleep and she was all alone. *My husband killed a little girl*, that's what she told me over and over again. She knew what you did. And she knew what you were.'

'You—' Blackslade is stunned to his core.

'I made sure I was there when she was going to call,' I hiss. 'I made sure I was there every single Friday night. She was talking to me…' Blackslade realises what I am about to say just before I say it. 'She was talking to me when you murdered her, you bastard.'

'No,' says Blackslade. 'You can't…'

'I can,' I spit. 'And I fucking did. I have a recording.'

'You bitch.' The fury in Blackslade's eyes is terrifying.

'I went to the police that Friday night.' I am pure rage now. 'I spoke to a Detective Constable Tremayne and I told her that I heard a woman being strangled while I was speaking to her. What do you reckon? I think that if I'm dead, and your wife has disappeared, there might be yet another major investigation into Coraton.'

For a moment, I think Blackslade will lunge at me. I think he will attack me himself. But I watch him contain himself – only just – and that gives me an idea.

'Kill her!' he shouts over my shoulder at Amber. 'Just fucking kill her now. Get it over with.'

'No!' I spring at him. Blackslade is not expecting it. I claw wildly at his cheek. Blood… I feel blood on my fingers.

'You bitch.' He leaps back. The gun is pointing at me again. But we both know what this means. Blackslade's DNA is under my fingernails now, and it will be impossible to explain all this as simple self-defence by Amber.

For a second, Blackslade is staring at me. His lips are drawn back with anger, his teeth are bared. He looks animal with rage.

'You killed my daughter,' I scream at him. 'You killed Lyra. You killed Victoria! And now you're planning to kill Amber and Ryan too!'

Blackslade is staring at me, and for a moment, he is not paying attention to Amber at all. There is a blur of movement in the corner of my vision and a ravening, screaming harpy leaps forward. Amber plunges her knife deep into Blackslade's chest at the same moment that his gun goes off.

The gunshot roars in the little room.

And I feel an agonising pain.

79

The bullet has hit my left arm, I realise slowly. Just above the elbow. It hurts. It really hurts, but I am not dying. I push myself until I am sitting upright and slump against the wall.

Blackslade, on the other hand, may well be dying. He is lying on the floor, and blood is trickling across the flagstones.

'You bastard...' Amber is standing over him. In a swift motion, she kicks the gun across the kitchen, far out of his reach. I don't think Blackslade will be reaching for it anyway. The knife is deep in his chest, rising and falling with his breathing, which is laboured. Blackslade looks down blearily.

'The kids!' Amber's head turns. From upstairs, there is movement, the high-pitched tones of scared children.

Ryan and Amber move as one, sprinting up the stairs. *Don't worry. It's just a stupid accident. No, stay upstairs for a little while. We need to tidy up.*

There is a cut to my head, I realise. It must be from when I threw myself to the floor as Amber leapt at Blackslade. Blood is trickling down my face. I try to rub it away.

Blackslade's eyes have closed now. His chest, I see with mixed feelings, is still heaving. I am not going to attempt first aid on that man, even if his chest stops moving.

Upstairs, I can hear Ryan on the phone. He must have dialled 999. 'Rose Cottage, Coraton. We need ambulances. Ambulances and police. Someone's been shot.'

Gabriel Blackslade opens his eyes. I watch them flood with pain, consciousness returning like a burn.

'Don't you move,' I whisper. 'Don't you dare move.'

Blackslade turns his head far enough to know it is me. He breathes out in agony and closes his eyes again.

'You killed my daughter,' I whisper. 'You killed her.'

Slowly, Blackslade opens his eyes. For a long time, he stares at nothing, and then his eyes move around to me. 'Yes,' he says quietly. 'Yes, I did.'

He doesn't apologise. It could never be enough, anyway. But that admission, after everything, is something. I watch Blackslade's chest heave up and down and wish he was dead.

'Why?' I ask, after a few moments. The word fades away in the silence of the kitchen. 'Why did you do it?'

'I…' For a moment, I don't think Blackslade will say anything. I think that he will remember all those years of criminal training and stay silent. But he does speak. Maybe he thinks he is dying, and there is no point in clinging on to his secrets. Maybe he is dying. 'I just couldn't stop myself,' he says. The knife moves up and down. 'I know it was wrong. And I know you won't believe me, but I am sorry. I saw her, and I just couldn't stop myself.'

The pain is unbearable. I feel tears fill my eyes. I stare up angrily at the kitchen's black-beamed ceiling and force my voice to be unemotional.

'You killed Elizabeth Wrenscott, too.'

His head jerks up. 'How did you…'

I watch him connect the dots slowly. Victoria knew, somehow. Maybe he even told her. And Victoria told the Good Listeners. Victoria told me.

'You don't know what it was like,' he speaks very quietly. 'Always being on the outside. Elizabeth and Lawrence, they were given everything they wanted, living in their beautiful house. With Ferdie and Georgia loving them and sending them to the right schools and everything being perfect. It was all just so… *charmed*. I hated it and I wanted it, all at once. Elizabeth was so spoiled. She was the centre of everything, all the time, like a little doll. And Georgia… She knew who I was. To Ferdie, I mean. So she couldn't let me… I was always on the *outside*.'

I think to myself that Blackslade had clearly known the Wrenscotts quite well, and not every wife would have permitted that much. Georgia had been generous, considering.

'I was never like *them*,' Blackslade half-admits.

'Kimlock trains,' I say.

Blackslade's head jerks. 'I couldn't work out…' His voice is becoming a gasp. 'I couldn't work out why you asked about them.'

I imagine him bidding on the mint-condition *Azalea*. It seems impossible now. 'I heard that Lawrence Wrenscott liked Kimlock trains,' I half-lie.

'Our father used to give Lawrence Kimlock trains,' whispers Blackslade. 'I always wanted them.'

I wonder why Ferdinand Wrenscott never married Donna Blackslade, even after she had his child.

I think Victoria has already told me. *He calls her horrible names. Horrible words. He thinks she's so far beneath him.*

I guess that Ferdinand Wrenscott was an old-fashioned snob back then. And a few years after that hiccup, he married squire-worthy Georgia.

'No,' I say coldly. 'You were never like them. You were more like your mother.'

That hurts him, even now. 'My mother was a whore,' he snaps. The anger jerks through his body and he winces. 'She was a nobody. A nothing. She never… She fucked all those men. Everyone knew. They would come to our house and…'

As he speaks, there is something in Blackslade's voice that jolts me. And I know that there is a chance that Blackslade will admit something to me, and only to me. Because at this moment, I am not Lyra's mother. At this moment, I am a Good Listener.

'Your mother didn't keep you safe, did she?' I keep my voice calm. 'She didn't protect you. She let men into her house, didn't she?' Just for a second, Blackslade's face contorts. 'Did one of those men come into your room at night?'

I think of that small boy, unloved and unprotected, hurt and hurt again in all the different ways. I think of him watching that pretty little girl, so loved by all. So protected. Safe and sheltered, almost all of the time.

Blackslade gasps, and in that second, I hear all the misery, and all the years of despair. And it is too late now. It is too late for any of us.

All I can do is listen.

'You killed Elizabeth,' I say quietly. 'And it ruined Ferdinand and Georgia's lives.'

'Yes,' he says.

I think that he couldn't have had a better revenge on the Wrenscotts if he'd planned it, and maybe he did.

'And you killed Victoria.'

'I loved her, you know?' He is almost mawkish. 'When we were first married, I really loved her. I thought things could be different. We had known each other since we were just children. She was always sweet. A bit shy, a bit nervous. But we both always wanted more than just… Coraton. I went away to university and after that, I was in London, doing my tenancy. But I would come back to Coraton every so often and that's when we met again. We started seeing each other and then I asked her to marry me.'

I wonder if there was a sort of comfort in someone who knew his past – or most of it – but was prepared to conspire in hiding it.

'You changed your voice,' I say. 'You both did. Got rid of your accents.'

'We needed to fit in. You don't know what it's like. The bar. That whole world. It *matters*.'

I think of Victoria in her smart boots and her expensive cashmere, trying so hard.

'And eventually, you moved back here.'

'Harepath House went up for sale.' Even now, I see the glow in his eyes. His pride at taking over the seat of the Wrenscotts. 'The moment I saw the advert, I knew I had to have it. I had to.'

I think about the pair of them moving back to Coraton. Back to the Wrenscotts', sorrow-filled domain, back into the Wrenscotts' shadow.

'We should have been happy in that house.' Blackslade is filled with self-pity. 'I wanted so badly for us to be happy. I thought I could force us to be happy.'

'That's not how it works.'

'It was impossible with Nell living in the same village.' Blackslade twitches at the memory of Nell. 'She'd take the piss out of us. Tell us we were snobs. Jealous, I suppose. She probably thought we should be living in some pigsty like her and that appalling husband of hers.'

'So you both stopped seeing Nell?'

'Victoria never wanted to go out much anyway. She started drinking more and more,' said Blackslade. 'I tried to stop her. I tried to help her. But she was so ashamed of it. She stopped leaving the house, she stopped doing anything.'

Now that Blackslade is talking, he is finding it hard to stop. The floodgates are open.

'She was scared of you,' I say. 'You hit her. You hit her on several occasions.'

'I wanted her to stop drinking.' He sighs. 'I was trying to help her. Poor Victoria. She never had any friends, really. She never had anyone to talk to.'

He doesn't seem to realise that Victoria might have been lonely because of Harepath's grandeur rather than despite. I imagine that when he tried to talk to his wife, all he did was scare her.

'And then,' all of a sudden, Blackslade's voice is pure menace, and I am glad Amber moved the gun far from his reach, 'then, she betrayed me.'

He stops, the fury quivering in the air between us.

'Did you tell her about Elizabeth?' I ask coolly.

'No.' His voice is affable again. 'But she clearly guessed. I was talking to her about Georgia teaching the little girls to dance around the maypole, and I think there must have been something in the way I said it.'

I wonder if Victoria had guessed long ago about Blackslade's father. She was clever, Victoria. Clever and lost.

'Where is Victoria's body?' I ask a moment later, because I think Blackslade may well tell me in these moments of broken chaos. And if he doesn't tell me now, before he dies or the haze wears off, Victoria will be lost forever.

His eyes fix on mine. 'The wood, of course.' Every word is a struggle now. 'She's in Abbot's Wood.'

I imagine that ancient wood torn apart one more time. 'Where?' I ask urgently. 'Where exactly?'

Blackslade won't say; perhaps in his daze he can't even remember. But I will find her.

And then I feel a horror that is so sharp that I think I may faint. Lyra. That day on the village green just before she died. Dancing around the maypole. Thrilled at being asked to join in. With the same blonde hair as Elizabeth, the same charm.

And Georgia, smiling down at her. Georgia, encouraging her.

'Did you see her that day?' My rage blazes up again. 'Did you see my daughter dancing on the village green?' Blackslade's eyes meet mine and he doesn't have to say anything. 'You bastard,' I whisper. 'You complete bastard.'

'I didn't want to.' Each word is a painful gasp. 'I fought it. I tried… But no one can understand… No one. Elizabeth, it's as if she's inside my head. It's as if she is a part of me. She was everything. And then suddenly, it was as if she was alive again, dancing, smiling. Lyra smiled at me, and I let myself believe… I let myself… I only meant to talk to her.'

I can't listen to him. I can't bear to listen to his lies.

'Stop it,' I say. 'Stop talking.'

'Elizabeth is everywhere,' he says. 'Every day and every night. I've always been scared that it would happen again, somehow, and I wouldn't be strong enough to stop it. And suddenly she was alive again. My Elizabeth. My father's Elizabeth. And I couldn't… I couldn't…'

There is madness in his eyes. I stare at the wall, at a splashy painting by one of Amber's children, and the anger pours over me in uncontrollable waves.

The stairs creak and Amber is next to me. She has a small first aid kit in her hand. Blackslade seems to have passed out.

'Sorry,' Amber says quietly, 'about earlier.'

The words are hopelessly inadequate and enough.

'I'd have done the same,' I mutter.

We smile weakly at each other in a sort of understanding and I wince as she puts a dressing on my arm. She looks across at Blackslade. His eyes are closed.

'He can take his chances,' she says firmly. 'How are you feeling? Do you want to move onto one of the chairs?'

'I'm fine,' I say.

'Nine nine nine said the ambulance would be here very soon, but I guess that the roads are bloody icy by now.' Amber sits down. 'Poor Victoria.' It seems to hit her for the first time that Victoria is dead. She drops her head into her hands and rubs her temples hard. 'Poor, poor Victoria. She never had much of a chance, did she?'

'I know,' I say. 'And those poor kids.'

'It's like a nightmare,' she says. 'Gabriel Blackslade… I never would have thought it. Never.'

Upstairs, the children have settled down. Incongruously, it sounds as if Ryan is reading them a story.

'Are your kids alright?' I ask.

'They'll be okay.'

We contemplate the kitchen, exhausted.

'What did Blackslade tell you before I came down here?' I ask Amber to distract myself from the pain in my arm. 'What did he say to Ryan before I came to Rose Cottage?'

'What Ryan told you.' Amber shrugs. 'That you'd turned up at Harepath and announced you were in love with him, and then gone totally mental.'

'Bastard.' The thought makes me shudder.

'Blackslade stitched us up,' says Amber. 'Completely. That business with Ryan's phone and Blackslade taking it up to Abbot's Wood – Ryan thinks you might be right. We were talking about it just now upstairs. Ryan could never understand what happened that day. He just thought he must have missed his phone in his trouser pocket or something, because he found it when he was back at home. But it was all so chaotic that day, and he was wearing his work trousers, you know, the type with about ten sets of pockets. He thought he must have had it with him and just not realised. He had done that before – thought he'd lost it and then I'd find it when I was doing the laundry.' Amber's eyes meet mine. 'Ryan's pretty, but he's not the brightest.'

'Didn't he wonder what the hell was going on after the phone showed he was in Abbot's Wood?'

'Ryan was just shit-scared at that point,' Amber says. 'He'd already said he was with Lawrence and Jordie, and they all just decided they had to keep to their story as much as possible. Just adapt it a bit. If Ryan had turned round and said, "Actually, there's something a bit weird about those phone records," it would have opened a whole can of worms. He never really understood what the phone records meant anyway, to be honest, all the GPS-this and the pings-that. Jordie's dad was going mental at them all, too, saying he couldn't believe they'd been so stupid.'

'And then Lyra was found in Abbot's Wood.'

'By then, they were all having a total meltdown,' Amber says. 'The lawyers stayed calm though. They actually managed to convince Ryan that it was helpful. That the phone records proved that Ryan hadn't been near the body.'

Every fibre of my being is repulsed by the thought, but I wonder if Blackslade put the phone down while he was out in Abbot's Wood. Perhaps he decided it would be better for everyone if Ryan's phone didn't lead the police directly to my daughter's body. Too obvious perhaps. I suppose it was also possible that he simply hoped that Lyra would never be found. Perhaps that was Plan A and Ryan's ruin was Plan B.

I look across at Blackslade, slumped on the floor, and I think I could kill him with my bare hands.

With an effort, I turn back to Amber. 'So Ryan had no idea that Blackslade had killed Lyra?'

'God, no!' Amber looks appalled. 'Gabriel just said that Victoria had run off and you'd gone completely mad about the whole thing. I don't know whether he was trying to hint at the idea that you might have killed Victoria. Jealous or something.'

'I suppose he might have wanted to keep that option open,' I say drily.

'Then he told us this thing about you having something else on Ryan killing Lyra, although he said he didn't know what it was. Ryan panicked. Thought you'd linked him to Lyra's death somehow. He's spent ages already with everyone thinking he was a murderer. He couldn't bear it all starting again. Gabriel can be so persuasive. You know what he's like.'

'Ryan was lucky, really,' I say. 'I imagine Blackslade thought he'd be in jail by now. If Ryan hadn't said he was with Lawrence and Jordie from the very start, and if they hadn't gone along with it... If either of their phones had been moving at the time...'

For a moment, I think Amber is going to be the one to kill Blackslade. 'Imagine deliberately setting someone else up for that crime. Imagine going to jail for that if you hadn't done it... It was so calculated.'

I remember something else. 'By the way, did something change?' I ask. 'Did something happen a few months ago between you and Ryan?'

A few months ago – a lifetime ago – when Nell thought that Ryan and Amber's relationship had deteriorated. A few months ago – a lifetime ago – when Victoria Blackslade started calling the Good Listeners.

'Why?' Amber looks blank.

'You and Ryan seemed to be fighting a lot more recently,' I try to remind her. 'As if something had changed.'

'Oh.' Amber's face clears. 'It was stupid, really. I'd never thought that Ryan had done it, you see. I know he can be an arsehole, but... Not that. Never that.'

There is still a sad glint of loyalty in Amber's eyes.

'Okay,' I say. 'So what changed?'

'I was talking to Victoria one day,' she says. 'Just chatting really, while I was doing some ironing. I was saying that me and Ryan were thinking about getting a new puppy. And Victoria said, didn't we already have a dog? And it surprised me, really, that she hadn't heard about our puppy. About Ryan searching for it that day. But I suppose Victoria was so lonely out at Harepath, how would she know?'

Ryan's activities out in the woods had never been reported by the media, I remember. Perhaps Victoria only ever knew what

Blackslade told her about Lyra's disappearance. Perhaps – consciously or unconsciously – she never wanted to know.

'Had you never talked to her about it all before that?' I ask.

'No.' Amber is certain. 'Victoria was hardly the chatty type, was she? And, of course, no one ever mentions anything about that day to Ryan and me. It's all just whisper, whisper, whisper behind our backs.'

Amber stops, the outrage stuffed back down. Perhaps she is realising, slightly too late, that I am not the person to grumble to about the impact of Lyra's death.

'So you told Victoria that your puppy went missing that day?' I prod Amber. 'That it just disappeared.'

'Yes,' says Amber. 'Then she asked what sort of puppy it had been, and I said it was a little terrier. And then I said, "Didn't you know? That's why Ryan was up in Abbot's Wood that day, with Jordie and Lawrence. They were out searching for the puppy." And Victoria just looked really shocked and said – almost without thinking – that Jordie hadn't been with Ryan. That Jordie had been fixing the fencing between one of the Harepath fields and one of the Meldons' fields.'

'What?' The word jolts out of me. But then I think back to the layout of the study. If Victoria was working at Blackslade's desk that day, she would have been able to look across the fields towards the Meldons' land. She would indeed have been able to see Jordie working away, his tractor parked nearby, loaded up with whatever was needed to fix the fence.

But, I think slowly, Emma – Victoria – also told me that she lied to the police. The Blackslade version of events was that it was Gabriel Blackslade working in his study that day, and presumably that is what Victoria told them. So Victoria never told the police what she saw. And that meant that Ryan and Jordie's alibi stood.

'What did you say to Victoria after she said that?' I ask.

'Well, I suppose I panicked a bit. I told her that it was impossible that Jordie had been working on the fences all day, because Ryan had sworn that Jordie was with him in Abbot's Wood all the time. I told her that Ryan's actual phone records had shown that he was up in Abbot's Wood. That Ryan *had* to have been up there with Jordie.'

'I see.' I don't, still, not quite.

'By then, Victoria was looking at me as if she'd seen a ghost,' says Amber. 'And I suddenly realised Ryan's whole story was total bollocks. Jordie hadn't been with him at all. And if Ryan had lied about Jordie, for all I knew he had lied about Lawrence being with him too. I'd thought all along that Ryan had an alibi, and suddenly he didn't at all. Victoria was looking horrified because she thought that I was married to a murderer.'

I can vividly imagine Amber's shock.

But I can imagine, too, Victoria's terrible moment of comprehension. Victoria must have suddenly realised that the terrier puppy found by her children was the Dallyns' puppy. But how did the puppy end up abandoned close to Harepath? And why did the puppy never get returned to the Dallyns?

Victoria wasn't staring at Amber in horror because she had realised that Amber's husband was a murderer. No, Victoria was staring in horror because she was realising that her own husband's story made no sense at all.

And perhaps she was also realising that there was only one person who'd had the opportunity of taking Ryan's phone up to Abbot's Wood. And it hadn't been Ryan.

Both women came away from that conversation believing that their husbands might have murdered Lyra.

And shortly afterwards, Victoria made the first call to the Good Listeners.

'Ryan went nuts when I told him that Victoria had seen Jordie working on the fences when they'd all claimed they were up in Abbot's Wood,' Amber is saying. 'Absolutely crazy. I suppose he couldn't cope with me suspecting him, as well as everyone else.'

'He would have been terrified too,' I say. 'Victoria could have blown all their alibis at any moment.'

'Yes,' Amber agrees.

No wonder, I thought, that things had been fraught in the Dallyn household. Ryan must have been paralysed with fear, while Amber was concluding that she was living with a murderer.

There is one more thing that I don't quite understand. It feels like a decade since I paused outside this house, although it was only just over a week ago. *It's all fucking Jordie's fault. He needs to keep his fucking mouth shut.*

'Did Ryan find out that someone else knew that Jordie wasn't with Ryan that day?' I ask. 'Just over a week ago. Just before you went off to your sister's?'

But even as I ask the question, I realise what the answer will be. I was walking home from Harepath the Thursday before last, and that was the day I had asked Blackslade those questions: about Linnet, about Ryan's illegitimacy, and, by the way, whether Amber has a sister.

I wonder if those questions fatally unnerved Blackslade. Amber was at Harepath that Thursday, and it would have been straightforward for Victoria to get her into conversation.

'Victoria spoke to me that day,' Amber says stiffly. 'She came to me, very worried. She said that one of the kids had mentioned that they had seen Jordie working on the fences that day, and that they might have mentioned it to some other Coraton kids.'

I guess that Blackslade must have forced Victoria to lie somehow, or perhaps he forced his children. I remember Emma's last desperate words: *He set him up. He set him up and he's forcing me to help him.*

'That pushed me over the edge.' Amber is crying suddenly. 'It meant that the story about Ryan's alibi being bullshit was about to go all the way around the village. I knew he would be arrested this time. I thought he'd be in jail for the rest of his life. We had a huge fight that evening. Worse than we ever had before. And the next day, I loaded the kids into the car and off we went to Lauren's.'

Amber left on the Friday morning, I thought bleakly. And that evening, Emma called the Good Listeners for the last time. That evening, Emma was killed.

'Amber!' Ryan shouts from upstairs. 'The kids want you.'

Amber and I look at each other and I wonder if she will ever leave Ryan. Obediently, she scurries up the stairs.

When she has disappeared, I sit in silence. After a moment, Blackslade opens his eyes. Slowly, he moves his head until he is looking at me.

'People talk to you,' he says, and there is something wry in his face.

'I suppose so.'

'Victoria,' he says, 'never found it easy to talk to anyone.'

In the distance, I hear the howl of a siren. Someone is coming at last. I close my eyes briefly, shutting him out.

'Victoria did find someone to speak to,' I tell him, 'in the end.'

80

The police get the scene disentangled quite fast. Coraton is wide awake now, watching agog. The paramedics take Blackslade away, the police walking warily alongside the stretcher.

Detective Tremayne is there, off to the side, waiting for her moment. Detective Tremayne with her chestnut eyes.

'Gabriel Blackslade killed Lyra,' I tell her. 'And he killed his wife, too. Victoria Emmeline Blackslade. I think her body's up in Abbot's Wood.'

Detective Tremayne's eyes narrow. 'Your Emma? The woman you made a statement about?'

'Yes,' I say to the police officer. 'There's a recording of her murder. Up at my house.'

'A recording?' Detective Tremayne is listening to her radio. The police are at the Harepath House now, and there are two Blackslade children there and Linda. No mother, though. No wife. No Victoria.

'I'd spoken to her before at the Good Listeners,' I say. 'Several times.'

Tremayne gives me five seconds of the bright chestnut eyes. 'Okay.'

'I think you should also look again at the murder of Elizabeth Rose Wrenscott,' I add. 'She died in 1991. She was strangled and she was found in Abbot's Wood, too. I believe that Gabriel Blackslade killed her when he was thirteen years old.'

'Okay,' she says. 'Okay.'

I find that I am sitting on the bank opposite Rose Cottage, a flurry of activity all around me, a paramedic peering at my arm. The Dallyn kids are rushed out and taken away for tea and chocolate biscuits at Nell's house. I gaze up the hill. In the dawn light, the moor is russet-frosted with the first snow of the winter.

There is a thought that keeps nearly coming into focus, before vanishing again. I watch the police officers gingerly start the process of analysing Rose Cottage. The scene of crime officers move with especial care.

Something about Blackslade's voice.

There is something about that voice…

Some of the time, Blackslade speaks with the rolling vowels of Devon. Although most of the time, he has an upper-class clip.

There is something about that voice…

Different memories are twining together. Different scenes tangling and twisting into one. *Something about that voice.*

I come to a sharp halt.

Gabriel Ferdinand William Blackslade.

William.

Will Harper, coming to the Good Listeners' centre.

But there was a Bill, too. Although I never thought his name was Bill. I remember Bill's words though. *And now… now I can't stop.*

I listened to Bill.

Some bloke she was seeing… How am I meant to be normal after that? I just want to be normal.

I listened to Bill and I told him: *None of that was your fault. None of it.*

Then there were those notes in the red file, too. *Billy, was raped, but can't tell anyone.*

* * *

And there was a Liam once, too… A Liam in Cullompton Services. A Liam who…

I tried to talk to my wife. But the way she looked at me… They'd all be better off without me. Do you believe in forgiveness?

I believe that there is good in everyone… Please, Liam, if you want me to call an ambulance, you have to tell me where you are.

Liam's sudden will to live. *Please help me… Please. I don't want to die…*

That Devon accent echoing again.

I'm evil. I'm evil… And I'm scared I might hurt someone else.

I think Gabriel Blackslade called the Good Listeners.

I think I spoke to Gabriel Blackslade over and over again.

And all I did was listen.

I think of that one Wednesday morning shift when I spoke to both Liam in Cullompton Services and a drunk Victoria. Blackslade must have been driving to court in Bristol or Taunton. And Victoria knew she would have a few hours alone. Both of them reaching out, both in despair.

I think of Victoria, and of her half-bravery, and of her horrible death. I think of her children, alone, lost.

Victoria tried. She did her best.

And her killer will be brought to justice, after all.

I think of Gabriel Blackslade, not using his first name – too distinctive. Not using Ferdinand either – my *father.*

Only ever letting the smallest part of himself call out for help. I feel an anger that is halfway to pity.

The man I wanted to kill.

The man whose life I saved.

There will be hours of questions, I know. There will be searches and statements and jargon and accusations.

But I will prove what happened. Even if Victoria's body is never found, I will give the police my recordings. I will tell them to search the attic. I will tell them about the Good Listeners' files. I will show them the eBay packaging label. I will give them every single shred of evidence.

I know that Amber will tell the police what she heard, and what she saw. Ryan, too, may be persuaded to tell the whole truth at last.

And if only for the attack on me and the Dallyns, Lyra's killer will go to jail for a very long time.

That will be enough.

It will have to be enough.

I realise that Nell is there. Nell, stunned, exhausted, her eyes filled with grief for her sister.

'It was him,' she says again and again. 'It was him all along. Victoria. My poor sister. She was living with a monster.'

'Are the children alright?' I ask.

'They'll be okay,' Nell says firmly. 'Poor little things. But they will be alright. Pauly and I will make sure they're alright.'

Soon, I think, I will go back to my stone-built cottage. I will go back to the little house where Lyra spent some of the happiest moments of her short life, and I will find a way to leave.

I know the truth, now.

I know, too, that Coraton will be part of my life forever. Not least because there is Nell, a new and unlikely friend.

But I know, also, that I will be able to find a new life beyond Coraton.

Detective Tremayne is standing a few feet away. She too is looking up at the tor, far above Coraton.

'You did it,' she says. 'You can breathe now, Clara. You can breathe at last.'

EPILOGUE

Just over a year later, I return to Coraton. Lyra's birthday. I will always return to Coraton for her birthday.

It is February and the daffodils are purposeful green spears. The cherry trees will blossom soon.

We gather at Lyra's memorial.

Late last night, in the frost-touched darkness, I walked up to Abbot's Wood.

It took time for Abbot's Wood to give up its secrets, but Victoria was found in the end. In the last year, Abbot's Wood has reclaimed the patch where she lay. For months afterwards, the ground was crushed by dozens of pragmatic feet. The wood was measured and photographed, tested and prodded. The ferns were trampled and the mosses squashed.

But eventually, everyone left, taking their Day-Glo tabards and their flashing cameras.

And, slowly, gently, the wood healed.

I lay in the cold close to where Lyra was found, looking up at the sky through a filigree of bare branches. In the moonlight, the colours of the wood were lost, and it became a land of greys and darkness.

When I closed my eyes, the air filled with sound. The river chattered and the leaves rustled and somewhere, far away, an owl was hunting.

As I stand at Lyra's memorial now, I can see the last of the snowdrops on Victoria Blackslade's grave.

I came back for Victoria's funeral, too.

* * *

I glance at the little group standing around Lyra's memorial. Lucas is there, exhausted and infinitely happier. Almost a year old now, safe in Ashley's arms, Jessamy is singing a wordless, tuneless song that pierces the silence of the graveyard.

Ashley catches my eye. *Sorry*, she mouths.

It doesn't matter at all, I smile back.

Jessamy thinks I am smiling at her, and grins back delightedly. Her smile is Ashley's, which I am grateful for. But Jessamy doesn't hurt the way I once thought she would.

Nell is beside Ashley, with flapjacks in her bag. She suggests one to Ashley with her eyebrows.

As Jessamy chomps on the flapjack, I watch Nell's eyes flicker to the bright white gravestone with the fading snowdrops. There is no lichen blurring these gold letters yet.

Victoria Blackslade, beloved mother, much missed sister, and no mention of her wifehood.

Cecily Blackslade's eyes are on the bright grave, as are Caspar's.

Caspar has been hard work, Nell has told me during one of our many conversations over the last year. Sodding hard work.

Devastated by his mother's death and certain – absolutely certain – that his father had nothing to do with any of it.

The police have been slowly and compassionately disabusing Caspar of that notion.

Gabriel Blackslade is awaiting trial for murder. He was not granted bail.

I gather that with his trained brilliance, he is not making the process easy for the police or the CPS. But they are confident, still confident.

Most of the time, I try not to think about Gabriel Blackslade at all. But sometimes I think of Liam, of Billy, of Bill.

They are all living at Harepath: Cecily and Caspar, Pauly and Nell, Tabitha and her small brother Reuben.

Cecily and Caspar couldn't bear to leave the grand old mansion, and there wasn't enough room for them all in the half-built house.

'We won't make any decisions until the court case is over,' Nell decided briskly. 'For now, Cecily and Caspar are happiest there. They can decide what to do with Harepath when they're older.'

Living in Harepath has apparently inspired Pauly. The half-built house is almost finished, and every time I visit Harepath, Pauly is fixing a slipped slate or repainting a window frame.

'I hadn't realised,' Nell admitted in one of our calls, 'how much Gabriel had chipped away at his confidence. Victoria did it too, I think, although Pauly won't say that. I think Pauly felt as if one sister had married up and one had married down, and that everything was his fault. That was all bollocks, of course.'

Sally has come along to the gathering at Lyra's memorial, too. Since that last quiet shift, she has kept me updated on Good Listeners' gossip, although not about the Callers, of course. *Manon and Austin have started going out! They began chatting during a quiet patch on an overnight shift, and now she's thinking about moving in with him!*

I often stay with Sally when I come down to Devon. Her farmhouse is only a couple of villages over from Coraton, and I enjoy the chaos of farming life.

Frank and Maria Fenton-Brown have made the journey down to Devon. 'Never got to that part of Dartmoor before,' Frank announced when I invited him. 'And afterwards we could push on through to see Bob Carlyon and his blue *Primrose*!'

I suspect every resident of the New Forest has now heard about Frank's triumphant involvement in bringing Lyra Brennan's murderer to justice.

The Fenton-Browns' kindness has remained a touchstone of happiness.

These days, I am back in London and it feels as if it is where I belong. Josh Aarons' next book has required hundreds of hours of research, keeping me busy and absorbed.

Josh has also encouraged me to feed some of the research back into my own PhD. I will find a way of getting that finished.

Rachel and I have rented a flat together and it has felt like home from the day we moved in.

Rachel is here too, of course, her lips moving silently with the reading.

At the head of the memorial stone, Georgia Wrenscott is reading aloud.

Georgia doesn't need the thin piece of paper in her hands to recite these sentences. The words flow from her as if they are part of her soul. *There is a time for everything, and a season for every activity under the heavens...*

As she speaks, Georgia's eyes are fixed on her own daughter's grave. Lawrence and Ferdie stand behind her, quietly loyal.

Hailey Meldon died a few weeks after Victoria was found. Jordie hasn't come today. He can't face the graveyard, he said. Not yet. Sorry.

Ryan Dallyn is not there either.

Amber split from him – for good, it would seem – not long after that night in Rose Cottage. She and the children moved into Harepath's nanny annex shortly after Linda went to live with her sister in Bournemouth.

All six children spend most of their time building tree-houses in the wood, Nell says approvingly. It's a bloody commune.

Before Georgia's reading, we placed flowers on the three graves. Harepath camellias: a flurry of pink, brave against the grey of the afternoon.

Elizabeth. Victoria. Lyra.

In their camellia cloaks, the three graves are beautiful. The camellia shades swirl from white to ballet slipper, from coral to the deepest boldest scarlet.

Three graves, united in beauty, after everything.

For a second, Georgia's voice hesitates. But then she goes on, her voice sure and true. *A time to love and a time to hate, a time for war and a time for peace.*

'A time for peace,' Georgia repeats, looking straight at me and smiling. 'It is a time for peace.'

Later, I walk out to Abbot's Wood one last time. I sit at the root of one of the ancient oaks and I close my eyes against the darkness.

I listen to the cry of the owl and the whisper of the river and the rustle of the trees. I lean back against the oak and it is then, just for a moment, that I am sure that I hear the smile in my daughter's voice.

ACKNOWLEDGEMENTS

I am a raging geek and I like to keep track of word counts. That means I can see I wrote the 79,377 word first draft of *The Good Listener* in two months between 23 September 2023 and 24 November 2023.

Given that our children were two and four at the time and we were in the middle of near-demolition and rebuilding of an entire house, all I can say is that Jonny, you are the best, kindest and most supportive husband in the world. None of this would happen without you. Thank you so much for letting – no, *encouraging* me – to run off and write my mad stories. I love you. (And you're gorgeous too.)

There are so many other people who have also been wonderful and supportive and *funny* along the way too. Nicky and Simon Heyworth are top of that list. Andy Pearce and Emma Faraday, you are simply fab.

I wouldn't get through a day without the women at the front of this book, and Flic Fitzgerald and Sarah Mahmud, you are my superheroes.

It has been pointed out to me that my first four novels were about sexy international journalism, and my fifth was about a suave (but deadly) dinner party on Dartmoor... and this one is about a loner living at the top of a muddy track in the middle of nowhere. If this trajectory carries on, the next book is going to be about one lunatic skipping about on the top of a tor. Luckily, this doesn't actually reflect my day-to-day Dartmoor life. I am so so so glad to have so many wonderful women in my life. Bronwen Foster-Butler, Bryony Mudd, Cath Brown, Catriona Ward, Charlie Llewellyn, Chloe Brooks Warner, Chloe Monk, Eve Stone, Harriet Knox, Miriam Kelly, Bex Hilton – I am genuinely looking forward to getting old and strange (older and stranger, perhaps) with you all. As always, I KNOW I am being useless and leaving people out. Sorry!

I am also insanely grateful to the wonderful people who look after my children. Katharine Lloyd, Elizabeth Robertson and Rebecca Bletcher – thank you for being fantastic teachers. Knowing that my children are happy and safe with you is all-important! Thank you also to Mrs Sylvester, the English teacher who inspired me.

Jo Katz, thank you for reading this book early on and giving me your own inimitable feedback.

Alison Hennessey – I can't believe this is the sixth book we have worked on together. What an adventure… Thank you so much for everything. And I am very glad your edits on this one were as brisk as always: 'the first two thirds are great, but then…' As always, everyone at Bloomsbury had been wonderful – especially Emily Jones, Therese Keating, Isobel Turton and Fabrice Wilmann. Huge thanks, too, to Andrew Gordon and Georgie Smith at David Higham.

The Samaritans are not The Good Listeners, and vice versa, but they do share several traits. This book is obviously heavily fictionalised, but I hope it has captured some of the kindness and generosity of helpline listeners. If you, or anyone you know, have ever been helped by the Samaritans, do please support them here https://www.samaritans.org/donate-now/ if you can at this time.

A NOTE ON THE AUTHOR

A former investigative journalist, award-winning thriller writer Holly Watt now lives in Devon with her family.

@holly.watt.author